Hampden DuBose

Memoirs of Rev. John Leighton Wilson, missionary to Africa and Secretary of Foreign Missions

Hampden DuBose

Memoirs of Rev. John Leighton Wilson, missionary to Africa and Secretary of Foreign Missions

ISBN/EAN: 9783337124427

Printed in Europe, USA, Canada, Australia, Japan

Cover: Foto ©Raphael Reischuk / pixelio.de

More available books at **www.hansebooks.com**

MEMOIRS

OF

REV. JOHN LEIGHTON WILSON, D. D.,

MISSIONARY TO AFRICA,

AND

SECRETARY OF FOREIGN MISSIONS.

BY

HAMPDEN C. DuBOSE, D. D.,

(For twenty-three years a Missionary in China,)

AUTHOR OF

[IN ENGLISH]: *"The Dragon, Image, and Demon; or, The Three Religions of China"*; and *"Preaching in Sinim."*
[IN CHINESE]: *"The Rock of Our Salvation"* (translated); *"A Sketch of the Life of Dr. Plumer"*; *"The Street-chapel Pulpit"*; *"The Illustrated Life of Christ"* (with no picture of our Lord); *"Twelve Pictorial Sheet Tracts"*; *"Introductions to the Bible, the Gospels, etc."*; *"The Gospel 1,000 Character Classic,"* etc., etc.

RICHMOND, VA.:
PRESBYTERIAN COMMITTEE OF PUBLICATION.
1895.

TO THE

EXECUTIVE COMMITTEE OF FOREIGN MISSIONS,

FAITHFUL IN SERVICE, ECONOMICAL IN FINANCE,

EARNEST IN PRAYER,

FREELY GIVING BOTH TIME AND LABOR,

AND

FILLED WITH LOVING SYMPATHY

FOR THEIR FELLOW-WORKERS IN THE FIELD,

THIS VOLUME IS INSCRIBED.

PREFACE.

AT the opening of the Synod of South Carolina in 1890, a memorial address was delivered on the life and character of Dr. J. Leighton Wilson, from the text, "King in Salem, priest of the most high God." Some members of his family requested that a brief memoir be prepared. For three years the subject was frequently on the mind, but during the last mission year, from September to June, not more than twenty-four hours were given to the work at home. It was on boat trips and during three summers that the materials were collected and arranged. In the language of China's sage, the writer can say of this biography of the missionary sage of the South, "I am an editor, not an author." In narrative portions, copying from missionary journals, frequently two sentences were condensed into one for the sake of brevity. Could he have visited the relatives, conversed with the friends, and sought information personally, instead of by epistle, no doubt the pages might have been enriched by many incidents. To compensate for this, friends have been kind enough to say "they were glad that Dr. Wilson's life was to be written by a missionary."

A kind Providence watched over the pages that were sent to a distant land, especially over the old letters from Africa, yellow with age. When on the passage to China, during a storm, the baggage was immersed in lubricating oil, and one trunk was broken to pieces and the contents well soaked. The letters were in the other trunk, else they would have been illegible.

We are indebted to the venerable Rev. Dr. C. C. Baldwin, of Foochow, now nearing his jubilee, for the loan of the old volumes of the *Missionary Herald;* to our *compagnon de voyage*, Mr. G. L. D. Paine, of Boston, for the gift of *Missions and Science;* and to the Rev. B. F. Wilson for furnishing the portrait of his great-uncle.

Valuable aid has been received from the Rev. J. B. Adger, D. D., Rev. J. J. Bullock, D. D., Mrs. J. N. Craig, Mrs. Anna Eckard Crane, Rev. R. L. Dabney, D. D., Dr. Cary Gamble, Rev. E. M. Green, D. D., Rev. M. H. Houston, D. D., Mr. John J. James, Miss Alice Johnson, Rev. J. A. Lefevre, D. D., Rev. W. J. McKay, D. D., Rev. W. W. Mills, Mr. Leighton C. Mills, Mrs. John S. Moore, Mrs. Essie Wilson Price,. Mr. Wm. Rankin, Rev. C. A. Stillman, D. D., Rev. and Mrs. J. L. Stuart, Rev. J. N. Waddell, D. D., LL. D., Rev. J. D. West, D. D., and Mrs. Jennie Woodrow Woodbridge. The two contributions received from Drs. Adger and Dabney were very touching, as they were written by amanuenses, as their eyes can no longer behold the light of the sun. With the exception of a few incidents, what they have written is indicated by quotation marks.

Some of those who labor for the spiritual welfare of the colored people may elect to keep a volume specially for circulation among them, as the subject of this sketch was their friend and benefactor.

We are indebted to the Rev. H. T. Graham for revising most of the chapters, and to the Rev. R. E. McAlpine for the revision of the others, and to the Rev. Dr. W. J. McKay and Rev. Dr. E. M. Green for correcting the sheets as they passed through the press.

H. C. D.

CONTENTS.

8   CONTENTS.

John Leighton Wilson, D. D.

CHAPTER I.

Life in Salem and a Godly Ancestry.

THE noble pioneers who carried the glad news of salvation to Asia, Africa and Oceanica, and laid the foundation of missionary work in reducing the languages to writing, translating the Bible, establishing schools, and organizing churches, have fallen asleep, and it is fitting that those who have entered into their labors study their lives and character in order that they may be incited to greater activity and more earnest consecration in the Master's service. It is also due to "the generation to come" that we tell of the ardent piety, heroic deeds, and manifold toils and trials of the early missionaries, that they, too, may have a strong faith in the power of the gospel to convert the world. The sweet psalmist of Israel, "the anointed of the God of Jacob," sang:

" Which we have heard and known,
    And our fathers have told us,
    We will not hide them from their children,
    Telling to the generation to come the praises of the Lord,
    And his strength, and his wondrous works that he hath done.
    For he established a testimony in Jacob,
    And appointed a law in Israel,
    Which he commaded our fathers,
    That they should make them known to their children,
    That the generation to come might know them, even the chil-
        dren which should be born,

Who should arise and tell them to their children;
That they might set their hope in God,
And not forget the works of God,
But keep his commandments."

A large portion of the Bible is devoted to biography. The gospel in all ages has been exhibited in the daily walk and conversation of the true Israel. God has chosen the historical method of illustrating the precepts of the word; and, selecting the holy men of Israel as the exponents of particular graces, has in the Scriptures given us the portraits of his saints. When we preach Christ, we preach him as manifestly set forth in the lives of his disciples. In comparing John the Baptist with the prophets who had gone before, and also with the "little ones" who understood the wondrous redemption purchased upon Calvary, the Saviour leads us to infer that the saints under the New Testament dispensation may, even while here below, rise from one plane of glory to another; and that in the character of one disciple there may be exemplified the greatness of Abraham, the pathos of David, the wisdom of Solomon, the enthusiasm of Isaiah, and the consecrated statesmanship of Daniel. The reader can in these pages study the work of the Holy Spirit in its moulding influence as it brings one of the sons of the kingdom into conformity with the mind and will of Christ.

Scotch-Irish Ancestry. The subject of this memoir could rejoice in the covenant blessing of a holy ancestry.

In the year 1734 there came to America in one vessel a colony of Presbyterians, who settled in Williamsburg County, South Carolina. These were the Wilsons, Jameses, Gordons, Friersons, Witherspoons and Ervins, and from these six families sprang Leighton Wilson, whose ancestry was wholly Scotch-

Irish. In the early history of the republic, the sterling character, inflexible courage, perfect honesty and wise conservatism of the Scotch-Irish settlers rendered them pillars in the temple of state. But most of all, their constant appeal to the law and the testimony, their strict observance of the Lord's day, and their rigid enforcement of family discipline, made them worthy citizens of the commonwealth.

Salem's Plains.

The country which they settled as a home for themselves and their children was perfectly level; not waving or undulating, but absolutely flat, save beside the water-courses, which flowed through the swamps, filled with the bay, the water-oak and the cypress, and beautified by the flowering dogwood, the honeysuckle and the jessamine. On the uplands, except now and then the hickory and the oak, there is but one tree, the tall, long-leaf pine, whose foliage never rustles in the wind, its grand trunk rising fifty or eighty feet before a limb is extended, and its burrs peerless cones, adorning these umbrellas of the forest,. while the straw which covers the ground furnishes the softest carpet.

The homes in the earlier years of the century were plain, but comfortable. The house, a frame building of two stories, was faced on the four sides with a wide piazza, from which small rooms were cut off. Each home was provided with a book-case, in which was found Scott's or Henry's Commentary, the Family Library, the

Books.

Presbyterian standards, a number of volumes of sermons, and ancient and modern histories. The voice of prayer and praise was heard morning and evening, the children were taught to work and to obey; they were instructed in the Catechism and the Holy Scriptures, and brought up in the nurture and

admonition of the Lord. It was a godly community.
There was a church in every house.

Hospitality.   Salem's hospitality was far-famed. The
people were "lovers of hospitality." The
belated traveler had but to rein his horses at the door,
and he received a hearty welcome. Few "calls" were
made; it was usually "to spend the day," and not infrequently "to stay a week." For the noon-day dinner the
bill of fare was stereotyped: a ham and large chicken-
pie, rice and corn bread, a great variety of vegetables deli-
ciously prepared; this followed by dessert and coffee.
In the morning a saddle-horse to ride over the plantation
was placed at the disposal of the visitor.

The church was the centre of the community, the
axis around which their hopes and joys revolved. The
people believed in religion, talked of religion, taught
religion, and made religion their chief concern. They
gave double honor unto those who labored in word and
doctrine, and counted their ministers as "holy men of
God," who, as undershepherds, were to lead them into
the "green pastures." They gave heed how they heard,
and the good seed fell into good ground and brought
forth abundantly. They loved the sanctuary of Jehovah;
they "offered in his tabernacle sacrifices of joy," and
worshipped the Lord in "the beauty of holiness." A

Mount Zion.   large handsome church, erected forty years
ago, with its porch upheld by massive Doric
columns, is now the Mount Zion of that Presbyterian
region, but before that time there was a square frame-
building with its high box-pulpit, and it was in this
sanctuary that the subject of this memoir worshipped
in his youth.

On the Sabbath the grove was filled with horses and
vehicles, as the people assembled for worship; but what

means that mighty chorus of voices that rises in such
delightful harmony? Lo! it is Afric's sons underneath

Afric's Sons, the great arbor, who lift up the voice of
praise to their great Creator. The minister
first preaches to them; then they fill the spacious gal-
leries of the church and join in worship with the white
congregation. Twice a year hundreds of colored com-
municants surround the communion tables to celebrate
the dying love of their Saviour and Lord. Each master
and mistress returns home on Sunday to assemble the
servants to catechize and instruct them. The minister
goes to some neighboring plantation and again preaches,
and often during the six days of the week in the evening, while the flaming pine-knot lights up the darkness,
he addresses the sons of Ham. They receive him as an
angel of God, join with him in the service of song, listen
to his exhortations, and when he departs they hold the
stirrup as he mounts and bid him God-speed. Delightful was the relationship between the white pastor and
his sable parishioners. This was Salem, the home of
the Wilsons, and in the midst of these surroundings was
the childhood of the Missionary-Secretary spent.

The study of the family tree is interesting. We can
trace the lineaments of this Master in Israel in the faces
of his ancestors:

WILSON.	JAMES.
Robert Wilson *m.* Mary Gordon.	William James *m.* Elizabeth Witherspoon.
Roger Wilson *m.* Mary Frierson.	John James *m.* Mary Dobin.
	John James *m.* Mary Ervin.

William Wilson *m.* Jane E. James.

JOHN LEIGHTON WILSON.

Three (and perhaps four) of those first-named above
crossed the Atlantic together in the ship which landed

the colony in the Carolina wilds. Robert Wilson, the founder of the Wilson family, of Black River, was born in 1710, or a century (less one year) previous to his great-grandson. As an illustration of how "a little one may become a thousand," it may be mentioned that his son Roger was one of five children, and his grandson William one of ten, so the near relatives of John Leighton were legion. Of the two elder Wilsons the writer knows only of their reputation for eminent piety. They served God in their generation and he blessed them and their children. The Gordons and the Friersons were among the staunchest of the families of the Palmetto State. A large colony of the latter removed to Maury County, Tennessee.

History deals more fully with ancestors on the maternal side. William James was born in Wales, near the close of the seventeenth century, and on account of the persecutions of the Stuarts removed to County Down in Ireland. He afterwards joined the colony which emigrated to the Sunny South, and was one of the original elders of the Williamsburg Church, the mother of Presbyterianism in Eastern South Carolina.

His son, John James, also became a Presbyterian elder, and was a member of the original session of the Indiantown Church. He was in the prime of manhood when the Revolutionary struggles of the colonies began. He raised a company of volunteers, and this, with some others, formed the original brigade of partisans which, under the magnificent leadership of Francis Marion, immortalized itself in the struggle for American liberty. He has left a name around which tradition has gathered many stories illustrative of mental vigor, personal intrepidity and patriotic ardor. His son, Captain John James, appears to have inherited, in no small measure, the same traits of character, and was also distinguished for the conspicuous part he bore in achieving the liberty of his country." He had seven sons and daughters; and as the teacher may be made illustrious by his pupils, so may the father be honored by the character and virtues of his children.

William E. James.

One of the sons of Captain James was William E. James, who for thirty or forty years was a member of the session of Darlington Church and one of the leading elders in the Synod of South Carolina. He was a man of stalwart frame and commanding presence, blessed with great wealth and noted for his liberal support of the gospel. He was never absent from the weekly prayer-meeting, and was exceedingly gifted in public prayer. His petitions were marked by their fervor, appropriateness and variety of expression, and were almost wholly in the language of Scripture. He was an efficient teacher and superintendent of the Sabbath-school. For ten years the writer sat in his class and can testify to his aptness to teach. He specially remembers when at the age of twelve the Book of Romans was studied, and how lucid were Mr. James' explanations. Though two and thirty years have passed since *we* sat with the watchers the night previous to his burial, yet it is a privilege to testify to our personal indebtedness to the religious instructions of this great and good ruler in Israel.

Miss Lavinia James.

To the two brothers specially mentioned here there was given a sister, who was summoned in 1830 to act the mother's part to the two little daughters of Rev. R. W. James; and, when these were grown and married, to go in 1846 to the home of her brother William and care for his five motherless ones. A lady of great loveliness and amiability of disposition, and of marked energy and executive ability, she managed well the affairs of their households, and all of those whom she lovingly served rise up and call her blessed. This handmaid of the Lord labored much in the church, and was a succorer of many, especially of her beloved nephew on the coast of Africa. Another and younger sister, Sarah, was the mother of Rev. Dr. E. M. Green, who was to the subject of this memoir, his own son Timothy in the faith.

Rev. Robert W. James. Rev. Robert Wilson James, the eldest uncle of Leighton Wilson, was born June 3, 1792; graduated at the South Carolina College in 1813; began the study of theology under the Rev. James W. Stevenson, D. D., of Tennessee, and completed the prescribed course at Princeton Seminary in 1817. The next year he was called to the pastorate of Indiantown and Bethel Churches. He then accepted a call to Salem, Black River, where he labored till the time of his death, thirteen years afterwards. "He held in fine combination an active, penetrating intellect, a resolute will, sound judgment, and great gentleness and benevolence of spirit—a well-rounded man. Social and hospitable, he won and kept a large circle of friends. His manner of presenting and enforcing divine truth was highly original. He thought his own thoughts, and spake his own words. In the courts of the church his intellectual ability, wise counsel, and gentle deportment found ready recognition. His opinions, carefully matured and forcibly uttered, often determined the most important questions. While his peers readily accorded the esteem to which his merits entitled him, his younger brethren looked up to him with affectionate veneration. He was one of the original founders and earnest supporters of Columbia Seminary. He prepared very care-

Preaching to the Sons of Ham. fully his discourses for the ignorant sons of Africa who flocked in great numbers from the large plantations on the river to hear his simple, lucid, earnest, and forcible presentation of gospel truth. He was largely instrumental in his own Synod in arousing a zeal in their spiritual welfare; and it is probable that his profound interest in their spiritual condition was the means of directing the missionary enthusiasm of his young neighbor and kinsman, J. Leighton Wilson, toward the dark continent.''

This is but a brief sketch of the life and labors of one of the most eminent ministers of South Carolina. It is introduced specially to show the early influences brought to bear upon the subject of this memoir. Here was a sedate and pious youth, with his mind partially fixed upon the ministry as his future calling; what more natural than that his uncle, so well known for learning and piety, should be to him a pattern he might safely imitate? He visited frequently at his home, had access to his rare and ample library, sat under his ministry, listened to his counsels, and spent one winter under his roof. The nephew was the minister's friend and young companion. Blessed relationship!

His Father. Mr. William Wilson, Leighton's father, was a planter. Like the patriarch Jacob, he was ''a plain man dwelling in tents,'' which we mean only figuratively, for the frame house in which his distinguished son was born and died was the first house in that part of the country that was glazed and ceiled. He was a noble specimen of the Presbyterian eldership, a pillar in the house of the Lord. He feared God and commanded his children after him; was just and honorable in his dealings with his fellow-men; gentle and kind in his family relations, and exerted a wide influence for good in the community in which he lived. He placed a high value upon education, and sought to confer upon his children the highest and choicest blessings of this life and of that to come. He was a man of wisdom and prudence, possessing "an excellent spirit," and, like Enoch, walked with God.

He married Miss Jane E. James, the eldest daughter of Capt. John James. It is an old adage that the son frequently inherits the moral qualities from the father and the intellectual from the mother, and in the subject of this memoir we find a happy blending of the gifts and graces of both the house of Wilson and the house of James. The gentleness and goodness, the purity and piety of the one; the splendid physique, the wide intelligence, the sound judgment and strong common sense, the active energy, and the executive ability of the other. He possessed the nobleness of heart of the paternal, and the sterling qualities of mind of the maternal, side of the house. He was a Wilson in humility of soul, simplicity of life, loveliness of character, and consecration to the church ; but it was the James' blood coursing through his veins that made him a Joshua to the Southern Church in her days of poverty and desolation.

Besides the missionary to Africa, there were born in the house of William Wilson three sons, William, Samuel, and Robert. The first of these settled in Marion County, and the other two on the right and left of the old homestead. He had also three daughters : Mary, Mrs. Flinn Wilson ; Martha, Mrs. W. E. Mills ; and Sarah, who never married. The last was a lady of remarkable intelligence, and the special correspondent of her absent brother. She was a great friend of the ministers ; among these one of the most beloved was the late Dr. Plumer.

On the 25th of March, 1809, there was joy in the
home, for a man-child was born there, and a few weeks
afterwards the godly parents, at Mount Zion, presented
him to the Lord. The father called him "John Leighton," after the pious and eminent commentator, pro-
phetic of the mantle of holy living and burning zeal
which should fall on his shoulders. The young mother's
words no doubt were, "I have lent him to the Lord; as
long as he liveth shall he be lent to the Lord"; and as
she returned home with the babe in her arms, she sang:

> "Mine heart exulteth in the Lord,
> Mine horn is exalted in the Lord:
> My mouth is enlarged over mine enemies;
> Because I rejoice in thy salvation.
> For there is none beside thee;
> Neither is there any rock like our Lord."

How little did Hannah know of the future of the
great judge and prophet who anointed the first two kings
of Israel! In like manner Jane James Wilson scarcely
imagined the conspicuous place in the world's evangelization that would be filled by her darling boy, now by
dedication and baptismal seal a minor in the household
and kingdom of Christ!

CHAPTER II.

Home, School, and College.

A CHORUS of voices sang "Home, Sweet Home" around the Wilson fireside. A godly and worthy father; a gentle and loving mother; strong, manly brothers, full of life and generous impulses; and three sisters, intelligent, affectionate, and winning; it was the abode of peace and joy. There was plenty with frugality, an abundance of earth's stores with the economical expenditure of the same; perfect contentment with the added blessing of godliness. They visited among relatives and friends living in the neighborhood, entertained with lavish hospitality, and the younger members of the family enjoyed the pic-nic, the social gathering, and the pleasant holidays. Amidst these happy surroundings was Leighton's childhood spent.

The Southern Boy. He grew to manhood not in the busy mart or in the counting-room on a crowded street, but upon his father's plantation, as free as the bird that flies in the air, or the squirrel that leaps upon the limbs of the tree. The boy on the Carolina farm at an early age learns to ride and drive a horse, and to feed and curry him. He can plant the kitchen garden and use the spade and the hoe. He can grasp the plow handle and drive the furrow through the broad acres, and knows how and when to plant, "chop," pick, gin, and pack the cotton, and can by muscular strength turn a five hundred pound bale on its end. He can climb the tall trees, set traps for birds, hunt rabbits, fish in the streams, bag a covey of partridges, shoot deer, and engage in a hundred athletic sports of the field and forest. It was by this out-door exercise that the subject of this sketch grew in stature to the height of six feet one inch, rather heavily built, with broad shoulders and a splendid chest, and laid the foundation of that remarkable physical strength which served him for nearly twenty years in the African jungle and for over thirty years in the mission-rooms.

His early education was conducted in the log schoolhouse in the country, and there is a family tradition that, in order to be free from interruptions, he would climb a pine tree to study his Latin. Without vouching for the truth of the story—for to ascend the straight, smooth trunk of the monarch of the Southern forest is no easy task—it goes to prove that Leighton at an early age developed studious habits, and that in his first days at school he had classical teachers. His father was long since laid in the grave, but were it possible to call up his shade, we would like to inquire what there was about this son that caused him to pay such special attention to his education. He must have seen something in the boy which seemed to forecast his future. To

Academy.

pursue his academic studies he sent him to the fine school at Springville, in the adjoining county of Darlington, and after that to Scion College or High School at Winnsboro, S. C., at that time under the superintendence of a noted teacher, Dr. Samuel Stafford. At this institution, in the olden time, many of the distinguished men in the State were educated. He also spent one winter under the instruction of his uncle, the Rev. R. Wilson James, who, as we have noticed in the previous chapter, was not only distinguished for his preaching ability, but was also eminent for his learning. Perhaps it was he who first suggested to his father the expediency of giving Leighton a finished education.

The next step proved the father's wisdom. At that time the reputation of the South Carolina College at Columbia for a high standard of scholarship was well established, and there was a distinguished and accomplished faculty teaching in her classic halls. Yet unfortunately, the president, Dr. Cooper, was an avowed infidel! His influence against religion was being felt through the State, and the young men of the commonwealth were being tainted with skepticism. It was not till after some years had passed that public sentiment became so strong that he was ejected from his position, and a chair established for teaching the evidences of Christianity.

College.   Mr. Wilson, the elder who feared God, resolved that he would not expose his son to any influence that would shake his faith in the truth of the gospel, so he sent him in 1827, at the age of eighteen, to Union College at Schenectady, New York, then under the able presidency of Dr. Nott. It was a costly undertaking. When young Wilson was near graduation he sent to his father for his travelling expenses home and says: "If I come all the way by land it will cost $250. If by water to Charleston $40 less will answer. I shall be content to follow either course that you suggest."

Before he entered college, probably previous to the time he went to school at Darlington, he united with the people of God on profession of his faith in Christ, under the pastorate, it is supposed, of Mr. Harrington. Among the Presbyterian families of Salem, it was not infrequent that the children of the covenant at an early

age came before the church session and took upon themselves the vows that believing parents had made for
them in infancy. He was a consistent and exemplary
member of the church.

He entered the junior class at Union College in the
fall of 1827 and graduated in the summer of 1829. His
ocean voyages began in his boyhood, for he took his
passage at Charleston and sailed for New York. A few
of his college epistles, addressed to his sisters, have
come down to us after the lapse of threescore and five
years. His first letter tells of two severe maladies, sea-
sickness and home-sickness, but he soon regains his
spirits and writes of his surroundings: "I am well
pleased with the college and the young men here. I
have a good many warm friends in the place, and have
had repeated exhibitions of the sincerity of their friendship for me."

He writes to his sister, March 1, 1828: "When I first
came to the college I had but one acquaintance, Sydenham Witherspoon, and I felt like a lost sheep, but since
my acquaintance has become more extensive I feel better pleased. I found one South Carolinian here; his
residence is Charleston. He is an amiable young man,
and I feel much attached to him because he is from my
native State." We will hear the report of the "amiable
young man," now a venerable octogenarian, and more
than once in this volume will he speak of his friend.
The Rev. Dr. John B. Adger writes: "My first acquaintance with Leighton Wilson was at Union College, Schenectady, New York. I was then a mere boy, having
recently professed religion. I was not particularly intimate with him, but both coming from South Carolina
we were naturally drawn together. There came with
him a friend of his from Alabama, named Sydenham

Witherspoon. Wilson impressed me greatly
Sedate, Sober and Solid. by his sedate, sober and solid character. He
was at that time a professing Christian, and
so was Witherspoon, who impressed me as being of a
very light and frivolous disposition. I venture to make
this statement, because on his return to the South he
became one of the most eminent, godly, and greatly
useful ministers of the Presbyterian Church, whose name
and memory are still dear to thousands of Christians in
Alabama.''

Day of Prayer. Of the observance of the day of prayer for
colleges in February, 1828, Leighton Wilson
writes : ''Day before yesterday was set apart
as a day of fasting and prayer for colleges. At night
Dr. Nott gave us a long, eloquent, and impressive address. Of the present Senior Class two-thirds will enter
the ministry.''

Catskill. During the summer of 1828 many of the
students went on a tramp to the Catskill
Mountains. The prospect from the summit of the
highest peak was particularly delightful to a student
from the flat lands of the Palmetto State. He writes to
his youngest sister: ''I will give you an account of the
march we cadets of Union College made the first of July.
With our knapsacks on our backs and muskets on our
shoulders we set off from Schenectady to Albany, a distance of twenty miles, and lodged in the Academy the
first night. The next morning we went aboard a steamboat, and in a few hours landed at Catskill, about twelve
miles from the mountain-house to which we were des-
tined, and which we reached in the evening. Being so
much elevated we very sensibly felt a change of tem-
perature, and found it so cold we had to throw our
cloaks around us. When we got to the highest peak of

the mountain we had the most splendid prospect that I ever enjoyed. We could see a vast extent of country and a great number of cities and towns. We went three miles further to see the falls of the Catskill River, very celebrated for their beauty. The waters fall nearly three hundred feet, and when we got below they presented an enrapturing prospect. Thursday, much gratified with what we had seen, we returned by the same route, reaching Schenectady Saturday evening.

A Walk of Forty Miles. "Our excursion gave us a fondness for walking. Sydenham, myself, and a few others set off on foot to visit the falls of the Mohawk, where this river empties into the Hudson. We were very much pleased with what we saw. Sydenham and I returned by a very circuitous route. We went to the junction of the Mohawk and Hudson, crossed the river, went down the east side to Troy, recrossed the river and reached Union College after night, somewhat fatigued, but delighted with what we had seen in a walk of forty miles in one day. We spent about fifty cents apiece. The remainder of the vacation I expect to devote to reading and writing." This walk of forty miles proves that he had the physical preparation for a messenger whose feet were to bear the glad tidings.

We can readily imagine the affection of a college boy of nineteen for his three younger sisters who look upon him as a prodigy in manliness and learning! He takes special interest in the cultivation of their minds, and writes : "I do not read as much of miscellany as I should like to, for I can read but little else than what is connected with my studies. I hope you all three will devote yourselves to this invaluable pursuit. You have not a select library, but still there are a good many books in it from which you might derive a good stock of knowledge. It would be unnecessary for me to point out the worth of knowledge. The pleasure that would arise from its possession would amply compensate for all the trouble you had in amassing it. You can appreciate the value of knowledge when you are in possession of it, and I know of no more direct way of obtaining this than by reading books. Those persons who do not possess a natural taste for reading are compelled to acquire a fondness by the sacrifice of considerable pleasure, but an acquired taste for reading I think more desirable than a natural one. Those who delight in reading from infancy read only for amusement, without any regard for improvement, but those who have acquired a taste read with both these ends in view. From reading you will learn many valuable lessons that will be highly useful to you in future life.''

Again his letters talk of home: ''I often revert to scenes at home. It gives me inexpressible pleasure to indulge in recollections of home. I can picture our dwelling, with everything that pertains to it: the little shade trees in the yard; the little live oak in front of the milk house; the large pines on every side of the house; these are present before my mind at this time, and you can scarcely imagine what pleasure there is in indulging in these ideal dreams. But however much pleasure there may be in contemplating these objects, there is pleasure vastly superior of going into the house and taking my seat at the fireside with you all and taking part in the chit-chat, but, above all, the privilege of kneeling together around the family altar. This is the place to enjoy a foretaste of heaven.''

During his vacation he writes of his religious work: '' I have charge of a Sabbath-school, which occupies much of my attention on the Sabbath.''

Towards the close of his college course he says: "I have been very busily engaged the last month, and am still quite busy. Commencement is only seven weeks off, and between this time and that I have more to do than I shall be able to accomplish. At present my time is devoted to the study of Hebrew, and besides this I have a speech to prepare.

"I am waiting for a letter from father to determine by what route I shall return home. If I come all the way by land I have promised a friend to spend a week or two with him in Pennsylvania. I have likewise promised a friend in Virginia to pay him a visit. I have had the offer of introductory letters to individuals near Dr. Rice's seminary in Virginia if I should wish to stop there on my way home. . . . I wish to visit Dr. Rice's seminary on my way home, as it is probable I am to spend some time there. Dr. Nott is intimate with Dr. Rice, and recommends me to study under him."

The brief record reveals the fact that he was a good and faithful student at college, that he had as his friend and counsellor its pious and scholarly President, whose influence was felt by him during life, and that he had the ministry in view, at least that he felt in some measure the call to preach, though the question of his life-work was not fully determined. He graduated at the age of twenty, and his immature years in part account for his immature views of duty. Some, as Jeremiah, in the days of their childhood hearken to the voice, "I ordained thee a prophet unto the nations," but with a far larger number it is not until after they have reached the age of manhood that they respond to the call, "Go, preach." It is natural to suppose that for years he had thought of the ministry as his life's work, but more in the light of a profession which he would prefer to law or medicine, than with a burning desire to make known the glad tidings. We call special attention to this phase of his religious experience, as it probably accurately represents that of multitudes of our Christian young men just as they are leaving the academic halls.

Of what he did the next few months there is no record. They may have been spent quietly at his father's home, reviewing his studies and in general reading. After the absence of two years, he enjoyed the society of his brothers and sisters, and the many playmates of his youth. The winter he spent with his uncle, Mr. James, was mentioned above for the reason that in the paper Dr. Wilson read before the semi-centennial of Columbia Seminary he mentions having "spent one winter under the instruction of his uncle, Rev. Robert W. James, of Indiantown." Mr. James moved from Indiantown to Salem during the time young Wilson was at college. If the winter in question was spent at Indiantown and not at Salem, then it was previous to his college course; but as the paper was written a half-century after the time referred to, and as only a few lines further on the mistake is made of saying that he "entered the seminary in 1830" instead of 1831, we incline to the opinion that the winter spoken of was the one following his graduation, and if so, he was the better prepared to profit by the instructions of the sweet preacher of Harmony and to enjoy the hours in his library. The pastor, no doubt, found the society of the earnest young student, his favorite nephew, very congenial.

CHAPTER III.

Spiritual Preparation.

DURING the latter half of the year 1830 Mr. Wilson taught at Mount Pleasant, an island in the Charleston Bay, only a little separated from the main land. He writes : " My school is small, the place is pleasant and healthy, society good, and I have great facilities for studying. I spend Saturday night and Sunday in town, teach a Sabbath-school class in the Second Presbyterian Church, and have formed a good many acquaintances in the place. I make Mr. Adger's my home when in town. He is the father of my old college-mate, John B. Adger. The young man himself is in Princeton, but his friends have been unusually kind and attentive. There is more domestic happiness and harmony in this family than I have ever seen in any other. Love appears to be the ruling principle, and peace the consequence.''

''For a month past (he writes to his sister, August, 1830) my mind has become clouded. God has hid his face from me, and if I really ever had a hope, for the present it is absent. We have had preaching here for more than a month by a Presbyterian clergyman by the name of Osborne. He is a plain, pungent, and zealous preacher.''

"I have been (September, 1830) generally well in health and my mind has been occa-
Knowing the Terror of the Lord.
sionally distressed since I wrote last, but at present all is clear. I have recently had eternity brought nearer to me than it had ever been before.

I have had conceptions of eternal misery that have made me tremble. I have had views of the deceitfulness and obstinacy of my heart, of which I had no previous conception. Some time since, when I was in deep anguish of spirit, after hearing a very solemn sermon, the services were closed by requesting all those who had a hope in the Redeemer to rise to their feet. I was left in my seat. The thought entered my mind that such might be the case at the judgment-seat of Christ, and I had scarcely conceived this when I imagined myself surrounded by a beloved father, mother, sisters, brothers, and an innumerable host of friends, all dressed in white robes and wearing glittering crowns, coming to bid me an eternal adieu. I could almost feel the pressure of the grasp. I next turned to the destiny that might possibly be mine. I rolled years upon years, and centuries upon centuries, until my imagination was exhausted. My feelings were so much tortured that I could no longer bear to think myself the subject of it, so I placed another on the wheel of time and could hear him exclaim, as century after century passed, "Is there no end?" and the reply was, "Eternity." But the obstinacy of my heart withstood all this, and it was weeks before my stubborn will would yield.

Tasting the Powers of the World to Come.

"We had a four days' meeting in August, when Drs. Leland, McDowell and Palmer, and Mr. Gildersleeve assisted Mr. Osborne. Many from town attended. Dr. Leland is much roused and doing wonderful good. Dr. McDowell has just returned from another meeting with increased zeal, though zealous before. These four ministers are very precious to me indeed."

"I feel that God has directed me to-day (October, 1830,) to write this letter unto you, my dear sisters, for I wish to give you a few hints as to the preparation which I think you should make for the camp-meeting, and the manner in which you should spend your time while encamped. I was very anxious to be with you a few days before the meeting commenced, but I shall not be up (if at all) before the meeting is advanced. Depend upon it, such seasons as are just before us are few, and should be precious indeed. Surely as we approach this solemn test of our lives we shall see these things in the clear light of God's countenance. You must make necessary arrangements before you go there; you must have cares while you are there; but suffer not these things to absorb your attention. A close, prayerful examination of the heart is necessary. What progress have you made in grace? Have your attachments for the world become less? Determine to wrestle with God for a blessing, for a renewal of your spiritual strength, and may you be enabled to say before you leave, 'It is good for us to be here.'"

This era in his religious experience has been termed his conversion, and it would appear from his own words that he considered this to be the beginning of his religious life. It may with good reason be held that he had never before experienced a change of heart, and now for the first time he knew his Saviour; but we do not incline to this view, for on the other hand we have before us a child of the covenant at an early age giving himself to God, leading an exemplary life at school, giving God thanks for a prosperous journey, known in college by his walk and conversation, teaching a mission Sabbath-school, longing for "the privilege of kneeling around the family altar," and talking to the President of the college about studying for the ministry; if the tree is known by its fruits, do not these appear to be the fruits of the Holy Spirit? Instead of the time of the new birth, may it not have been a season for the deepening and quickening of his religious life? Here is a young man having just reached his majority, teaching school, reading literature, and enjoying religious society, "at ease in Zion." The Lord had a great work for him to do as the apostle to the Gentiles, so he leads him into the Arabian desert; or that he may follow in the footsteps of his Master, he is sent into the wilderness; or that he might be like Abraham, who "went out not knowing whither he went," the "horror of a great darkness fell upon him." God used an humble preacher as an instrument to bring him before the judgment-seat, and after he had experienced the joys of light and salvation he decides immediately that henceforth he would live for dying men. Does it not seem a period of apostolic preparation? But whatever may have been his previous state, he was now a changed man. The old days of formalism had passed away. Religion was now to him a living reality, for he knew the power of Christ's resurrection, and henceforth "Beheld his glory, the glory as of the only begotten of the Father, full of grace and truth." He received at Mount Pleasant the baptism of the Holy Ghost. He was anointed for his life-work. With the vows of consecration fresh upon him, he resigned his position in the school and entered at once upon his biblical studies.

CHAPTER IV.

In the Theological Hall.

JOHN LEIGHTON WILSON entered the Theological Seminary, Columbia, S. C., January, 1831, at its formal opening, and was a member of the first class which graduated from that institution. His teachers were Dr. Goulding, "a polished scholar and impressive preacher," and Professor Howe, who was permitted to teach successively fifty classes in the seminary. He was one of the most eminent biblical scholars of the nineteenth century. With a seraph's tongue he approached in prayer the mercy-seat, and in his love and tenderness exemplified the character of the "beloved disciple." He was the intimate and life-long friend of his first pupil, and in many points of character there was a marked resemblance between the two.

Classmates. Among his classmates were the genial Francis R. Goulding, the author of the *Young Marooners*, and who, in the pastor's study, invented the sewing-machine, either simultaneously with or previously to Howe, who obtained the patent; William Moultrie Reid, who was recommended by his Brother Wilson to his home church, Mount Zion, where he labored for forty years, and was known and honored as "Father Reid"; J. M. H. Adams, who was accepted by the American Board, but was hindered from entering the mission-field by the determined opposition of his family; and James L. Merrick, a man of devoted piety, who labored for seven years in Persia.

At that time the central building was the only one of any size on the grounds, as the halls on the right and the left, with their comfortable dormitories, had not then been erected; but though in narrow quarters, contentment reigned in the hearts of the students. He writes: "I have changed my room to one in the basement story of the large building, and have Julius DuBose for my room-mate. Our room is large, and we will have two small bed-rooms formed in it, besides a place ·for sitting and studying. I hope we shall stir up one another and provoke each other to growth in grace and all good works."

The effects of the meeting at Mount Pleasant were permanent. His early reading at the seminary was the works of Baxter and John Newton and the Life of Brainerd. His college letters to his sisters were about the cultivation of their minds; those from the seacoast discussed the establishment of female character, but his seminary epistles had one burning theme, and that was the development of the spiritual life. He closes one of these with the words, "Give me the blessing and presence of God, and I would sooner be in the deserts of Africa or the cold regions of Greenland than in the most refined society and affluent circumstances without the comforts of religion."

"Your very interesting letter (writing to his sister, February 27, 1831,) is before me, and gave me more than a little pleasure. When you say you have been *revived* I feel that my prayers have been answered and my strongest desires satisfied. If I had the whole world at my disposal I would not wish to confer anything upon you that would exclude the enjoyment of religion and the hope of heaven. For my own part I would rather live in the lowliest hut with the enjoyment of God than in the most resplendent palace on earth without a hope of heaven. . . . I tremble for myself when I contemplate the solemn relationship which I bear to those of my fellow-creatures about me. We either attract by our consistent and Christian deportment, or we repel by unbecoming behavior and indifference for their spiritual welfare.''

To his sister: ''COLUMBIA, *June* 29, 1831. Suppose an angel from heaven were permitted by God to visit this earth and was allowed to do all the good he could in the space of thirty or forty years, do you suppose the angel would ever be found idle? No, he would be flying from one end of the earth to another and proclaiming the glad tidings of salvation everywhere. Paul was an active man, but were he permitted to return to this world again he would desire to be more active than ever before.

''A few days' meeting has been appointed here the last week in July, and Christians are looking forward to a revival of religion. Our vacation will commence August 1.''

Work among the ignorant settlers on the sand hills around Columbia has been carried on by successive classes in the seminary. The young student writes, October 27, 1832: ''I attended my sand hill Sunday-school this morning, and had a large and interesting school.'' As he was a member of the first class in the seminary, it is likely he was one of the founders of the Barhamsville Church.

CHAPTER V.

The Missionary Volunteer.

WE read in the gospel history that when Andrew beheld the Lamb of God the first thing he did was to find his brother Peter. That was no doubt the best day's work for the church Andrew ever performed. His example has been followed by many young disciples.

Adger Called. Two students at Princeton were taking an evening walk when one broached the subject of Foreign Missions. It was a new thought to his companion, who afterwards found that the speaker had committed himself to work in heathen lands. We do not know his name, but the listener, who was John B. Adger, soon felt that he was called to go far hence to the Gentiles. He thus writes of what happened over sixty years ago: "It was in the year 1830, after I entered Princeton Theological Seminary, that my intercourse with Wilson, my old college-mate, was renewed by letter. He was then living at Mount Pleasant, near the city of Charleston, reviewing his college course and carrying on his studies with the assistance of Rev. Dr. Leland, who ministered then to the Presbyterians and Congregationalists of what was called Christ Church Parish. At that time, as his letters informed me, his religious feelings were at a low ebb. I had myself, after my graduation in 1828, passed through a year of great spiritual declension, but coming to Princeton Seminary in the following year with a view to entering the ministry, I found myself in a new atmosphere of religious life. I was led to abandon all hope of having been converted at college, and my experience of religion became very much deepened. Naturally our correspondence related largely to these matters, both on his part and on mine. Afterwards becoming myself deeply interested in the idea of Foreign Missionary Work, that also became a subject of our letters. Years afterwards he told me that it was then he first began to **A Word in Season.** think of devoting himself to this work. I consider it the greatest honor of my life to have had something to do with initiating his interest in this sublime enterprise.

"Subsequently Wilson went to Columbia Theological Seminary, of whose first class he was a member. I continued at Princeton. Our intimacy became more close and our correspondence very lively. Gradually each of us was brought to the conclusion of devoting our lives to the foreign propagation of the faith. He was appointed a missionary to Africa, and I to the Armenians of Asia."

In the memorial adopted by the Synod of **Revival in the Seminary.** South Carolina it is said: "During his seminary course there was a deep interest awakened among the students in regard to the claims of the heathen nations upon the church of God for the gospel of Jesus Christ, and Leighton Wilson, with others, responded promptly to this call and devoted himself— mind, soul, and body—to the great work of foreign missions."

He writes to his sister, January 19, 1832: **The Student Volunteer.** "I suppose you were all apprised of the subject of my last letter to father, but I hope you will all cheerfully consent and be proud to see me so

much honored as to be a foreign missionary. If a man
of the world were appointed to negotiate for our government with some other nation of the earth he would feel
honored, and everybody else would look upon him as an
honored and distinguished man; and ought not that man
to feel honored who is commissioned by Jesus Christ to
proclaim the glad news of salvation to those who sit in
the dark places of the earth?

"I have looked at the subject now for more than a
year, and there appears to me stronger reasons for my
becoming a missionary than for many who go, and one
of considerable importance is that our family, those dearest to me on earth, have been made the subjects of grace.
Are we not laid under infinite obligations to him who
has loved us with an everlasting love, and ought I now
to hesitate about obeying his command, ' Go, teach all
nations'?

"I do not think of going away to a foreign country
because there is nothing to be done at home, but because there is more to be done in those places where the
Christian religion is unknown. If I had them at my
disposal I could put more than one hundred ministers to
work in South Carolina, but I could set 500,000 to work
in the missionary field.   Pray for the heathen world; St.
Paul admonishes us to 'pray for all men.'"

"I have received (he writes January 9, 1833) a letter
from Dr. Wisner with regard to my communication to
the American Board, and he requested me to procure
testimonials of my character and qualifications for the
work of missions.   Dr. Wisner intimated that it might
be my duty to visit Africa on an exploring tour and return to this country.   A missionary station is contemplated on the Niger.   The people are degraded enough,
still they are our *brethren*.   But however degraded they

are in their moral character, and whatever they may be in their customs and habits, I am willing to labor, live, and die for them."

Dr. Wisner. The letter of Dr. Wisner, one of the Secretaries of the American Board, of the date January 5, 1833, to which he refers, is as follows: "I was much gratified yesterday by the receipt of your letter of the 25th ult. Glad to have the evidence that you have *made up your mind* that, Providence permitting, you will be a missionary, and that you will go to Africa; on a mission to which country, by young men from the Southern States, my heart has been for some time set. Your letter I regard as an offer of yourself to the Board for such a mission, and as such I will communicate it to the Prudential Committee when I shall receive the testimonial of your professors." It was on Christmas, 1832,

A Christmas Gift. that this theological student, not yet twenty-four years of age, offered himself for the foreign mission work. The first desires to go to the Dark Continent sprang up in his heart when as a child he listened in the negro cabins to the stories about Africa handed down by tradition, and now in the strength of early manhood he offers himself for the work.

Young Adger in Columbia. On June 29, 1832, he wrote to his sister: "I expect my friend John Adger here in a few days. He has been at home spending his vacation and returns to Princeton by land." Of this visit hear the voice of Leighton Wilson a half-century afterwards before the assembled alumni of Columbia Seminary and a crowded audience in the First Presbyterian Church: "The seminary has always been pervaded by a deep and earnest missionary spirit. One of her professors (Dr. Adger) was himself a foreign missionary for many years, and it was his constant aim to promote a missionary spirit in the hearts of the young men under his care. We must be allowed to make special mention of his interest in this cause, whose semi-centennial we to-day celebrate. The speaker feels that it is due to himself, as well as to this venerable father, to give utterance to the feelings of profound gratitude which he has always felt towards him for the kind interest he took in him when inquiring about the path of duty; for the wise counsel he gave to him when he knew as yet nothing of the trials and perils of the missionary life; and especially for the heart-felt prayers that he offered to God that his young servant might be guided into the path of duty. If the speaker ever knew what consecration to God meant, it was while he and this venerable father were kneeling in prayer in the foundation-room of the seminary building. To his memory, even in the deepest wilds of Africa, that south-west corner room has always been a place of peculiar sanctity."

In 1892 Dr. Adger writes of his friend and brother: "In choosing his field of labor, his mind and heart were turned to Africa, not only because it had been a very much neglected portion of the world by Christian nations, but also because he believed that America, and especially the South, owed it to Africa to send her the gospel, inasmuch as so many of her dark-skinned children were held in bondage there." "I know it was also a leading

Reflex Influence.
motive with him in devoting his life to foreign missions to exert some reflex influence upon the Christian people of his native State in extending and deepening their interest in the spiritual condition of their slaves."

The lives of Adger and Wilson were linked in the first

beginnings of their personal interest in the work of foreign missions, in their service in different fields under the American Board, and in later years in their own land they were again united in the conduct of that great work. Their hearts were knit together as those of David and Jonathan.

CHAPTER VI.

Seeking a Helpmeet.

"I HAVE made up my mind," he writes from the Seminary to his sister Sarah, October 27, 1832, "to go to Synod and thence to Savannah. I suppose you know for what. Francis Goulding has made me believe that Miss B. is the next to the best girl in Savannah; Mary Howard, his own, not only being the best in Savannah, but also in the world. Mrs. Baker thinks these two sisters very intelligent and amiable girls, and from the concurrent testimony of a great many I have come to the conclusion it is worth while going down to see them, being determined to judge for myself. In most cases there is a mountain of parental objection to be climbed, and nothing is more painful than to think of tearing away a girl from the bosom of unwilling parents. In my projected scheme no such difficulties are to be encountered. The young ladies have already made up their minds to the work of missions, and they have no parents to say they shall not go. I am trembling for fear I shall be suspected. I will write you again after I return from *Headquarters*."

The "Miss B.," referred to above, was Miss Jane Elizabeth Bayard, daughter of Nicholas Bayard, M. D., and Miss Elizabeth McIntosh, who was born on Cumberland Island, off the coast of Georgia, January 8, 1807, on her mother's plantation, which had been given by Congress to her grandfather, Gen. Lauchlin McIntosh, for distinguished services rendered during the Revolutionary War. By Dr. Bayard's second marriage there were two daughters, Jane and Margaret. When they reached the ages of thirteen and ten respectively, their parents died and they were sent by their half-brother, Col. Nicholas Bayard, who was then a young man, to their uncle, Mr. Andrew Bayard, of Philadelphia, who for years stood for them *in loco parentis*. Instead of the life of luxury in their Southern home, with maids to perform every service, the carriage waiting at the door and the servants treating them as princesses, they were taught to be independent and useful, and withal a wealth of love was showered upon the orphans.

After completing their education they returned to Savannah, where, as young ladies of many accomplishments and considerable wealth, they were much in society. Afterwards Jane consecrated herself to the Lord and became an active and efficient member of the church. The sisters, becoming interested in the Sandwich Islands, offered themselves to the American Board to be sent there. If our information is correct, they were not accepted, for the reason that it was considered inexpedient to send unmarried ladies to foreign fields.

Suitors. There appeared upon the scene about the same time two young suitors. One, the Rev. James R. Eckard, a former acquaintance and friend in Philadelphia, who sued for the hand of Margaret and led her to India, and the other, Leighton Wilson, who received the consent of Jane Bayard to go with him to Africa.

From Synod, whither he was going, as mentioned in the letter given above, he made his way to Savannah, and on Sunday morning he overheard a young lady in the Sabbath-school teaching a class of negroes, this was his first sight of the one whom he afterwards claimed as his bride.   After a pleasant visit he returned to the seminary and wrote (December 18, 1832): "I have yours spread before me, to be perused the third or fourth time.   You say, 'And now I leave kindred, friends and happy country, and uniting my destiny with yours seek a home in some savage land.' . . . I am exceedingly annoyed by my brethren here.   'What did you go to Savannah for?'   'It is surprising that you should have gone to see the colonists sail, and come back the day before the ship started.'   Suspicion is fixed upon me, and every look, word and gesture is closely analyzed. I suppose this is one of the constituents of the *blessed torments of love.*"

CHAPTER VII.

The American Board and Western Africa.

IT is difficult for us to look at foreign missions as they were known and understood in the United States sixty years ago. The views of God's people were very primitive, and even the Presbyterian Church considered the great commission as binding in a very modified degree. The A. B. C. F. M. represented the whole American Church, and *The Missionary Herald*, with a limited circulation, was, if we are not mistaken, the only magazine in the United States devoted to the propagation of the faith in foreign lands. There was no monthly concert, no regular missionary sermon, no annual collection. The ideas of the church with regard to the heathen were very much like China's ideas about foreign countries before the five ports were opened. By the masses almost nothing was known of the habitable globe, save of England and America. In a discourse preached by Dr. Howe at Salem Church on Black River, urging an effort to evangelize the benighted tribes of the earth, he alludes to the circumstances under which Dr. Wilson went to the Dark Continent, and says: "When did our Presbytery send its first missionary to the heathen? In 1833. He went away amid misconceptions, sneers, and bitter words on the part of many, and but a few months ago planted his feet on barbarian shores."

The South and Missions.

Though this was the case, yet from 1833–'36 the Southern churches contributed largely of their means, and a number of her young men

entered upon the work themselves.   Among these
were Rev. Samuel R. Houston, D. D., Rev. George
W. Leyburn, and Mr. Venable of the Synod of Virginia;
Rev. T. P. Johnson and Rev. Alexander E. Wilson,
M. D., of the Synod of North Carolina; Rev. George W.
Boggs, Rev. John B. Adger, D. D., Rev. John F. Lan-
neau, Rev. J. L. Merrick, and Rev. J. Leighton Wilson,
D. D., of the Synod of South Carolina.   The wives of
all these, with one or two exceptions, were also from the
South.

The early history of the *formative period* of the mission
to Western Africa is preserved in young Wilson's letters
to Miss Jane E. Bayard, of which extracts are given below.   The first of these were written from Columbia
Seminary:

"I mentioned Dr. Wisner's letter.   It contains a very
feeling appeal in behalf of Africa, and urges me very
strongly and affectionately to undertake a mission to that
continent.   I do not know that I could, even if I had
not previously thought of it favorably, have resisted such
an appeal.   He states that a gentleman from New York
has just written to him that he would support a mission
to that country for five years.   Now, Jane, I am thinking of writing to him in a very few days and offering
myself to the Board for this mission.   I am now only
waiting a letter from Adger."

December 29, 1832.   "Are you ready to hear that I
have 'volunteered for war'?   I have, but it is to the
American Board and to contend with the powers of
darkness in Africa.   I have been preparing to wield 'the
sword of the Spirit,' and have neither skill nor wish to
handle the broadsword.   I do not know how you came
to infer that I was a nullifier, for I am sure I have very
carefully avoided taking any side in politics, feeling that

they were altogether out of the range of the ambassador of peace.

"I mentioned above that I had offered myself to the Board.   Yes, Jane, I have placed you and myself at their disposal to be sent to the heart even of savage Africa.   I told Dr. Wisner I would hold myself in readiness to obey any command of the Board after April, provided he should give us three months' notice in case he should require us to leave the country during the next year.   I feel a great load of anxiety removed from my mind by this step.   I commended the case to God and the responsibility of acting into the hands of the Board, and feel confident that all will be done aright.   I feel particularly encouraged by your willingness to go with me to the dark regions of Africa."

"I received a letter from my friend Adger yesterday, in which he explicitly tells me that he does not feel it his duty to go to Africa; one of his reasons being the want of constitutional qualifications.

"I cannot be induced to turn away my eyes
A Suffering Continent. from Africa.   My heart is fixed upon that *injured, neglected* people, and I rejoice yours is also.   Our lives in that country must be laborious indeed.   We must be subject to many trials and deprivations, but, Jane, this is food for the children of God. Englishmen can penetrate the heart of the country for wealth, and shall we not go for the love of Christ?"

"Since I wrote last (Columbia, January 7, 1833) the long-expected letter from my father has been received. The suspense caused me no little anxiety, as I was afraid that his being called upon to give his consent to my
Go, My Son. placing myself under the care of the Board would prove too much for him.   But I was most agreeably disappointed.   He gave me his full and

hearty consent, but in very affecting terms, like the patriarch giving up his youngest son. 'Go,' he says, 'and if I am bereaved, I am bereaved.' Nothing has contributed more to his cheerfulness than our engagement."

Who is sufficient for these things? "You speak of your want of qualifications to be a missionary. You have not a more affecting sense of your wants than I have of mine. In vain I have searched and examined myself to find something that would recommend me for such an undertaking. I have despaired of it, and have laid myself at the feet of the Master, to be disposed of as he sees fit. I see you would like to contend for 'the lowest seat,' but if you take it I will not get any at all.

"The lines I promised to copy for you may not be new to you, but they were to me, and if some poor African converted by our instrumentality should express such sentiments it would make us very happy."

"INDIAN HYMN.

"In de dark wood, no Ingin nigh,
　Den me look heben, send up my cry
　　'Pon my knee so low.
　Den God on high in shining place
　See me at night with teary face,
　　De preacher tell me so.

"He send he Spirit, take me care,
　He come heself to hear me prayer,
　　If Ingin heart do pray:
　He see me now, he know me here,
　He say poor Ingin, neber fear,
　　Me wid you night and day.

"Den me lub God, wid inside heart,
　He fight for me, he take my part,
　　He save my life before:
　God love poor Ingin in de wood,
　Den me love God, and dat be good,
　　Me pray him two times more."

"COLUMBIA THEOLOGICAL SEMINARY,

"*January 17, 1833.*

"Dr. Wisner suggests 'going to Liverpool on an exploring tour before marriage.' To this nothing but a very plain providence could induce me to consent. When I leave the country, I do not wish to return; the pain of *one parting* from friends is *enough*. Besides, I cannot bear the idea of leaving my beloved Jane behind me for so long a period. But in all these things I feel it to be our duty to be patient and resigned.

"I have just read a letter from my friend Adger. He says now that 'he is still open to conviction about going to Africa'; if no exploring is to be done, and if a healthy situation can be obtained for the mission, where females can live and labor, he may yet go. If we could have him for an associate we would be highly favored. He is a very dear friend and an invaluable man."

Monthly Concert.

"The last Monthly Concert (February 26, 1833) was one of the most interesting meetings I ever attended. The case of Brother Pinney and his departed associate was the subject of remarks, and the whole audience, a very large one, was melted to tears."

His letter of February 16, 1833, to Miss Bayard contains extracts from the first letter he received from Mr.

Dr. Anderson and Dr. Wilson.

Anderson, one of the Secretaries of the American Board, who was appointed to conduct the correspondence with the mission to Africa.

This was the beginning of very intimate official relations, which were continued for twenty years, of the highest mutual regard and esteem and of the warmest personal attachment. The Secretary desired to obtain the services of several Southerners for Africa, as he considered they would be better adapted to the cli-

mate. The interest in the early days of Columbia Seminary in foreign missions was very
intense. Several of the students of the first
and second classes gave the subject the most serious
and earnest thought. Some of those to whom the way
did not appear to be open to enter the foreign service
lived to preach for forty and fifty years in their native
land.

Columbia Seminary.

His letters say: "The Board is very anxious to commence the mission next fall, but seem to regard it as
all-important that there be another minister to go with
us. Mr. Anderson thinks that I ought to go to Boston
and study the elementary parts of the Arabic language
with Mr. Eli Smith, the only man in the United States
who can teach it. But I think myself, if there is a prospect of our going next fall, it will be the wisest course
for me to acquire some knowledge of medicine."

"Rev. and Mrs. G. W. Boggs have been
heard from. They reached Bombay in good
health and fine spirits and were ready to commence their labors. The news caused quite a sensation
in this place, as they have many friends here. There is
quite a missionary spirit in Columbia. At the last
Monthly Concert the house was crowded."

Missionaries to India.

"The next letter, or the one after the next, I hope
will be a *living epistle*, which you may read over and
over again if you choose."

Mr. Wilson was licensed to preach at a meeting of
presbytery held at Walterborough, which is one of the
oldest towns in the southwestern part of South Carolina.
Half of the State was then within the bounds of the
venerable Presbytery of Harmony. The young semi-
narian found it a convenient place to assemble with the
"brethren," as he was within a day's ride of a "sister"

whom he expected to "lead" to a distant land. Not long after this he started for Andover, going by sea from Charleston.

Separation. He writes: "Your letter gave me the first information of Brother Eckard's and Margaret's engagement. It did not surprise me, but I am not unaffected in view of such an arrangement. I see it will be no ordinary trial for you, but I feel assured that the same grace which makes you willing to go to distant lands will sustain you both under this trial. Rely upon your Saviour for support and he will not forsake you. Though you will be *far, very far* apart, and separated for life, still you have a *common Master* and the *same throne of grace*. Be happy then, my beloved Jane. All is well if the Master bids you go to Africa and Margaret to Ceylon!

"I am staying here (in Charleston) at the home of Mr. Adger; it is a pleasant family. Brother Adger arrived yesterday. I believe his mind is made up to go to the Mediterranean. Brother Adams spent one day with me since I wrote to you. He has offered himself to the Board."

"A letter (Boston, May 24, 1833) from Mr. Anderson to Brother Eckard will reach Savannah a day or two before this, informing him that he must leave Boston by the 29th of June. This arrangement will no doubt hurry him away sooner than he expected, and has no doubt filled you with peculiar emotions. It shall be my constant prayer between this and that time that you and Margaret may be enabled to bear your separation with calm, Christian composure. Look to God for sustaining strength. Overlook the short space of your separation to a glorious reunion in heaven, when you will not only meet, but will be allowed to show to each other many redeemed souls from among the heathen as the wages of your life. Endeavor to be cheerful and happy, my dearest. Men may look on the scene and wonder, some may deride, but the Master smiles.

"The views of the Board with regard to the African mission are now quite definite. It is expected that I remain in this place and Andover until September, studying Arabic and making preparations for the exploring tour. It is expected that Brother Adams and I leave this country in December, with the expectation of returning by May or June of the following spring. They have determined to send us to Liberia, and we will explore from that point."

"Andover, June 7, 1833. I share largely, my beloved Jane, in your bereavement. Margaret is dear to me as a sister, and I cannot contemplate a separation from her for life without peculiar emotions. She is an only sister of my dear Jane, and how can I contemplate a separation that will affect her so much without participating largely myself? This morning especially I have been enabled to exercise contrition of heart for past sins and unfaithfulness, and to lay myself at the feet of Jesus, desiring to be disposed of to his glory, and commending myself, my Jane, Margaret, Brother Eckard, the African mission, all to his care and blessing. I expect to be with M. and Brother E. when they sail, though it is to afford me a melancholy pleasure."

"I usually stay (June 21, 1833,) with Dr. and Mrs. Wisner when I am in Boston, and find their house a very pleasant home indeed. They are remarkably pleasant and kind. Mr. Anderson is a lovely man, and his wife an excellent lady. I have stayed one night with them. They live about six miles from Boston.

Andover.
"Andover is a beautiful place, and in many respects very pleasant. I am allowed all the privileges of a resident graduate, but have no connection with the institution. My time is taken up in the study of Arabic and in acquiring information about Africa. I have pressing invitations at various places to preach every Sabbath."

Don't Go.
" I received (July 3) a letter from Mrs. Eckard, and she said she had written to you urging us to give up the African mission. I could regard her scheme in no other light than fanciful, and framed with too much indifference to the poor, benighted Africans to deserve a very serious consideration. Many hard things have been said about us, as, ' Going to martyrdom,' ' Pursuing shadows,' etc.

"I have had repeated and free conversations with both Dr. Wisner and Mr. Anderson on the subject of our future field of labor, and they, with all the members of the Prudential Committee, are *decidedly* of the opinion that we ought to go to Africa, a place where a mission ought to be established, and which they think is suitable for females. Our lives may, and probably will, be shortened, but such is the transcendent importance of that mission that it seems to me our duty to commence it, even should there be no possibility of our living more than *ten years*. Besides, my dear, my heart is strongly drawn out towards the *poor Africans*. If we do not care for them, who will? And if we cannot go as missionaries to Africa, who can?

"I was informed by Dr. Wisner last week, and subsequently by a letter from Brother Adams himself, that he is cut off from the fond hope of accompanying me next fall. His parents are more decidedly opposed to his going than they were before he offered himself to the Board.

His mother, it was thought, would not *survive* his going, and he has very *wisely* declined to go at present. He has had to pass through very deep waters.

"The plan now proposed is that I go without any other white man, if none can be found before the time of sailing. I am authorized to procure two suitable negroes in this country, go to Liberia in October or November, and there get Philip Moore and Charles Henry, both you know to be substantial men, to explore the adjoining country. I shall not be exposed to savage violence, and the dangers of the climate will not be greater than they would be if I had a white companion.

"In order to execute the plan above stated, it is necessary for me to visit home in two weeks and return by the middle of September to Philadelphia to attend the annual meeting of the Board, and after that leave the country as soon as an opportunity may offer.

"An application has been made to the Board for me to become *Governor* of Liberia; what think you of that, Jane? 'Governor Wilson'—how does it sound? I love the privilege of preaching the gospel too much to give it a serious consideration."

"You will be informed (July 21) by a letter from Margaret of my arrival in Philadelphia. We went out to Germantown this morning to see your cousin, Theodosia, and Mrs. Henry. They gave me a very warm grasp and treated me as kindly as if I had been their *real cousin*. I have been a good deal with Margaret and Brother Eckard. They are both cheerful; Margaret as much so as I ever saw her. She has told me a great deal about you. Brother Eckard is to be ordained to-morrow night, and it is to attend this I have delayed two days longer. To-morrow night I expect to take my last leave of them."

There is no record of the young licentiate's movements between the date of this letter, July 21, and September 8, but it is quite certain that he visited the
sea-coast of Georgia and also that he spent a brief season
under his father's roof.

The Presbytery of Harmony was convened at Mount
Zion Church during the week preceding the second Sabbath of September. The meetings of the judicatories of
the church have always attracted the Presbyterians of
Black River, and they would assemble in large numbers
to hear the preaching and listen to the discussions, dinner being served in the shade of the overhanging trees
in the spacious parks around the sacred tabernacles.
The *one* feature of this meeting was the ordination of a
Ordination.   missionary, an event hitherto almost unknown
in the State. It was in the home church,
amidst the friends of his youth, a large circle of relatives
and a mighty assembly of godly people. The newly-
ordained bishop writes, "Late Sunday night, 8th September, 1833. This is the eve of my ordination, and it
has been a solemn and interesting day. An impression
has been made on my mind and the minds of friends not
soon to be forgotten. My uncle, Mr. James, preached
the ordination sermon and Professor Howe delivered the
charge. My own feelings, dear Jane, were moved by
the tenderness of friends and by a lively sense of the responsible and honorable work before me. I could freely
have given vent to my feelings in tears, and how, you
ask, could you avoid it, whilst the whole audience was
bathed in tears, a weeping father before me, and the
speaker scarcely able to give utterance, because of his
intense emotion? I felt it all-important to repress these
tears and exhibit to the assembly an example of unmoved
composure and cheerfulness.

"That afternoon I preached in the grove to the negroes on the subject of missions. Afterwards an old colored man, eminent for piety, came to me and said he believed it was in answer to his prayers that I was going to Africa, and that he would add to his prayers one dollar (he is very poor) for the spread of the gospel in that country. There was an immense number present and deeply interested in the exercises of the day. When I was done preaching they came up one by one to shake hands with me, but their weeping and sobbing became so wild and disorderly, that I was compelled to take leave before I had told the tenth part 'good-bye.' Such scenes affect me not a little.

"I found my father's family well and cheerful. We lodge under our roof to-night *eight preachers and four elders.*"

On the following Friday he commenced his journey by stage to Philadelphia. He went by private conveyance to Camden, in the adjoining county, and writes, September 13, "I am thus far on my way to the North, and am waiting for the stage. This morning I took leave of my beloved father, mother, brothers, and sisters. All were affected, but none, I believe, regret the event. My father gave me a pressure of the hand and uttered a benediction at our parting, which will never be forgotten. I wish you knew him, that you might help me to love him. And now, when I turn my eyes backward to my native home and to the dear object of my love at Fair Hope, my heart is almost absolutely bowed down with sadness. Yet when I turn my reflections upon the great object of my mission, when I remember who it is that bids me ONWARD, the short time of my absence, and the prospect of soon doing good to *poor, benighted Africa,* my heart recovers its wonted cheerfulness. Ever remember that you have an earthly friend who loves you with a *pure* and *deep affection*. Time and distance cannot diminish but increase it. It is a true remark of the influence of absence upon affection, 'A strong wind will extinguish a candle, but fan a torch into a blaze.'"

"Dr. Ely's study, Philadelphia, September 21, 1833. I sit down to write to you this morning with a *cheerful heart*. Why should I not? God has preserved my health and life through the dangers of another long journey. He smiles, I believe, on the cause of our beloved Africa. Day before yesterday I was detained part of the day in Baltimore, and having nothing else to do, I *Maryland Colonization Society.* went to the Maryland Colonization office, where I received information about Africa and our mission which encouraged my heart.

"The M. C. S. is about to plant a new colony on the coast of Western Africa, to be located at Cape Palmas, two hundred and fifty miles south of Monrovia, and presenting, as we all think, a much more eligible site for the commencement of a mission than any place in or about Liberia. The society in Baltimore is anxious to have a mission started with the commencement of the colony, and they hold out strong inducements for us to go there. I communicated to Dr. Wisner and Mr. Anderson the substance of what I had learned; and they, with myself, are decidedly in favor of that point, and my instructions to-morrow night will be to go directly there.

"My plan will be to go to Baltimore and embark with the first party of emigrants for the new colony, which will consist of about twenty men with the agent, and it will probably be three or four weeks from this time. The agent of this new colony is Dr. Hall, a practicing physician. He is an excellent man, and has been in Liberia for some years.   Besides this, an old Columbia friend and classmate, by the name of Wyncoop, met me here yesterday and offered to go with me on the expedition. The Secretaries heartily approved of the proposal.   He is one of the best of men, and my most intimate friend while in Columbia.   I know no man more pleasant and companionable.   He will attend the theological seminary on his return.

"I expect to receive my public instructions to-morrow night in Mr. Barnes' church.   The occasion is anticipated with much interest in Philadelphia."

The following extracts from the instructions of the Prudential Committee, given at a meeting held over threescore years ago, will prove interesting to the reader. For years the American Board had been desirous of giving the gospel to Africa, and now the stalwart young Southerner stands before them to receive the solemn charge:

"Eight years ago the Board, by a formal resolution, enjoined it upon the Prudential Committee to embrace the 'earliest opportunity' for establishing a mission in Africa.'   They have attentively observed the indications of Providence, but until within a few months

The Pillar of Cloud.

past no cloudy pillar was seen to invite our labors.   It has been towards Western Africa that the Committee have looked with the most intense desire to labor for the spiritual good of that benighted continent.   Since that time, until your disposition to consecrate yourself, dear brother, to the liberation of Africa from her thraldom of ignorance and sin became known to the Committee, no man offered his services to the Board whose constitution and habits were thought to be adapted to the climate, and who was at the same time willing to encounter the perils of that field.   But now the time appears to have come for us to enter the arena of that spiritual conflict, which is to extend itself with invincible power, until Africa shall rejoice under the peaceful reign of Jesus Christ.

"The Moravian mission, in the frozen regions of Greenland, is situated on one extreme of nature; where men, surrounded by icebergs and barren mountains, and dwelling on the verge of animated being, labor hard to collect the far-scattered elements of life. You will be on the other extreme; beneath the burning zone, with the soil teeming around you with vegetable life, and with the tribes and nations of men, so many and so populous that the light once enkindled may radiate from people to people with reflected and multiplied brightness. Though many a white man hath found an untimely grave, better is it, if God so order, to preach the gospel under the burning line than beneath the frozen pole. The stream of your life may be shorter, but it will flow with a broader, deeper current.

"Though you have been inured to a Southern clime from your infancy, and are supposed to possess a constitution in a good measure inured to the climate of Africa, your mission is planned with a view to save you from all unnecessary exposure of health and life.

"On the morrow, by leave of Providence, you will repair to Baltimore, and there, you will, if possible, make arrangements for sailing in a vessel belonging to the Colonization Society of Maryland, and soon to proceed with emigrants for a new colony at an advantageous location at Cape Palmas. It is intended, should the Head of the church favor our designs, that one of our first stations be at this place. . . . .

Keep Your Health.

"The Committee would most affectionately and seriously enjoin upon you *to take good care of your health.* Never suffer yourself to be anxious. Anxiety is fever in the mind, and in Africa it will quickly exert a sympathetic influence through the body. Calmness of soul is invaluable everywhere, but to you its importance, merely as a safeguard for the health, is greatly enhanced.

"An object of prime importance, in respect to the inland parts of Western Africa and the central portions of

Explore. the continent, east of the Niger, *is the exploration of the country with a view to missionary operations.* None of this vast region has up to this time been explored with this end in view. . . .

"The stand for you to take, dear brother, when friends remonstrate with you for hazarding your life in Africa, is that of mild, but firm expostulation. 'What mean ye to weep and break mine heart? For I am ready not to be bound only, but also to die at Jerusalem for the name of the Lord Jesus.' Thus expostulated the great apostle to the Gentiles, and when they saw he 'would not be persuaded,' 'they ceased, saying, The will of the Lord be done.' So let his will be done by your mission to Western Africa. You have our affection and our confidence, and you shall have our prayers. You shall have the prayers of God's people in every part of the land, and he who commanded the gospel to be preached in Africa, as well as the other portions of this wide world, will be with you to the end."

Writing to Miss Bayard from Baltimore, October 9, he says, "I am now staying at the house of the Rev. Mr. Hamner, a Presbyterian preacher from Virginia, who is building up a new church here. He is a wealthy clergyman, but, unlike many of that class, he is humble, pious, and active.

Preaching on "The last Sabbath I was in Philadelphia I
Missions. preached morning and afternoon for Dr. Skin-

ner's people, and attended a missionary meeting that night at Dr. Ely's. Sabbath after next I am to preach on the subject of Missions, in Mr. Nevins's church, in this place. The Sabbath after, in Washington city."

Baltimore, October 16. "A carpenter has commenced our house. It is to be thirty-four feet long and nineteen feet wide, with a passage of eight feet running through the middle and dividing it into two large rooms. One of these is to be a sitting, eating, school and "palaver" room. The other will be divided in two, for a sleeping-room and a study. The building is to be a story and a half high, so as to make two sleeping chambers upstairs. There will be two piazzas, running the whole length of the house. These are necessary to protect the walls of the house in the rainy seasons. Its cost is eight hundred dollars. A carpenter in Liberia will put it up."

A House for Africa.

To his sisters: October 24, 1833. "My affections cling to my dear friends at home. Home has numberless endearments for me, and if *my mere preference* was concerned, there would be the place of my future abode. When I turn my eyes over my native country, my heart is almost possessed with a desire there to live, but when I survey *dark, benighted Africa*, when I reflect that her sons and daughters are ignorant, when I remember the judgment before which these Africans are soon to stand, when I remember the command of Christ, all my desires to remain at home vanish, and I am ready, yes, cheerful and happy in making all these sacrifices; yea, I believe I would be ready to sacrifice my life for the glory of God and the salvation of my fellow-creatures!

"I have expended about $200 in purchasing beads, razors, scissors, knives, clothes, jew's-harps, etc., for Africa. I suppose if I were to

A Pedlar's Outfit.

come to South Carolina with such an equipment I would be regarded as a good Yankee pedlar.''

Alexandria, November 6. To Miss B: ''We hope to sail from Baltimore the last of next week. My heart is sad sometimes when I think of leaving you behind, but nothing else causes a single regret.''

Kind Ladies. Baltimore, November 23. To his sister, Mrs. Mills: ''Almost every day for the last week or two, when we come up to our chamber at noon, I find on my table some present or other: a jar of pickle, a canister of home-made ginger-cakes, a can of preserves, etc., 'with the compliments of Mrs. ———.' We rejoice to receive these little presents, for besides the comfort they will afford us they indicate an interest on the part of those who give, for the sake of the cause we have undertaken.

''Last Monday night we had a prayer-meeting, specially for the success of the African mission. The meeting was large, and the interest manifested was very deep; many tears were shed, and I trust much good was done.

The Dying Love. ''Communion will be administered in one of the churches here to-morrow, where I expect to join the Christians for the last time before I embark. I rejoice that this opportunity of once more celebrating the dying love of Jesus is afforded me.''

November 24. ''I was called upon to go to preach to the negroes, which I could not refuse to do. This forenoon I preached for Mr. Hamner; immediately after I went and joined the people of God, in celebrating the Lord's Supper at Mr. Nevins' church, and felt it to be a privilege to renew my covenant engagement with the Master the day before I embark.''

CHAPTER VIII.

First Voyage to Africa.

REV. J. L. WILSON sailed for Africa, on his exploring tour, November 28, 1833. He writes to Miss Bayard, "The pilot, who is conducting our ship out to sea, will probably leave us to-morrow, and I take this opportunity of letting you know that we are under full sail for Africa. Our quarters on board the vessel are small, but comfortable. Our cabin is not more than seven by ten feet, and in only one corner can I stand upright. We have nothing but common berths in which to sleep, about six feet long and two and a half wide, and all opening into the cabin. This cramping I could bear, if there was one spot about the vessel where I might kneel down in secret to hold communion with God, but there is not. We are compelled to pray either in a lying position, or kneel where many eyes may be upon us. Our cabin passengers consist of Dr. Hall, Mr. Hersey (assistant agent of the new colony), Mr. Wyncoop, and myself. Then there is the captain and his crew, and, besides, about twenty emigrants on board. Two African goats, four pigs, and a large quantity of ducks and fowls, constitute the remainder of our livestock. The good ladies of Baltimore have provided every little thing necessary for our comfort. I rejoice to tell you that my spirits are good; I feel more like a foreign missionary to-day than I ever did before. You are seldom out of my mind. I do not believe that *distance*, *time*, *wave* or *wind*, will be

able to separate you from me. I expect to be employed
chiefly on the voyage in teaching the children and in
instructing the adults in the Bible; also with the study
of Greek, Hebrew, and medicine."

"Not only has our voyage been long (Brig *Ann*,
January 11, 1834), but in many respects disagreeable.
Storms, calms, head winds, rough seas, and sea-sickness,
constitute all the variety we have had; but what was
more distressing than all these outward difficulties was to be shut up to the company of
a man (our captain) who is profane, vulgar,
and utterly despises religion and religious men; but we
have abundant reason to thank our Father in heaven
that he has thus far brought us safely, protected us from
sickness and danger; and, although we have been compelled to dwell in the tents of the wicked, God has shown
that he can manifest himself to us in any place.

"We have been sounding the coast for the last four
days, but we have not seen any land. Africa's birds
have been flying around us and her weeds and flowers
have been floating about the ship for some days. Yesterday I could but say to myself, 'You wandered so far
from your native home, not because your father's house was not dear, not because America
does not spread an inviting field for your labors,
not for want of love for Christian and refined society, not
because Africa is fair and inviting in itself, but because
a voice from heaven calls, and the bleeding sons of this
injured land plead for her; therefore will I go, yea, go
with cheerful heart."

Near Cape Ann Shoals, January 22, 1834. "Yesterday afternoon we had a pleasing proof that we were quite
near the African coast, when a native canoe, which had
by some means got loose from the shore, came floating

along quite near to us. This morning at four o'clock
the captain came down from the deck in great trepida-
tion, and informed us that he had got into water only
seven fathoms deep. The first glance at his chart con-
Shoals!!   vinced him that he was in the midst of the
Cape Ann Shoals, one of the most dangerous
places on the African coast. He rushed up again to
anchor the ship, but found that he had got into deeper
water, and concluded he was on the outer edge of the
Shoals, which proved to be the case. Had we been
going at a rapid speed we should have run upon the
shore, and would have been exposed to the most calamitous consequences."

"We reached this place (Monrovia, January 28) after a
tedious voyage of sixty days. The two missionary families who sailed from Norfolk reached here about a month
before us, and most of them are already down with the
fever."

Later.   "When we arrived at Cape Palmas, an immense number assembled about the place of
our landing. Our boat stranded and we were carried
ashore on the backs of natives. Several of the head
men of the town met us at the water's edge to escort us
to the king's palace. As soon as our whole company
had landed, we moved forward in a regular procession,
each one of us having a staff-man to clear the way. The
procession was a compound of the novel and
First Recep-   ludicrous. The most heartfelt joy was mani-
tion.
fested by the immense multitude who were
accompanying us, and the loud noises which they made
by their unintelligible jabberings, together with the
dingling of bells and chains which they wore about their
necks and ankles, were almost deafening. We were
conducted through a great many winding streets (if,

indeed, they deserve the name of streets) before we
reached the king's headquarters.   The houses

Avenues.

are very compact, so as to render it impossible
for more than one person to pass between them at the
same time.   They are generally of the same size and
appearance, being of circular form, with high thatched
roofs.

"We were apprised of our proximity to the king's palace by the immense numbers that were assembled about
the place.   We found his majesty sitting on a low stool
under the roof of one of his houses, with a small striped
umbrella held over his head.   He retained his seat, but
shook hands cordially with each one of us.   He is a fine
looking man, very stout, and with a dignified, sensible

*King's Rai-
ment.*

appearance.   The only clothing he wore was a
striped cloth fastened around his loins and extending down to his knees.   He had a string
of beads around his neck, several iron bracelets on his
wrists, and at least a half-dozen coarse iron rings around
each ankle.   Immediately behind him stood his wives.
Seats were furnished us around the king, under the
vertical rays of the sun.   This, together with the number of human beings who wedged up every avenue
through which air could pass, made the place almost
intolerably warm!"

*Report to the
American
Board.*

After spending some time at Cape Palmas
and making arrangements for the establishment of the mission, Mr. Wilson prepared his
report to the Board, which was in substance,
"That they had visited Cape Mount, Monrovia, Cald-
well, Grand Basse, Grand Sisters, Rock Town, and Cape
Palmas, and had had opportunities to see and converse
with the head men of all the intermediate towns of any
considerable importance along the coast.   Of these places

Cape Palmas was by far the most suitable place for the location of a mission. The Agent of the Maryland Colonization Society had purchased a tract at Cape Palmas embracing twenty miles square. The site chosen for a mission settlement is a half-mile distant from a very populous native town, and is on an elevated ground fronting the sea. Six acres of land have been tendered the mission by the Agent of the colony. The elevation of the ground, its apparent healthfulness, and its distance from both the colony and the native settlements, render it as suitable a place as could be desired.

"Any apprehension of violence from the natives towards a missionary establishment is greatly relieved by the consideration that the people manifested a strong desire for the education of their children, and that they had taken all the pains they could to impress upon the mind of the king the fact that the mission is distinct from the colony, and will be identified with the interests of the natives.

"There are within the bounds of the newly-purchased territory three native towns, embracing a population of not less, perhaps, than three or four thousand. One of these is about twenty miles from the American settlement, and is a place well known by merchantmen as an important trading mart. It is situated at the mouth of a large river and commands more intercourse with the interior tribes than any other town on this part of the coast."

The young pioneer collected a vast fund of information about the social status of Western Africa, the vices of its inhabitants, the prevalence of polygamy, the dialects of the land and the relation between the interior and the maritime tribes. These topics are fully discussed in his report to the Board.

His next letter was written on board the ship *Jupiter*, New York Harbor, April 13, 1834: "We left the coast of Africa on the 10th ult., and have had a speedy, and, so far as a kind captain and good ship accommodations could render it, a pleasant voyage home. I was attacked with the fever a few days after we set out, and was confined to my bed about ten days. Since then, however, I have been constantly improving, and my health is quite good. I have given orders for the erection of the mission-house on a high and elevated spot of land, not more than a half-mile from a native town of 1,500 inhabitants."

Steamboat between Providence and New York, April 25, 1834: [To Miss Bayard.] "This morning Mr. Wyncoop and myself parted, after being together constantly for the last six months. Evening before last our report was brought before the committee and acted upon. The mission is to be commenced at Cape Palmas. Two ordained preachers and three lady teachers are to be sent out, and I am sent forthwith to the South to procure the persons. *It is more than I can do by myself, so you can calculate on taking an agency with me.*

"The Prudential Committee think it best for me to see the officers of the Maryland Society, so I shall go to Baltimore, thence to Charleston, and from that place to Savannah, where I hope to see her who is *very dear* to me, and after that I hope not to be separated till death does its work!"

The voyage down the coast was made in safety, and, in Savannah, Georgia, on May 21, 1834, John Leighton Wilson and Jane Elizabeth Bayard were united in marriage. They lived to celebrate their golden wedding. They were a very happy couple, for during a voyage of five months no tidings were received from either party, and now they were to walk the path of life together.

The Bride. Mrs. Wilson was tall, with a figure rather slender and very graceful; with light hair and blue eyes; a soft, mellow voice, which always spoke in modulated tones, and a pleasant smile to light up her attractive face. She was very gentle in manner, and exceedingly prudent in speech. She was blessed with excellent health throughout her lengthened years, and this caused her to look brightly on life. It was the quiet repose of her soul that rendered her disposition so homelike, and her companionship so restful to her husband. In all his thoughts and plans and labors she sympathized, and only eternity will reveal the results of her wise counsels.

The young people were welcomed at the old homestead in Sumter, and friends and relatives listened with delight to his lectures and talks about his voyage across the sea, and about the sights and scenes in the equatorial land of our brethren in black. Mr. Wilson's time was much occupied in obtaining from local doctors valuable suggestions about the treatment of fevers and the more common diseases. A distinguished physician in Camden gave him some very practical hints, for which, forty years afterwards, he expressed great gratitude.

CHAPTER IX.

Seven Years at Cape Palmas.

THE *Missionary Herald* says: "The Rev. John Leighton Wilson received the instructions of the Prudential Committee in the Central Presbyterian Church, Philadelphia, on Sabbath evening, October 19, preparatory to his embarkation, with his wife, for Cape Palmas, in Western Africa. He also received an appropriate farewell address from the Rev. John McDowell, D. D., the pastor of the church." **Farewell.** The young missionaries sailed November 7, 1834, in the schooner *Edgar*, Captain New.

Writing from near Monrovia, December 14, 1834, to Miss Theodosia Bayard, he says, "I suppose your first inquiry is, 'How has Jane borne the journey?' I am sorry to tell you she has been sea-sick most of the time. Her sickness has been severe and prolonged. When the weather was pleasant she was always on deck and in cheerful spirits. The captain is a man of considerable intelligence, has made himself quite companionable, and has been attentive to all our wants. Our accommodations are good, and in everyway our situation **Wedding Journey.** is as pleasant as we could reasonably expect in any vessel. Our progress on the voyage has been unusually expeditious. I have been able to preach only once, and do not enjoy the Sabbath on the sea as on dry land.

"We anchored at Gorèe the 7th December, after a voyage ot thirty days. The sight of land, and especially the continent of Africa, was quite refreshing. Gorèe is a French settlement, situated on a small island about six miles from the mainland. The highest point is occupied by a fort, and the remainder of the island is very densely covered with small stone-houses, with flat roofs. The streets are narrow; more like alleys than streets. The place abounds in fine fish, and we have purchased oranges, limes, bananas, and cocoanuts, which were quite a treat to us all. I bought a fine little horse at this place for my wife, and the captain has been good enough to take it down without charge.''

In a letter dated January 10, 1835, he describes how demonstrative the people were on their arrival: ''Our reception by the natives was, in their way, quite triumphant. We were carried ashore in the largest canoe about the cape, rowed by twelve or fifteen native men, who sang and rowed with great spirit from the time we left the vessel till we reached the shore. The king was the first to pay his respects, and has been particularly kind and friendly ever since. I made him a small present, in compliance with the universal custom of the country, and he, in return, presented me with a bullock. The natives generally pretend to feel interested in our object and claim me as *their man*, in distinction from the colony. They received us with loud acclamations of joy. More than five hundred of them are now around our door.

An African Welcome.

''The situation of our house is remarkably pleasant. I do not know that I have ever seen any place where the beauty and grandeur of nature are more harmoniously united. On the south we have a boundless view of the ocean, and the sea rolls on the beach with such tremendous and majestic power that our house is constantly jarred by the breaking of its

Beautiful for Situation.

mighty billows. On the east there is a salt lake eight or ten miles long, and we see at one view three native towns and the colonial settlements. The north presents an extended plain of the richest verdure, through which winds a beautiful fresh-water stream, which, from our piazza, may be traced to a great distance.''

Mrs. White, who arrived Christmas, 1836, in a letter which remained unfinished at the time of her death, which occurred in January, writes: ''When we reached the beach we found Mr. and Mrs. Wilson waiting with open arms to receive us. We came immediately to Fair Hope, the name of the mission premises, and found it as beautiful a location as the eye could desire to rest upon. We have found everything, as far as external experiences are concerned, much more pleasant and delightful than we had imagined in our most sanguine moments. I do not think there can be a more delightful spot in the world than the one that is now our home. My eyes, I am sure, will never tire of looking at the broad ocean and listening to the beating surf that breaks almost at our feet. There are two windows in our room, and from one we look out upon the sea, the little island where the natives bury their dead, Cape Palmas, the native towns, and Hoffman's river. From the other, we see a lovely salt lake and the verdant plain. Sing Sing and Newburg are justly called beautiful, but they do not equal Fair Hope. The scenery here is quite different from both these places, but much more attractive. The landscape is more mild and soft, with its gentle undulations and placid lake, its lofty waving palms and running vines that carpet the earth with flowers, while the wide-extended expanse of waters presents a sublime spectacle.''

Mr. Wilson ·ontinues, ''The natives are generally a

spirited people, and their character as a community has
been materially improved since the Americans
Law and have come among them, principally, I think,
Order. from the rigid manner in which the governor
of the colony has punished theft, both among them and
the colonists. Theft and lying, however, must still be
considered as crying sins in this land of darkness."

Though the mission premises were located at Cape
Palmas with a view to the healthfulness of the situation,
yet they were in sight of the tall, dark forests and dense
jungles that line the coast of Africa; and the miasmatic
influences were soon felt by the foreigners. He writes,
"We all expect to have the fever in a few
African weeks, but I apprehend no serious conse-
Fever. quences from it." January 26: "Since writing the above we have all had the fever. My wife was
the last to take it. This is the seventh day since she
was attacked, but no symptoms of dangerous illness are
discoverable. The rest of us are convalescent, yet we
all expect occasional relapses. The fevei is severe, and
we all suffered much for a week or ten days, especially
myself. We do not feel at all discouraged, nor do I consider the fever here as an insuperable obstacle to white
men living and being useful in this part of Africa."

"Under date of March 17," says the *Missionary
Herald*, "information has been received that Mr. Wilson, in consequence of too early and great exertion while
recovering from the attack of the fever, suffered a re-
lapse by which his life was brought into great danger.
Through divine mercy there was a fair prospect that he
would recover."

Later: "Intelligence has been received from Mr. and
Mrs. Wilson at Cape Palmas, dated June 15th. Mr.
Wilson had not recovered from the repeated attacks of

the fever which he had experienced previous to April, and his health was precarious."

Writing to his wife, May 29, 1842, Mr. Wilson recalls these days: "I look back upon different periods of our life with feelings which I cannot, and will not, attempt to describe. None of these, however, brings with it such affecting and overwhelming thoughts, as that, when you, a lonely female on the coast of Africa, watched over what you supposed would be the pillow of your dying husband." Recently married, thousands of miles from a Caucasian settlement, the young wife, herself recently recovered from a severe attack of Africa's scourge, ministers beside the couch of her husband, who now tosses in his delirium, and it seems that the candle of life is soon to go out. But the Lord had merciful designs towards Africa, and spared the life of the young missionary.

The Lonely Watcher.

He says, in a letter dated August 24, 1836, "Since I wrote last our general health has been good, and we have been subjected to little or no inconvenience on account of sickness. When I say *good health*, you must not understand me as speaking of what you would call in America *good health*, but *good African health*. We have frequent attacks of chills and fever, but are not confined to our rooms for more than a few hours, and are able the next day to resume our duties."

Good African Health.

The season of acclimation passes by, and his epistle of May 18, 1840, says, "My own health is as good as it probably would have been in America. I was for a time quite a dyspeptic, but obtained permanent relief by abandoning the use of coffee and tea, and by the habit of daily labor in my garden. You will probably be surprised to hear me boast that I have the

Garden.

finest garden in Western Africa. The country around us is very poor, and it would be impossible for us to live with any degree of comfort without a garden. We have cabbage, tomatoes, okra, onions, beets, squash, cucumbers, melons, corn, peas, sweet potatoes, beans, etc. We have also a variety of fruit trees advancing rapidly to a state of maturity. But the moral vineyard engrosses our thoughts and attention.

"Our winter has just set in, the rain falls in torrents, the winds howl around our house, and the ocean roars tremendously. Whilst we are putting on our warm clothing you are throwing off yours."

In his home letters he says, "I have recently secured, what I have been wanting ever since I came to Africa, a milk cow. The natives regard these as more precious than gold, and it is with extreme difficulty that they can be induced to part with them. The idea of milking them seems not to have entered their heads until I came here, and my fondness for milk appears to them most strange and unnatural."

Milk.

When a vessel brought the mail, which was sometimes once in six months and again at the end of twelve, it was the practice of Mr. and Mrs. Wilson to open one letter or paper a day, so as to make the pleasure last as long as possible. Truly, in their isolated condition, on the shores of equatorial Africa, they appreciated the words of the wise man, "As cold waters to a thirsty soul, so is good news from a far country." He mentions in an epistle, May 5, 1836, the reception of the United States and Indian mails: "We have just received letters from home, and Jane has also had one, not a little cheering, from her sister on the continent of Asia."

The American Mail.

The mail sometimes was the bearer of sad tidings. Mrs. Wilson wrote, ''By a paper that has just reached us, we see that Mr. James is no more. Mr. Wilson was much affected, although your letters had prepared him for the event.''

Death of Rev. R. W. James

It is said that for five years Mrs. Wilson never saw the face of a white woman, except the wife of an English missionary, who came to their house from the ship and died after three weeks illness. In after years, speaking to a niece of their home life, she said: ''Your uncle and I determined, when we went to Africa, that we would keep up the more minute courtesies of life and be particular about our personal appearance; so every day, after he got through with his school duties and I with mine, I put on a clean calico dress, put up my hair in the way he liked it, and we paid those delicate little attentions to each other which are apt to be neglected after some years of married life; and I was ever afterwards thankful I began that way in a hot and debilitating climate.''

A Lonely Life.

One incident at Fair Hope illustrates the idle stories that sometimes go home about the extravagance of missionaries. Once their cousins sent them from Philadelphia a box containing a fruit cake and a variety of preserves. Mrs. Wilson put some of each kind on the table, thinking that their guests, the officers of a man-of-war, would enjoy them after a long cruise along the coast. One of the number, though he knew perfectly well where these delicacies came from, reported to the Mission Rooms, in Boston, that the missionary's salary ought to be reduced, as they were living in luxury. Mr. Wilson was written to on the subject, and it is needless to add that his explanation was satisfactory.

Fruit Cake.

A Practitioner. One department of his labors in the Dark Continent was the medical work. Most of these years without a doctor, it was necessary for him to treat the numerous diseases that were brought to him, both by the white man of the sea and the black man of the jungle. He became a specialist in the African fever, having studied the subject most carefully, and his long experience and practical knowledge made him eminently successful. Frequently ship captains with a sick crew applied to him for medical aid, as it was known that he was skilful in treating the cases which occur so frequently on the African coast. He was of great service to European voyagers in teaching them the use of the medicines so needful in that climate. In one of his home letters he asks that a box of sassafras, which grows so abundantly on the edge of the Southern swamp, be sent him.

Mrs. White wrote thus of what she saw: "This morning Mr. Wilson was walking through a native town and met a man who said he wanted to see him. When Mr. Wilson asked him what he wanted, he replied that he had a little baby that appeared to be sick, and it had cried ever since it was born. He had been to the native doctor and asked him what to do for the child. He replied, 'Take the child to Mr. Wilson and let him hold it in his arms for a little while and it will get well.'"

Dr. Wells, the brother of Mrs. White, writing fifty-six years afterwards, says: "In my sister's sickness, especially as the end drew near, she could not bear to have Mrs. Wilson out of her sight. Both Mr. and Mrs. Wilson were all that parents could have been in caring for the dying missionaries, and mourned for them as if they had been near kin-folks. And, indeed, they were of the same family, 'the household of faith.'"

He saw African life in all of its phases. A
Deceiving the Ignorant. man once came to the native village claiming
supernatural power, and said he would prove
it. He would cut himself with a knife and the blood
would flow, but he could wash off the blood and there
would be no scar on his body. That night by torch-
light the natives formed a circle, and this man danced
and leaped around and apparently cut himself with a
knife, and the blood flowed profusely. Mr. Wilson
watched the performance and saw a man in the crowd
chewing a red root, and as the imposter passed by he
would spit on him. He immediately seized the man,
explained the trick, and sent him away with sundry exhortations about deceiving his countrymen.

Soon after his arrival, being engaged in some
"Board Talk." sort of carpentry at some distance from his house,
he found that a needed tool was wanting. As
an African lad stood near, watching his movements, he
thought of sending for it by him; but as he could not
send a verbal message, he wrote on a piece of board the
name of the desired implement and gave it to him to carry
to the house. The messenger understood by signs what
he desired, went immediately, and returned bringing the
article, evidently wondering at the transaction. As he
handed him the tool, he remarked, in his native tongue,
"Board talk."

One day he saw a large crowd of natives
Arresting an Execution. and joined them to hear what was the matter.
He soon found that they had, for a trivial
offence, arrested a man and condemned him to be executed. He spoke to the people about how trivial the
misdeed was, and ordered the man to be released. They
immediately obeyed. This incident illustrates the immense control he had gained over those who lived within

the sphere of his influence.   Mrs. White noticed this and wrote, ''Mr. Wilson has gained an immense influence over the natives, and can do with them just as he pleases,'' and mentions the riot described in the next chapter.

He was frequently away from home, on journeys into the interior.   He writes, November 3, 1836: ''There is much need of a missionary to itinerate among the settlements around.   He might, without going more than thirty miles from Cape Palmas, embrace within the sphere of his labors more than fifty thousand souls; and no people in the world, so far as human foresight may determine, are more ready to receive the gospel.   They have no religion that deserves the name; they are simple-hearted and will receive anything that falls from the lips of a white man with implicit confidence.   I have recently performed a tour of more than one hundred miles into the country.   I set out with the intention of reaching the Kong Mountains, but was taken sick and had to retrace my footsteps.   I penetrated the country farther than any one ever did from this part of the coast; and the wonder of the people, when for the first time they saw a white man, was very great.   With the exception of one place I was treated with great kindness.''

Itineration.

''We have experienced'' (Cape Palmas, June 21, 1837) ''much of the goodness of our Heavenly Father, but not without afflictions.   One of our teachers, as we humbly trust, has been removed from earthly toils to heavenly rest; while another, from an attack of palsy, has been disqualified for school work.''

'' A few weeks ago a Portuguese vessel was wrecked at a neighboring town, and, as usual, the cargo became the booty of the people.   Unfortunately

Rum.

a large portion of it consisted of rum, and the whole country has been in a state of intoxication.   They speak of such an event as a 'God-send,' and no argument can shake this long-cherished and fond maxim.''

''We have had an opportunity'' (May 21, 1841) ''lately to see many of our countrymen, having been visited by two men-of-war, the *Cyane* and the *Grampus*.   On board of these vessels there are always a number of respectable and intelligent Americans, and, in a few cases, pious men.   We are daily expecting to see three or four steamboats from England, on their way to open the heart of Africa to the influences of missions and civilization.''

Fellow-countrymen.

''Mr. Wilson and I'' (writes Mrs. Wilson, September 22, 1841) ''have just returned from a short voyage down the coast, where we were received by the English missionaries with great kindness and hospitality.   These friends came to Africa in February, and in seven months four out of the eight have been numbered with the dead.   One gentleman at the British forts, hearing we were on board the vessel just anchored, came off for us, telling us his wife was quite sick.   We hastened on shore, thinking we might be of some use or comfort to her, as they had had no medical attendant and there was no white female in twenty miles.   On our arrival at the house we found her quite ill, but did not think she was so near her end; she died that evening.

A Short Voyage.

''We left home in the barque *Union* from New Orleans, but while at Annamabo we heard that Captain Lawlin, our long-tried friend, was to be at Cape Coast in a day or two.   We left Captain Ryan with many thanks for his kind attentions, and went by land to be ready for the *Atalanta*.''

The Mission Compound. Mr. Wilson writes, April 21, 1837: "Our settlement at Fair Hope begins to assume a conspicuous appearance from the sea, and somewhat resembles a pleasant, airy, country village. It embraces, besides our own house, two other small but neat dwellings, a handsome church, 25 x 40 feet, a printing-office, study, storehouse, and a dormitory for our boys. In addition to this, we expect soon to build a house for female children."

Mrs. Wilson, the Teacher. "The progress of the children" (November 3, 1836) "in the schools is most satisfactory. Some of those who have only had three months' instruction can read with tolerable ease. All this I attribute, under the blessing of God, to Mrs. Wilson's talent for teaching, and the happy faculty she has of making every one about her cheerful and contented.

"When we first made an attempt to collect native children, their parents were indifferent about sending them. They offered various objections, 'It will take too long to learn.' 'It was true that book was good palaver, but they would be dead before their children would get any advantage from their education.'"

Later: "Jane has the charge and supervision of the native schools, both male and female, and is very fond of teaching. Much of my time is devoted to preparing books for the press. A vocabulary of the language is now in the printer's hands.

"The vessel, which has just arrived, has brought two Episcopal missionaries. One of them, Mrs. Paine, is married. If her life is spared, Mrs. Paine will be a great acquisition to Jane's happiness and comfort.

"'Tell all the colored people 'How-d'ye' for me. I would do them good if it were in my power.

6

King David's Servants.   ''Some of the Episcopal missionaries attempted a short time since to penetrate the country from this place, but they had not gone more than ten miles when they were arrested by the natives and sent back. Gov. Russworm soon followed in their footsteps, expecting that his *gubernatorial dignity* would carry him through, but both himself and aid-de-camp, and also King Frerman, were arrested, stripped of their clothing, and sent back in a state of nudity.''

Coming to Church.   ''We have recently formed ourselves into a church ; and on last Sabbath I administered the Lord's Supper for the first time. . . . . I have commenced preaching through an interpreter. The audience on Sunday afternoons has been small, but quite as attentive and orderly as I could expect. The king leads the way in attendance, and has said they will work no more on Sunday, after they have housed the present crop of rice. We attach very little importance, however, to these outward signs ; our sole reliance is upon the efficacious influence of God's grace.''

A Southerner was admirably suited for work among the Africans. Leighton Wilson was reared in the midst of African people ; he knew their character, could measure their impulses, and had the eye to discern the double-face, the one for the white man and the other for those of their own color. He, too, sympathized with them in their affectionate, demonstrative disposition, and their trusting, confiding nature.

Mrs. White gives her impressions of the last Sabbath of 1835 : '' On last Sunday afternoon we attended service with the natives. Mr. Wilson speaks to them through an interpreter. The scene was more interesting than I had imagined such a one could be. The audience consisted of about twenty native children from the schools, with about as many men, among whom were the king and several of his head men. A number of women stood at the windows and looked in during most of the service. Mrs. Wilson's school is extremely interesting. She has twenty-five native children, and they spell and define remarkably well. There are now in the day-schools more than a hundred children, and the number could be increased to any extent whatever, were there teachers enough to instruct them."

The following summary of their seven years' work at Cape Palmas was afterwards given by Dr. Wilson: "A church of forty members organized; more than a hundred youth educated; the Grebo language reduced to writing; a grammar and dictionary of the language published; the Gospels of Matthew and John translated, and six or eight other small volumes published in the native language."

The Dying African Boy. When at home on furlough in 1846, in an address delivered at Darlington, South Carolina, he said that after working for years, with little fruit of his labors, there was a boy converted who was a great help to him. After awhile the boy was taken sick, and he left word with the nurse if he became worse in the night to send for him. He was awakened at midnight, and when he came to the door of the house the boy was praying to the Lord Jesus to grant him forgiveness of sins and bestow upon him dying grace. Soon after he entered the room the sufferer breathed his last. He said he was never afterwards sorry that he went to Africa.

CHAPTER X.

In Perils and with Cannibals.

IN the early part of 1836 the young missionaries were exposed to great danger in an anti-foreign riot in Africa. The *Missionary Herald* has the following account of it from Mr. Wilson's pen: "The affray was between colonists and the natives. The direct cause was the imprisonment of an old and much-venerated man. The faith of the officer of the colony was broken, and the old man was sent to jail. Feelings of the deepest revenge were excited, but they did not burst forth till one or two days afterwards. A lad was brought before the magistrate, found guilty of stealing, and sent to jail. The Americans, knowing that there was much excitement in the native towns through which they had to pass with the prisoner, deemed it necessary to go in a considerable body and well armed. As was apprehended, a scuffle ensued, but no great injury was sustained, except a few hard blows and some slight wounds, and the prisoner was lodged in jail. Before the escort could return, the natives rallied in a body of four or five hundred, to cut off the Americans from the cape, where all their guns and ammunition were deposited. A party was sent to force open the jail and turn out the prisoners.

The colonists, seeing them sallying out in such dread array, fled to our house for refuge. This act of cowardice emboldened the mob, and they directed their course to the mission premises in pursuit of the fugitives. Their appearance at

Five Hundred Savages.

this time was imposing beyond description. Picture to yourself a band of five hundred savages, armed with guns, cutlasses, and spears, intoxicated with revenge, and intent upon shedding blood; and when you connect with this scene hundreds of demoniacal voices, fierce yells, war-horns and bells, you may have an idea of what I wish to describe. I found it necessary to place myself before our front gate to prevent bloodshed within our very doors. Here I was treated with far more deference than I had expected. They were surprised that I was so confiding as to place myself unarmed in their midst, and not one single individual offered the least disrespect. By the assistance of one or two head men I succeeded in rallying the whole mob, and made them a talk. At the close of this they agreed to seat themselves where they were, and remain so until the king and myself could go and have an understanding with the agent in relation to the cause of dissatisfaction.''

The bearing of Mrs. Wilson at this critical juncture was only casually referred to in the *Herald*, no doubt because she ever refused to have her name mentioned in print; but the story of her heroism has come down to us by family tradition. As it was necessary for Mr. Wilson to go with the king, it involved leaving his young wife surrounded by the black throng of wild, naked savages. He felt it to be his duty to go, but hesitated on her account, when this brave woman said: ''My dear, I came here to be a help-meet, not a hindrance, to you; go, I feel sure God will protect me. I am not afraid.'' She took her stand at the gate, and by her self-possession, quiet demeanor and commanding eye, for hours held the wild mob in check, and quieted them so much that they afterwards were far more willing to listen to reason, though still bent on revenge and bloodshed.

The *Missionary Herald* continues: "While we were gone to meet the agent, a party from a different quarter went to the jail, forced it open, and turned out the prisoners. The whole of the mob then put themselves together and came to meet us, determined, if their demands were not granted, to rush in a body upon the big guns, which they knew were only guarded by six or seven Americans. Our communication was satisfactory, and the mob, for a time, was quelled. My house became an asylum for twenty-five or thirty Americans; and I found it necessary to be up all night to prevent aggression, as the fever of excitement had not yet cooled. Some of the colonists, who were the particular objects of vengeance, we found necessary to lock up in our pantry and other places of privacy. No disturbance, however, took place during the night, and the next morning a palaver was called. The king took the high ground to denounce the authority of the American governor and to contend that he should not remain at Cape Palmas. At this juncture I found it necessary to bring all the influence I had to bear on the case, and several hours elapsed before I could get them even to give the governor a hearing. He had been here only a few weeks, and had had very little opportunity to become acquainted with the people and to acquire influence over them. As soon as he obtained a hearing, the current of feeling was changed, and the palaver amicably adjusted. I am disposed to think the natives cling to us as their friends more closely than ever. I write that you may know that we are not troubled or distressed by every storm that passes across our horizon."

We come now to other scenes of interest in the career

of the pioneer missionary. It was not sitting in a
pastor's study in the beautiful land of America
that he read about cannibals, but on more than
one occasion this young hero of the cross

Man-
Eaters.

came into personal contact with the man-eaters. In a
journey, made a short time after his arrival in Africa, he
says: "I made particular inquiry about a report we
frequently hear, that there are man-eaters not far from
this place, and I am inclined to believe it is true. Several
men here, of whom I made inquiry, have unhesitatingly
attested the fact; and a man who had just returned from
that section to Demale declared, without knowing that I
had been inquiring on the subject, that he had left the
people in a town that morning in consultation whether
or not they should eat a criminal then held under arrest.
It is said they eat nothing but criminals and captives
taken in war, but every feeling in the human heart
revolts at this melancholy attainment in the annals of
cruelty and inhumanity."

Of a journey made two years after his arrival, he
writes: "Bolobo is a slave-holding country. I should
not have known that such a practice existed if I had not
met two slave-dealers, who came while we were there to
deliver up a slave. They had come from a two days'
journey in the interior. They unblushingly acknowledged the perfidious manner in which they captured the
slave they had just sold. He came from a friendly
village on a visit to relatives, and just at that time an
order for a slave arrived. The dealers fixed upon this
man as their victim, waited until he was asleep, seized
and bound him, and in the night hurried him away.

These two men acknowledged that their countrymen were in the habit of eating human
flesh, thus confirming the suspicion that there

Human
Flesh.

were cannibals within fifty miles of Cape Palmas. There was nothing about their appearance that indicated uncommon severity of character, except that they filed their teeth, and the heartless indifference with which they could relate their abominable practices. When they discovered my disgust and abhorrence, one of them attempted to shield himself by the shameless apology that 'meat was meat.' "

Some years later he was upon an exploring tour far in the interior, and with only a few native attendants. He was made sick by drinking water from a mountain stream, and was suffering from an attack of dysentery, and in a very weak condition he lay down in the middle of the day under a tree near a village. One of his escorts told him that he overheard some of the natives **Without Salt.** saying that when the men came home from their farms (to dine) they would kill him and eat him, and that he was so white he would not need salt. He was far distant from human help, and a long journey lay between him and the coast, but he prayed most earnestly, and then asked himself, "Why am I here? In whose service am I engaged?" He immediately felt, "I am in Christ's hands, and under his protection." At once all trembling fear passed away and he arose from his hammock, and striking his stick forcibly on the ground, he said to his company, "Get up, let us go," and he passed on feeling that he was immortal till his work was finished. Sublime and heroic courage marked his career in Afric's wilds.

CHAPTER XI.

The Death of Colleagues.

ONE of the most delightful privileges in mission life is to welcome new laborers fresh from the home-land with the fire of youth, the enthusiasm that new scenes beget, and a burning zeal for .the spread of the truth. Another source of pleasure is the growth of a mission: to see year by year new recruits come to the field and the work enlarging and spreading. Let us reverse the picture, and we catch a view of *Anticipation.* pioneer life in Western Africa. After two years of lonely watching, waiting, and working, the subject of this sketch wrote: "Our hearts begin to beat high with expectation of the arrival of Mr. White and his company, but the Lord only knows whether we are to receive them."

The story is best told in the words of the survivors: "I have to relate," writes Mrs. Wilson, "the death of our beloved associates, Mr. and Mrs. White. They arrived on Christmas day, just two years from the time of our landing here, and we received them with joyful yet trembling hearts. For two weeks our intercourse was delightful, and we really were very happy, for they were pious and intelligent. At the end of that period the fever laid its hand upon these dear friends. In four days our brother left us for a brighter world, and his dear partner lingered eighteen days. You can little imagine how desolate we are, and how this stroke has bowed us to the ground!"

"Our house is indeed a house of mourning," writes Mr. Wilson, January 28, 1837. "God has taken our dear Brother and Sister White to himself. They were permitted to pass this way, and tarry only a few weeks with us on their journey to their heavenly home, and we believe that they are in those mansions which Jesus has gone to prepare, and ere this fully understand and devoutly adore that Providence, which interposed between them and their anticipated usefulness in benighted Africa. We have been almost overwhelmed by the waves of grief which have successively and so rapidly passed over us. They were both taken off in their first fever, and within a month after their arrival. Mrs. White was taken first with fever, which was not at any time very virulent; but she was taken with what is known in this disease as a 'sinking spell,' which seems to be nothing more than the suspension of the nervous action throughout the system. On the 23d she was seized with quinzy, and became speechless and unable to swallow. Her fever rose higher than it had ever done. She lay in a state of insensibility all day, and in the evening about 9 o'clock, in the midst of a burning fever and high pulse, the silver chord was loosed, after an illness of eighteen days. Mr. White was taken ten days after his wife. The fever at its commencement laid hold on its victim with a grasp that no human power could detach. On the fifth day, to the doctor's great consternation and our deep grief, it was obvious that death had laid his sceptre upon our dear brother, and in the course of half an hour he sank without a struggle or a groan into the arms of death. He left no dying testimony to cheer the hearts of his friends, but he has left a living testimony of his attachment to his Saviour and his devotion to the cause of humanity and religion. One of the last sentiments he penned was, that he felt no solicitude about the issue of his expected sickness. I shall never, I can never, forget the kindlings up of his countenance whenever the salvation of this people was made the subject of conversation. The day of his burial all the natives suspended their labor and amusements. The corpse was borne to the place of interment by four native men, followed by the king and a great many others. Our own feelings, under this afflictive dispensation, are indescribable. I trust it has humbled us more than any previous event of God's providence, and has taught us to feel that there is no hope for Africa except in the almighty arm of Jehovah. We received our dear brother and sister in the first instance with joyful, but trembling hearts, and now our worst fears have been realized, our prospects have been clouded, and all our plans of operation have been overthrown. We dread the influence which we fear will be exerted upon the church at home by this event. If it awakens sympathy and excites prayer, it will advance the cause of the Redeemer in this benighted land; if it causes despondency and confirms those in opposition who have been faithless, the consequences will be exceedingly calamitous."

October 27, 1841 : "You will, my dear parent, brothers, sisters, and friends, sympathize with us when you hear that God has, in his inscrutable but wise providence, taken from us, by death, our dear Christian brother and fellow-laborer, Dr. Wilson. This truly afflictive event occurred on the 13th instant, from epidemic dysentery, after an illness of nine days. It was truly profitable to attend the death-bed of one who was so eminently prepared for

this great and solemn change.   His mind was unusually
clear and his spirits tranquil and composed.   He seemed
to meet death as a familiar friend, and looked upon it as
the gate of endless joy.   His mind, for months before he
was attacked with his last illness, seemed to have been
prepared by the Spirit of God in a remarkable manner for
the great change.   Many of our family have had the
same disease with which he died.   It is sometimes good
for us to feel that we are treading upon the verge of
eternity.   One of Dr. Wilson's practices would be profitable for us all, viz., to commit to memory one or more
verses from the portion of Scripture which we daily read.
The day preceding his death he spoke of the work in
which he was engaged as very important, and hoped
that the church, notwithstanding the many afflictions
with which the Mission had been visited, would never
abandon it.   He said he did not then, nor had he ever
for one moment regretted his coming to this part of
Africa.   He suffered much with thirst, and said: 'How
happy are they who quench their thirst at the fountain
òf living waters!'   He sent to the native town for three
or four young men, and calling them by name, said:
'I am about to die; I am going to Jesus Christ.   I beg
you never to forget those things which I have taught
you, but to attend to the salvation of your souls.'   After
they left he soliloquized: 'Well, the Lord is about to
take down this tabernacle, but, blessed be God, we have
a building of God, a house not made with hands, eternal
in the heavens.'   He desired us to sing the Grebo hymn,
'Jesus, dear friend, to thee I lift mine' eyes.'   When
asked if he knew the persons around the room, he said,
'No, no, no.'   'Do you know Jesus?'   'Yes; dear,
precious Saviour, I look to him.'   These were his last
words.   We buried his remains, according to his desire,

under the shade of two beautiful trees at Fishtown, which had been the scene of his labors."

Mrs. Wm. Walker. Mr. and Mrs. William Walker arrived at Cape Palmas February 3, 1842. Mrs. Walker died on the 3d of May. On the last day of her sickness Mr. Wilson very tenderly expressed to her our fears that she could not remain long with us. "Then you think I must die soon," said the young bride. She did not seem at all disturbed, and lay quiet a few moments. Then the thought of home and friends rushed upon her mind, and she exclaimed: "Oh! my father and mother, my brothers and sisters." She was reminded of the Saviour. "Oh, yes," she said, "he is a great and precious Saviour." She proposed having prayers, and Mr. Wilson led in prayer. Her countenance was as calm and serene as the beautiful morning that was just dawning. She said: "Tell my parents and friends that the time since I left America has been the happiest of my life. Tell them that I do not now, on my dying bed, regret coming to Africa." Her passing away was like a setting sun; it seemed to fade away into the twilight of heaven.

Rev. Jno. M. Campbell. Rev. John M. Campbell sailed January 1, 1844. He arrived at Cape Palmas in good health, but while waiting for an opportunity to proceed to the Gaboon, he was seized with the acclimating fever, and after an illness of nine days, died at the Episcopal Mission house on the 19th of April. Nine years before this the Macedonian cry from the interior of Africa was wafted to his ears. He listened; his heart was moved with compassion, and he responded, "Here am I; send me." He immediately left his farm and commenced a course of study. From that time till his death he ceased not, day and night, in private and public, to plead the cause of the African Mission.   During his sickness, Mr. Bushnell, his companion on the voyage, inquired, "Are you willing to die?"   He replied, "Yes, I rejoice to depart, while I mourn for you that remain. But, brother, do not give up the work; be not discouraged, though two, who started with you, are so soon taken away."   [The other was Mr. Crocker, a Baptist missionary, who died at Monrovia *en route*.]

Rev. B. Griswold.   Rev. B. Griswold arrived February 3, 1842, and closed his earthly labors July 14, 1844, after an illness of eleven days.   "A short time previous to his death he made a tour to the Pongwe country and encountered fatigue and hardship.   Before he was fully recovered from the effects of this journey, he was called upon to perform a surgical operation at night.   The exposure connected with it seemed to be the immediate cause of his death."   "His purpose to go to a heathen land," says the *Missionary Herald*, "was formed at an early period in his academic studies. In reply to the question, 'What led you first to think seriously of the subject?' he said, just before his departure for Africa, 'When I was a lad a good man who came to my father's house to solicit aid for the missionary cause remarked to me as he was leaving, *I shall not ask you to give anything, for I hope you will give yourself.*'"   Mr. Wilson writes, "The funeral exercises were attended by one of the largest and most serious assemblies I have ever known in the Gaboon."

Mrs. Walker.   While Mr. and Mrs. Wilson were absent on furlough, the report of the mission said: "When the year 1848 opened there were only two members of the mission on the ground, and in April the number was still further reduced by the death of Mrs. Walker, leaving her bereaved husband to bear the heat and burden of the day alone, and yet he was not alone, for the sustaining presence of him who has said, ' Lo, I am with you alway,' imparted strength equal to his day.''

"My hand" (writes Rev. J. L. Wilson, Feb-
Mrs. Gris-   ruary 6, 1849) "almost refuses to report the
wold.
death of Mrs. Griswold [formerly Mrs. Dr. A. E. Wilson].   That one so cheerful, so energetic, so useful, so obliging, that one, humanly speaking, the least likely to become the victim of disease, should be so suddenly taken away, is one of those dispensations of Providence which cannot be explained, and we must be dumb before the Lord.   Her death occurred on Wednesday morning, after an illness of little more than four days. At the commencement of the disease there were no symptoms of virulence, and on Tuesday morning a favorable crisis showed itself, but towards evening the disease developed unexpected violence, and although the strongest methods were resorted to, in less than eight hours she calmly resigned her spirit into the hands of her Saviour.   There were lucid moments when she spoke sweetly of her confidence in Jesus.   But no dying testimony was needed in her case.   She had given the highest proof of her attachment to her Master, by her devotion to his service while in health, by her kind and affectionate deportment to her associates in the mission, and by her untiring efforts to promote the spiritual welfare of the heathen around her.''

Mr. Wilson wrote again, in 1850:   "Mrs.
Mrs. Bush-   Bushnell brought from the United States the
nell.
seeds of pulmonary consumption.   She enjoys a placid and happy state of mind, and is calmly waiting for her Master to bid her come away.''   She died February 25, 1850.

Just after the subject of this sketch left the field, his

young colleagues, Rev. and Mrs. Rollin Porter, were
called from the field of their choice and ended
their earthly labors; the wife on the 6th and
the husband on the 16th July, just a year after
they landed at the Gaboon.

Rev. and Mrs. Rollin Porter.

Thus one-half of those who joined the mission during
these sixteen years were removed by the hand of death,
while one or two others returned to the States on account of health. How constantly the thought of the
"decease that was to be accomplished" was before the
the founder of the mission, and how inexpressibly sacred
were his relations to colleagues from whom he feared he
might at any time be separated by the grave! How this
feature of his missionary life tended to develop that exquisite sympathy and tenderness he ever manifested
towards his brethren and sisters in heathen lands! His
character was in a large degree moulded by the circumstances by which he was surrounded during the first two
decades of his service in the foreign field, and ministering beside the dying couches of his beloved co-laborers
developed the gentleness of a disposition naturally loving
and affectionate.

The Holy Dead.

The holy dead on Afric's shores speak in
living voices to the Christian church. These
truly took their lives in their hands and went
out expecting to return no more. All those named
above were cut down in the spring-time of life—the
bridegroom and the bride sleeping side by side under
the burning sands of equatorial Africa! A half-century
has passed by, and yet the tear is dropped in loving
memory of the young martyrs who died in the service of
Christ.

CHAPTER XII.

The Manumission of his Slaves.

A MISSIONARY'S life was not chosen by Leighton Wilson and his wife for the sake of gain. Mrs. Wilson was an heiress, but she cheerfully gave up all her possessions for the privilege of personal service in the foreign field. At the time they were sent to Africa all Presbyterians went out under the American Board, which was located at Boston. It was at this place, and about that time, the movement for the abolition of slavery began, which resulted thirty years afterwards in the overthrow of the institution.

Before his first voyage to Africa, under date of October 24, 1833, Mr. Wilson writes to Miss Jane E. Bayard, who was at Savannah, Georgia: "I would say about your negroes, by all means, if possible, colonize them. For I hold that every human being, who is capable of self-government and would be happier in a state of freedom, *ought to be free*. I am not, however, a friend of immediate and universal emancipation, for the simple reason that all negroes are not ready for freedom, and would be worse off in that than in their present condition. My opinion is that you should colonize them, but it must depend on three things—their fitness, their willingness, and the place to which they are to go."

Writing to his sister from Cape Palmas, March, 1838, he says: "In a former letter it was mentioned that all Jane's slaves were about to emigrate to Africa. I believe I am still the owner of two. I have serious scruples about retaining them as slaves, now that a way is open to set them free. I have, therefore, made a proposition to Dr. Anderson to take John to Boston, and have him taught some mechanical art in reference to coming out here. And I have likewise proposed to give up the girl if he can find any one to take her, and I have told him if such openings offered, he could correspond with you. *I wish it distinctly understood, that neither of the children are to be removed, without both their own and their mother's consent.*"

In a letter to his father, July 17, 1843, he says: "In this I enclose certificates of freedom for John and Jessie. I find that the Missionary Society will sustain serious injury unless I give them up. The Prudential Committee think I have done all my duty to them. If they prefer to remain on the plantation as heretofore, then let them do so, with the distinct understanding that they may leave at any time they desire."

His position was severely assailed in the New England papers by those who knew nothing of the circumstances of the case. These effusions caused him no little sorrow of heart, as appeared in the following *Jeremiade*, a letter to his wife, from whom he had been separated a year; the long absence causing him to look at the clouds which he imagined covered the horizon.

Evil
Spoken of.

"I suppose you have seen and heard a great deal in the States about my *slave-holding*. Thank God, I have a *clear conscience* in his sight, and I do not fear the fury of misguided abolitionists. But what a pass have I, who hoped to have spent a useful but not an ostentatious life on heathen ground, come to! The colonists say I am their enemy. The English traders say I am secretly laying the foundation of a new colony on the Gaboon. By the colonization societies in America I am looked upon as a secret plotter against them. The people of the South—those who know me—suppose me to be a rampant abolitionist. While the abolitionists of the North denounce me as a *vile slave-holder*, or, to use their modest language, *man-stealer*."

At the meeting of the American Board in 1842, "Mr. Greene read several memorials and other papers on the subject of the connection of the American Board with slavery." The committee to whom they were referred, brought in the following paper: "In reference to the case of the Rev. John Leighton Wilson, a missionary of the Board to West Africa, it is stated in a letter from Mr. Wilson, and subsequently to his entering on the missionary work, that he sustained the legal relation of owner to a number of slaves, who fell to him in consequence of a bequest made to him before his birth; that he had offered to emancipate them, either in this country or in Liberia, and had done all which he deemed suitable to terminate a relationship painful and burdensome to himself; while they had steadfastly refused; and that he was, at the time mentioned, desirous still to emancipate these slaves, if any mode could be pointed out which should be just and kind to them. Whether Mr. Wilson has emancipated them, or what their situation has been during the last six years, or what it is now, your committee have no information. They understand, however, that the secretaries of this Board have written to him, making inquiries as to these points. With their present want of information, your committee deem it necessary to say nothing more than that Mr. Wilson appears to have intended to act conscientiously and humanely relative to the slaves under his care. Still, if his relation to them is not already terminated, it is very desirable that it should be, with as little delay as circumstances will permit.''

The following letter places the matter in a clear light:

"MISSION STATION, GABOON RIVER, W. A.,
"*January 23, 1843.*

"*Rev. Rufus Anderson, D. D., Secretary A. B. C. F. M.:*

"MY DEAR BROTHER : Your letter of March 17, 1842, making further inquiries about my *slave-holding*, was handed me by Mr. Walker, who arrived here December 1st.

"By legal inheritance, I am the legal owner of two slaves. One of these is a man of eighteen or twenty years of age, and the other, if I mistake not, is a girl of twelve or fourteen. Their grandmother and her posterity were entailed upon my mother and her posterity before I was born. At the age of twenty-one I found myself their owner, and this ownership was involuntary.

"By marriage I became joint owner of about thirty more, but, as it was repugnant to my own feelings, as well as others concerned, measures were adopted before I left the country, which have since resulted in the emancipation of the whole of these. It was made optional with them to go to the North, to Africa, or to any other place where they could enjoy their freedom. They made choice of Africa, and, though I have had reason since to regret that they did not go elsewhere, it is nevertheless a relief to myself and all concerned that they are in a state of freedom.

Choosing Africa.

"In relation to the other two, who are in *voluntary servitude*, I would remark, that I have used every means, short of coercion, to induce them to go where they could safely accept their freedom. Some time before I left the United States, I obtained the

Voluntary Servitude.

consent of the boy to accompany me to Africa, with the expectation of educating him for a teacher. And an application was made to the Prudential Committee that he be allowed to go, to which they consented. But before the time of embarkation arrived the boy showed a disposition to be vicious, and at the same time manifested a decided repugnance to going to Africa. He was advised to go to one of the free States, and the advantages of this course were distinctly set before his mind, but he refused. His sister was at that time too young to have any discretion and nothing was said to her.

"Some time in 1840, if I mistake not, I wrote to you and requested that you would obtain, if possible, a situation for these two slaves, where they could be educated and made free. At the same time, I requested that you write to my family, and I expressed the hope that the slaves might be prevailed upon to accept freedom. By the same mail I wrote to my sister. From you I received no answer, but from my sister I learned that the slaves were decidedly opposed to leaving the place of their nativity, and that the parents and others thought the proposition unkind.

An Unkind Offer!!

"Subsequently I wrote to Dr. Armstrong, of New York, and my friends at the South, but from neither party have I yet received any answer. Lastly, I deputed my wife, who, I presume, is now in the United States, to prevail on these slaves to move to one of the free States.

"I desire no profit in any form from their labors. Those who emigrated to Africa were brought here at private cost, involving an expense of several thousand dollars. The only object I have in alluding to this fact is to show that I am not a

Thousands of Dollars.

slaveholder for the sake of *gain*, and that, so far as I have funds to dispose of in the cause of humanity, they have been appropriated *chiefly* to promote the happiness and comfort of those who have been in bondage. I do not see it my duty to use *force*. They have the liberty of choosing for themselves, and I have endeavored to communicate such light and information as will enable them to choose wisely. This seems to me the best liberty that is in my power to confer. If I withdraw my protection from them and allow them to become public property, it seems to be very questionable whether I am in the line of duty.

"If my connection with the Board is a source of embarrassment or perplexity, I shall feel very sorry for it. When I offered myself to the committee I had no other desire than to spend my life in making known the unsearchable riches of the gospel to the miserable and degraded inhabitants of Africa, and after having spent eight years among them, and having, as you know, endured no ordinary trials and difficulties, I am still free to say that I have not now any other desire than to continue in this good work. But the interests of the Board and its widely-extended missions are too precious to come into competition with the right of any one individual, and rather than be that individual I would welcome the cold clay, which shall hide me from the notice of my fellow-men. If, therefore, you feel that my connection with the Board is prejudicial to its interests, either now or at any future time, I will retire from your service without any other than feelings of sincere esteem and affection.

"Very truly and affectionately,

"J. LEIGHTON WILSON."

No Thought
of Self.

The Rev. Dr. John B. Adger, who was at that time a
missionary of the American Board at Smyrna,

Letter from Dr. Adger.

writes of those days: "About the time we
went to the mission field began the great anti-
slavery movement in New England, and the publication
of *The Liberator* by William Lloyd Garrison.   Soon after
Dr. Wilson's departure for Africa he thought proper to
manumit his slaves, all except one boy, and these were
sent to Liberia at great personal expense.   Whether Dr.
Wilson was influenced by doubts as to the lawfulness of
the relation of master and slave I cannot say, but think
it more probable, that, as he contemplated, in becoming
a foreign missionary, a life-long absence from the United
States, he supposed he was better providing for the slaves
he loved by sending them to Liberia.   It seems, however, that he changed his mind on that subject, for years
after he told me he greatly regretted what he had done.
He soon lost sight of them after they landed in Liberia,
and he never knew what became of any of them.

"He had been a good many years, I think, laboring
on the coast of Africa for the good of the negro before
the abolitionists began their assault upon the American
Board, on account of his connection with that society.
The fact that they had in their employment, as a missionary, a man from South Carolina still owning one
slave boy, although he had manumitted many, gave
them an opportunity to arouse a great deal of opposition
to the Board amongst the good Christian people of New

England.   Dr. Anderson told me of the per-

Dr. Ander-
son's Love.

secutions which the Board had undergone on
Dr. Wilson's   account.   He   spoke   in   the
highest terms of this great missionary.   He said the
Board had stood faithfully by Dr. Wilson, and never did
surrender him.   As for himself, he averred that '*he would*

have seen the American Board shivered to pieces before he would turn his back on Leighton Wilson.' The reader can judge how furious and bitter that zeal was which could condemn and malign and hold up to scorn such a man as John Leighton Wilson for the crime of retaining one boy in a thoroughly scriptural relation, when he manumitted all the rest of his slaves, and *when this boy persistently refused to accept his freedom.* It was a war to

The Attack.

the knife, and the knife to the hilt, which was carried on against the Boston Board. The assault greatly diminished for a time its pecuniary resources, and their whole work, their great and glorious work abroad, was made to suffer. The attack was vigorously repelled by the Board, and Wilson was defended to the last, but the battle was over his person all the same.''

This was the condition of affairs at Boston. In Salem,

Uncle John.

the boy John, caring nothing for the strife afar off, lived happily under the care and protection of Mr. Samuel Wilson. He was taught the carpenter's trade, and, it is said, received pay for his services. As his head grew gray he was known as ''Uncle John,'' who boasted that he had ''gone through the Seminary'' with his young master, and would talk as grandly as if he had taken the full course with ''Mars Leighton.'' He always lived on the plantation, and was a faithful, kind, and trustworthy servant. When the Federal armies passed through the country during the war he helped to hide the valuables and to take care of the horses concealed in the swamps, and several times when Dr. Wilson was compelled to leave home he placed John in charge of his family and property. All during the troublous times ''Uncle John'' was as true as steel. He was sent with aid to Columbia after it was burnt during its occupation by Sherman's army. Dr. Wilson loved to praise John's skill in managing two four-horse wagons, laden with bacon and meal, in the rainy season through the swamps and over the sand hills between Mayesville and Columbia, a distance of fifty miles, and of the gratitude of good old Dr. Howe, who had had nothing to eat in two days, and how these supplies brought joy to the homeless families of noble birth who were sheltered at the Seminary. "Uncle John" was the hero of the hour, made so by the prompt dispatch of Dr. Wilson. His wagons, laden with provisions from his home, were the first to reach the starving women and children in the city once, beautiful with parks and gardens, but then, alas! sitting desolate in ashes!!

CHAPTER XIII

The Itinerant Missionary.

THE object of the American Board in planting its first mission on the western shores of Africa was that this should be the headquarters for a line of stations to extend far into the interior. They were fortunate in having a man with the spirit of Caleb, "to spy out the land," and bid the people "Let us go up at once and possess it." Mr. Wilson made repeated journeys up and down the western coast for twenty-five hundred miles, became familiar with the African ports, obtained information about the country and studied the character of the maritime tribes. He was also acquainted with the ship-captains trading along the coast, and acquired valuable information as to the commercial relations of the Europeans and Africans. But it was to the interior he cast his longing eyes, and wished to know about the heart of the country as well as its seaboard. For the double purpose of exploration and evangelization he was in "journeyings often." Extracts from the published accounts of his journeys will be given. The first journey was five months after his arrival in Africa.

To the Interior.

"This morning (June 6, 1834) we left home at eight o'clock, and the day was favorable for walking. After crossing the little river which runs into the sea near the Cape, we passed over a rolling country for several miles and entered the rice-fields. We were not a little surprised both at the extent of the cultivation and the quality of the rice. Portions of it had attained its full growth and was as good as any I had ever seen in South Carolina or Georgia. We commenced what may be considered a complete specimen of African travelling. Our road was a mere foot-path, not more than ten or twelve inches wide, and so entirely covered over by grass and shrubs as not to be traced except by those who had frequently travelled it. About 4 P. M. we arrived at a beautiful town by the name of Granbahda, where we spent the first night. In many respects it excels every other town in this part of the country for beauty, cleanliness, and the openness of its streets. It is situated on rising ground, and is surrounded by a high spiked wall. The outskirts are overgrown with beautiful groves of lime and sour-orange, which were laden with ripe fruit. Their beauty may be more easily imagined than described. As we approached the gate of the town, which is nothing more than a hole three feet high, and wide enough to admit a full-grown man, we passed a company of youngsters quietly engaged at their games. As soon as we entered the enclosure, one yell started hundreds of voices and brought around us the whole town's people, so thronging the way as to make it difficult for us to reach the chief's residence.

The City Gate.

"After winding about awhile we were seated under a shade tree in front of his majesty's house. Here we were walled in by a solid body of human beings, which excluded all fresh air, and almost deafened us with their loud and unrestrained clamors. I begged the people to go away, for awhile at least, that we might have a little fresh air and be quiet. To this they strenuously objected, saying that I would go away early the next day, and they would not have another opportunity to see me. Had we resorted to our house, they would have followed us and made that an intolerable retreat.

"When you look at one of their houses from
A Grebo House. without, you are reminded of a small pyramid,
resting upon a base not sufficiently large to support it, but when you enter its low door you are surprised that you can stand erect in any part of it, and
would compare your situation to the interior of a hollow
pyramid.   The hollow, however, is not continued up to
the apex.   There stand four posts in the centre, supporting a circular scaffold, upon which the roof rests, and by
which it is held in its place, resembling a pointed cap
which covers a man's ears and eyes.   The walls of the
house are plastered with a mortar made of clay and cow-
manure.   The other parts present the appearance of
glossy-black, caused by the smoke of the fires.   The loft
is a store-house for rice and other articles of food.   There
are also frames suspended from the loft in which the
women pile up their fire-wood.   The ambition of the
head of the house is to display his crockery; so basins,
bowls, and plates are suspended around the lower part
of the wall in horizontal lines.   Their only bedding is a
thin mat, with a block of wood for a pillow, and these are
all they have to offer a guest.

"About one o'clock, June 7th, we reached
Beautiful Scenery. the first settlement in King Neh's domains.
For a mile or two we made a gradual ascent,
when the country became hilly and the views exceedingly beautiful.   On reaching the summit of some high
hill we were often constrained to halt and survey the
beauty and grandeur of the scenery.   Its enchantment
was heightened, doubtless, by the richness and verdure
of the rice which crowned the numberless hills around
us, and we could scarcely realize that we were in the
country of an uncivilized people.

"June 8.   The next morning Neh had assembled all

his chief men and sent for me to receive in their presence a 'royal dash.' I took my seat, and a
dead silence for several minutes ensued, the
chief having his eyes fixed upon the ground.
After awhile he raised his eyes, and said the calf and the
goat, which were standing near by, were for me. I then
presented four yards of red flannel, four cotton handkerchiefs, a few beads, a looking-glass, a razor, and a knife.
The articles were carefully scrutinized and accepted.
The people were disappointed that I brought no tobacco,
and the king himself told my head man to tell me pri-
vately that I must bring tobacco the next time I came.''

In 1836 we have an account of another tour.
"A short time since, Teddah, king of the Bolobo country, visited Cape Palmas to see and shake hands
with the American people. Neither he nor any of his
suite had ever seen the face of a white man, and the feelings of curiosity with which they approached the settlement can scarcely be imagined. I thought it expedient
to interest the king and his people in our mission, and
accordingly took the most effective means of accomplish-
ing the end, by making him a present. He received the
gift with undisguised pleasure, and appeared delighted
at the prospect of having a white man to visit his country,
and he did not leave my house until he had obtained repeated promises that I should come to Bolobo. I left
home to fulfil this engagement.

"Bolobo lies to the east of Cape Palmas, and embraces
an extent of country about forty-five miles in circumference, with a population of about three thousand. Kay,
the residence of Teddah, is thirty miles from the Cape.

"Our path led us directly over the summit of a conical
hill, three hundred and fifty feet above the surrounding
plain. The scenery from the highest point was grand and

beautiful beyond anything I had expected to see so near the sea-coast. The compass of vision in every direction could not have been less than thirty miles. To the north we could trace the cloudy summits of lofty mountains, and in every direction the view was fine.

"An hour's walk brought us to a second village, called Boobly, situated on an elevated nook of land formed by the curvature of a noble stream of water. The path, for some distance before we reached the village, was over-hung with lime and sour-orange trees, the natural beauty of which was much heightened by the abundance of the ripe fruit with which their branches were laden. We halted a few moments, and the people clustered thick around to see a white man. Straight hair is with them the wonder of wonders ; and if they have no fears of violence, it is with difficulty you can keep their hands off. While seated here I involuntarily took off my hat, which raised a prodigious shout of wonder and admiration from the simple-hearted by-standers.

A White Man.

"The people of Kay had heard we were coming, and were on the *qui vive*. Now they were about to enjoy the long-wished-for sight of a white man. The children met us in great numbers some distance from the town, and the whole population was assembled within the gate. Our entry was honored by the beating of the town drum and a heavy discharge of musketry, an honor shown only to kings and white men. We were soon conducted to the front of the king's house, and were walled in by a solid mass of naked human beings. Many climbed to the roofs of the houses to get a peep at the stranger. I was urged to take off my hat, which caused another loud yell. No menagerie could excite closer observation than does a

A Naked Wall.

white man on his first visit to some of these bush towns. Every action is scanned with shameless scrutiny. If he eats, they want to see how a white man eats; if he sleeps, they want to see how a white man looks with his eyes shut; if he walks out he is followed by a gang of noisy boys and girls. The traveller acts the wisest who sits down and bears it calmly.

"In the morning I found Teddah and his head men assembled to thank me for my visit and to proffer their country's hospitality. A handsome bullock was brought out, and the king pronounced it mine. Another man with a drawn knife stepped forward and asked if I would have it killed. I told him he could kill it, and before I could get out of the way it was slaughtered within a few feet of our door. Soon after this work of death was accomplished, which from the barbarous mode of infliction made me feel uncomfortable, a man brought a large bowl of smoking blood and inquired if I wanted it. I turned away with no little abhorrence, but was relieved in some measure when my head man said that the people did not drink it before it was boiled.

Barbarian Hospitality.

"I requested Teddah to assemble the people at some convenient place that I might preach to them. It was twelve o'clock before they all gathered. We repaired to an open space in the town. The king took his seat near me, and the people formed in an oblong square in front. I need scarcely say that my feelings were deeply engaged when I found myself, a minister of the living God, surrounded by five hundred human beings, not one of whom had heard the name of Jesus or the glad tidings of salvation."

Preaching.

After speaking of the slave trade and cannibals he continues: "There is nothing beautiful about the situation of Kay. That the soil is very rich is indicated by the height of the banana and other plants. I saw near to the town an enclosure of rich and beautiful tobacco, which, I think, is indigenous to Western Africa.

"During our stay of two days we were treated with the utmost kindness and hospitality. The children loaded us with cherries, bananas and other fruits without asking or expecting anything in return. I thought, however, their object was similar to that of boys handing nuts and cakes to monkeys to see how they would eat.

"Were I adequate to the task, I might amuse you with an account of an African dance, but its superlative ridiculousness scarcely admits of description. Perhaps, however, if one of the children of nature were allowed to peep in upon the scenes in one of the brilliant ball-rooms of America, he would think his own amusemant equally rational. The two sexes here never dance together. An open space in the centre of the town is kept swept for the dancers. The drums beat, and the leader appears and scampers about like a wild horse. He is followed by forty or fifty others, who move around the ground in single file in a long, stiff trot. The music then begins, and each one strives to excel the others in the rapidity of his movements, at one time leaping and then again squatting. Each dancer has a set of bells around his ankles, the astounding noise of which seems to impart supernatural agility. Every muscle of his body is brought into violent action. The head is thrown backwards and forwards, and the countenance is made to portray, in rapid succession, every passion of the human soul. At one moment you see the man so overwhelmed with fright that his eyes are ready to start from their sockets; again you see his face covered with smiles, and in the twinkling of an eye it has gathered a storm of anger.

"On our journey homewards we found that two adjoining settlements had been on the point of war, and, though the dispute had been settled, they had not laid aside their trappings. As we passed through the neighborhood the woods resounded with the rattling of their war-bells and with their savage yells. I scarcely know an object more frightful than an African warrior in full attire. His face is dyed jet-black, which is in striking contrast with his snow-white teeth, and his body is completely covered with the skins of wild beasts, cartridge-boxes, and daggers; and when he assails an enemy he expects to gain half the victory by the fright he may occasion."

In April, 1836, Mr. Wilson started on a tour to the Kong Mountains, but on account of the opposition of the natives and serious illness, the farthest point he reached was one hundred and twenty miles from the coast.

He writes, "I have always entertained the opinion that it was important to the successful prosecution of missionary work in Western Africa that a station should be established in the interior as soon as possible. I thought the Kong Mountains might possess peculiar advantages in relation to health, and, from such fragments of information as I could gather from the people hereabouts, I was induced to think those mountains made a sweep to the sea-coast, and were not more than two hundred or two hundred and fifty miles distant. The beach people represent the intermediate tribes as cannibals, and suppose that a passage through their dominions would be utterly impracticable. I knew also that the country was broken up into innumerable tribes or clans, and that my progress would be liable to be arrested.

S

"Baffron, the slave dealer I met with the second day, mentioned the name of a man whose tribe stretched from the river almost to Pah, and said if we could get him as our guide we need apprehend no difficulty. While speaking of this man, whose name was Podih, his arrival was announced, and he expressed much pleasure at having the honor of conducting a white man through his country.

"The next day we proceeded up the Cavally. Our attention was frequently arrested by the gambols of monkeys in the trees overhanging the river, and occasionally we started an alligator from his sunny repose. The beautiful pea-fowl was seen bounding from tree to tree, and numberless birds cheered our progress by their sweet notes, while the lofty and wide-spreading tree-tops afforded us a grateful canopy from the rays of the burning sun. About one o'clock we came to a small native town, and were passing by on the other side, when the people urged us to come near the bank that they might see a white man. One or two hundred persons gazed on the anomaly with wonder and amazement.

Birds of Plumage.

"After crossing a mountain, the next day found us at Grabbo. Here the reception was suspicious, for when the 'palaver drum' was beaten we saw a large concourse of men, most of them armed with guns and cutlasses, assembling at the council house. After the reasons for the visit were given, the people appeared satisfied. Being much fatigued and exhausted, I determined to retire earlier than usual. A light was ordered, but this attracted the people in great crowds. After allowing them to satisfy their curiosity, the house was cleared and the doors closed. What appeared shyness at first now gave way to unrestrained curiosity to

Suspicious Reception.

see 'how a white man sleeps.' Several times the crowd was dismissed, but the right of gazing in the doors the rabble stoutly maintained, and when the shutters were closed they were wrenched off and carried away.''

Mr. Wilson was taken severely ill in the night, and as the jealous and threatening movements of the people continued, the next morning it seemed hazardous either to proceed or to remain, so he decided to go back to the coast. He says: ''We continued about ten miles further to the north to reach the Cavally, where we hoped to get a canoe and make the falls of the river that night, but at that place every effort to procure one failed, and the people were intent upon detaining us. At Santon the inhabitants were startled by the arrival of a white man, and for a time the surrounding country Savage Yells. was filled with their screams and savage yells. We went to a shade tree in the middle of the village, and I could scarcely stand upon my feet until a pallet could be spread, so faint and exhausted was I by the long walk which I had taken. Here the people walled me around so completely as to exclude almost every breath of air. It was in vain I told them that I was sick, and I fell into a sound sleep amidst the thunder of surrounding voices. This was a day of trial, suffering, and disappointment, above any that I had ever experienced. My sickness increased, and I found it necessary to throw myself upon the grass for rest three or four times during the morning's walk.''

This is the occasion probably referred to when the subject of this memoir delivered ''the charge'' to the writer at his ordination by the Presbytery of Harmony, in the church of Darlington, South Carolina, April 8, 1871. After an eloquent sermon by the venerable Dr. Plumer, which moved the congregation deeply, Dr. Wilson spoke with impassioned fervor, the tears rolling down his cheeks. Testifying to the abiding presence of the Master with his disciples, he said: "Once on a journey under the equatorial suns of Africa, sick, weary, and exhausted, I threw myself down in the shade of a tree, feeling that

The Light. this might be the place where I would breathe my last, when suddenly a bright light seemed to shine around me, and lit up the tree under which I was lying. I arose refreshed and invigorated, and pursued my journey." Thus did the angel of the Lord appear to his young servant amidst the wild jungles, and when surrounded by the black savages, and make "the flame of fire out of the midst of the bush" a token to him that he had surely seen the affliction of the African people, and had heard their cry and known their sorrows, and that he who had sent him to the Dark Continent would be with him even to the end of the ages.

The journal continues, "After three o'clock we came in sight of the next village, and the last one in this direction which belongs to the Tabo people. Here we concluded it was best to try and reach Yapro, the head town of a kind and hospitable people, and accordingly started for that place.

The Catskills of Cape Palmas. "Yapro crowns the summit of a high mountain and affords the most magnificent and imposing prospect that I have ever seen. The view is not unlike that enjoyed from the top of the Catskill Mountains, except this, that here it is sublime and unbounded in every direction. The Cavally River may be traced in all its meanderings to a great distance, and innumerable spiral mountains are seen rearing their bold and lofty peaks towards the clouds. None of these, however, could rival the one on which I stood, for height and beauty.

"For a missionary station, I think the falls of the Cavally decidedly inviting. The country is densely populated, the land is mountainous, the air is pure and apparently healthful, and there is every reason to believe that a missionary would be gladly and cordially received. My heart swells with emotion when I contemplate this vast and interesting field for missionary enterprises between the sea and the mountains. Its hills and valleys teem with inhabitants, but they are men without virtue, without the knowledge of God, and as ignorant of Jesus Christ and the way of salvation as if no redemption had been provided. The evil one, in the panoply of the false prophet, has invaded the country on the opposite side of the mountains, is day by day acquiring new trophies, and marching with a rapid pace towards the western shores. Nothing is needed, with the blessing of God, but Christian men to arrest his progress and possess the country."

The Eye of the Chris-tian Soldier.

In 1843, the missionary went with Toko, a noted trader, on a trip up the Gaboon River. The latter had been deputed to settle some pecuniary claims, amounting in all to fifty dollars, between parties at the Gaboon and some of this tribe which resided fifty miles in the interior. These had seized some men from the coast, who had no concern in the matter whatever, put them in stocks, and sent word to their friends that, unless their claims were settled immediately, the prisoners would be sold into slavery. The boat in which Mr. Wilson and Toko made their journey was hewn from the trunk of a single tree, but was finished in style that did credit to the ingenuity of the ship-builders. Passing up the stream for some distance, he speaks of Passall's town: "The place is situated on a low marshy spot, and is made up of twenty-five or thirty shabby, dilapidated old dwellings, which scarcely looked like the habitations of men. The major part of the houses on each side of the street seemed to be arranged under a continuous roof, having the appearance of two long sheds. The inhabitants of the town, in their general appearance, correspond exactly with what might be expected of the tenants of such abodes. With the exception of old Passall himself, there was not, as far as I saw, a single healthy-looking individual there; and it is questionable whether another settlement could be found on the river, where in so small a compass there was a greater concentration of all sorts of diseases.''

The chiefs of the Gaboon are in the habit of obtaining certificates of good conduct from the captains who trade on the river. Passall produced a bundle of these, but there was one stain upon his character which no credentials could remove. About two years before this time an English man-of-war despatched a boat up the river in pursuit of slave junks. The officer in charge, instead of returning the same day, according to instructions, resolved to explore the main branch of the river without a guide or any adequate means of defence. Having sailed all night, he landed at Passall's residence in the morning, and while the party were eating breakfast the house was surrounded, and three out of five were massacred. The remaining two were detained till they were ransomed. Mr. Wilson slept three nights in the room in which this deed of cruelty and bloodshed had been perpetrated.

After describing the payment of the claims, the release of the prisoners and the general feelings of good-will manifested by all parties, he adds: ''The scene at night was impressive in the highest degree. The full moon was pouring her rich effulgence upon the broad placid bosom of the river, whilst the tall trees stood in silent majesty over our heads, and seemed to be living spectators of what was transpiring underneath. It was a scene in a heathen land, and yet, around, beneath and above us were some of the most remarkable displays of the beauty, majesty and grandeur of God's creative power. And man, that active, restless being, is here, and though unknown to all the world besides, he is nevertheless urging forward his little interests with the same earnestness and intensity of feeling which are experienced in the most exalted stations. But how circumscribed the range of his thoughts! How little of God does he know! How profoundly ignorant of Jesus Christ and the way of salvation! And he is the living representative of innumerable generations, who have lived on the same spot, engaged in the same pursuits, and gone down to death in the same moral midnight. But is there no brighter prospect for those who are now alive and those who, in a few years, are to occupy their places? May we not believe that the time is rapidly approaching when this vast moral and intellectual waste shall be reclaimed? Is there any extravagance in thinking that the voice of strife and discord, the song of the nocturnal dance and the cry of war, which have resounded along the banks of this river from generation to generation, shall be turned into anthems of the most exalted praise to God and the Lamb?"

The Annual Report of the American Board, a half century ago, says: "With the Prudential Committee it has ever been a leading idea in regard to the Gaboon Mission *to reach the interior* at some point above the peculiar fever influences and beyond the tangled forests of the coast regions. When, under the guidance of God's good pro-

vidence, the mission shall reach such a point, where it
can make a home and centre, and there gather converts
and educate native preachers to go forth with the Word
of Life in all directions, then will its grand idea be realized.''

In the notes on his journey as given above, Mr. Wilson continues: ''During our short sojourn we
met with a number of men entirely different in
their features and general appearance from those in this
part of the country. Some of these were said to have
come five, and others ten or twelve days' journey from
the interior. They were known as the Pangwe tribe.
They were on a visit to this part of the country, which
is as near to the sea-coast as they have ever ventured.
Hearing of us at this place, they came in considerable
numbers to see a white man. Those whom we saw,
both men and women, were vastly superior in their personal appearance to the maritime tribes, and if they are
to be regarded as fair specimens of their people, I have
no hesitation in pronouncing them the finest Africans
with whom I have met. They wear no clothing, except
a piece of cloth made of the inner bark of a tree, which
is fastened around the loins by a cord. Neither do they
covet cloth. They jeer at the bushmen of this region by
telling them they wear clothes to conceal their personal
defects and their external diseases. Both men and women braid their hair with a great deal of taste; the latter
braid the hair on the forepart of the head in two rows,
which lie over the forehead not unlike the frill of a
cap. The men are of medium stature, remarkably well
formed, healthy in appearance, and manly in deportment. They had knives, spears, travelling-bags, and
other articles of curious and ingenious workmanship,
specimens of which we procured for a very small quan-

Pangwe.

tity of beads. All of their implements are made of native iron, which is considered vastly superior to any brought to the country by trading vessels. They represent their country as mountainous and healthful, and affirm that cutaneous and other diseases common to the maritime tribes are unknown. They have never participated in the slave trade and, regard it with the utmost abhorrence. The westward border of what is known as the Pangwe territory is probably within one hundred miles of the coast, and from thence it may extend many hundred miles into the interior, and possibly spread over a large portion of the south side of the Mountains of the Moon.''

In the *History of the Gaboon Mission* it is said: "The brethren still have their eye directed to the Pangwes, but the difficulties in advancing from the coast have been found to be great. There are no caravans of traders and no roads; beyond the navigable rivers there is found only a narrow path through the densest forests.''

"I have recently returned," says Dr. J. L. Wilson in a letter to his brother-in-law, Mr. William E. Mills, September 2, 1852, "from an excursion among the Pangwe people to the distance of a hundred miles in the interior. We took the villages which we visited by surprise, and the women and children fled to the woods like deer. The men, however, stood their ground, and in a few minutes after we took our seats in the palaver house we were surrounded by several hundreds, armed to the teeth with spears and knives. They were orderly and listened to the glad news of salvation with intense interest. They wore no clothing except a narrow strip of cloth, but had fine musical instruments, and showed by various specimens of cutlery that they had much skill in working brass and iron. They wanted nothing in exchange for what I obtained except white beads and brass rods. There is some prospect that we will have one or more missionaries among the tribe next year.''

CHAPTER XIV.

The Absent Wife: First Days at the Gaboon.

CAPE PALMAS was selected by the American Board as their first station in Western Africa, and for the first few years its prospects seemed very bright. It was a colony under American protection, the colonists were colored men who had lived in America, and the location promised to be a permanent basis for future missionary operations. Had the territory been occupied exclusively by American freedmen, they would have been at liberty there to plant a Western civilization; but within the twenty miles square of the colony's jurisdiction there were numerous towns and a large native population, who found the governmental regulations a yoke very grievous to be borne. The natives, for the violation of the law, were brought before an American judge and sentenced according to English law, which incited them to rebel against the constituted authority. On the other hand, the colonists, a feeble band on a foreign shore, felt that they must use every precaution to secure the protection of their lives and property against the savage hordes which might at any day be hurled against them, so they enforced the law that every resident must be enrolled in the militia. Teachers, printers, and the larger boys from the school, though from neighboring tribes, were drafted for military service, and, as can be easily seen, the mission was placed in a false light before the natives of the country.

The author of *Western Africa* says: "In consequence of

"

frequent collisions between the colonists and the natives, which kept the minds of the latter in an unfit state to receive religious impressions, the jealousy with which the colonists looked upon the efforts of the missionaries to raise the natives in the scale of civilization and intelligence, and in consequence of legislation which had the tendency to embarrass the labors of the missionaries, in 1842 the mission was transferred to the Gaboon.''   In the *History of the Gaboon Mission* it is remarked: ''The leading objects of the colony with reference to the natives were not the same as those of the mission ; the native teachers and pupils in the schools, though from tribes owing no allegiance to the colonial government, were by the laws made subject to miltary duty, and, as a body, the colonists seemed to regard the missionaries with jealousy and ill-will.''

The position of Rev. J. L. Wilson was a very delicate

A Moses.

and trying one. Here were thousands of native Africans to whom he came to preach. They lived within the bounds of a foreign colony, and were ruled by Americans, who could not speak their language. Every complaint and appeal was taken to the senior missionary, upon whom they relied as their friend and counsellor. The government looked with jealousy upon one who possessed such unbounded influence and to whom every case was referred. He found much of his time taken up with keeping the respective parties at peace, and in settling satisfactorily the minor disputes that arose. It has been said by an eye-witness that the Africans ''looked upon him as a king,'' and thus they neglected to see the spiritual nature of his office, and that he came solely to minister to them in holy things.

He had much at Cape Palmas to make his situation desirable: the charming location by the sea, a fine garden, a large orchard of fine tropical fruits, and as agreeable surroundings as could be found on the West Coast.

Going Forth the Second Time. He had found only a spoken language, but had reduced it to writing, and had given to the people the beginnings of a literature. Now his tongue was unloosed, and he could preach in the vernacular the gospel of Christ; but it seemed best for the future interest of what was designed to be a great mission for it to be established in another location; and Leighton Wilson went forth joyfully to explore the coast, select a location, build houses, learn the language, commit its sounds to writing, and initiate various missionary enterprises.

The narrative of the beginning of the Gaboon Mission is very graphically described in letters to Mrs. Wilson, who, on account of feeble health, returned to the United States in 1842. Mr. Wilson went to the Gaboon on the *Grecian*, Captain Lawlin. On the return voyage, calling at Cape Palmas, Mrs. Wilson took passage for home. The letters from which these extracts are taken crossed the Atlantic five times and the Pacific once, and it was with feelings of reverence they were read, some of them fifty years to the day after they were penned. Their careful preservation during a half-century proves how joyful news was received by the slow sailing vessel!

Writing to his wife in the early part of 1842, he says: "I send an ebony walking-stick of native manufacture, the head of which is the tooth of the sea-cow. This please present to my father. I have procured two more parrots for you, which whistle sweetly and talk some Gaboon, and would learn English, I have no doubt, very easily. You must see to it that the sailors do not cheat you by taking yours and putting theirs in the place of them."

"Dr. Anderson told Brother Griswold before he left

America that he must never write a letter when he was unwell, or in low spirits, and although I am heartily convinced of the wisdom of the advice, I can hardly adhere to it, especially as I have been in the habit for so long a time of looking up to you, my dear wife, as my comforter and support in such circumstances. When I am in low spirits or in perplexity, it is as natural for me to go to you to unbosom my troubles and seek advice as it is for a child to go to its mother to supply its wants. The fact is, dear Jane, by myself I am no man at all, and what is more remarkable than all the rest is, that I have not known it until we parted. I really suppose if my companions could read my heart this afternoon they would reproach me with the epithet of 'baby.' But you won't, will you, dear wife? I really believe, were I not governed by a love to my Saviour and a desire to do good to the wretched inhabitants of Africa, I would return from this, or any other undertaking in the world, in the face of all the sneers and scouts that could be cast at me. As it is, however, I can and do go forward with manliness and courage, and for the most part with feelings of the utmost cheerfulness.''

''I was little aware how severe a duty I was imposing both upon you and myself when I proposed a separation of nine months or a year. You requested me not to forget you. You ought to have requested me not to forget everything else. And this memorable day, May 21, the anniversary of our marriage, as if my heart was not already sufficiently burdened, brings along with it such a tide of overwhelming and affecting associations, that I am almost unmanned. Yes, dear Jane, the eight happiest years of my life; yea, happier than all the rest of my days put together, is constantly before my mind, and leaves me in the exercise of feelings which I have no language to express. This precious silent Sabbath afternoon intervenes and gives me an opportunity not only to preach, but some hours to hold converse with my own heart and my dear wife. But, oh! the sorrow of being alone! Everything I see and handle reminds me of her who is dearer to me than life. If I open my chest, there are some things there that your hands have arranged; when I go to my state-room, one berth is vacant; when I speak to David, Frances, or Victoria, I am reminded that I have not only left you myself, but taken away your pets also. Old Peter and others are constantly saying, 'You no bring your wife dis time.' And thus everything has conspired to remind me of my sorrow and misery.

    "I have been disappointed in laying in the promised supply of cocoanuts, but I have stored away twenty or thirty of them for your homeward voyage. It will be well for you to get one or two bottles of Mrs. Dr. Wilson's excellent wine to use on the voyage, and one or two jars of pickles. I am inclined to think Captain Lawlin's stock of rice is small, and you better have a croo or two carefully cleaned and sent aboard. I have thus far failed to procure a milk goat, but will continue to make exertions, and I hope you will not have to quit the coast without one, as I am more and more convinced that it will be essential to your comfort and health. When I review the last eight or ten years of my life, I regard it as a scene of almost uninterrupted happiness, and you, my dear wife, under the good hand of God, I regard as the author of it. The period of betrothal was crowded with what may be regarded as the romantic, the imaginary, and the fanciful. The earlier period of married life were all fervor and glow; the longer and more natural part of our life has been the season of a steadily growing affection, which has rendered my life almost insupportable without you. If I have been happy, you have made me so; if I have been cheerful and useful, it is from the same cause. I am living and laboring in Africa, my dear Jane, because you cheered and animated my moments of despondency. If, therefore, you feel depressed and desolate at any time, be encouraged by what you have done for me and what you have done for Africa. If you are permitted to do no more in this land for your Saviour, feel assured that your life has not been thrown away.''

''I have been a day and a half on shore at this place (Elemena, June 2, 1842). There is one street, more than a half-mile long, arched with the umbrella tree, which is not only superior to anything at Cape Coast, but equal in beauty to anything of the kind which I have ever seen in any country. The native part of the town is very low, muddy, and repulsive. You have, without any figure of speech, to kick the dogs and pigs out of your way, and you will find naked children, sheep, and a gold taker or two in every porch which you enter.''

''At Cape Coast (June 14) we occupied the same room which you and I did on a previous voyage. In the same apartment we found the effects of one of our new missionaries, Mr. Wyatt, who died not many weeks since.

A Strict
Rule.

Mrs. Waldron has a school of sixty girls in the room back of our old quarters. No girl is admitted unless she wears clothes. The congregation at Cape Coast has improved very perceptibly both in numbers and in the respectability of its appearance. One-half of the women wear the European dress, and the same is about true of the men. There is a demand for schools and preaching in the country around, which the missionaries are utterly incapable of meeting.

"The Ashanti princes are on a visit to Cape Coast, and take their meals at Mr. Freeman's. He was kindly re-

One-tenth. ceived by the king of Ashanti. The carriage which Mr. Freeman took to the king cost originally $1,700, and the expense of taking it there from Accra was $1,000; in all, probably upwards of $3,000. The king made a present in return of about as many hundred dollars.

"I have procured a good drip stone, and will endeavor to have good water. I can hardly realize that I have gone one thousand miles in one direction, and that ere long you will commence a voyage four times that length in an opposite direction."

"Having made my appearance, my dear wife, on two previous occasions" (writing near the Gaboon, June 19, 1842) "since you commenced crossing the Atlantic, and having had no intimation of being an unwelcome visitor, I have prevailed upon old Neptune to be the bearer of one more dispatch, by the assurance that he would greatly gratify one whom I esteem and love more than any other on the face of the earth or the sea. He has acceded to my wishes this one time more, on the condition that I tax him no more during your present voyage, and to this requisition I stand pledged.

"I never felt a disposition to write poetry until since we parted, and I cannot account for my present inclination, unless it be that I find prose too tame and stiff a vehicle to convey the true feelings of my heart. I want a pen far more glowing than that which I habitually wield to give even a faint outline of what I feel for you. Your name and image are before my mind night and day, in company and alone, in dull spirits and in high, aboard and ashore, ever present and all-consoling. Without you this lower world has no attractions for me. If you

9

go before me to our Father's house, it will be a comforting thought that he will permit you, a pure spirit, to be my ministering angel.

"We are drawing near to the close of our voyage, and you can form some idea of the feelings of interest and anxiety which occupy my mind at this juncture. We left home with Cape Lahow and the Gaboon before our minds. We found difficulties in the way of occupying the first, and now only one remains to be revisited. How we shall find things there depends upon observations which are to be made in a day or two. If insurmountable obstacles are encountered, we shall have to commence our journeys afresh."

"Yesterday we made St. Thomas, and this morning (June 2, 1842) we were greatly surprised to find any land so near to the coast of Africa as high and picturesque as the mountains of this little island. Its appearance corresponds very nearly with what I should expect in approaching the Sandwich Islands. We coasted along the west and north all day, and had an opportunity to view all that was to be seen near the water's edge. The only appearance of civilization on the west side are a few obscure fishermen's towns. Small canoes came off, and brought plantains, fish, yams, etc., which were purchased at a high rate. We rounded the northwest corner late in the afternoon, and had a full, though distant, view of the castle and town of St. Ann De Chaves, which, I believe, is the chief settlement on the island."

"We arrived here, my dear and beloved wife, yesterday at midday, and this forenoon (June 23, 1843) we had a general palaver in relation to the object of our visit. The people gave their hearty assent to the planting of our mission, and, as I found no serious obstacle to the occupancy of the place, it has accordingly been decided that I remain and commence operations. I trust that the hand of God has been with us, and his praises are continually on my lips. Every view of the prospect before us is cheering, except the absence of her who is dearer to me than life. This is *bearable only* because I believe it is the will of our Heavenly Father. Taken altogether, it is not only the greatest, but, I believe, greater than all the sacrifices which I have ever been called on to make put together.

First Views of the New Station. "The Gaboon is a new chapter in my African experience. Things are very different from anything we have ever seen before on this continent. The river itself (I think it should rather be denominated *a bay*) is a noble one, and, opposite the place we are to live, is greatly enlivened by beautiful sail-boats flying in every direction. The towns are small, but very compact. The largest we have seen does not contain probably more than five or six hundred inhabitants. The style of building, compared with anything you or I have seen before in Africa, is unique. The people, taken together or *en masse*, I believe, are more civilized than any natives I have seen before on the coast. The men wear shirts and cloths which reach to their ankles ; a few wear coats, shoes, and vests. The females wear cloths which cover almost the whole of their bodies.

Selecting a Lot. "The country along the river is thickly wooded, and the towns are so completely enveloped in plaintain groves as not to make a very conspicuous appearance. The situation which I have chosen for the missionary premises stands immediately in the rear of what is called King Glass' town, on ground considerably elevated and about a half-mile from the water's edge. The location is airy, and, though not so beautiful as Fair Hope, is nevertheless what you would call a pleasant one. Near to it is a spring of water, better than any I have ever drank on the sea-coast. Captain Lawlin's old friend Toko has a drip stone and a cooling jar, so that for a day or two past we have luxuriated upon pure and cool water.

And to Knowledge, Experience.

"You know I am too well schooled in African matters to be sanguine in relation to any outward appearance. Still, I am greatly deceived (humanly speaking) if our prospects as a mission are not very encouraging. I shall enter upon my work here with much valuable experience, and I trust with increased ardor. My earthly happiness, under the good hand of God, will be consummated when my beloved wife returns once more to cheer and animate my heart."

"In relation to the two communications I am to send you, one of them might with propriety be denominated 'Homeward Bound' and the other 'Home as Found.' . . . .

Humble Quarters.

The house in which I live contains six rooms. In front is a large parlor, with a small room cut off its end Behind these are two rooms, twelve feet square, one of which I use as a bed-room; its ground floor is covered with mats. In the rear are two other small rooms. Helen is cook, but next week she will be put to washing, and I will have a hired cook. I shall have one boy to bring wood and water. A third is to be employed as my fisherman, and promises to furnish a daily supply for the mission families. A fourth is to be market-boy, to purchase plantains, yams, chickens, etc. Each of these is to receive about twenty dollars *per annum*. Plantains and yams are the staple articles of food here.   There is an abundance of corn, and as soon as I can procure a mill to grind the staff of life, it is pretty certain that you and I will not starve.

"The parlor which I am occupying is furnished with a half-dozen chairs, a few chests, a good table and a lounge.   The walls are ornamented with several handsome pictures and a new gilt-framed mirror.   I use one of the real old-fashioned Windsor chairs, and to prevent dampness arising from the dirt floor, I have a mat spread over the place where I usually sit.

"You can scarcely conceive with what pleasure I visit King Glass and others here, and feel perfectly assured that they are expecting nothing by way of dash for any kindness they may extend to me.   As yet I have made no dashes, and expect to make none.   There is a degree of manliness and independence here which is unknown on the windward coast.

Farewell. "And now, my dear wife, I must bring these scribblings to a close, though it is a task from which my feelings have recoiled ever since I began. There is one word peculiarly hard for me to write, but it must be done, and it will be done with as much Christian cheerfulness as could be expected in the nature of the case.   And now I must write that dread word, and thanks to my Saviour who has given me grace and strength to do it cheerfully and with a spirit of resignation, so, my much-loved wife, *farewell and farewell.*"

Imagination. "When I took leave of Captain Lawlin and others on the evening before departure, it was with the hope and expectation that I should see nothing of the *Grecian* the next morning (July 18, 1842), and such proved to be the case.   I went down to the beach and looked, but no vessel was in sight.   I returned, and imagination commenced her work.   She soon overtook the ship and hurried her onward.   Flying ahead, it fluttered around and around that precious and to me indescribably dear freight which she was to receive at Cape Palmas.   I thought of you, and felt for you in the vessel's unavoidable delay in reaching Cape Palmas, and of the anxious surmises and conjectures you would form to account for that delay.   I thought of you as the *Grecian* heaved in sight, and the mixed emotions with which you would hear the first tidings.   I followed you up to your chamber, and looked upon your countenance as you broke open my letters, and almost reproached myself in audible language for penning things which you would almost be sure to attribute to low spirits and dejection on my part. I thought of you in all your preparations for embarkation and in taking leave of some who are dear to us both.   I thought of you in your sea-sickness, and involuntarily dropped a tear because I was not there to tender you my sympathy.   I have anticipated your arrival at Philadelphia and have seen you enjoying the affectionate greetings of a numerous circle of dear friends, and feeling the bracing influence of an American climate.

"You must not suppose that I returned from the beach with feelings of dreariness or dejection.   No, just the reverse.   I have been permitted to enjoy much of the presence of my Saviour, and who can be low-spirited or feel desolate in such society as his?   Besides, my time and attention have been so completely engrossed in making preparations for the reception of the brethren from Cape Palmas, revisiting the adjacent towns on the river, and studying the language, that I have not had time to feel lonely. There are vessels here nearly all the time.   Some of the captains have very little sobriety and virtue; others, however, I have found to be worthy men, who are not only friendly to me personally, but also feel disposed to advance the work in which we are engaged.

"In relation to domestic affairs, I get along not only quite as well, but also a great deal better than I expected. I have a daily supply of fish, both fresh and dried, fowls, salt beef, kid, plantains, yams, sweet potatoes, tomatoes, eggs, etc.

"I find the people still decidedly civil and kind. There is not a day in which I do not receive a present of a basket of groundnuts or some sugar-cane. These gifts are made without any expectation of a return. In a social point of view, the natives are elevated far above those on the windward coast, but still they are heathen in the full sense of the word. The belief in witchcraft, the practice of polygamy, and a thousand other kindred vices are as common and as inveterate as at Cape Palmas or any other place in the world.

"I have made agreements for building all *A Cheap House.* the houses which we shall need for the present, and the materials have been, for the most part, collected. The house in which we are to live independently of the doors and windows, will cost about eighty dollars. The site has been selected and cleaned away, and a new road has been cut. The women of the two towns, of their own accord and without any compensation, labored for two days in clearing the grass and rubbish from the hill. I have visited all the settlements on the river in this immediate vicinity, and am more and more pleased with the prospects opening around us."

With the picture before us of the missionary's mansion, built of bamboo with a thatched roof, and costing fourscore dollars, it may be an appropriate time to relate an incident. Seated in his and Mrs. Wilson's room in Baltimore, the conversation turned on missionary residences, when the Secretary suddenly said, "DuBose, we had a nephew in China; he sent us the photograph of his house, and we were so ashamed of it we never let any one see it;" and, turning to his wife, "It is put away somewhere now, is it not?" "Yes," she replied, as if it were an unpleasant topic, "*I keep it hid.*" The nephew was a better preacher than an architect, and the house he built was quite a modest abode, constructed without due reference to the beauty of its proportions and for a moderate sum of money; but, situated upon the side of a Chefoo hill, the prospective was fine, and as "distance lends enchantment," the camera represented it as a handsome mansion. Hence the aged couple thought it was too much of the "earth earthy" for a disciple of him "who had not where to lay his head."

The Audience Interested.

His letters to Mrs. Wilson continue: "To-day (Sabbath, July 24) instead of preaching to three small towns separately as heretofore, I made a successful effort to bring the people together at King Glass' house, and spoke to them all at the same time. I preached to them on the ascension, the second coming, and the judgment, and I am not aware that I ever witnessed greater astonishment. I was hindered at almost every step by inquiries, which discovered not only excited feeling, but serious reflection. One asked what time Christ would return to judge the world. Another came to the very natural conclusion that those on the left hand of the Judge would greatly exceed those on his right."

Then and Now.

July 27. "The commencement of a new mission here brings to my remembrance many things associated with the early part of our residence at Cape Palmas. Then I was much excited by the novelty of the situation and driven forward by mere ardent impulses. I was zealous, sanguine, and in many things impetuous. I was inexperienced, unacquainted with the African character, drew wrong inferences, and fell into a great many mistakes. *Now* I labor under very little excitement. African life has its shades and changes, but in all important matters it is the same all over negro-land. What I am wanting in youthful ardor and activity I trust is more than made up by a more mature experience, by a more sober and rational view of things, by a feeling of a greater weanedness from this world, and by a more abiding desire to glorify God. All of my aspirations after personal aggrandizement are gradually yielding, I trust, to steadier devotion to the cause of Christ. I am conscious of no desire to live except for the advancement of the Redeemer's kingdom and the salvation of souls. And I trust it will always be so."

August 7, 1842. "Since I wrote you last I have had a slight attack of intermittent fever, such as you have seen me have fifty or a hundred times. During the continuance of the attack I had a soft couch to lie on. Mr. Dorsey prepared good tea for me. I had a gilt bowl, one which Captain Lawlin gave me, to drink it out of, but the *sweet presence* of my wife was wanting to make that sick couch a happy place. The attack gave way to the usual remedies of quinine, blue pill and hot coffee.

"Although I have felt my loneliness very keenly at times, God has been pleased to show me that it has been ordered by him, and is good for my spiritual welfare. It has afforded opportunity for much serious reflection, and given me the means of testing the sincerity and strength of my religious principles; it has brought heaven nearer to me and made me feel that it is my home.   I have thought upon the goodness of God in times that are past, and especially in the gift of a wife who is in every way suited to me, and has made me a happy husband for eight precious years.

"You will be surprised, perhaps, when I say I have not had a *palaver* of any kind since my arrival here which has caused me the least anxiety.   How different this is from my previous experience in Africa you need not be told.

A Black Stain.   There is one serious stain upon the character of this people, however, and that is, their participation in the slave trade, in which I find them more seriously involved than I had at first imagined. But this vile traffic is doomed to have its end, and though it is most seriously to be regretted that this people have anything to do with it, yet it should not occasion surprise so long as white men are engaged in it, and place before them the strongest inducements to take part also."

Visit to Conig Island.   August 12.   "Day before yesterday, my beloved wife, without much forethought or preparation, I determined to visit Conig Island, which is situated in the middle of the Gaboon River, sixteen or eighteen miles from its mouth, and about that distance from the mission station.   I performed the voyage in a native sail-boat.   Our company consisted of my interpreter, my steward (*i. e.*, my housekeeper, who designated himself by that appellation), four oarsmen, and four other boys as passengers.   We left this place about 3 P. M., and had scarcely shoved the boat from the beach when two large, awkwardly-made, but effective sails were spread, and our little craft moved off and up the river as a 'thing of life.'   The sails were set, not to be touched again until the voyage was ended. Then followed a scene truly African : The boys huddled around a few smoking embers on the forepart of the boat and smoked their pipes. After this they stretched themselves at full length and had a general sleeping match. We sailed along the north bank and had a pretty clear view of all that was to be seen near the water. Thick jungles, grassy fields, forests of tall trees, and the wide streets of the native villages almost buried in plaintain trees, alternately revealed themselves and afforded much entertainment. As we neared what is called 'Round Point,' the banks of the river gradually rose, and the surrounding country became more imposing. As we doubled the point, a scene of transcendent beauty presented itself to our view. The river turned suddenly towards the north-west and stretched out in a straight direction far beyond the reach of the eye. Conig Island, with its high and lofty hills clothed in the richest green, presented itself directly before us. Several large tributary streams poured into the river on our right and left, the mouths of which were indicated by high bluffs and projecting masses of rock. Several native villages, most of them situated on the sides or summits of high hills, were distinctly seen, whilst the situation of a great many more, some as far off as fifteen or twenty miles, were identified by the presence of tall trees or by projecting points dividing the tributary streams. We landed about sunset at the south-east end of the island, near to a small but beautiful village, situated at the base of one of the tallest of Conig's hills. I was hospitably entertained by the head man. His house, though not so large as others I have seen on the river, is decidedly the neatest, and has an air of comfort and civilization. Yesterday morning I ascended to the top of the highest hill before the sun was up, and the view was really enchanting. We reached home about four o'clock hungry and fatigued. You, my dear wife, occupied my first thoughts, after throwing myself upon the couch. Always, after returning from fatiguing walks, you were at home to cheer me and listen to the incidents of my travels. This time I quieted my mind by resorting to my pen."

Submission.   "I am not aware, my dear wife, that I ever felt more grateful for the Sabbath (August 14) or enjoyed it more than I have this. I have experienced a state of mind to-day which I have not before enjoyed to so full an extent since I parted from you. It is a hearty feeling of submission to the will of God in the disposal of both you and myself. And the attainment of this state of mind, I do not know how abiding it will be, has freed me from a needless and sinful burden of anxiety. We can be happy Christians only when we can say 'thy will be done,' and the more we have the grace of acquiescence, the happier we will be."

January 15, 1843. "The brethren from Cape Palmas arrived here about the 1st of December and brought two letters from you, one written before you left Cape Palmas and the other from Monrovia. I shall begin to look very steadily for you after the 1st of May. I hope you will muster all your handkerchiefs and aprons, and fasten them to the yards of the vessel to quicken her pace. Should you touch at Cape Coast, this letter will be handed you, and though of the same date with one you will have received at Cape Palmas, I trust it will not be uninteresting. For me to write the same things to you, my dear Jane, is not grievous, and I believe you will read them over and over again without weariness. The brethren tantalize me not a little about the time of Captain Lawlin's return. One says 'June'; another, 'July,' while Brother G. has the effrontery and hardheartedness to say 'August.'"

The next epistle to Mrs. Wilson was dated, "At sea, between Gaboon and Cape Palmas, February 25, 1843."

No Tidings. He writes: "I am now on my way to Cape Palmas, where I expect to await your arrival, and if you ask, 'Why I come'?—the answer is ready, 'I could not help it.' I left our affairs in such a condition at the Gaboon that they would not suffer by my absence. Some things were to be done at Cape Palmas that will depend on such instructions as you will bring from the Committee; and, above all and beyond all, I have come thus far to meet and cheer you, for if you have felt as I have, you will greatly need it. That uncomfortable word *possibly* will force itself upon my mind. And what a calamity, what an overwhelming trial, if, upon arrival at Cape Palmas, I shall be told that Captain Lawlin has already passed down. That is not all. Imagination will be busy at times, and I may be told that the arrival of the *Grecian* in America has never been heard of. If I should receive the most afflictive tidings, I should have to bear it, so far as those around me are concerned, *without a single sympathizing tear.* At such times how refreshing it is to remember that there is one above who is touched with a feeling for our infirmities. I would not be one of those who follow the world as their chief good; no, not for ten thousand worlds!"

The following letter to his "parents, brothers, and sisters," written June 2d, 1843, presents very vividly the anxious love of a husband waiting for the absent wife: "I have been here nearly three months, **Return!** **Return!!** though when I left the Gaboon I hoped it would not have been that many weeks, and yet Jane has not arrived. I am in hourly expectation, but God alone knows when she will get here. I have been anxious enough about her, as you can readily imagine. I did hope to have seen her by the first of April, but April has come and is gone! May followed, and that is gone!! The anniversary of our parting has come and gone; so has the anniversary of our marriage, and yet my dear wife has not yet arrived. One vessel after another has heaved in sight of Cape Palmas; a greater number passed by, some up and others down the coast. I have made excursions in one direction, then in another. I have read all the books in the neighborhood; some for instruction, some for amusement, and others for personal improvement. I have written tracts in the Gaboon language, and had them printed. I have walked until my shoes are almost worn out; looked for vessels until my eyes are sore; have waited until my heart is almost faint; dreamed and dreamed again, but still my dear Jane is not here.''

Later, June 23: "Last night a letter was placed in my hands from my beloved wife, dated 'Monrovia, June 15,' which stated she would be here in the course of four or five days. This has filled my heart with joy and gladness. 'I love the Lord because he hath heard my voice and my supplications.'

"The box, which was made up for us in Darlington, has been received in good order. The contents are very valuable, and will be highly useful.''

"You, my dear father, and the rest of the family, will rejoice with me (Gaboon, July 17) when you hear of the safe arrival of my wife in Africa. I doubt not that her visit to America will be of permanent benefit to her. Jane has told me so much about Sumter that I feel as though I had paid you a visit myself. Things, persons and events stand out so distinctly before my imagination that I can scarcely realize I have been absent nearly ten years.''

CHAPTER XV.

Life at the Gaboon.

REV. J. L. WILSON writes (to the mission rooms), July 26, 1843, "It is now nearly six weeks since I commenced a residence in this place. I have visited most of the chiefs in this vicinity, and found them already interested in our mission, or with a little explanation have made them so; and there are none of those whom I have visited who have not either promised to send their sons to our schools when organized, or requested that schools might be established in their towns. The people continue to be civil and friendly, and have of their own accord rendered some important aid in our preparations for building. All the experience I have acquired and the observations I have made, induce the belief that we have entered upon an interesting and promising field, and that we were conducted to it by the unerring hand of our Heavenly Father. My health has been uninterruptedly good; we have excellent water and the situation of the mission premises will be open and airy. My time has been chiefly spent in visiting the surrounding country, attending to the erection of houses for the mission family, and in studying the language.

Bamboo. The buildings will be constructed throughout of bamboo, and if we can secure a sufficiency of boards to lay the floors, they will not only be commodious, but airy and comfortable."

The *Missionary Herald* says, "A letter from Mr. Wilson, August 23, 1843, states that the prospects of the mission continue to be encouraging; that Mr. Walker had commenced a new station twenty-five or thirty miles up the river, and that Commodore Perry had offered to render the missionaries any assistance that might be in his power.''

On November 25, 1843, the pioneer writes, ''*Preaching the gospel* we make our leading business. We maintain stated preaching at six different places, with occasional services at a still greater number. All the schools have been kept up thus far in buildings belonging to natives; but a house has just been erected at King Duka's town with a front hall twenty-four feet square, which is to be used as a school-room and place for religious worship. These houses are put up in native style at an expense of about sixteen dollars; the garden fence and place for cooking will bring it to about twenty dollars.''

Sixteen Dollars for a School-House.

He writes to the American Board, January 29, 1846, ''The time has come when more ought to be done to place the mission on a firm and broad foundation. The Gaboon is now a French province and likely to continue so. So long as we shall be permitted to carry on our operations in quietness and peace, the mission ought to be strengthened and reinforced. At the same time, we ought to commence another station beyond the jurisdiction of the French. That station might be opened at Cape Lopez, sixty miles south of the Gaboon; or at Cape Saint Catherine's, one hundred miles still further south, at both of which places the Gaboon language is spoken.''

New Stations Needed.

Soon after the settlement of the mission at the Gaboon was made, the *Missionary Herald* says, ''A very full and interesting description of the country and the noble Gaboon River, of the character and condition of the people, and of the encouragements to missionary work has been received from Mr. Wilson." The report, speaking of

Gaboon Merchants. trade, says, "The native merchants, through whose hands the trade in ivory, redwood, ebony, bees-wax, and gum copal passes, are, for uneducated men, much more respectable than any I have known in Africa. Some of them are frequently trusted with goods by the captain of a single vessel to the amount of three or four thousand dollars, and, as a general thing, they are honorable and punctual in discharging their obligations. There are a few who transact business to the amount of twelve or fifteen thousand dollars a year. How they manage a business of this extent in the smallest fractions and driblets, without the aid of written accounts, is very surprising! It is done with the utmost accuracy, without any other aid than memory.

Houses at the Gaboon. "The houses are constructed almost entirely of bamboo. Poles are fixed in the ground about a foot apart, and bamboo reeds are tied horizontally to these, and this forms the body of the house. The roofs are covered with leaves of the same. They are spacious, well lighted and ventilated, and with the exception of dirt floors, they are as comfortable habitations as most persons would desire. The house in which King Glass resides is sixty-six feet long and twenty-seven wide; others in the same town are very nearly as large.

Politeness. "In their intercourse with white men they are uniformly civil and polite, and carefully avoid anything like obtrusiveness. It requires only a very partial knowledge of their character and disposition to make a white man feel perfectly safe among them. Unfortunately, for their morals, they have not always found the best patterns of virtue in the whites with whom they have had intercourse. It is mortifying to observe that many of the vices of heathenism have not only been sanctioned and encouraged by the example of Europeans, but a great many, peculiar to civilized countries, have been grafted upon their character.

Progress Towards Civilization. "There is probably no people on the West Coast of Africa who have made further advances towards civilization than those who reside upon the Gaboon, unless it may be some who have been long under Christian instruction. And it may be questioned whether there are any of this description who have all the urbanity of manners and kindliness of feeling uniformly manifested by natives on this river."

King Glass. King Glass, as the African chieftain was popularly known, always proved himself a firm friend of the missionary. When Mr. Wilson started on his long evangelistic tours, he always left Mrs. Wilson in the care of King Glass, feeling perfectly confident that he would do all in his power to afford her protection. This sable ruler was a great thief, and Dr. Wilson's parting injunction was, "Jane, look well after King Glass, and see that he does not want anything." The old man used to boast that "the minister thought so much of him that he told the white woman to look after him."

When Mrs. Wilson returned to Africa she took as an assistant teacher a colored girl whom her mistress had educated. This girl was a great help to her, and also very companionable, and in the evenings, when Dr. Wilson was busy or absent, they would talk about Savannah, and the people they knew there, and both felt happier for their conversations.

Dr. Wilson's life in Africa was devoted to philan-

thropy.   The sick and suffering, the needy and destitute,
the traveller and sailor, the widow and orphan,
Philan-   all found a refuge under his roof.   He showed
  thropy.
kindness to hundreds of the white race who
visited the equator.   He and Mrs. Wilson wished to adopt
a little Portuguese girl, who was left on their hands, and
who lived with them for some months, but she was afterwards claimed by her relatives in Portugal, and they
very reluctantly had to give her up.

Among those who enjoyed the blessings of associating
with these good people was the great African traveller,
Du Chaillu.   Du Chaillu.   He, when a boy, made their
house his home, and his father requested Mrs.
Wilson to teach Paul the English language, and it was
a source of great enjoyment to her to have the monotony
of their African life broken into by the merry company
of this bright French boy.   Dr. and Mrs. Wilson were
warmly attached to him, and he, with all the strength of
his ardent nature, returned their affection.   He always
called them father and mother.   From the time they
adopted him as a protegé, till the day of their death,
they entertained the highest regard for his character for
truth and honor.   In his book on Africa he speaks at
length of the home-life at the Gaboon and Dr. Wilson's
work in the dark continent.   On hearing some one say,
"Dr. Wilson was narrow," he exclaimed, "Dr. Wilson
narrow!   He was as broad as this broad earth!!"

Of the visits of the men-of-war, Mr. Wilson writes,
January 20, 1844: "This river is the south-
American   ern cruising point of our squadron.   The
  Squadron.
Decatur is now in the river, and Captain
Abbott has shown us the utmost kindness.   The officers
of the Decatur think the natives of the Gaboon the most
interesting and promising specimens of the African race

they have met with on the coast. Commodore Perry has sent us a kind salutation; he promises himself to pay us a visit in the course of a few months." The *Missionary Herald* says: "During his stay at the Gaboon, Commodore Read showed Mr. and Mrs. Wilson many attentions. He expressed a willingness to do whatever he could for the mission. He left a letter for the French Admiral, which occasioned a correspondence between the latter and Mr. Wilson."

They now and then had European visitors. He writes (October 15, 1850), "Captain Brown, of the *Lowder*, brought his wife out with him, and she is staying with us at present. She is a member of one of the Presbyterian churches in New York.' Again, "We have an English lady staying with us, and this is the fifth or sixth lady visitor we have had in a year past, so you see we are not exactly out of the world."

Visiting Ladies.

Mr. Wilson remained for twelve years on the coast of Africa before he returned to the United States on furlough. When he was Secretary in Baltimore, in an epistle to the writer, August 15, 1879, he says: "I was invited home once, after being seven years in Africa, under the impression that missionaries could not live at all in that country. I felt if I acceded it would be the death of missions to that country, for a long time at least, and I preferred to die at my post rather than imperil that great cause I remained over twelve years, and missions are going on there more prosperously than anywhere else."

Furlough Declined.

In his home letter, dated "Gaboon, W. A., February 6, 1846," he writes: "In my last I mentioned that we were expecting to return to the United States in the early part of the spring, but Mr. Bushnell, whose health is very poor, will return with Captain Lawlin, and Mr. Walker, my only other associate, has not yet arrived. I regret this delay an account of the very great age and infirmity of my father, whose face I desire very much to see once more in the land of the living."

September 23, 1846: "My last was written in February, and since then no direct opportunity to convey letters has presented itself. I often think of you and pray for you, and neither time, distance, nor the multitude of cares and labors, which press upon me day by day, can either deface or diminish the affection I feel for all the dear ones at home."

The next spring he was permitted to enjoy his first rest from the toils of missionary life. The

Vacation.

Missionary Herald says: "In accordance with a rule, which the Prudential Committee have recently adopted to preserve the health and prolong the lives of our missionaries on the western coast of Africa, Mr. Wilson is now on a visit to this country. He arrived at New York, accompanied by Mrs. Wilson, June 21. There was, however, another reason for his return. He wishes to call the attention of American Christians to the condition of Africa, and to induce some of our young ministers, and candidates for the ministry, to take part

Need of La-borers.

with him and his associates in efforts for its evangelization. For some time past our mis-

Appeal of the A. B. C. F. M.

sion has been in a languishing state. If we attempt anything we should conduct our operations upon a scale commensurate, in some measure, with the greatness of the undertaking; and it specially behooves us to relieve the brethren, at present connected with the mission, from a position as hazardous as it is trying. During the absence of Mr. Wilson, the responsibility of its cares and labors rests upon Mr.

Walker, as it had previously rested for months and years upon Mr. Wilson. Is it right for the churches to leave such a burden upon these brethren? If this mighty continent is to be regenerated by the gospel of Christ, ought not Christians of every land and every hue engage in this work? Will you permit this honored servant of our common Lord, who has just come to our shores burdened with the interests and the wants of Africa, hoping to obtain a few helpers in his work of love to her fallen children, yet fearing a disappointment, to return to his adopted country in loneliness and sorrow, if not in despair?''

In an appeal to the churches, at the time he was on furlough, the subject of this sketch says: ''During the last four years at the Gaboon, a large amount of religious truth has been stored away in many minds, the influence of which is beginning to show itself in certain outward reformations, such as the partial observance of the Sabbath, more general abstinence from intoxicating drinks, and greater punctuality and honesty in their commercial transactions. Towards the missionaries they have uniformly been kind, the object of the mission is more clearly understood, and we think they manifest an increasing interest in the continuance of our operations. . . . . . . Besides the villages nearer to the principal station, where the word of God has been dispensed steadily, there are fifteen or twenty settlements more remote, where there has been occasional preaching, so that the people over a considerable extent of country have been initiated into the first principles of Christianity, and thus the way has been prepared for more vigorous, systematic, and extended operations hereafter.

''Besides various elementary books, there have been

prepared a small hymn-book of forty-eight pages; a
Printing. volume of simple sermons of seventy-two
pages; a volume of extracts from the New
Testament of eighty-two pages, and a volume of Old
Testament history. All these are in the Mpongwe language, and printed in tolerably good style by a native
boy of our own training, who is not more than sixteen
years of age. We have prepared for the press a grammar, and an extended vocabulary of the Mpongwe; also
a small vocabulary and a few familiar sentences in the
Batanga language. These will be printed in the United
States.

"There has been much mortality among the Mpongwe
Intemperance. people during the past year—more than has
ever been known before—the principal part
of which is to be ascribed to intemperance and other ex-
cesses in past years, showing that what we are to do for
this and other branches of the African family ought to
be done with as little delay as possible. It is a painful
fact that the tribes on the western coast are gradually
disappearing, and it is still more painful, as well as un-
deniably true, to reflect that the means of their destruc-
tion has been furnished by our own and other Christian
nations. The great day of account may reveal, it may
be, that the number of the victims of intemperance in
Africa greatly exceeds those of the slave-trade. The
intervention of missionary influence alone will avert
these calamities. It is mortifying to observe that many
of the vices of heathenism have not only been sanctioned
and encouraged by the example of Europeans, but a
great many peculiar to civilized countries have been
grafted upon their character, thus the name of God is
blasphemed among the Gentiles.

"Among the Balkali tribe I found, what is seldom seen

immediately on the sea-coast, a large number of very aged men and women. This can be accounted for only by the supposition that they have recently emerged from the interior, and have not as yet been brought into contact with the blighting influence which modern commerce exerts upon heathen tribes. These people, though heathen in the full sense of the word, and frequently at war among themselves, were civil and kind to me, and listened with the utmost attention to the preaching of the word, which they had never heard before.

The Aged.

"The Batanga people, like the other two tribes, have been but little known to white men, until the last fifteen or twenty years. They are what may be called unsophisticated natives, that is, heathen of the deepest dye, but yet untainted with the vices of civilized countries. This people, though they have many cruel and savage practices, are mild and civil in their intercourse with strangers, and would be glad to have a missionary reside among them."

In speaking of the affinity of the language spoken on the east coast at Zanzibar to that of the Gaboon—*i. e.*, the similarity of the words—Mr. Wilson urged the establishment of a mission at the former place, and said: "If a station should be established there, it would be perfectly reasonable to expect that a line of missions might be extended from one of these points to the other in less than twenty years, and thus lay open one of the most interesting and extensive fields of missionary enterprise that can be found on the continent."

Trans-Continental Missions.

His appeal continues, "Those members of the mission family, who have tried both parts of the coast, are unanimous in the opinion that they now enjoy better health than formerly. We have had thrown upon our care at different times since we have resided at the Gaboon, as many as ten or twelve foreigners sick with fever, all of whom have had it mildly, and not one has died. The French have made an experiment on a much larger scale, and their statistics clearly show that the Gaboon, with the exception of the Gorée, is altogether the most healthy point occupied by them on the coast."

Health at the Gaboon.

Of his vacation, which was spent in South Carolina, we have no accounts. The following letter to Rev. John C. Lowrie was penned upon the occasion of the death of his brother, the Rev. Walter M. Lowrie, who had gone to Shanghai as a member of the committee for the translation of the Bible. As he was returning to Ningpo, the junk on which he had taken passage was attacked by pirates, and the young and gifted missionary was thrown overboard and drowned, August 19, 1847, about twelve miles southeast of Chapoo, in the Hangchow Bay. Rev. J. L. Wilson writes from Mount Clio, Sumter County, S. C., January 13, 1848:

Walter Lowrie Killed.

"The papers brought us yesterday the astounding intelligence of the death of your dear brother. If it is the slightest alleviation of the grief that you must all feel, be assured of our most cordial sympathies, and I have no doubt but that thousands of other Christian hearts feel equally as much. Your honored father must have been almost overwhelmed by this event. And yet, why should he? It was under the sovereign eye of a most merciful God that this deed of violence was perpetrated; and as inexplicable as it may be to us, I have no conviction more firmly made on my mind than that this very event will be overruled so as to subserve the cause of missions, and the salvation of the heathen, more effectually than even the life of your brother. My own aged father, who could more easily enter into the feelings of your father than most persons, could scarcely compose himself to sleep last night after hearing the painful intelligence; and if such were his feelings, what must have been those of your own family? God grant you all grace to recognize his hand in this event, and to exercise the most cheerful resignation to his holy will!''

Just previous to his third voyage to Africa, after a furlough of just one year, he writes to his sister, Mrs. Flinn Wilson, under date of May 5, 1848: ''I write to acknowledge the safe arrival of the box of hams, etc. I opened the box to take a peep at the hams and found them *black*, but perfectly sweet. As to the complexion, it was so much the better, as you know I am accustomed to *black* things, and they will eat much the sweeter for having been prepared by my own dear sisters. We have heard from the Gaboon, and our friends are all well. We will probably leave the country for Africa about the middle of June. Our company will consist of six or seven, possibly of nine or ten. Many others are now disposed to follow us. I have had to make a great many addresses since I was in New York, and am expected to speak three or four times at the anniversary next week. I often think of you all, my dear sister. The fact is, I did not know how much I loved you all until I turned my back upon you last.''

Loving Sisters.

''You will have some idea of the employment of my time (to Mr. and Mrs. Mills, June 6, 1848), when I tell you I had to preach four times last Sabbath in the largest churches in Boston. I addressed on the previous Thursday an

The Great Congregation.

audience of over two thousand five hundred persons, which was enough to try the lungs of a horse. I appear on such occasions for Africa. We leave this afternoon for Providence, from whence we expect to sail in a week. Governor Armstrong took us to Plymouth to see the rock upon which the pilgrim fathers first planted their feet. It is now almost buried, but it called up many exciting thoughts. We shall not think of you the less or pray for you the less when we are on the great deep or in Africa.''

His letters home, after a second separation, burn with affection for the loved ones far away. He writes (July 6, 1849), "I often think of my aged father walking on the confines of another and better country, and not infrequently almost covet his near release from the trials and sorrows of this lower world." Under date of "The Gaboon, October 15, 1850," he writes to his sister: "Your letter of June 5, announcing the death of our dear and aged father, was handed me last night. My mind was prepared to receive the intelligence by your previous letter of February 5, which had come to hand only a week before. And the dear man is gone! I can scarcely realize it! How many touching associations has the announcement awakened! That homestead, identified almost with our existence, how changed! The church he loved and frequented—how his absence will be felt! Ah! the joyous meeting in heaven; husband, wife, and daughter all embraced in the same arms of love! I can scarcely repress the desire to be there too, and instead of grieving I almost rejoice that our father is released from his intense suffering. And yet I can scarcely force my mind to the conclusion that I shall write his name on the back of no more letters—shall say, 'dear father,' no more. Be it even so, since thou, dear Father in heaven, has ordered it."

"I suppose it makes little difference to what member of the family this letter is addressed" (he writes to Mrs. Flinn Wilson, March 30, 1851), "as it is likely to be read by all. You see I have lived long enough among kings and noblemen to set due value upon anything I do or write. I hope you will all be considerate enough to appreciate my condescension. I send each member of the family an article on the slave-trade, which was published in England. We have now a good physician in our mission, which relieves me of much care and makes us all feel that we can better afford to be sick than formerly. A mission of the Assembly's Board has been established at Corisco, not more than forty or fifty miles from us. The brethren there are getting along very well, and feel encouraged with their prospects. We see them or hear from them every two or three weeks."

Corisco.

To his sister: "I was not a little surprised and grieved to see in public print the article against the American Board, but I am glad the communication was disapproved by Harmony Presbytery. The charges and intimations against the Board are unjust and undeserved. I have received distinguished marks of kindness from its officers, and ever since my connection with them they have honored me with their confidence. They have never imposed any restrictions upon me which would interfere with my preaching according to the standards of our church, or carrying out the discipline over the churches which I have formed. Nor have they ever given me any instructions which would interfere with those of the Presbytery. My *ecclesiastical relations* are unimpaired by my connec-

Love for the A. B. C. F. M.

tion with the A. B. C. F. M. They have always been prompt and cheerful in rendering me the advice and pecuniary aid which I have asked. When I have been recklessly assailed by abolitionists, even when a proposition lay before them for my withdrawal, if my connection was an incumbrance, they have fearlessly stood forth for my defence."

Again, he writes: "The Roman Catholic Mission has grown quite strong in point of members, but R. C. Mission. the only symptoms of life they manifest are the attacks they occasionally make upon our ministerial authority. They tell the people that we are not the true ministers of Christ, but somehow or other the natives cannot comprehend the arguments they adduce to prove this. They can much more easily understand us when we tell them 'that the tree is known by its fruits.'"

To illustrate how the seed sown may spring up and grow, we know not how nor where, the following incident, which occurred at the General Sow Beside All Waters. Assembly a few years before Dr. Wilson's death, is related: The delegate from the Reformed (Dutch) Church, who had been a missionary in India, was presented to the Assembly, and began his address with a graphic description of a death-bed scene which he had witnessed in that country. The dying man was an officer in the English navy, a devout Christian, and was passing calmly away in the full triumph of the Christian faith. He related to the speaker the circumstances of his conversion, which had taken place on one of his voyages in the naval service to the western coast of Africa. There he had met an earnest and consecrated missionary, and had been impressed no less by his noble Christian character than by his humble and self-denying work in that distant and obscure field of labor. It impressed upon him, as nothing else had ever done, the reality of the Christian religion which could lead a man to make such a sacrifice for the good of his degraded fellow-men. His personal appeals to him as he presented the claims of the gospel, enforced by such a character and life, were irresistible, and he was brought to consecrate his life to God. The interest of the vast audience increased as the narrative proceeded, and when the speaker ended by saying, ''That missionary never knew the result of his faithful effort to bring that soul to Christ, but I am glad to tell him of it to-day as he sits there before me, your venerable Secretary of Foreign Missions,'' the audience was electrified, and Dr. Wilson, who had not suspected until the last word, how the story would end, bowed his head, while his whole frame shook with emotion.

CHAPTER XVI

The French at the Gaboon.

THE bright prospects of the mission, within two years after it was founded, were somewhat clouded by interference from an outside quarter. While the ministers of peace were establishing friendly relations with the native chiefs and their tribes, and striving to obtain an influence over them for good, suddenly a storm-cloud arose. It was the grasping hand of France seeking to enlarge her domains by appropriating to herself a portion of the dark continent. A brief account of the events of these stirring times will illustrate how European governments fraudulently obtain control of African territory. Dr. Wilson's pen graphically describes these scenes in the *Missionary Herald*, and this chapter is in his words and those of the secretaries at Boston :

"It was evident even in 1843 that the French were exceedingly anxious to obtain a permanent footing on the Gaboon River. Having purchased a site for a settlement at Gua Ben, they endeavored to induce the natives in the vicinity to place themselves under French protection. They were particularly anxious that the territory of King Glass, in which the mission was located, should become a dependency of the French government, but the natives promptly rejected every proposition made to this end.

"On the night of March 27, M. Amoreux, master of a French merchant vessel lying on the other side of the river, came to King Glass, bringing with him a jug of brandy. He sent for another man, noted for his intemperance, and plied them both with brandy until they were intoxicated. He then called a son of King Glass, presented to the three a paper, purporting to be a letter of friendship to Louis Philippe, and expressing a wish that French vessels might trade here as usual. He did not say one word about his being an agent of the government, for he knew this would 'set the palaver' with all the head men of the village. King Glass, drunk as he was, signed the paper.

"M. Amoreux then hastened on board a French man-of-war, and early in the morning the vessel was lying off King Glass's house, firing a salute. The commander then came on shore, called on King Glass, and read to him the paper which he had signed. He then came to the mission-house and informed Mrs. Wilson (Mr. W. was up the river) that she was on French territory; that King Glass had signed a treaty ceding the sovereignty of his dominions to King Louis Philippe, and that she must look to the French for protection. Mrs. Wilson thanked him for his information and replied that, 'it was doubtful whether the territory was really ceded, and that the mission did not desire or need French protection.'

"As soon as the character of the paper became known to the people, they assembled at the king's house and spent the whole day in anxious consultation, neither eating nor drinking till the sun went down. They protested that the paper was improperly obtained, and that King Glass had no power to make any such treaty or cession of territory. The French knew that the treaty could not be finally ratified without the unanimous consent of all the principal men

expressed in general council, and also that all the head
men could have been assembled in two hours, so there
was no excuse for neglecting to consult with them.

"On the next day, M. Bouet, the Governor of Senegal,
and commander of the French forces on the west coast
of Africa, arrived in the river. A document, prepared in
the most respectful language, stating the circumstances
under which the signature of the king had been obtained,
and protesting against the instrument on the ground of
unfairness and deception, and also because King Glass
had no power to sign such a paper, was addressed to the
Governor. The king prepared another paper saying
that he had been grossly deceived, that no part of the
paper relating to the cession of territory was made known
to him, that it was an unofficial expression of friendship
to Louis Philippe, and that he had declined many former
pressing solicitations to cede the territory. He closes,
'We therefore appeal to your honor as a gentleman, and
to your sense of justice as a governor, to return to us
the paper which has been so unjustly obtained.' The
Governor looked at these papers a moment, just long
enough to see the subject, then tore them in pieces and
told the bearer to bring him no more English books.

"On Mr. Wilson's return, he, with his colleague,
called on the Governor to obtain from him a pledge that
the mission should not be molested or hindered in its
work. This he cheerfully granted, but declined hearing
a word from them in behalf of the natives, declaring
that the Africans should suffer for the insult they had
offered in refusing his invitation to partake of the dinner
he had prepared for them. The natives sent a respectful
remonstrance to Louis Philippe, and another to Queen
Victoria, asking the interference of the British government in their behalf. The missionaries took no part in

11

these counsels, nor gave any advice. They were present, however, when the documents were signed, and saw that they were correctly apprehended by the hundred head men who affixed their names.

"It will be seen from the above statements that it was the settled purpose of the French to gain the sovereignty of the country adjacent to the Gaboon, and where honorable negotiations had been unsuccessful, they did not hesitate to resort to measures which cannot be too strongly reprobated. The French claimed that King Glass surrendered the sovereignty of his dominions to the king of France March 24, 1844, but we have seen that *his signature of the document of cession was obtained by fraud.* On the fifth of May, 1845, a brig of war, Commander Fournier, arrived at the Gaboon River with instructions from the Minister of Marine to carry into execution the treaty." Mr. Wilson wrote, May 14, "They have seen one of their number seized and put in irons for carrying English colors on his boat, a thing which had been practiced from time immemorial." Under date of July 2 he writes, "King Glass's town has been under blockade for three days past, and no one knows

The Blockade.

when the blockade will be raised. We were the first to feel it, and, judging from a variety of circumstances, we are blockaded more vigorously than King Glass and his people. On Monday morning I sent my Kroomen to remove Mr. Bushnell, then sick, to this place. At that time no one knew of a blockade; indeed, three days before I had seen a letter from Commander Fournier disavowing any blockade. Notwithstanding this, my canoe was seized and my men made prisoners. On application for their release, the commander replied, 'Such individuals as reside at Glass's come under the denomination *de la France*, or her protection. I cannot recognize any other power.' The next morning an officer called to apologize, and said that the commander not being able to read English, did not know the boat was sent for a sick missionary."

Mr. Wilson further says, "On the 12th instant the *Tactique* was brought to this place. The people, in order to maintain their independence as far as possible, raised the French and English ensigns together. The commander came ashore and gave King Glass and some of his head men a pretty thorough berating for this seeming affront. He then came to Beraka, and after entering our house, somewhat unceremoniously, he introduced himself by saying that 'if another affront was offered he would certainly blow down the native towns, and, although he would not train his guns on our place, he would not be responsible for any mischief that a chance shot might do.' I replied that 'we had nothing to

Neutral.

do with the political affairs of the country; that if King Glass or his people voluntarily surrendered their country to the French, or if they were reduced to subjection by forcible measures, that we should *obey the powers that be*. But as the treaty had never been executed in a single point, as the natives denied the existence of any treaty at all, and as they had openly maintained their independence up to the present time, we should stand upon neutral ground until the contest should be decided ; and should any collision take place in the meantime between the natives and the French so as endanger our property or personal safety, we would rely upon the United States flag for protection.' He denied that there could be any neutrality in the case; that as we were not the *political representatives* of our country, we could have no *positive character* whatever ; that he was not bound to know that there were American citizens in the country, but still he said (and it was with a lofty air) if I was only waiting to see French authority established, in order to acknowledge it, I should soon be satisfied.

"Finding no disposition on the part of the people to acquiesce in their terms, the French resorted to stratagem. An embassy was sent by the commander to say that if King Glass would cause the French colors to be raised the next morning on a flag-staff sent from the vessel, he would weigh anchor and leave the coast. King Glass replied he had no objection to hoisting the French flag, but he preferred to furnish a flag-staff himself. The officer came the next morning and said King Glass might furnish the pole, but they would supply the rope and pulley; that an ensign was attached to the rope and he must have it hoisted when that of the man-of-war was raised. The king told him to send a man from the vessel to hoist the colors. The officer replied that if the colors were not raised on shore at the same time they were on board the vessel, the towns would be forthwith destroyed. The people resolved with one accord to abide the consequences, denouncing the heaviest penalties against the man who shall put forth his hand to perform the forbidden deed. The flag remained folded for a week, and the French kept up a desultory firing at such of the natives as went out to fish or were seen walking on the beach. The balls sometimes passed over our premises, but never so near as to endanger our safety or excite our fears until Sabbath, the 20th instant, when we could not mistake their intention to disperse the congregation that had assembled at our church for public worship.

"A second deputation was sent to say that the French were now convinced that the people were unwilling to submit to their rule, and that the commander would certainly weigh anchor the next morning and go away, provided they would hoist the French ensign upon a flag-staff of their own erecting. To avoid the possibility of a misunderstanding, the deputation was kept going to and from the vessel all day, and towards night brought back the *final, unequivocal* answer, that if they would raise the flag the next morning the vessel would go away. The next day the ensign was hoisted in due time, and the people expected the ship to weigh her anchor in fulfilment of the solemn promises given the day before, but instead, an officer was sent on shore to say that the flag-staff must be placed where formerly he had erected his, and furnished with rope and pulley. King Glass replied that he ought to be allowed to raise the colors where and when he pleased, provided no affront was offered to the French.

"Within fifteen minutes a party of Gorée soldiers made their appearance in front of one of the towns on the beach, whilst four boats, with armed men, shoved off from the man-of-war, and made a simultaneous attack upon the other two villages. About the same time a thirty-two pound shot was thrown into our church, where the commander had every reason to suppose that our school was assembled, and not more than fifty paces from our door, near which my family was standing. We could not mistake the intention of that shot, and, in view of the bloodshed and confusion with which we were likely to be surrounded, I determined to avail myself of the protection of the United States flag, and hoisted it over our dwelling. This caused the fire to become more intense, and brought the balls still nearer to our dwelling. Apprehending that this might be construed into an act of resistance and not as an expression of neutrality, and finding the lives of the whole family placed in imminent peril, I ordered the colors to be lowered.

Cannonading the Mission.

Whether it was a part of the preconcerted scheme for the man-of-war to cannonade the mission premises, whilst the sailors and soldiers carried on the work of devastation in the native towns at the foot of the hill, I will not pretend to decide.

"After the cessation of the fire of the heavy guns we were still more annoyed, and our lives placed in quite as much danger, by the bullets of the party who entered King Glass's town. Under pretence of firing at a body of armed natives at the head of the street, they managed to send a large portion of their balls through our yard, whilst it is capable of demonstration that had they been really intended for the natives, they were turned more than one hundred yards out of their course.

"How far a private citizen has the right to use the flag of his nation as a means of protection in such circumstances as we were placed in, I have not the means of knowing with certainty. The question has been referred to all the commanders of the United States vessels that have successively visited the river since these difficulties began—as Commander Abbott, of the *Decatur*, Tatnall, of the *Saratoga*, Bruce, of the *Trenton*, and Bell, of the *Yorktown*—all of whom had means of judging of the merits of the question, and it was the concurrent opinion of all of these gentlemen that we had a right to use the flag as an expression of our neutrality, and they all expressed the confident assurance that it would be respected by the French.

"I was compelled to decide between three courses: First, to raise the French colors; second, to raise the American colors; or, third, to have no colors. I had determined to adopt the last as the most becoming an

institution purely religious, and this was not abandoned
till after the cannonading of our premises was opened.
I had then to choose between a French and an American
flag as a means of protection. Had I raised the French
ensign I should have appeared before King Glass and
his people as recognizing French authority, which I had
no right to do, and what was still worse, the sentence of
death had been denounced against the man who should
do it without the king's authority. There remained
then only the one course which I pursued. The French
commander had been previously notified that the American flag would be raised in the emergency, *only as an
expression of neutrality, and as the means of protection
from violence.*

"It cannot be said, in justification of this outrage upon
a defenceless family, that it was unavoidable or acci-
dental. The position of the vessel was such that every
native house might have been demolished without throwing a single shot into our premises. If it be true that,
because we are not the *political representatives of our
country*, missionaries have no *positive character* (by
which, I suppose, is meant that they have no political
character distinct from the savage tribes among whom
they are found), then may they well be afraid to go
abroad at a time when France seems bent upon adding
to her realm every portion of the world, the inhabitants
of which are incapable of resisting her power."

Writing February 6, 1846, he says: "Since our cannonading last July we have experienced no further rude-
ness from the French. The admiral—one of the first
men in their navy—is expected in a few days, and if
practicable, I will have an interview with him in the
hope of placing the mission on a more permanent foundation."

September 23: "The French admiral has been here, and I have had several interviews and some correspondence with him, and though he has not done in every respect that which is perfectly right, yet the mission is placed on a better foundation."

The American Commodore. "Commodore Read, of Philadelphia, has been here, and treated us with very special attention. Not being able to come up the river, on account of the great draught of his frigate, he sent up the United States brig *Dolphin* for Jane and myself, and we spent a day and a night on board his vessel very pleasantly."

From that time the relations between the missionaries and the French at the Gaboon seem to have been very pleasant and cordial. At a later day the ruling powers requested Mr. and Mrs. Wilson to act as interpreters, and copies of the official records of the transactions between the French and Africans in their handwriting are now extant. The occupation of the country by a foreign power diverted for years the minds of the natives from the one great object of the mission, which was the establishment of Christianity, and this the missionaries deeply regretted.

In 1850, Rev. J. L. Wilson writes to his sister: "The French commodore has been very polite to us. Jane and I breakfasted with him one morning, and I received several visits and a great many notes from him during his stay. He expressed much interest in our work."

The following correspondence six years after the bombardment will be read with pleasure:

"GABOON MISSION, *October 15, 1851.*

"*To Charles Penang Commander-in-Chief
       French Naval Forces:*

"RESPECTED SIR: The undersigned, American missionaries residing at the Gaboon, desire to present their acknowledgments for the polite attentions you have extended to them personally, and for the interest you have manifested in the labors in which they are engaged. At the same time they would renew the assurance already made, that they have no other object in residing at the Gaboon except to promote the intellectual and religious improvement of the aborigines of the country.

Kindly Relations.

"We would also express our hearty sympathy in the successful efforts you have put forth to prevent the natives of this region of country from participating further in the foreign slave-trade, and we hope they will not be suspended until this wicked practice is entirely suppressed, etc., etc., etc.

"(Signed by)

"J. LEIGHTON WILSON,
"A. BUSHNELL,
"JACOB BEST,
"HENRY A. FORD,
"ROLLIN PORTER."

The following reply was received:

"GENTLEMEN: I have been highly gratified by the letter which you have done me the honor to address to me in relation to the measures which I have taken to arrest the slave-trade in the waters of the Gaboon. I am happy, gentlemen, in receiving the sympathies extended to me by men who are so honorable, and who enjoy with such good reason the esteem of the inhabitants of the country.

"One of the principal objects of France in establishing herself at the Gaboon is to introduce civilization, and you are largely contributing to this work. Gentle-

men, we shall regard as good compatriots and friends
those who, like yourselves, conduct the natives in this
path by their instructions and by their example, etc.,
etc., etc.

" PENANG,
"Commander French Naval Division."

CHAPTER XVII.

The Naturalist Discovering the Gorilla.

THE subject of this sketch was a child of the country and rejoiced in rural surroundings. During his residence near Mayesville, when he was secretary, in his early morning walks he delighted in gathering flowers, inhaling their fragrance, and in analyzing them. Botany was a favorite science, especially its practical study in the fields and woods, where to his devout mind each tree, and shrub, and flower revealed the beauty and excellency of the Creator's handiwork. When in early manhood his residence was transferred from the pine lands of Carolina to the shores of Africa, the luxuriant foliage of the tropics naturally excited his observation, and he made himself thoroughly acquainted with the flora of that continent. As a member of the Royal Oriental Society of Great Britain, he was frequently consulted on important scientific questions.

The fauna of Africa also invited his enterprising research, and he was able to make important contributions to the department of Natural History. The study of the animal kingdom in forests and jungles, which seemed to be specially made for the abode of wild beasts, was both pleasant and profitable, and furnished delightful mental recreation after his arduous philological and missionary labors, and tended materially to fit him for the ministerial profession, by furnishing comparison between the place of man in nature and in grace, and the beasts of the earth over which the Lord had given him dominion.

A half-century ago, before the story of the travels of Livingstone and Stanley were published, Dr. Leighton Wilson was an authority on African questions, and his name was not unknown in scientific circles in England and America. He was a light-house on the coast of the Dark Continent.

As a specimen of what he saw during his long residence, we give an extract of a letter to his wife, telling of a trip to Conig Island, in 1842: "There was one object well calculated to command the attention of any one who should arrive at the same time of the day that I reached the place. There stands just by the village a stupendous cotton tree, the wide-extended arms of which afforded a roost, one would think who saw them congregated and heard their deafening noise, not only for all the parrots in this part of the land, but all in Africa. From six to eight o'clock in the evening they were assembling and making a noise so great that, even at a distance of a quarter of a mile from the tree, two persons in conversation could not be heard without raising their voices. They have kept this roost, it is said, from time immemorial."

The study of the animal kingdom became a part of their home-life. Mrs. Wilson, seeing that the natives were cruel to animals, surrounded herself with them as pets, with the hope of teaching them to be kind and gentle to the brute creation. Her husband in one of his letters speaks of these, and mentions "an African deer, of the antelope species, an African wolf, and a porcupine." To the latter she fastened a little bell, much to the amusement of the natives. Watching the habits of these animals—for she had quite a collection—was a source of recreation to her in her lonely life. The black men would sometimes bring dangerous species to her to purchase, but these she declined.

In a home-letter (May 17, 1836), he speaks of an evening call made by one of the lords of the jungle:

Leopard. "We have again been visited by another of the terrible animals of Africa. Not many months ago we killed a huge snake, and a few evenings since a leopard intruded himself into our yard and carried off a full-grown sheep. It was not seen, as it entered at a late hour, but you can judge of its size and strength when I tell you that it leaped with the sheep in its mouth over two fences, neither less then eight feet high. They are frequently seen about the settlement, and sometimes they are very destructive to domestic animals, but never, or very seldom, assail a human being unless it is in their own defence. The teeth of the leopard are esteemed by the natives nearly as valuable as the same quantity of gold, and there is not an ornament they prize so highly. The man who has the courage and good fortune to kill one is raised to great favor with the people, and is ever afterwards an important character."

He writes thus of the king of the serpents : "The boa-constrictor is to be found in all parts of

Boa-constric-tor. Western Africa. Their chosen places of resort are in thick jungles or along the water-courses. They are fond of sunning themselves on branches of trees overhanging the water. They grow to an enormous size. The writer has never seen one more than twenty-five feet long, but it is said they attain to much greater length. They live upon deer, monkeys, and such other wild animals as they can seize, and when they have swallowed a full-sized sheep, or deer, they remain in a torpid state till it is digested. I assisted once in extricating a favorite yard-dog from the folds of

one of these monsters. The snake had stretched himself across a much-frequented path, and the dog, in the
act of jumping over it, was caught and held in its firm
grasp for more than half an hour. The snake commenced sliming the body of the dog from the head
downwards with the intention of swallowing it, and he
had more than half completed his work before his victim
was rescued. The dog received no injury, but it was
some weeks before the varnishing he had received could
be removed. The boa has no poisonous fang. Its teeth,
both of the upper and lower jaw, hook downward, so
that whatever prey he attempts to swallow must go
down, or the animal itself perishes in the effort to
extricate itself."

Mr. Wilson obeyed the royal preacher's command
about the "ant"—"consider her ways, and be wise."
After speaking of the species, which erect clay houses,
White Ants. or turreted tumuli, he says: "There is another species of the white ant, which make
their nests under the ground. These subterranean
abodes have as much mechanical arrangement as the
mounds. They usually emerge at night, and a box of
clothes is always a favorite object of attack. They cut
holes through the whole depth of clothing in the chest,
and it would look as if they were governed by a desire
to render every article useless to its human owner in as
short a time as possible. When they direct their aim to
some object in an elevated position, they always construct
a covered archway to it, which is seldom more than a
quarter of an inch in diameter, and is constructed partly
of the fine fuzz, collected along the surface over which it
is built, and partly by clay brought up from the ground
through the arch, their own bodies furnishing the cement
necessary to give it adhesion. I have watched them oc-

casionally, and found that they would raise the arch two
or three inches an hour. They are indomitably persevering. You may make a breach in the arch or tear
down the whole of it, and they will go to work immediately to rebuild. A drop of arsenic will cause them to
abandon their undertaking. To prevent their incursions,
it is common to raise scaffolds on small posts, on which
provisions are laid. By making an application of fresh
tar to these posts, once in two or three months, these
ants are kept down.''

The Drivers. He writes of the ''drivers,'' which are so
denominated from the fact that they compel
almost every other species of the animal creation to get
out of their way, or submit to the alternative of being
devoured. They traverse the country in trains quarter
of a mile long; and persons, about to step over the
train as it glides along under the grass, frequently start
back under the impression of its being a snake. The
soldiers, who always keep along the side of the regular column, the moment they receive a note of alarm,
set off with all possible dispatch for the point of danger,
while the main body is either brought to a dead halt or
turned backward. When about to cross a well-trodden
path, where they are likely to be disturbed, the soldiers
weave themselves into a complete arch, extending across
the whole width of the path, under which the females
and the laborers bearing the larvæ pass without the least

The Arch. exposure. The construction of the arch with
their own bodies is one of the most singular
and interesting facts to be met with in the history of
insects. One ant is raised entirely above the ground by
having one pair of its feet interlocked with the forefeet
of another standing upright, and the other pair in the
same posture on the other side of the arch. Any num-

ber of these arches are formed, and they are bound together by other ants, stretching themselves lengthwise with the arch, and serving as traverse beams to hold the different parts together.   The arch, when formed, holds together with the greatest tenacity, and looks like a beautiful network of beads.   I have frequently put the end of my cane under the arch, and raised it four or five feet from the ground without letting a single ant fall.   They will attack living animals with great vehemence, and there is nothing of the animal race that can effectually resist them.   A horse or cow shut up in a confined place would be harassed to death in a few hours, and would be entirely devoured, except the hair and the skeleton, in less than two days.

"In nothing is the ingenuity of these little insects more remarkably displayed than in the expedient to which they frequently resort in order to cross a little stream, on the sand-beach, after a shower of rain.   To plunge in it singly they would soon be swept away by the rush of the current.   They come to the edge of the water, raise their antennæ, point them from one direction to another, as if they were taking a scientific view of all the dangers of the crossing, then form themselves into a compact knot, or raft of a dozen or more, and launch upon the stream, having by previous observation made sure that they would strike a projecting bluff on the opposite shore.   I have watched them for hours together, and have seen raft after raft of these little creatures go over in safety, whereas, if they had attempted to get across singly, they would all have been swept into the river."

The Raft of Ants.

THE GORILLA.

Although Dr. Wilson's contributions to science were

considerable in several departments, yet his crown as a
naturalist was the discovery of the gorilla.   In Professor
Huxley's *Man's Place in Nature*, reference is made to the
indebtedness of scientists to the pioneer missionary.   Mr.
C. N. Chapin, of the American Board, writes: "It seems
to be true that Rev. Dr. J. Leighton Wilson first brought
the gorilla to the notice of American and European natu-
ralists.   The complete skeleton presented by him is in
the collection of the Museum of Natural History in Boston."   This was the first skeleton of the gorilla which
was ever taken to Europe or America.   In *The Illustrated Library of Wonders*, by Victor Meunier, the following account is given: "The reports of travellers
were imbued with exaggerations and errors; but beyond
what was erroneous and improbable, these accounts
agree in attesting the existence of an ape distinct from
the chimpanzee, larger, stronger, and more dangerous
than this latter, and of that there was no reason to doubt.
Attention was then aroused to the subject.   It was in
1846 that all doubts ceased.   It happened that at that
period an American missionary, the Rev. Dr. J. Leighton
Wilson, discovered at the Gaboon the skull of a new and
extraordinary kind of ape.   A narrow cranial cavity,
almost wholly behind the orbits of the eyes, and where
the cerebral convolutions had left but feeble impression;
jaw-bones of prodigious power, projecting in front, and
armed with formidable and deeply-rooted tusks; at the
extremities of the eyebrows, on the line of the parietal
bones, and at the junction of these with the occipital,
were enormous bony ridges; finally, very large and
arched cheek-bones; in a word, all the characters of besti-
ality carried to excess and united to those of strength
without equal among apes.   A learned American naturalist, Professor Jeffries Wyman, gave a description of it

12

in 1847, in the *Journal of Natural History*, of Boston. The discovery of Mr. Wilson did not long remain isolated, and the anatomy of the new quadrumane, to which Wilson had given the name of *gorilla*, became the object of the labors of Richard Owen in England, of Isidore Geoffry Saint Hilaire, and of Duvernoy in France. The interest still increased when the first white man who had seen a living gorilla face to face had made known his marvellous stories of the chase. This white man is an American of French origin, M. Paul du Chaillu.'' May it not have been the discovery of the missionary which first fired the heart of his young protegé and led him ten years afterwards to his adventures with the wild man of the forests, the marvellous accounts of which enriched the pages of science?

In *Western Africa* Mr. Wilson thus describes this formidable animal: '' It is almost impossible to give a correct idea, either of the hideousness of its looks, or of the amazing muscular power which it possesses. Its intensely black face not only reveals features greatly exaggerated, but the whole countenance is but one expression of savage ferocity. Large eyeballs, a crest of long hair which falls over the forehead when it is angry, a mouth of immense capacity revealing a set of terrible teeth, and large protruding ears, altogether make it one of the most frightful animals in the world. It is not surprising that the natives are afraid to encounter them, even when armed. The skeleton of one, presented by the writer to the Natural History Society, of Boston, is supposed to be five and a half feet high, and with its flesh, thick skin and the long, shaggy hair with which it is covered, it must have been nearly four feet across the shoulders. The natives say it is ferocious, and invariably gives battle whenever it meets a single person. I have seen a man, the calf of whose leg was nearly torn off in an encounter with one of these monsters, and he would probably have been torn to pieces in a very short time if his companions had not come to his rescue. It is said they will wrest a musket from the hands of a man, and crush the barrel between their jaws, and there is nothing, judging from the muscles of the jaws, or the size of their teeth, that renders such a thing improbable.''

Du Chaillu (Dr. Wilson's pupil), who was the first white man to see this animal, says: ''The roar of the gorilla is the most singular and awful noise heard in these African woods. It begins with a sharp bark, like an angry dog, then glides into a deep bass roll, which literally and closely resembles the sound of distant thunder. The underbrush swayed rapidly just ahead, and presently before us stood an immense male gorilla. He had gone through the jungle on all fours, but when he saw our party he erected himself and looked us boldly in the face. He was nearly six feet high, with immense body, huge chest and great muscular arms, with fiercely glaring large grey eyes and a hellish expression of face, which seemed to me like some nightmare vision. Thus stood before us the king of the African forests. He was not afraid of us; he stood there and beat his breast with his huge fists till it sounded like an immense drum, meantime giving vent to roar after roar. His eyes began to flash fiercer fire as we stood motionless on the defensive, and the crest of short hair, which stands on his forehead, began to twitch rapidly up and down, while his powerful fangs were shown as he sent forth a thunderous roar; and now truly he reminded me of nothing but some hellish dream-creature, a being of that hideous order—half-man, half-beast—which we find pictured by old artists in some representations of the infernal regions. He advanced a few steps, then stopped to utter that hideous roar again; advanced again, and finally stopped at a distance of about six yards from us; and here, just as he began another of his roars, beating his breast in rage, we fired and killed him.''

CHAPTER XVIII.

𝔗𝔥𝔢 𝔏𝔦𝔫𝔤𝔲𝔦𝔰𝔱.

THE writer of these chapters lives in the middle kingdom, where the language is considered a great obstacle to missionary labor. But here we find an alphabet, the most extensive on the globe; dictionaries to give the exact meaning of the characters; printing-presses which have for ages issued from stereotype plates their works by the thousands; schools by the hundreds of thousands, and a multitude of teachers ready to instruct the foreigner. How different with the subject of this sketch when he arrived upon the African shore! First at Cape Palmas and then at the Gaboon, Leighton Wilson began the study of the Grebo and the Mpongwe respectively, without an alphabet, a book, a printer, or a teacher. He reduced these languages to writing, prepared grammars and dictionaries, set up printing-presses, and taught the natives to read the words which for generations had been only spoken. Sixty years ago it was a heroic undertaking to attempt the mastery of a barbarous vernacular without a single help in beginning the arduous enterprise, but in two instances it was successfully accomplished.

As early as February, 1837, a little over two years after his second arrival, he writes: "Our printing-press is now up, and we have a modest and intelligent young man of color, who will be printer and teacher." In May, 1840, over five years after reaching Africa, he says: "I have mas-

tered the language so far as to dispense with an interpreter, but still find it hard to preach in this poor barbarous tongue.   I have completed the first part of the Grebo
dictionary.   We have recently printed a small volume of
Bible History, and I now have on hand the ' Life of
Christ.' ''   The late Bishop Payne, in his lectures on
mission work in Africa, always spoke of the broad
foundation laid by Dr. Wilson at Cape Palmas, in reducing the language to writing, in the translation of
Christian books, and in commencing schools and the
work of preaching among the people.

In the report of the mission for 1840, it is said, ''The
printing at the Mission Press embraces sixteen separate
publications, among which are a Dictionary, the Ten
Commandments, Bible History (two volumes), Life of
Christ, reading and spelling books for the school, a
hymnal, etc.   The number of volumes printed
Printing.
is 25,000, and the entire number of pages is
over 1,000,000.''   In the following year there were
printed the Bible History, Child's Book, Mark's Gospel,
Simple Questions, and a Grebo Reader; in all 9,000 volumes, or 381,000 pages in the Grebo.   ''The Grebo
language is taught in the seminary, and in
Grebo.
most of the schools.   The children can acquire
a sufficient knowledge of Grebo in a short time to read
it with profit and interest.   It may be remarked of this
language that it is not even yet thoroughly mastered by
any missionary on the ground, and there are frequent
occasions for slight alterations in the orthography of our
books.   The difficulties of reducing a language like this
to system and order, without any essential helps, are
known only to those who have made the experiment.
We have had to form our orthography from a constantly
varying and fluctuating standard, and all the grammati-

cal principles at which we have arrived have been deduced from a series of almost endless comparisons. There is no one individual in the community who could be followed as the guide in pronunciation, or as a correct standard in relation to the grammar of the language. The constant inquiries which are being made are daily shedding more light on the subject, and we trust it will not be long before all its principles will be evolved and thoroughly understood.''

The account of the second division of his literary labors on the western coast of Africa is very cheering to pioneer students of unknown tongues. In less than a month after his arrival at the Gaboon, he writes to his **Early Efforts.** wife: ''I find the language of the country here more pleasant to the ear, and, if I am not mistaken, much easier to be acquired than the Grebo. I have already made a vocabulary of four hundred words, have written down a good many colloquial sentences, and practiced on my morning and evening walks, repeating over and over what I have written down. I think I have acquired more knowledge of this in one month than I did of the Grebo in three. This is owing in part, I have no doubt, to my previous experience in studying African dialects, but much also to the intrinsic ease with which this may be acquired.'' Again (July 26, 1842), ''The language is radically different from all the dialects I have known anything about in Upper Guinea. It is harmonious, pleasant to the ear and easy to be acquired. I have collected something more than five hundred words, and shall continue to labor at it as my time and other engagements will allow.''

The next year, while he was waiting at Cape Palmas for the return of Mrs. Wilson from the United States, he writes : ''During the time I have been here I have prepared and had printed several little tracts in the Gaboon language, including a hymn-book, catechism, scripture precepts, etc.''

''In the early part of September last,'' writing from the Gaboon, December 26, 1843, ''I began preach-**Preaching at the Gaboon.** ing in the native language, and from that time my audience has steadily increased. You can form some idea of the difference between this and the Grebo language, from the fact that I never attempted to preach in the latter until I had resided four years at Cape Palmas, whereas I preach here after nine months' continuous residence.'' If the writer might express an opinion, the difference was not so much in the languages as in the linguist. He had served an apprenticeship of seven years at Cape Palmas, and had learned the art of studying an unwritten language. The ratio of progress is much as that of a doctor, after some years' practice, attending lectures and clinics, and that of an unfledged practitioner, who, for a similar length of time, listens to what he feels he may never have use for.

''We have been greatly surprised,'' he writes in the *Missionary Herald*, ''to find in this remote **Mpongwe Language.** corner of Africa, and among a people but very partially civilized, one of the most perfect languages of which we have any knowledge. It is not so remarkable for copiousness of words as for its great and and almost unlimited flexibility. Its expansions, contractions and inflections, though exceedingly numerous, and having apparently special reference to euphony, are all governed by grammatical rules, which seem to be well established in the minds of the people, and which enable them to express their ideas with the utmost precision. How a language so soft, so plaintive, so pleasant to the ear, and, at the same time, so copious and methodical in its inflections, should have originated, or how the people are enabled to retain its multifarious principles so distinctly in their minds as to express themselves with unvarying precision and uniformity, are points which we do not pretend to settle."

In western Africa he writes: "The first thing that is sure to arrest the attention of one who Ethnography. has had an opportunity to study the character and habits of the people in connection with their languages, is the remarkable correspondence that will always be found between the character of the different tribes and the dialects they respectively speak. The Grebo tribe, physically considered, is one of the finest of the races in western Africa. They are stout, well formed, and their muscular system is remarkably well developed. They stand erect, and when not under the influence of excitement, their gait is measured, manly and dignified. When engaged at work or in play they are quick, energetic, and prompt in all their bodily evolutions; they are fond of work, are capable of enduring great hardships, and, compared with most of the tribes of western Africa, are really courageous and enterprising. But they are destitute of polish, both of mind and of manners. In their intercourse with each other they are rude, abrupt, and unceremonious; when opposed or resisted in what is their right or due, they become obstinate, sullen, and inflexible. They have much vivacity of disposition, but very little imagination. Their songs have but little of poetry, and are unmusical and monotonous; besides which, they have very little literature in the form of ancestral traditions or fabulous stories. Their dialect partakes very largely of these general outlines. It is harsh, abrupt, energetic, indistinct in enunciation, meagre in point of words, abounds with inarticulate, nasal and guttural sounds, possesses but few inflections and grammatical forms, and is, withal, exceedingly difficult of acquisition.

"The Mpongwe people, on the other hand, are mild in disposition, flexible in character, courteous in their manners, and very deferential to age and rank. But they are very timid, irresolute, and exceedingly averse to manual labor. They live by trade, are cunning, shrewd, calculating, and somewhat polished in their manners. Their temperament is of the excitable or nervous character, and they are, altogether, the most imaginative race of negroes I have ever known. They have inexhaustible stores of ancestral traditions and fabulous stories, some of which, if embodied in suitable language, would bear comparison with the most celebrated novels and romances that have ever been presented to the world. These general outlines of the character, habits, and disposition of the people are no bad counterpart of their language. It is soft, pliant, and flexible; clear and distinct in enunciation, pleasant to the ear, almost free from guttural and nasal sounds, methodical in all its forms, susceptible of great expression, and, withal, very easy of acquisition." *

---

* To illustrate the relation of language and character, it may be mentioned that at Soochow, where the writer resides, the dialect is soft to the ear, musical in its rhythm, abounds in particles like the Greek, and is spoken with great rapidity. The people are small in stature, not noted for their physical strength; the young scholars looking more like school-girls than men. They are, however, courteous in manners, and gentle in disposition. The sons of Han, to the north of the Yangtse, are taller, stronger, and more soldierly in their bearing. The Mandarin which they speak corresponds with the racial features. It is harsher in sound, bolder in expression, and spoken with measured accent and great tonal emphasis.

Much of Dr. Wilson's time, when he was in Africa, was given to linguistic labors. As a gram-
Comparative African Philology. marian, he wrote grammars in both the Grebo and the Mpongwe. As a lexicographer, he published dictionaries in both these langauges.
He was an earnest student of the comparative vernaculars, and at one time or another a large number of colloquials were brought under his review. By his extensive travels, by the visits of natives of different tribes to the coast, and by his varied association with men and places, his attainments in comparative African philology were very extensive. The accounts given in the pages following show how eager he was to study other dialects, how industriously he embraced every opportunity for acquiring new words and phrases, and how rapidly he could form a simple vocabulary of an unknown tongue.

When he was on furlough in the United States he had printed a small vocabulary and phrase-book of the Ba-
Batanga Language. tanga language, which he prepared while on a brief visit to this people. He says: "This language belongs to the one great family, which undoubtedly prevails over the whole of the southern division of the African continent, but as a dialect it differs essentially from the Mpongwe. I have a vocabulary and series of colloquial sentences in the tongue that would be serviceable to a missionary who should think of locating among them."

In Dr. Wilson's appeal to the churches, while on furlough, he says: "We have recently made large collections of words in the different dialects on this part of the coast, especially of those spoken between the Bight of Biafra and Benguela, and we find that they are not only related to each other, but by comparing them with such vocabularies as we have of the languages of the Cape of Good Hope, Mozambique, and other parts of the eastern coast, we learn that, though differing from each other materially as dialects, yet that they all undoubtedly belong to one general family. The orthography of the Zulu, as furnished in the journals of our brethren laboring among that tribe, not only bears a strong resemblance to the Mpongwe, but many of their proper names are common to them and the Gaboon people.

"The most remarkable coincidence we have met with is the close affinity between the Mpongwe and the language spoken by the original inhabitants of the island and coast of Zanzibar. We have recently procured a vocabulary of this dialect from a native of Zanzibar, brought from the eastern to the western coast of Africa by an American trading vessel. From this man we obtained a vocabulary of more than two hundred words, as well as a few colloquial sentences. Of these a small number of words, as might be naturally expected, were evidently of Arabic origin, but of the remainder nearly one-fourth were identically the same, or differed very slightly. While these words were being taken down several Mpongwe men happened to be present, and the utmost astonishment was manifested by both parties on discovering the close affinity of their languages. Had this man remained in the Gaboon two or three weeks he would have spoken the Mpongwe with some ease."

On every visit to a new tribe the pioneer obtained by signs a list of nouns, and soon learned the leading verbs and connective particles. So fond was he of learning spoken languages, that had he remained in Africa another score of years he would probably have reduced to writing the principal vernaculars of the west coast.

Long experience had given him the key to the mastery of unknown colloquials. From the example before us, it is proper to infer, that though the gift of tongues is not in this age miraculously bestowed, yet it still remains the heritage of the church as she goes forth conquering and to conquer.

CHAPTER XIX.

The Author.

AFTER his return to the United States, Dr. Wilson published *Western Africa: Its History, Condition, and Prospects.* Dr. Livingtone pronounced it "the best book ever written on that part of Africa." In the Preface the author says: "The writer has spent between eighteen and twenty years in the country. He has had opportunity to visit every place of importance along the seacoast, and has made extensive excursions in the maritime districts. He has studied and reduced to writing two of the leading languages of the country, and has enjoyed, in these various ways, more than ordinary advantages for making himself acquainted with the actual condition of the people. He claims for his book the merit of being a faithful and unpretending record of African society." Our author was specially fitted to give an impartial and intelligent view of the Western Africans in that "the missionary is allied to one side by the ties of race and religion, and to the other by the interest he feels in the people to benefit whom he consecrates his life."

Though issued forty years ago, before the travels of Livingstone and Stanley marked literary epochs in the history of the Dark Continent, and the civilized world awakened to a knowledge of and interest in her sable sons, it still holds the position of a standard work. Two of its departments are very complete, namely, the historical review and that of the social life. The one is fixed in the centuries that have passed, the other is essentially unchanged. The Rev. Thomas Laurie, D. D., author of the "Ely Volume," says: "The best exposition of the contribution of missions to geography in Western Africa is the work of Rev. J. Leighton Wilson on that country. This is one of several similar works by missionaries, which we would like to put into the hands of any one who is 'not aware that missionaries had ever done anything for science.' It is written by no transient visitor, who 'could see nothing but the surface of things,' but by one who had spent more than eighteen years in that country, had visited every place of importance along the coast, and made extensive excursions in the interior. He had reduced to writing two of the native languages, and had more than ordinary facilities to become acquainted with the life of the people, their moral, social, civil, and religious condition, as well as their peculiar ideas and customs. It is not a book in which the writer is his own hero, but a treasury of facts drawn from all available sources, especially his own personal observation, thoroughly digested, well arranged and written in a style so transparent that the reader seems to look on the scenes and occurrences which he describes.

"Missions and Science."

One striking feature of the work is that, like Dr. Williams' *Middle Kingdom*, it is practically an encyclopædia. It describes the first discoveries of the Carthagenians and the Portuguese; the establishment of the English, French, and Dutch colonies; its natural scenery; the rivers, mountains, and lagoons; its climate; the rains, winds, and storms; its geography; Senegambia, the Congo, Guinea; the grain, gold, ivory, and slave coasts; its different tribes; their peculiar customs, domestic habits, dress (or the want of

African Encyclopædia.

it), and social condition; its various tribal governments; their kings, deliberative assemblies, revenues, armies, and wars; the gold mines along the coast; its trade in ivory, palm oil, and the various products of the country; its fauna and flora; the religions, superstitions, and human sacrifices. As a complete account is given of each province separately, and as this seems in part necessary, from the fact that so many segregated principalities occupy the coast, the reader notices a few instances of repetition, but the book is so replete with information and adventure, of wonderful scenes and striking events, all described very graphically, that he is given a view of the country and its people which cannot fail to be interesting and instructive. In *Missions and Science*, or *The Ely Volume*, twenty-three octavo pages are given to extracts from this work. Only a few notes can be made upon the vast number of subjects treated in *Western Africa*.

Our author commences with the Carthagenians, who sent out an expedition of sixty ships which sailed as far south of Gibraltar as the Pillars of Hercules are distant from the city of Carthage, and from their narratives, it is seen that they met with the Ethiopian tribes. He says: "It is an interesting historical fact that the negro race had reached the shores of the African continent more than two thousand years ago, and that they were then distinguished, not only by the same physical characteristics, but by many of the habits and customs that have been continued, with little change, even down to the present time. That this people should have been preserved for so long a period in constantly increasing numbers, and that in the face of the most adverse influences, while other races, who were placed in circumstances much more favorable for the perpetuation of their nationality, have passed away from the earth or dwindled down to a mere handful, is one of those mysterious providences that admit of no rational solution, unless it be that they have been preserved for some important future destiny."

"The coast of western Africa is singularly deficient in bays and harbors for shipping. For a dis-No Harbors. tance of fifteen hundred miles there is not a single bay, harbor, estuary, or indentation of any kind, where a vessel of any considerable size can be shielded from storms and the heavy swells of the ocean. Ships have to ride at anchor in the open sea, and, at most places, one or two miles from the land; while the lading and unlading must be effected by boats, and often through the heaviest and most dangerous surf. This must always be a serious impediment to the development of the commercial resources of Northern Guinea."

"There is another feature of this region that should not be overlooked. In consequence of the ex-Lagoons. posed position of the seacoast to the heavy swells of the ocean, the rivers and smaller streams are frequently obstructed, and form for themselves backwaters or lagoons. These lagoons are separated from the ocean only by a narrow bank of sand, which is thrown up by the other swell. They are sometimes two or three hundred miles long, but generally have only a few feet depth of water, and are seldom more than a quarter or a half-mile wide. One of these lagoons extends nearly the whole length of the ivory coast, and another along the greater part of the slave coast. They furnish great facilities of intercourse and commerce to the maritime tribes, but are too shallow for ordinary shipping."

"A belt of the densest wood and jungle of a hundred miles wide extends along the whole coast of western

Africa, and is no doubt the chief cause of the sickness which prevails in this region. Where the land has never been cultivated forest trees of giant size may be seen in every direction. At some points they are the only landmarks by which mariners can identify the situation of some very important native villages. When these natural forests are once cut down, the land is soon covered with a jungle of undergrowth which is almost impenetrable for man or beast. Beyond this belt of wood, or jungle, the country is more open, the air is drier and freer from miasma and the climate decidedly healthier"

Forests.

"At the European settlements the traveller witnesses strange and incongruous sights, the flowing together, as it were, of the waters of civilization and barbarism. The white man (rendered whiter still by the fever of Africa) and the African of darkest hue are seen in constant intercourse; the civilized African, with an intelligent countenance and clean attire, transacting business with a sable brother from the 'bush,' who has not clothing enough to hide his nakedness; the stately European dwelling, surrounded on all sides by grass-covered huts; the sound of strange and unintelligible languages, and various other contrasts between the descendants of Ham and Japheth."

White and Black.

"The physical aspect of the country, as might be inferred from its immense extent, is not only very varied, but presents some of the richest and most exuberant natural scenery to be found anywhere in the world. In the vicinity of Sierra Leone, the eye rests upon bold headlands and high promontories enveloped in the richest verdure. In the region of Cape Palmas there are extended plains, somewhat undulating, that are beautiful with almost every variety of

Scenery.

the palm and palmetto. On the Drewin Coast the country rises to high table-land of the richest aspect and of immense extent. The gold coast presents hills and dales of almost every conceivable form and variety, and as we approach the equatorial regions, mountain scenery of exceeding beauty and surpassing magnificence presents itself.

"Between the highlands of Cape Appolonia and the River Volta there is as much richness and variety of natural scenery as can be found in the same compass in any other part of the world. High ridges rising up gently from the water's edge and stretching back indefinitely into the country; hills of various size and of every conceivable form and outline; verdant fields with graceful undulations, and more or less extended, reveal themselves in succession; and the eye seldom tires in contemplating their varied outlines, or in beholding graceful palms and beautiful umbrella-trees, which are scattered in every direction over the surrounding country. No portion of the coast presents more varied or imposing natural scenery than the islands of Fernando Po and St. Thomas, and the adjacent islands of Kamerun, the height of the peaks being 8,000, 10,000, and 14,000 feet. The mariner, as he approaches, is strongly impressed by the bold outlines of their mountains, the rich verdant drapery in which they are clothed, and the immense height of their graceful and towering peaks."

Turning from nature to man, our author, by his long residence in two different parts of the country, **Ethnology.** and his extensive journeys, had an opportunity to study the relations of the different tribes which form the population of the coast. Their differences in figure, in complexion, in disposition, in social customs, in manner of life, in agriculture, in architecture, are carefully noted and minutely described, by one whose eye was trained to note the points of resemblance, proving their original unity, and the lines of divergence which followed their long separation and want of intercourse. When in the Dark Continent he studied the African. He says:

Not the Lowest. "The inhabitants of western Africa, though greatly debased by the multifarious forms of heathenism found among them, are not, nevertheless, to be ranked among the lowest order of the human race. Placed in contrast with the civilized nations of the earth their deficiencies are palpable enough, but compared with other uncultivated races of men they would occupy a very respectable medium. In their native country they have fixed habitations, cultivate the soil for the means of subsistence, have herds of domestic animals, show much foresight in providing for their future wants, have made considerable proficiency in the mechanical arts, and evince a decided taste for commercial pursuits."

To show that they occupy a medium position among the lower races, he presents the Krumen as an example:

Physique. "It would be difficult to find finer specimens of muscular development, men of more manly and independent carriage or possessing more real grace of manner, anywhere in the world. No one ever comes in contact with them for the first time without being struck with their open, frank countenances, their robust and well-proportioned forms, and their independent bearing, even when they have but the scantiest covering for their bodies. The most marked deficiency is in the formation of their heads, which are narrow and peaked, and do not indicate a very high order of intellectual endowment."

There is no part of the book more complete than that

which gives a picture of the manners and customs, the social life and habits of the people of Africa. He speaks

The Home. of the home life among the barbarous tribes:

"The Kru people, as a general thing, are cleanly in their persons and houses. All classes perform daily ablutions with hot water, and the adults often twice in the day. After the thorough application of water and the use of a coarse towel made of grass-cloth, they rub a small quantity of oil over the entire person, which imparts a bright and healthful appearance to the skin, and is no doubt greatly promotive of their general health. Their houses are small, and, though poorly lighted and ventilated, are almost always neat. Long before the sun is above the horizon may be heard the jingle of the little bells worn as ornaments, as the housewives hasten in merry bands to the spring to fill their pitchers while the water is yet cool. And during the whole of the day they may be seen engaged in pounding rice in mortars, or in preparing it as food for their lords, when they arouse from their slumbers and express a wish to partake of it."

"The strongest of all the natural ties are those between the mother and her children. Whatever other

My Mother. estimate we may form of the African, we may not doubt his love for his mother! Her name, whether she is dead or alive, is always on his lips and in his heart. He cares for no one else in times of sickness. She alone must prepare his food, administer his medicine, and spread his mat for him. He flies to her in the hour of distress, for he well knows, if all the rest of the world turn against him, she will be steadfast in her love, whether he be right or wrong. If there is any cause which justifies a man in using violence towards one of his fellow-men, it would be to resent an insult offered to

his mother.   More fights are occasioned among boys by
hearing something said in disparagement of their mothers
than by all other causes together.   This strong feeling,
so characteristic of the African race, probably grows out
of the institution of polygamy, bad as this in itself is.
The affections of the father are necessarily divided among
the different branches of his household, while those of
the children are concentrated more particularly on the
mother, who not only provides for them, but must de-
fend them in the litigations which constantly occur.''

''Polygamy prevails in every part of Africa.   In their
Many Wives. estimation it lies at the very foundation of all
social order.   The highest aspiration to which
an African ever rises is to have a large number of wives.
His happiness, his reputation, his influence, his position
in society, all depend upon this.   The consequence is
that the so-called wives are little better than slaves.
They have no other purpose in life than to minister to
the wants and gratify the passions of their lords, who
are masters and owners, rather than husbands.   It is
not a little singular, however, that the females, upon
whom the burden of this degrading institution mainly
rests, are quite as much interested in its continuance as
the men themselves.   A woman would infinitely prefer
to be one of a dozen wives of a respectable man than to
be the sole representative of one who had not force of
character to raise himself above the one-woman level,
and such is the degradation of her moral character that
she would greatly prefer the wider margin of licentious
indulgence.''

In speaking of the army of Dahomi, our author describes the woman's brigade: ''Most of the stouter
women are reserved for soldiers, and what is very remarkable, under the peculiar training to which they are

subjected, they are said to constitute the bravest portion of the king's army. The number of these at the present time is said to be about five thousand.

Female Warriors.

The king places implicit reliance upon their bravery, and prefers to be surrounded by them in times of imminent peril. They are thoroughly organized, have their own officers, and in all regular engagements have an important post assigned them. These Amazons use muskets and all other implements common in African warfare. They become very athletic and masculine, and retain no true feminine refinement. When they would reproach each other for imbecility or cowardice, they say: 'You are a man.'"

The following description of the wealth of the king of Ashanti is given: "The king makes frequent displays of his riches, but especially when he receives distinguished visitors from a distance.

The Gold of Ashanti.

On the reception of the English embassy, he was seated on a throne incased with massive gold, his person enveloped in richest silks and wearing many ornaments of pure gold on his neck, arms, wrists, fingers, ankles, and toes. His attendants and ministers at the same time made a still greater display of belts, gold-hilt swords, hatchets, scales and weights, horns, dishes, stools, and innumerable other articles of pure gold, all belonging to the royal treasures. Each caboceer is permitted, once in his life, to make an ostentatious display of his wealth in the streets of Kumasi. This is a gala day, the brightest and happiest in his sublunary existence. He decks himself, his wife, his children, and his dependents in his richest robes and with the gold ornaments, and then parades them through the streets, and concludes the exhibition by a grand feast, to which all of his friends are invited."

A considerable portion of the book is devoted to the discussion of matters relating to trade commerce, and a complete view is given of the exports of western Africa.

Ivory Trade. It is said, "The natives of this part of the country are unsurpassed for their cunning and shrewdness; and trade, for which they have an ardent love, is the very sphere in which that cunning and shrewdness is called into exercise." This is specially seen in the ivory trade: "Sometimes a man living at a distance from the port gets possession of a large and valuable tooth. It is the largest one the oldest resident of the country has ever seen; so large that a cat has raised a brood of kittens in the hollow end of it. The measure of the tooth, both its circumference and length, is sent down to the coast. A ship happens to be in port, and the captain hears so much about it he concludes it must be marvellously large. Such a tooth will add materially to the value of his cargo, and it will be gratifying, both to his owners and to his own pride, to have taken home the largest tooth of ivory that ever left the coast of Africa. The demand made by the owner is less than half its value, and the captain dispatches a messenger. When it is brought part of the way a claim is made for an additional payment, and when it is quite near the coast, the factor tells him there is a fetich mountain that will not let it pass till some more money is paid. The next message is that the tooth has actually reached the beach, but the party who brought it down refuses to give it up unless remunerated for his trouble. The irate captain has no alternative. When the famous tooth is laid on the deck he sees he has been over-reached, but the parties are all out of sight. The native merchant, whose sincerity and honesty the captain never suspected for a moment, may have had the tooth in his house from the beginning of the negotiations, and used all this subterfuge and trickery merely to get a better price for his ivory."

The author treats fully of the gross and dark superstitions of the land, of which only one or two examples will be given here. He says: "Witchcraft is a prominent and leading superstition among all the races of Africa, and may be regarded as one of the heaviest curses which rest upon that benighted land. A person endowed with this mysterious art is supposed to possess little less than omnipotence. By his magical arts he can keep back the showers, and fill the land with want and distress. Sickness, poverty, insanity, and almost every evil incident to human life, are ascribed to its agency. Any man is liable to be charged with it. Every death which occurs in the community is ascribed to witchcraft, and some one consequently is guilty of the wicked deed. The priesthood go to work to find out the guilty person. It may be a brother, a sister, a father; there is no effectual shield against suspicion. Age, the ties of relationship, official prominence, and general benevolence of character, are alike unavailing.

"But terrible as witchcraft is, there is a complete remedy in the 'red-water ordeal.' This, when properly administered, has the power, not only to wipe off the foulest stain from injured innocence, but can detect and punish all those who are guilty of practicing this wicked and hateful art. The people who assemble to see it administered form themselves into a circle, and the pots containing the liquid are placed in the centre of the enclosed space. The accused comes forward with a cord of palm-leaves bound round his waist, and seats himself in the centre of the circle. After his accusation is announced, he makes a formal acknowledgment of all the evil deeds of his past life, then invokes the name of his god three times and imprecates his wrath, in case he is guilty of the crime laid to his charge.   He then steps forward and drinks freely of the 'red water.'   If it nauseates and causes him to vomit freely, he suffers no serious injury, and is at once pronounced innocent.   If, on the other hand, it causes vertigo and he losses his self-control, it is regarded as an evidence of guilt, and then all sorts of indignities and cruelties are heaped upon him.   They spit upon him, pelt him with stones, and in many instances he is seized by the heels and dragged through the bushes and over rocky places till his body is shamefully lacerated and life becomes extinct.''

As a teacher of religion, our author made himself familiar with the religious views of the people among whom he came to labor.   He says of the fetich:

Fetich.

"A fetich may be made of a piece of wood, the horn of a goat, the hoof of an antelope, a piece of metal or ivory, and needs only to pass through the consecrating hands of a native priest to receive all the supernatural powers which it is supposed to possess.   One of the first things which meets the eyes of a stranger, after planting his feet upon the shores of Africa, is the symbols of this religion.   He steps forth from the boat under a canopy of fetiches, not only as a security for his own safety, but also as a guaranty that he does not carry the elements of mischief among the people.   He finds them suspended along every path he walks; at every junction of two or more roads; at the crossing-place of every stream; at the base of every large rock or overgrown forest tree; at the gate of every village; over the door of every house, and around the neck of every human being whom he meets. They are set up on their farms, tied around their fruit trees, and are fastened to the necks of their sheep and goats, to prevent them from being stolen.''

The practice of demonolatry is universal : '' On the gold
Exorcists. coast there are stated occasions (generally at night) when the people turn out *en masse*, with clubs and torches, to drive away the evil spirits from their towns. At a given signal, the whole community start up, commence a hideous howling, beat about in every nook and corner of their dwellings, then rush into the streets with their torches and clubs like so many maniacs, beat the air and scream at the top of their voices, until some one announces the departure of the spirits through some gate of the town, when they are pursued several miles into the woods and warned not to come back.''

The resident missionary was impressed with the truth
**Human Sac-
rifices.** of the psalmist's words, '' The dark places of the earth are full of the habitations of cruelty.''

'' The practice of offering human sacrifices to appease evil spirits is common, but in no place more frequent, or on a larger scale, than in the kingdoms of Ashanti and Dahomi. Large numbers of victims, chiefly prisoners of war, are statedly sacrificed to the manes of the royal ancestors, and under circumstances of shocking and almost unparalleled cruelty. At the time of the death of a king, a large number of his principal wives and favorite slaves are put to death to be his companions and attendants in the other world. Among the darkest features in the history of this people are the cruel and bloody human sacrifices which are annually offered. The savage and atrocious cruelties practiced on these occasions are perhaps without a parallel in the history of the world.''

Just at the present time, when the attention of the Christian church is turned to the Congo Free State, it will be of interest to present an epitome of the rise and fall of the Roman Catholic missions in that country, which are so fully described in *Western Africa:*

The Roman Church in the Kingdom of Congo.

"The circumstance which, above all others, has contributed to give interest to the kingdom of Congo is the fact that it has been the stage upon which has been achieved one of the most successful experiments ever made by the Church of Rome to reclaim a pagan people from idolatry.   For more than two centuries, this kingdom, according to the testimony of the missionaries themselves, was as completely under the influence of Rome as any sister-kingdom in Europe, so that, if the inhabitants of that country are not now, in point of civilization and Christianity, what the Catholics would have them to be, or all that a pagan people are capable of being made under her training, the fault lies at her own door.   She had the field to herself, and for two hundred years enjoyed facilities and advantages for propagating her religion among this people which she can scarcely ever expect to have again in any future efforts she may make.

A Grand Experiment.

"San Salvador, the capital and metropolis of the whole kingdom, was situated in the province of Pemba, upon the summit of a high mountain, and not only enjoyed a magnificent prospect of the surrounding country, but was reputed healthy even for Europeans.   It was not only the residence of the king, but was the headquarters of the missionaries, as also of a large number of Portuguese merchants, who resorted thither on account of the facilities it offered for trade. For many years a bishop and his chapter, a college of Jesuits, and a monastery of Capuchins, were supported

San Salvador.

in San Salvador at the expense of the Portuguese government. Besides a cathedral of large dimensions, there
were ten smaller churches, to which the ordinary names
of St. Johns, St. James, St. Michael, St. Anthony, etc.,
were given, all of which contributed materially to beau-
tify this otherwise barbaric city.

"On his third voyage to Congo, Diego Carn, the original discoverer, took with him twelve missionaries of the
Franciscan order, who are regarded as the founders of
the Christian religion in the kingdom of Congo. Count
Logno and his nephew, the king of Congo, were among
their first converts. For a time the latter showed great
zeal in promoting the new religion among his subjects,
but as soon as he found that he was required to give up
the multitude of wives and concubines with which he
was surrounded, and be married to a single wife, he re-
nounced it, and returned to the religion of his fathers.
His son, Don Alphonso the First, not only embraced
Christianity himself, but did all he could to promote its
interest throughout his realms. His brother, Pasanquitama, was a man of very different spirit, and finding
there was a popular dislike to the new religion, availed
himself of it to raise a rebellion against the king. The
armies of the two brothers had scarcely engaged in battle when St. James was distinctly seen fighting on the
side of the king, and victory, of course, soon turned in
his favor. Pasanquitama was not only beaten, but was
made a prisoner. He refused to ransom his life by embracing Christianity, and was accordingly executed.
Soon after this signal victory in behalf of Christianity, a
large reinforcement of missionaries was sent out by the
Society *de Propaganda Fide*, and in the course of fifteen
or twenty years the entire population of Congo was
gathered into the pale of the Roman Catholic Church.

"About the middle of the sixteenth century the labors of the missionaries met with serious interruption in consequence of an invasion of the country by hordes of the war-like Giachi. The army of Congo, though large and well-disciplined, was scattered like chaff before these savage invaders. San Salvador was burned to the ground, and the king and his people had to betake themselves to the 'Isle of Horses,' on the Zaire, for safety. In this extremity the king of Congo appealed to Don Sebastian, king of Portugal, for help, which was promptly granted. Six or eight hundred Portuguese troops were dispatched, and after several engagements, in which the Giachi showed great bravery, the savages were driven from the country and the king restored to the throne.

"The missionaries returned to their labors, and having been reinforced by new recruits from Europe, not only re-established the Catholic worship in all the provinces of Congo, but extended their labors into the neighboring districts. . . . There was also, it is probable, a religious motive which prevented the Portuguese from seizing upon the country. Congo had received the Catholic religion at a very early period after its discovery, and its sovereigns, with one or two exceptions, had always showed as much deference for the authority of Rome as those of Portugal itself. All of the kings had been crowned according to the Catholic ceremonial, and the crown itself had been bestowed by the Pope as a testimony of their loyalty.

"It is not easy to say how much civilization there was in Congo in the days of its greatest prosperity. . . . The missionaries and the Portuguese residents no doubt did something to change the general aspects of the country. Wherever they went they planted gardens, cultivated fruit trees, and built substantial houses, both for private dwellings and places of public worship. The king and some of the chiefs followed their example, but the mass of the people continued to live in bamboo huts; they cultivated only the indigenous vegetables of the country, and were always clad with the scantiest apparel, while there were vast hordes of the poorer people who had no clothing whatever.

"For a period of two centuries paganism was interdicted by law, and the severest penalties were inflicted upon those who were known to participate in the observances of any of its rites. There were periods, too, in the history of the country, when it would have been difficult, if not impossible, to find one adult in the whole kingdom who had not, in infancy or afterwards, been introduced by baptism into the church. The number of churches and other places of public worship was very considerable. In the entire kingdom, it is probable there were not less than one hundred consecrated churches, and perhaps two or three times as many other places where the priests were in the habit of performing baptism and celebrating the mass. The king and his chiefs always vied with each other in their attendance upon mass, and there was scarcely a single outward ceremony of the church which they did not scrupulously perform. Wherever the priests went it was the duty of the chief to send a messenger around the village to notify the people of his arrival, and direct them to come and have their spiritual wants attended to. The common people might be seen in long trains bearing logs of wood to the convents, or scourging themselves with unrelenting severity in the churches, as acts of penance. One of the missionaries states that in one of the villages he entered the mothers rushed upon him 'like mad women' to have their children baptized. The authority of the priests in matters political as well as ecclesiastical was established on the firmest basis.   There were no acts of penance or humiliation inflicted upon the sovereigns of Europe when Rome was in the zenith of her power that these missionaries had not the satisfaction of seeing the humbler chiefs of Congo subjected to; and one can readily imagine with what awe it must have struck the simple-minded Africans to see the Count of Logno, the most powerful chief of the kingdom, prostrated at the church door, clothed in sackcloth, with a crown of thorns on his head, a crucifix in his hand, and a rope about his neck, while his courtiers, clothed in their most brilliant robes, were looking on.

"But what has become of this church with all of its resources and power?   Where are the results of this spiritual conquest that cost so much?   The friends of Rome must acknowledge that they constructed a spiritual edifice in the heart of this pagan empire that could not stand in its own strength; the moment the hand which reared and for a time upheld it was taken away, it fell to pieces.

"In accounting for the downfall of Romanism in Congo, something, no doubt, is to be ascribed to the decline of the Portuguese power.   It was under her fostering hand that the church of Congo first rose to power and importance.   The time came, however, when Portugal had no more treasures to bestow upon the church, and as little power to control the political affairs of the state.

"Another cause was the countenance the Roman Catholic religion always extended to the foreign slave trade. The missionaries participated in the traffic themselves. By an arrangement with the civil authorities, all persons convicted of celebrating the rights of the ancient religion, were delivered up to the missionaries and by them sold to the first slave vessel which entered the river, and the proceeds were distributed to the poor. The number of individuals thus convicted was very considerable, so that vessels engaged in transporting slaves to Brazil could always depend upon the missionaries to give them material aid in making up their complement of slaves.

"Another cause of the downfall of Romanism was the character of the religion introduced into Congo. One would naturally suppose that going among a people so deeply debased and so utterly ignorant of everything pertaining to Christianity, the missionaries would have taken special pains to instruct them in the principles of the Catholic religion before introducing them into. the church. It is but natural to suppose that they would have translated the word of God into their language, established schools for the instruction of the youth, and employed all the ordinary means for diffusing Christian knowledge among the people. But the world knows that such a course is no part of the policy of Rome. The missionaries introduced all their rites and ceremonies. The mass was celebrated with due pomp; the confessional was erected in almost every village; penances of all grades and kinds were imposed; children and adults alike were required to count the rosary, and the people *en masse* soon learned to make the sign of the cross, and most readily did they fall into the habit of wearing crucifixes, medals, and relics."

They introduced substitutes for heathen customs. Instead of interdicting to every person at birth some one article of food, they commanded "that the parents should enjoin their children to observe some particular devotion, such as to repeat many times a day the rosary of the *crown* in honor of the blessed virgin, to fast on Saturdays, etc." Instead of guarding their fruit trees

14

and fields of grain with fetiches, the people were recommended "to use consecrated palm-branches, and here
and there in their patches of corn to set up the sign of
the cross."   "It was the great error of the Roman missionaries that they presented to the benighted inhabitants of Congo a system of superstitious observances so
nearly allied, both in spirit and form, to the one which
they aimed to extirpate. . . . It was important for
the people to enjoy the favor of the missionaries, and
they had no fears that their own religion would be con-
taminated with Romanism. If they showed all due reverence for the rites and ceremonies of the Romish Church
in the presence of the missionaries, they were not the less
punctilious in performing the rites of their own in their
absence. As but few of the missionaries ever made
themselves acquainted with the language of the country,
the natives had special advantages for playing off this
double game. It cost them no effort to appear to be zealous Roman Catholics, when in reality they were the most
besotted pagans on the face of the earth."

The missionaries hoped to strengthen their position
"by the exercise of their pretended miraculous gifts, . . .
but whenever you enter the precincts of the unknown
and the mysterious, the realms where the imagination
alone can travel, there is no place where the negro feels
more at home, and the endless variety of fantastic ima-
ges, which he brings forth from these mysterious regions,
shows that here he has no rival. The missionaries, therefore, when they addressed themselves to the task of
working miracles, little knew how egregiously they were
to be outstripped "

"Corporal punishment was the favorite instrument
of discipline, and it was administered without restraint.
The slightest deviation from the prescribed rules of the

church was punished by public flogging, and it was not uncommon for females, and even mothers, to be stripped and whipped in public. Sometimes these castigations were inflicted by the missionaries themselves.''

"We have no certain information of the process by which Romanism ceased to be the religion of the country. We can only compare the Roman Church in Congo to a magnificent edifice that fell to pieces because it had no foundation upon which to rest, or to a beautiful exotic that withered away because it had taken no root in the soil of the country.''

CHAPTER XX.

Suppression of the Slave Trade.

THIS chapter presents one of the most interesting and striking features of the life of the pioneer missionary of the American Board to Western Africa. It sets forth distinctly his influence on the world's civilization.

Writing to Miss Theodosia Bayard on his second voyage to Africa (December 14, 1834), he says: "We anchored at Gorée after a voyage of thirty days. The sight of land, and especially of the continent of Africa, was refreshing to us, yet not without melancholy reflections. Gorée, like many other spots on the coast of Africa, has been the scene of much inhumanity and cruelty. It was once a most extensive slave-market, and although the trade has been suppressed at this place many years, I fancied I could almost see traces of human guilt upon her mouldered wall. Indeed, the stone walls which were originally reared to confine the slaves still remain, a monument of the sufferings of the Africans and the reproach of the Christian name."

On a journey in the interior in 1836, speaking of two men who had just disposed of a slave, he says: "I asked them if they did not think it wrong to capture and sell their fellow-men as slaves? They said, 'No; that no white man had told them it was wrong.' How affecting to trace the footsteps of white men in Africa! I have reference to slave-dealers, who form the great majority of those who have visited her shores! They are to be traced in wars, in bloodshed, in tumults, in distress, in misery, and in everything that can degrade and render savage the heart of man."

On another journey in 1836, he says: "At Cavally we met a white man by the name of Baffron, who was engaged in the slave-trade, and we had to take lodgings in the same house. He is in the employ of the far-famed Peter Blanco, of Gallinas, and if I am correctly informed by this man, that notable trader has between fifty and one hundred vessels engaged in transporting human beings from the continent of Africa to the West Indies."

Peter Blanco.

In 1840 he writes to the *Missionary Herald:* "The increased efforts of the English government to suppress the slave trade is to be regarded as one of the most auspicious events connected with the improvement of this country. Although the direct trade in slaves has been carried on only at a few points along the coast, yet there is scarcely any part which has not in some way or the other been afflicted by its endless train of evils. They have not brought slaves to this vicinity for many years past, but it has been a favorite resort for the purchase of rice for the slave factories, and the article which the purchasers have usually given in exchange for rice has been rum, the influence of which upon a community like this needs not to be told. Last week Lord Francis Russel, commanding the Brig *Harlequin*, anchored at this place, bringing with him a slave vessel taken on the leeward coast, and while here he took a second slaver that was passing by, and chased several others. About the same time the corpse of a native boy was washed upon the beach near to this place, and the only reasonable conjecture is that it was thrown overboard by a slaver when pursued to avoid being condemned if captured. This is a common piece of cruelty in the annals of the slave trade.

In *Western Africa*, Dr. Wilson says: "Up to the beginning of the seventeenth century the trade in slaves was confined almost entirely to the Portuguese. The English, French, and Dutch, as yet, had nothing to do with it. All these nations were then acquiring colonial possessions in America, and it was not long before they came to the conclusion that the Portuguese and Spaniards had adopted the true policy of rendering their West India plantations valuable by the introduction of African slaves. They found little or no difficulty in quieting the public conscience by placing an appeal to humanity. The aborigines of Africa were living in the midst of the darkest heathenism, and it would be an act of humanity to transfer them to a different soil, where they might participate in the blessings of the gospel. No sooner did the matter assume this aspect than the energies of all three of the nations, like pent-up waters, burst forth, and not only deluged Africa with the most frightful calamities, but had well-nigh swept away its entire population."

In 1672 a new company was chartered under the name of the "Royal African Company" of England, with ample powers to protect and foster the African trade. This company did not confine itself to the gold coast alone, but acquiring a footing in various other parts of the country, soon became very extensively engaged both in the slave trade and in other branches of commerce. They imported large numbers of slaves into the British West Indies, and were able, it is said, sometimes to trust planters to the amount of £100,000.

"During the greater part of the eighteenth century

England was the chief actor in that traffic in men which
she now denounces so bitterly, and has ex-
Assiento
Contract. pended so much money to suppress.   The
contract for supplying the Spanish colonies
with slaves was transferred from the French to the English company.   An agreement was formed between the
Spanish government and this company, well known as
the 'Assiento Contract,' by which the company was to
have the exclusive right of supplying the Spanish colonies with slaves for the term of thirty years.   During
this period they bound themselves to furnish one hundred and forty-four thousand, or about four thousand
eight hundred annually.   They were at liberty to import
as many more as they could dispose of, but they were
bound by contract to furnish not less than this specified
number.   They bound themselves, besides, to pay the
king of Spain two hundred thousand crowns, and also
thirty-three and a half crowns on every slave imported
into the country.   They were, moreover, required to pay
the king of Spain and England each one-quarter share of
all the profits.

"It can readily be seen that the trade became the engrossing business of the Royal African Company.   It is
estimated by Badinel, who had the best means of inves-
tigating the subject, that the number of slaves taken from
the coast of Africa by this company between the years
1713 and 1733 was fifteen thousand annually, or three-
hundred thousand in all, about one-half of whom were
taken to the Spanish, and the remainder to the English
colonies of America.   Between 1733 and 1753 the average number exported annually was about twenty-thou-
sand, or four hundred thousand in the term of twenty-
years."

"McPherson estimates the number taken from Africa

in 1768, through all sources, as ninety-seven thousand, of whom the English transported sixty thousand, and the French twenty-three thousand. Badinel states that the number exported from the coast in 1798 was not less than one hundred thousand, of whom fifty-five thousand were taken by the English, twenty-five thousand by the Portuguese, and fifteen thousand by the Americans. These were the evil days of Africa, but the evil had reached its highest point. A feeling of indignation had arisen, both in Great Britain and in the United States, against this iniquitous business. The English have undoubtedly led in opposing and crushing this cruel practice. When public opinion had been thoroughly aroused to its injustice and inhumanity, a very general desire was awakened in the British mind to repair the injuries that had been inflicted on that ill-fated continent.''

''In virtue of a bull of the Pope, a slave market was opened in Lisbon, and as early as 1537 it is said that not less than ten or twelve thousand slaves were brought to this place, and transported from thence to the West Indies. This was denominated as the 'carrying trade,' and we need scarcely remind the reader that from the time it was set in motion up to the present hour it has been the object of engrossing attention to the Portuguese nation. If we cannot but admire the energy and courage they displayed in bringing to the knowledge of the civilized world countries which were not known to exist, equally impossible would it be not to execrate the meanness which would induce them to sacrifice the inhabitants of those countries to the cupidity of the rest of the world.''

The Pope's Bull.

''In Africa, where men are seized for the first time and converted into property for the purpose of gratifying their fellow-men, it assumes a char-

Horrors.

ter of aggravation which it does in no other part of the world. In the earlier years its victims were procured in wholesale numbers by war and violence; villages were surprised, and the entire population seized and sold into slavery by their more powerful neighbors. This system soon gave place to another, which, though not attended with the same outward violence and bloodshed, has nevertheless proved more injurious to the country in the course of time than the one it supplanted. Few are now taken to the markets kept open along the coast, except those charged with some crime, and the most prolific source of accusation is the charge of witchcraft, a thing so subtle and indefinite that it may always be substantiated on the most precarious evidence, and so pliable at the same time that it may be made to cover the most barefaced acts of injustice and cruelty. The writer has more than once known a company of men, on the mere suspicion of witchcraft, to seize upon one of their own number, sell him to a slave dealer, and divide the proceeds among themselves, when it was not only obvious to others, but acknowledged by themselves, that there was a strong probability that they would all in a short time be disposed of in the same way. He has known two friends (professedly so, at least) come to a slave factory on a mere pleasure excursion, and while one was secretly negotiating for the sale of his companion, the intended victim has had the adroitness to escape with the money and leave the other to atone for his duplicity by a life of foreign servitude.''

Writing to Mrs. Wilson from the Gaboon in 1842, he speaks thus: "I have visited all the settle-

Slave
Factory. ments on the river in this immediate vicinity.
There was one scene in these excursions which particularly affected my heart. I refer to the in-

terior of a slave factory on the opposite side of the river. I cannot enter into details, but suffice it to say my curiosity will never prompt me again to visit a similar scene of human degradation. Think of four hundred and thirty naked savages of both sexes, of all ages, sizes and conditions, brought together in one enclosure, chained together in gangs of twenty, thirty, or forty, and all compelled to sleep on the same platform, eat out of the same tub, and in almost every respect live like so many swine. More than this, on the *middle-passage* they must have quarters still more circumscribed, and live on much scantier fare. God reigns, and this vile traffic in human beings must come to an end.''

If we consider that for two centuries white men ravaged the coast of Africa, and slavers carried as freight to distant lands captive men and women, we can form a better estimate of this terrible traffic. What utter demoralization there must have been amongst the tribes adjacent to the coast, or living along the great rivers! How the European incited the black savage to deeds of rapine and violence, and wars and crime marked the advance of commerce! Its advocates can only be estimated by the numbers borne forcibly from their native land. The figures tell us that the victims of the slave trade were numbered by the millions.

It was in the closing stage of this epoch that Leighton Wilson exercised a deciding influence in the annihilation of this infamous traffic. Efforts were being made to withdraw the British squadron from Africa, under the allegation that little or nothing had been done in putting an end to it. This feeling in England caused him to prepare a paper which was sent to a wealthy merchant in Bristol, who placed it in the hands of Lord Palmerston. The Premier directed an edition of ten thousand to be printed in various forms and widely distributed in prominent circles. It is also to be found in the *United States Service Journal*, and in the *Blue Book*. The monograph proved clearly that the squadron had accomplished a great deal, and urged that only the fastest ships should be stationed on the coast. Lord Palmerston informed Mr. Wilson that after the publication of his article all opposition in England to the retention of the African squadron ceased, so in directing the movements of the British navy the humble missionary was on this occasion the foremost of admirals. Only very brief extracts are given from this historic document.

The Premier's Testimony.

"Previous to the period when this traffic was declared to be illegal by the British Parliament and the government of the United States, it was carried on very much in the same way as lawful trade is at the present time. Vessels which came out for slaves 'ran down the coast,' touching at all the principal settlements, and purchasing such slaves as were offered for sale, until their cargoes were completed. In some cases whole cargoes were collected by kidnapping the natives who came off in their canoes to trade, and sometimes by capturing other slave vessels that had completed their cargoes and were ready to sail, but had not the means of self-defence. Besides, there were a few points along the coast occupied by the British, as well as other European governments, intended to facilitate the same trade. In this way the whole coast, from Senegal to Benguela, was, more or less, voluntarily or involuntarily, implicated in it. When the trade became illegal, the Spaniards, Portuguese, and others, who determined to persist in it, had to adopt a new mode of operation.

Paper on the Slave trade.

They could no longer perform their usual voyages along the coast without multiplying the chances of being seized as prizes and having their property confiscated. It became necessary, therefore, to erect barracoons on those parts of the coast where slaves could be collected with the greatest ease and in the largest numbers; and at the appointed time the vessels returned and took away these slaves without being detained on the coast more than twenty-four hours, and in some cases only a single night. The points thus occupied at one time could not have been less than forty or fifty. The English have never had any treaties with the Spanish, Portuguese, or Brazilian governments that would authorize them to destroy these barracoons. Hence they have been compelled to do what they could by guarding the coast and seizing slave vessels in their vicinity. But as the number of the places occupied by the slave trade greatly exceeded the number of cruisers employed to watch them, and were seldom less than fifty or a hundred miles apart, it will readily be seen that the cruisers had a difficult task to perform, and the frequent escape of slavers was inevitable. At the same time, the profits of the trade were so great that the escape of a single slaver would cover the loss of three captures.

"Notwithstanding all these disadvantages, such have been the diligence and activity of the officers of the squadron, that they have forced the trade out of more than three-fourths of the strongholds which it once occupied. Let any one open the map of Africa and ascertain the places where slaves are now collected and shipped, and compare the number with what it was twenty or twenty-five years ago, and it cannot result in anything short of profound surprise.

"From Senegal, near the borders of the Great Desert,

to Cape Lopez, a few miles south of the equator, a distance coastwise of something like twenty-five hundred
miles, there is now, with the exception of three factories
on what is called the slave coast, no trade in slaves
whatever. In fact the trade, with the exceptions just
made, is now confined to what is called the Congo
country, in which there are not more than eight or ten
points where slaves are collected and from which they
are shipped. If we add to these the three above mentioned, we have, on the whole coast, not more than
twelve or fourteen; whereas there were, even within the
knowledge of the writer, nearly four times this number.
More than two thousand miles of sea coast, and that
forming the frontier of the best and fairest portions of
the African continent, have been relieved from this unparalleled scourge; and, perhaps, more than twenty
million of human beings, interiorwards, have been restored to comparative peace and happiness by the operations of the squadron along the coast. And how has all
this been achieved? We reply, by a process in itself
perfectly natural, and in exact accordance with the ex-
pectations of those who originated the enterprise. Take,
as an illustration, the history of the slave trade in the
Bight of Biafra. All who have investigated the subject
know that the rivers Benin, Bonny, Brass, Kalabar, and
Kameruns were once the chief seats of this trade. It is
through these rivers that the Niger discharges itself into
the ocean; and as the factories near the mouths of these
different branches had great facility of access to the heart
of Africa, it is probable that the traffic was carried on
more vigorously here than anywhere else on the coast.
But at present there is none of it. This part of the coast
having been subjected for several years to a virtual
blockade, not only did the Spaniards and Portuguese

find themselves under the necessity of relinquishing it, but, at the same time, the natives saw they could derive a larger and more certain profit from lawful commerce, and consequently turned their attention to the manufacture of palm oil.

"In relation to the objection that there has been no material diminution of the number of slaves exported from the coast, we have more than our doubts. The time has been when tolerably accurate statistics might be collected on this subject, but we do not see how this can be done at present. There is no one on the coast of Africa who can furnish anything like accurate information; and as most of the slaves which reach Brazil are smuggled into places where there is the least likelihood of their being detected, we doubt whether there is anyone there that can furnish information upon which more reliance can be placed. It is the policy of those engaged in the traffic to make an exaggerated impression, for they hope to put an end to the efforts of the squadron by convincing the English nation of the hopelessness of the undertaking. Our own impression is that the number of slaves exported has vastly diminished, perhaps in a ratio very nearly proportioned to the extent of sea-coast which it has lost. It is utterly incredible that the number of slaves now concentrated at a dozen or fourteen points can be compared with what it was when the whole coast was taxed for this purpose.

"The squadron has also been operating in an indirect way by the influence it has exerted in promoting lawful commerce and the countenance and protection it has extended to the European settlements and the American colonies on the coast, and especially for the indirect aid it has afforded to the cause of Christian missions. In these different ways the British squadron has done more, perhaps, to emancipate Africa from the thraldom of the foreign slave trade than by all other methods put together. Without this all the prize ships that have been taken, and all the treaties that have been formed, whether with the chiefs of Africa or with the different governments of Europe, would have been comparatively worthless.

"Lawful commerce (and by this term we mean trade in the natural products of the country in opposition to the slave trade) owes its existence almost entirely to the presence and influence of the British squadron. Previous to the period when a check was given to the slave trade, the lawful commerce of Western Africa consisted of small quantities of gold-dust, ivory, and bees-wax, and did not amount annually, it is presumed, to more than £20,000. The insignificance of this trade, however, did not arise from any poverty in the natural resources of the country at that time, for they were as considerable then as they are now, but to the influence of the slave trade. During the prevalence of this traffic, the African seas were almost wholly given up to piracy. No vessel could carry on lawful commerce without the constant liability of being plundered. If these vessels were armed for self-defence, as was attempted in some few cases, the expense was so great that it consumed all the profits of the voyage.

"Another thing that operated equally to the disadvantage of lawful trade was the fact that the natives of the country were so much engrossed in furnishing victims for the slave trade, that they had neither the time nor the taste for the tamer pursuits of cutting dye-wood or manufacturing palm oil. Indeed, the excitement connected with capturing and selling slaves was always more congenial to savage natures; and had it not been for the obstacles interposed by the presence of the British squadron, we scarcely see how their attention could have been diverted from this to pursuits so different and so much less congenial to their natural tastes. We do not pretend to give statistics, but suppose it is entirely safe to say that the annual exports from Western Africa at the present cannot be less than £2,000,000. Regarded merely in a selfish point of view, England will be repaid for every dollar she has expended upon this enterprise, not only in the market she will have created in Africa for her manufactures, but likewise in the immense amount of valuable products that will be brought to hei own shores from that country. But if these results acquire importance in connection with commercial enterprise, how must they appear when contemplated in the light of humanity!

"All that has been said in relation to the importance of the squadron in developing the commercial resources of the country, and in promoting the cause of civilization, may be applied with equal force to the countenance it has lent to the cause of missions. The writer is not aware that the officers of the squadron have been in the habit of regarding any mission stations on the coast as under their special protection, but the mutual good feeling that has always existed between them and the missionaries, the readiness which they ever have manifested to repress all lawless violence, and especially the peace and quiet which they have restored to those parts of the coast where the missionaries are laboring, are favors and advantages more highly appreciated than the officers of the squadron have any idea of. Africa can never enjoy any high degree of internal prosperity without the aid of Christianity.

"More recently, but from a different source, we have

heard the opinion gravely expressed, that the most certain and effectual way of breaking up the traffic will be to let the Brazilians have unlimited access to the coast of Africa, and so glut their own markets that slaves will become comparatively valueless. We confess we have never heard this latter sentiment avowed without feelings of mingled astonishment and indignation, and have scarcely been able to refrain from exclaiming, Treason! It means that after toiling so long for Africa, we have come to the conclusion that she is not worth contending for, and therefore deliver her over to the destroyer without condition or mercy. Who can tell how many slaves it will take to glut the market of Brazil? The half of the population of the continent of Africa would scarcely be sufficient to supply the demand that would spring up under such circumstances.

"If the government of Great Britain would give efficiency to this enterprise, and bring the slave trade to a speedy termination, vessels of a better class should be designated to this service than those which have been stationed on the coast for a few years past. The writer pretends to no personal knowledge of the sailing qualities of vessels; but an article has recently appeared in the *London Times* by one of the commanders who has been in the service, in which it is conclusively proved that a large number of the vessels in the African service for a few years past have been of the poorer class, and utterly unfit for the kind of service in which they are engaged. None but the fastest sailers can be of any real use. Those employed by the slave traders are the fastest that can be procured, and to send in chase of them second or third-rate cruisers is but to subject the officers of the navy to disappointment and mortification. A small number of the fastest sailers would be more effective, and accomplish the undertaking with much more certainty."

Thus ends this great state paper. His voice was heard by the English nation, and her people accepted the three conclusions: First, That the squadron had done much for Africa; Second, That it must be continued till its work was accomplished; and Third, That the fastest ships be placed in this service till the slave trade come to an end.

In a letter to his brother-in-law, Mr. Mills, dated September 2, 1851, he wrote: "I sent you six months ago a pamphlet on the slave trade which was written for circulation in England, with the hope of contributing to arrest the efforts that were then made to withdraw the squadron and leave the slave trade to itself. The English government has renewed its efforts, and sent out a better class of vessels, and have already brought this wretched traffic to a standstill. There are now not more than six or seven places on the coast (out of thirty-eight or forty where it was carried on a few years ago) where slaves are still collected for exportation. This renewed effort, I have been assured, has resulted in some measure from the pamphlet just mentioned, which to me is ample satisfaction for the labor spent in preparing it."

The Appeal had its Effect.

In his last letter from Africa to the *Missionary Herald* he says: "The English squadron has very nearly put a final end to the slave trade. All its strongholds in the vicinity of the Congo have been abandoned. Indeed, I now know of but three points on the whole coast where it is still continued. The year 1851 will probably be the historic period of the breaking up of this protracted and wicked contest. The English Admiral and a large number of his vessels are now at Cape Lopez (the place which has served as an outlet for all the secret slave trade carried on in this river for three or four years past), and will, no doubt, effectually abolish it before he leaves.''

The long night of woe to the unhappy sons of Darkest Africa was ended, and the dawn of a brighter day was ushered in. For this happy consummation, Leighton Wilson toiled and prayed, and then rejoiced!

CHAPTER XXI.

Secretary in New York.

THE missionary who had so long withstood the power of the African suns, had at last to seek a change of climate by a return to his native land. The annual report of the American Board for 1852, says, "Mr. Wilson went to Africa nineteen years ago. During the last year his health has evinced a stong tendency to give way, and it was to escape a dangerous crisis in his constitution that his brethren urged upon him and Mrs. Wilson a homeward voyage. Our brother and sister have long borne the burden and heat of tropical days, but were never more interested than now in their African labors. It is remarkable that the influenza, from which Mr. Wilson suffered in October, extended as an epidemic along a thousand miles of the coast."

Failure of Health.

He had written to his family, March 15, 1851: "When the last American vessel left this place I was sick with liver complaint. My sickness was not of long continuance, and I am now quite as well as usual." It seems that his malady continued during the coming twelve months, for the next letter that has come to our hands is dated Pittsburg, Penn., August 13, 1852, and was addressed to his brothers and sisters: "It is a sore trial that I cannot go at once to the South, but both Dr. Hodge, of Philadelphia, and Dr. Post, of New York, have advised me to try the mountain air of this region, and thus far their advice seems to be good. My strength and general health have improved very perceptibly. Indeed, I am better now than for two years past. I am not fully decided about my future movements, but will remain up here till after the meeting of the American Board, September 7; then visit the theological seminaries in New York and Princeton, and after that go South. I hope by that time your turkeys and hens will be very fat, for if my health continues to improve up to that time, I shall be likely to make large depredations in that department. Perhaps as you have a railroad to Charleston, you are sending all your poultry there, and I may find myself reduced to Yankee straits in South Carolina.''

The winter of 1852-'53 was probably spent among his friends and relatives in Sumter county. The Presbytery of Harmony elected him a commissioner to the General Assembly of 1853, which met in Philadelphia. This, we are inclined to think, was the first one he had ever attended. On his long journey to the city of ''Brotherly Love,'' how little did he imagine that he would attend the highest court of the church successively for the next thirty years. The Board of Foreign Missions held its annual meeting during the sessions of the General Assembly. As their work was rapidly extending in different parts of the world, it became necessary to increase the force in the office by the election of another secretary. Here was present a missionary of twenty years' experience in the field, just entering the prime of manhood, a representative minister from the South, and one whose health would probably prevent his return to the equatorial regions. As he had never been in the service of the Presbyterian Board, he had no official connection with its annual meeting.

Mr. William Rankin, his associate in New York, says,

"My first acquaintance with Dr. Wilson was at the General Assembly of 1853 in Philadelphia, of which body we both were members, he representing the Presbytery of Harmony. When the report on Foreign Missions was read before the Assembly he made the principal address, and before the final adjournment a special meeting of the Board was called, and after a statement of the increasing labors of the office, on motion of the Hon. Walter Lowrie, Sr., Dr. Wilson was chosen third secretary. He was considered the fittest man for the post. After obtaining a release from the service of the American Board he accepted the appointment, and entered upon the duties in September of the same year."

After the Assembly Dr. Wilson writes to his sister from Pittsfield, June 15, 1853, "We have been driven here by the pressure of the summer heat, and really it is almost intolerable here. Before leaving New York I had two physicians examine my liver, and they have both confirmed the opinion of Dr. Jeffries, of Boston, that I must not think of returning to Africa for the present, and probably, they say, not at all.

"In my last I mentioned that I had been elected one of the secretaries of the Presbyterian Board in New York, and my mind is tending to the conclusion that I ought to accept. The appointment was unsought and unexpected, and, therefore, I suppose it ought to be considered as providential. I can do more for African missions at this post than at any other in the country. Dr. Anderson has written strongly against it; he says I ought to work with the American Board if I remain in this country."

He is led to accept the position and enters upon its varied and multiplied duties. But what a change!

Instead of Toko, King Glass, and the hordes of naked savages, he had for his associates in the Presbytery of New York and in the Executive Committee, Drs. Philips, Potts, Janeway, Spring, J. W. Alexander, W. J. Hoge, and such elders as Robert Carter, Robert Stuart, James Lenox, and a host of worthies like unto these. Instead of his thatched cottage at the Gaboon, built at a cost of $80, he lived in a large residence in the grandest city of America! Yet his heart pined for the mission field. The writer, when not ten years of age, remembers hearing his mother say, "Dr. Leighton Wilson lives in New York in a house of nine rooms, provided with every comfort and convenience, but he says he would rather be in Africa."

He was associated in the office with the Hon. Walter Lowrie, and his son, Rev. Dr. John C. Lowrie, the Secretaries of the Board. With the latter he was connected by marriage. Their friendship was very deep and warm. Twenty years after Dr. Wilson came South, Dr. Lowrie visited him in Baltimore to confer with him about mission work in Africa, and to urge that our church establish a mission on the Congo.

His Associates.

This period in the life of Dr. Wilson is singularly wanting in detail, for which two reasons are assigned: First, Those associated with him thirty-five or forty years ago have for the greater part entered into rest; and Second, The writer of these pages, after the task was undertaken, was not able to visit the Mission Rooms in New York, but he is happy to be able to present two letters, one from an honored servant of the church who was Treasurer of Foreign Missions for nearly forty years, and the other from the venerable Rev. Dr. John D. Wells, for one or two score years the President of the Board of Foreign Missions in New York.

Mr. Rankin writes: "Dr. Wilson's great work was in
Africa, and afterwards as the executive officer
of the Southern Committee of Missions, yet
he filled an important place during his eight
years' residence in New York as one of the Secretaries of
the Board. Soon after his removal to the city he purchased a residence in what was then the upper part of
the city, where he and Mrs. Wilson entertained their
guests, returned missionaries especially, and their hospitality was unbounded. I can speak feelingly of this,
for an invalid sister-in-law, residing in the West, and
coming to New York for special treatment, was invited
to make their house her home, and she remained there
for several weeks. This was a token of his regard for
me, and I am assured our attachment was mutual.
Though seldom meeting in later years, I could feel no
abatement of my affection for him.

"He visited our Indian missions in the Southwest,
and when he withdrew from the Board, in a private interview with Walter Lowrie, at the request of the latter,
he promised to use his influence with the Southern
churches to look after their educational and spiritual interests, and his appointment as Secretary of the Southern
Committee enabled him more fully to discharge this
trust. On leaving New York he sold or exchanged his
house for one in Savannah, and also disposed of his
church pew, both at a great pecuniary sacrifice.

"When the new Brick Church (Dr. Gardiner Spring's)
was dedicated, Dr. and Mrs. Wilson identified themselves
with it, purchasing a pew. Before that, they attended
the Madison Square Church, as it was convenient to his
residence. Dr. Wilson was a man of warm social influences, lovable in disposition, and it was a pleasure to
be his daily associate at the Mission House. As a Sec-

retary, he was regarded as unexceptionally efficient, courteous, and sympathetic. His heart was in his work, and he gave all his energies to it. He was unusually popular. He addressed Synods and the General Assembly frequently, and with great acceptance.

"From the first he was the Recording Secretary of the Board, and these records are an enduring memorial. He also edited the foreign department of the *Home and Foreign Record.*

"The entire body of the Presbyterian Church of New York were his friends, and every one who knew him loved him and regretted his voluntary withdrawal. It was a sad day to many when he left all these surroundings, but God had work for him to do in the Southern Church, the foundation of whose Foreign Missions he laid. You have a noble subject for biography, and may his grand portraiture be an inspiration to you and every reader of your pages."

The following letter is from the aged Rev. Dr. John D. Wells, of Brooklyn, New York: "I rejoice to know that a sketch of the life of Dr. J. Leighton Wilson is to be prepared. It is due to the grace of God, the church at large, and the great cause of missions that his name and works and influence should be kept in loving remembrance; and that Mrs. Jane Wilson, his beloved wife and co-worker, should be closely associated with him in this sketch to be prepared. My first knowledge of them came from letters written from Cape Palmas, Western Africa, January, 1837. My brother-in-law, the Rev. David White, and my sister, Helen M. White, missionaries of the A. B. C. F. M., were received in their house with open arms, December 25, 1836. In my association with him I could never forget how joyfully he and Mrs. Wilson welcomed them in their African home, and how tenderly they ministered to them in their sickness, until they closed their eyes for the final sleep, mourning for them as if they had been nearest kindred. The letters of my sister, written during the few days of the sojurn of herself and husband with Mr. and Mrs. Wilson, tell strongly of their loving kindness and of their great work in behalf of the people of that part of Africa, both adults and children. I cannot read these letters—the last she ever wrote addressed to me and left unfinished—without many tears. I have now in my possession precious autograph letters from both Mr. and Mrs. Wilson written to my mother and myself, that laid bare their hearts and endeared them to us before we had seen them. Mr. Wilson and Mr. White were acquainted with each other in this country, having been a short time together in Union College. Indeed, it was their strong personal attachment that had much to do with deciding the great question of Mr. White's proposed field of labor. They were friends and brethren here, and did what they could to become fellow-laborers in Africa. When Mr. and Mrs. Wilson returned to this country, we had the great joy of seeing them face to face and entertaining them at our house.

"The notice of my election to the Board of Foreign Missions bears date May 12, 1854, and was written by 'J. Leighton Wilson.' From that time till his voluntary withdrawal in consequence of the war, I saw him in the Executive Committee of the Board almost every Monday morning. And a sorrowful change there was to me when he withdrew, for I loved him with no ordinary love, and never knew any change of affection consequent upon the course he took in obedience to his conscience and his love for his native state. His Society was always pleasant and inspiring. He was a wise, strong, consecrated man, filling a large place as Secretary of the Board after filling a large place as missionary in Africa. His book on *Western Africa* is still referred to on all the matters with which it deals. He was a large man every way: in stature, in endowments, in acquisition, in character and in conversation, and served the great cause which the Master made great and laid upon the hands and hearts of his church under a world-wide commission and a precious promise of his own presence. I think Dr. and Mrs. Wilson had as large and loving interest in this cause as any persons I have ever known.

"We here knew how faithful he was in the service of the Board, how wise in counsel, how acceptable and efficient in speech and with his pen, and how considerate and kind in all the associations of the office, and how pleasant and loving in social fellowship. I was very glad when he was made Secretary of the Southern Board, and am sure that he has left the impress of his wisdom, energy, and consecration on the work which passes into other hands while he and Mrs. Wilson rest in the Father's house."

The Rev. Dr. Dabney writes, "In the spring of 1858 I was invited to preach the annual sermon on Missions before the Presbyterian Board. As I was but little known in New York, I surmised that my election was due to Dr. Wilson. I was invited to lodge at his home during this visit, and was entertained by him and Mrs. Wilson with unaffected, simple, and elegant hospitality. It was from this time I dated my intimacy with him, an intimacy which I have ever counted one of the chief honors and blessings of my life, and which was only interrupted by his death."

Dr. Dabney.

The late Dr. Bullock says, "My intimate acquaintance with him began in the winter of 1860-'61, in New York. He was honored and beloved by all the brethren with whom he was associated in that great work. It was a noble body of illustrious men who composed the New York Presbytery at that time. Dr. Wilson was regarded as a wise counsellor and a most efficient Secretary. He avoided discussing political questions with his brethren, as he knew they were not in sympathy with him or his people."

Rev. J. J. Bullock, D. D.

Dr. Waddel writes, "The General Assembly of 1857 met in Lexington, Ky., and I was a member of that body. At that time and place I met with Dr. Wilson and many others from the Northern States. A lady member of my family, who was an invalid, accompanied me with a view of meeting some person among the delegates from New York, in whose company and care she might prosecute her journey to that city, and place herself under the treatment of an eminent physician. As my engagements at the University of Mississippi at that time required my return to Oxford, if possible, on the adjournment of the Assembly, it was a matter of great importance to us that I should meet with such an opportunity. I felt that a kind providence had highly favored us in meeting with Dr. J. Leighton Wilson and wife, who kindly took charge of her to their hospitable home in New York city.

Rev. John N. Waddel, D. D. LL. D.

"During the following vacation in the university I visited New York, and we were so fortunate as to be received into the family as guests, and to be regarded as members of the household, enjoying all the privileges of a most delightful home. While spending this brief period of association with them, I had unusually favorable opportunity of studying the peculiar traits of Dr.

Wilson's character, not only in his home and in his private life, but in the occasional visits I paid to the office of Foreign Missions. In this way I saw in him what I regard as unusual: the manifestation of a prevalent, unvarying, and calm sincerity and kindness of heart in his intercourse with all he met. Let not this, however, be interpreted as that he was habitually 'all things to all men.' On the contrary, he was earnestly true and consistent in his treatment of every special subject and topic of discussion. Yet this earnestness of manner conveyed his views on each point without arrogance of style or self-importance. He never forgot for an instant the respect due to the views of all and every one with whom he might at any time be brought in contact.

"The combination of personal traits in his character and disposition was striking in its varied presentation. While there was always a careful preservation of dignity of manner, the result of a consciousness of what was appropriate, yet this was perfectly natural. Every one felt in his presence an absence of restraint, at the same time realizing most profound respect for him. One other trait is worthy of note, and that is a pleasing and joyous humor in which Dr. Wilson occasionally indulged, which, never transcending the limits of propriety, always enhanced the enjoyment of his society."

In the spring of 1854, during his residence in New York, the degree of Doctor of Divinity was conferred upon him by Lafayette College at Easton, Pennsylvania.

Lafayette College.

The Cawnpore massacre occurred June 27, 1857, while he was in the Mission Rooms at New York. When he heard the details of this terrible calamity, and that four of their own missionaries, with

Cawnpore.

their wives and children, were butchered in cold blood, it
was too much for his spirit to bear. It was a crushing
blow, not only to his soul but to his body, and the writer,
a mere child at that time, remembers hearing it said that
"it made Dr. Wilson sick, and that he had to take to his
bed." Never was the unity of the members of the body
more fully illustrated than by the sympathetic love that
this beloved disciple had to his brethren who were bearing the heat and burden of the day in distant climes.

One of the leading events in the joint administration
of the Rooms was the planting of a mission in
Brazil. The Rev. A. G. Symington appeared
before the Board and asked to be sent to that country.
Up to this time the Presbyterian missions had been
established in purely pagan lands, where the nations were
worshipping dumb idols. The proposition before them
now was to go to an empire where Roman Catholicism
was the established religion, and it was opposed by a majority of the Board. Dr. Wilson appeared as the advocate of Brazil. He pleaded that the young brother was
so extremely anxious to go to that field, and that his
mind and heart were so stongly drawn to its evangelization, that it should be regarded as the guiding hand of
Providence. Its first proposal was from Rev. Dr. Dabney,
who, by correspondence, "had before suggested to him
the policy of a mission to the American papal states, dwelling upon the peculiar dependence of these benighted popu-
lations on the Protestantism of their own continent, upon
the proximity and commercial relations with our own
country, and upon their partial preparation for the gospel
in the possession of languages cognate to our own, their
similar civilization and their defective knowledge of the
true God. The founding of such a mission was also
argued from the example of the apostles, who, begin-

ning at Jerusalem, always first directed their missionary efforts to the Jews of the dispersion, and obtained from them, notwithstanding their partial apostasy, the readiest and most abundant fruits.''

The Board acceded to the advice of their honored Secretary, and agreed that a *small mission* be planted in that land. It did not continue small. The Presbyterians have numerous churches, well-established schools, a religious literature, a theological seminary, and an organized synod. The inauguration of this work was one of the results of Dr. Wilson's administration.

Soon after he entered the office, by the treaty of Commodore Perry, the Sunrise Kingdom was opened to civilization and the gospel. His family physician was Dr. J. C. Hepburn, who for several years had been a missionary at Amoy, China, but was now practicing his profession in New York city. Dr. Hepburn was not only his doctor, but also his personal friend and a constant visitor at his home, and their conversations naturally turned towards this newly-opened country. The Secretary, no doubt from seeing the physician's great interest in the subject, suggested that he go to Japan. What a work this great lexicographer and Bible translator accomplished in eight and thirty years!

During his eight years in New York, Dr. Wilson was gaining an experience most valuable for his future work in the South. He was in a mission house, thoroughly organized in every respect, and was one of the executive officers of a Board fully equipped for the world's evangelization. He had had the experience of a score of the early years of manhood in the hardest of mission fields. Now he was being trained for his future and greater work in circumstances likely to develop all the powers of his heart and intellect.

He was not there, as in Africa, with his thoughts limited to one field of labor, but he viewed the wants and conditions of men upon all continents, and the whole human race passed before his range of vision.

The duties of his office were confining, but he always took regular exercise. As he lived "up-town," it was two and a half miles to Centre street, but he walked, both going and coming, and so had the needed recreation. He never allowed his body to suffer from sedentary habits.

One of his nieces writes of his home life: "Mother took us to see them, and uncle begged so hard to have us stay during the winter that she consented. I had for a companion a daughter of a missionary to India, and a most delightful two months we had. He returned from his office at 4 P. M., and dinner was served immediately, after which I would bring his slippers and dressing-gown for him, and he would lie down."

Home Life.

Far away in Africa, a missionary mother, about to die, committed her little daughter, with golden ringlets, to Mrs. Wilson's care. This child took their name, and knew no other parents than Dr. and Mrs. Wilson. She called them father and mother, and they always spoke of her as their daughter. Every evening when he came from the office he had a romp with Nelie (Cornelia) before he entertained his guests. She was a pearl in their home, their constant companion, the sharer of their joys and sorrows, and inherited the wealth of their love. They gave her the finest educational advantages, and she became an accomplished musician, which added much to the charms of the old homestead in Sumter. Under their gentle tuition she developed all the finer and lovelier graces of woman-

The Adopted Daughter.

hood, and their heart-tendrils twined around the beloved daughter by adoption. What they were to her, such loving, kind and indulgent parents, all who visited at the house knew, but the pleasure her presence and society gave to them cannot be measured. It was many years afterwards that her father, the Rev. Dr. De Heer, returned from the mission field, and as he folded his daughter in his arms, exclaimed. "Is this my little curly-headed girl?" She married in 1871 Mr. Joseph Scott, a gentleman of fine education, a successful planter, and an efficient elder of the Mount Zion Church. Several children were given them, some of whom were taken away at an early age, but two lovely daughters remain to make glad their lives, one of whom bears the name of her adopted grandmother, and upon whom will no doubt fall the mantle of her graces and goodness.

CHAPTER XXII

Charles Hodge and Leighton Wilson.

THE subject of this memoir writing to Miss Bayard, May 18, 1833, said: "An uncle of mine, a friend of Prof. Hodge's, and the Professor were together a few days since, when the latter inquired about '*a certain Wilson* in South Carolina who was going to marry his *cousin?*' Mr. James told him that Wilson was a nephew of his. Prof. Hodge said, 'There is not *a finer girl in the world* than my cousin.' 'Nor is there a better man in all the world than my nephew,' said Mr. James.''

Owing to the proximity of New York to Princeton, and the frequent visits of the Secretary to the Seminary in order to see the students who were candidates for missionary orders, the warmest personal attachment was formed between the great Professor of Divinity and his missionary brother. They were spirits eminently congenial, and for a series of years bound in bonds of the closest friendship. The fact that Dr. Wilson favored the election of Dr. Hodge's son, Dr. Casper Wistar Hodge, to a chair in Princeton Seminary, is mentioned in Dr. Hodge's memoir.

In no respect has church history brought the two nearer together than in the remark of the Princeton theologian to Rev. Dr. Samuel B. Jones, that "Dr. Leighton Wilson was the wisest man in the Presbyterian Church, and had more of

The Famous Dictum.

the apostolic spirit than any one he ever knew." When Dr. Wilson resigned his office as Secretary and came South, Dr. Hodge repeated the same in substance when he said, "Our wisest man is gone out from us."

Towards the close of their personal association there occurred a long correspondence, only very brief extracts of which are here given. The following was written by Dr. Wilson to Dr. Hodge on the day previous to the secession of South Carolina:

23 CENTRE STREET, N. Y., *December 19, 1860.*

Dr. Hodge:

MY DEAR BROTHER,—Your article on the "State of the Country" did not reach me until yesterday. I have read it and re-read it, and I do not regard it as a "fire-brand," as Dr. Boardman does. If it contains some things that would irritate the Southern people, it also contains much to soothe and command their respect. Dr. Thornwell, I understand, is preparing an article on the same subject, and I would not, if I could, abridge your liberty. [Then follow many pages.] But I will not pursue this subject further. Perhaps I have already said a great deal more than you bargained for, or are ready to read. I desire and pray most earnestly for the preservation of the whole Union. If the North will concede what is just, and what the South imperatively needs, the Union may be saved. Otherwise, we go to pieces. There are certain things in your article which the North ought to hear, and there are others which the South ought to hear. But whether upon the whole it will do more good or harm, I am not prepared to say. One thing I know, if my heart and your arm were united, and we could carry out our desires, the North would soon be compelled to relinquish some of her unjustifiable positions.   As it is, my only hope is in God, and I love to lay the matter before him.

Yours as ever, truly and affectionately,

J. LEIGHTON WILSON.

Dr. Hodge replies:

PRINCETON, *December 20, 1860.*

J. Leighton Wilson, D. D.

MY DEAR PRECIOUS FRIEND,—Your letter fills me with despair.   That a man so wise, so gentle, so good as you are, one whom I unfeignedly regard as one of the best men I ever knew, should evidently approve of what I consider great crimes, and disapprove of what I consider the plainest principles of truth and justice, shakes all confidence in human convictions.   I never felt so deeply before that opinions are not thoughts, but feelings. . . .   The difference is in the medium through which we look at the same truth, and the bearing we give it in present circumstances. . . .   If we, who love each other and who sincerely desire that truth and justice should prevail, thus differ, what must be the case of those who are not thus united, or who are animated by feelings of mutual enmity !   My article was designed for the North as well as the South.   So far as the North is concerned, it was designed to show that all condemnation of slave-holding as sinful, and all abuse of slaveholders as such, is un-Christian and wrong; that all attempts to produce dissatisfaction among the slaves are criminal, and that, to avoid the necessity of disunion and the terrible consequences, the North should concede everything possible.   I do not see how the Union can be preserved on the principles which appear to me to underlie, your whole letter, and therefore what good men

should unite in laboring to accomplish is that the disunion should be peaceable.

Your affectionate friend,

CHARLES HODGE.

Dr. Wilson to Dr. Hodge:

MISSION HOUSE, 23 CENTRE STREET, N. Y., *Dec. 22, 1860.*

Dr. Hodge:

MY DEAR FRIEND AND BROTHER,—If the difference
of views between you and myself on the general state of
the country is the cause of despondency on the one side,
it is of real heartfelt grief on the other. I have always
looked upon the contest going on between North and
South for years past with interest, and my sympathies
have always been with the South as the injured party.
So long as those who stood up for the rights of the South
were a majority at the North, I felt no uneasiness, but of
this great conservative majority, I have seen prop after
prop taken away, till the foundation seems really to
crumble.

I believe that you and thousands like you would suffer a hundred deaths rather than overwhelm your brethren at the South, but I cannot regard the leaders of the
party in power in any other light than as hostile to the
interests of the South. I do not expect to pursue this
correspondence further. I am afraid that the time for
argument has gone by, but whatever may happen, I
trust I shall always regard yourself as one of the dearest
friends I have ever had. God save us from terrible
times and scenes.

As ever, your affectionate brother,

J. LEIGHTON WILSON.

Dr. Hodge replies :

"PRINCETON, *January 3, 1861.*

"MY DEAR DOCTOR:—I am deeply grieved that my article gives you so much concern.   .   .   .   I am willing to do anything to promote peace, but I cannot suppress or repress my convictions.   I believe that what I have written will commend itself as true to nine out of every ten of its readers.   Your whole mind is turned towards the South.   You seem to forget that God has a people at the North, and that their sympathy and confidence are worth maintaining.

"Yours affectionately,

"CHARLES HODGE."

When in 1861 Leighton Wilson bade the General Assembly in Philadelphia a "sorrowful farewell," no heart was more pained than that of Charles Hodge.

CHAPTER XXIII.

The Patriot.

THE following pen-picture of a scene in the life of the Missionary Secretary is by the Rev. Dr. J. J. Bullock, the octogenarian, recently passed away:
"I met him in the early part of 1861, and his heart was deeply troubled as he saw the storm gathering, for he was an eye-witness from day to day of the intense excitement of the people, and the tremendous preparations they were making to overwhelm the Southern people, if they dared to declare their independence. He knew also the weakness of the South compared with the more populous and powerful North. I left New York in February to go to Washington to see if the Peace Convention could do anything to prevent war between the two sections of our beloved country. I called to bid Dr. and Mrs. Wilson good-bye. I shall never forget the appearance of the grand old Christian patriot when he said, 'My brother, we know not what is before us. You see the great power and the tremendous forces of the North, their intense hatred of secession, and their fixed determination to crush the South if they do not yield to the Federal government. I pray God to avert the storm and save us from the hands of civil war; but if it comes, my mind is made up, I will go and suffer with my people.' He did go, not to conquer, but *to suffer with his people*. He uttered these words with tears in his eyes and with a trembling voice. I thought I had never seen a more heroic spectacle of mingled tender-

ness and intensified courage to do and suffer as God
wills."

Dr. Dabney writes of two months previous to that
time: "He came to Union Seminary in December, 1860,
to become acquainted with our students and interest them
in Foreign Missions. I had returned from a laborious
evangelistic excursion in wretched weather, and was confined to my house by indisposition. I remember the
sympathetic kindness with which he visited me. Lincoln
had been elected on the free soil issue, and South Carolina and the Gulf States were moving towards secession.
Most of us in Virginia, though deprecating the free soil
movement as a great injustice and folly, desired not to
make the election of Lincoln a *casus belli*. I well remember my surprise when Dr. Wilson developed pretty
warm sympathies with the Carolina movement, which
we deprecated. He had been visiting some Western and
Southern Synods upon missionary affairs, and had come
from Tennessee and North Carolina to our seminary.
He reported agitation everywhere, and the spirit of determined resistance as rife in the districts he had visited.
The Union men in the North were loudly proclaiming
that the agitation in Carolina and the Gulf States was the
work of politicians, and did not express the real feeling of
the home people. We, in Virginia, had been endeavor-
ing to hope that this might not be true. I remember
distinctly my thoughts in my sick chamber when Dr.
Wilson left me: Here is a grave, conscientious, and en-
lightened citizen, a godly and moderate man, whose
home and livelihood are in the North. While I have
been secluded in my study he has been travelling extensively in both sections and has felt the heart of both.
He is no trading politician with electioneering ends to
subserve, he feels and judges in the fear of God. If,

then, such a man has given up the Union under its present administration, the schism must, indeed, be hopeless.''

One of his nieces writes of those troubled days: ''The next long visit was when I went to stay with them while uncle came South before moving in 1861. I went some weeks before he left, and remember the harrassed look in his dear face when trying to make up his mind what was his duty, also the calm that would come over it after retirement for prayer that he might be guided aright. He sold his house in New York, and our aunt, with their adopted daughter, came to stay with us in Easton, Penn., where we were then living. By the time they were ready to come South the state of public feeling was so excited that father had great difficulty in getting them through to Kentucky, to Dr. Stuart Robinson's care. They, however, reached South Carolina safely.''

First Troubled, Then Calm.

The following anecdote illustrates his sympathies at that time. One day after the *Star of The West* left to reinforce Fort Sumter, it was reported that the vessel had gone in without any trouble. Just then a friend in New York asked him to go and have some oysters. He replied, ''I do not want any oysters, if after all they have said in South Carolina they have allowed the *Star of The West* to go to Fort Sumter without any trouble.'' Very soon another report came, that the *Star of The West* had been fired upon and had left the harbor. He immediately went to his friend and said, ''All right; I will go with you for the oysters.''

Star of The West.

After he had bidden farewell to the Board of Foreign Missions, sitting during the sessions of the Assembly, and settled his accounts to the last penny, he turned his face southward and passed into Virginia at Alexandria on the very last day before travel was closed.   He came without a home, a position, or a salary.   In his memorial before the Synod, Dr. Cozby says, "Dr. Wilson was associated with many dear and honored friends in New York, whom he was loth to part with; but when the bugle notes of war sounded, and his native State called her sons to arms in defence of her dearest rights, his patriotism was stirred to its profoundest depths, and he hastened home to cast in his lot with his people and share their welfare or their woe."   He rented a small farm-house near his paternal home, and his family lived in the neighborhood during the four years of the "cruel war."

Dr. Wilson witnessed at Philadelphia the passage of the famous "Spring Resolutions" by a vote of one hundred and fifty-four to sixty-six in the General Assembly of 1861.   The Presbyterian Church made the following declaration:

"*Resolved*, That this General Assembly, in the spirit of that Christian patriotism which the Scriptures enjoin, and which has always characterized this church, do hereby acknowledge our obligation to promote and perpetuate, as far as in us lies, the integrity of these United States, and to strengthen, uphold, and encourage the Federal government in the exercise of all its functions under our noble Constitution, and to this Constitution in all its provisions, requirements, and principles, we profess our unabated loyalty," etc.

Spring Resolutions.

An able writer has said, "This paper, from its very terms, was simply a writ of ejectment of all that portion of the church within the bounds of the eleven States which had already withdrawn from the Federal union."   The Rev. Dr. Charles Hodge, with a large number of his brethren, protested against it, and declared that the Southern churches were driven "to choose between allegiance to their State and allegiance to the church."

After the passage of this resolution forty-seven Presbyteries withdrew from the old church, and sent commissioners to the General Assembly of the Presbyterian Church in the Confederate States, which was organized December 4, 1861, in the city of Augusta, Georgia. It was opened with a sermon by the Rev. Dr. B. M. Palmer, of New Orleans, who was chosen Moderator, and "was composed of men who fully represented the ability, the learning, and the piety of the whole church." Dr. Thornwell was the ruling spirit, and by his side were Drs. Adger, Bocock, S. R. Houston, Kingsbury, Lyon, McFarland, R. H. Morrison, Pratt, J. B. Ramsay, Waddel, J. S. and J. R. Wilson, and a host of worthies, with such prominent Ruling Elders as J. D. Armstrong, Wm. A. Forward, Job Johnstone, J. G. Shepherd, T. C. Perrin, Wm. P. Webb, and heroic men of like stamp.

Dr. Leighton Wilson was a commissioner from Harmony Presbytery to this court, as well as to the Assemblies of 1863 and 1865. He was ready with the first report on Foreign Missions, for by advice of the Presbyterian Convention which was held in Atlanta during the previous summer he was appointed to visit the Indian missions. His report was full of instruction and full of enthusiasm. The missionaries in that region were the first to cast in their lot with the South, and the religious work among the Indian tribes had in the providence of God been thrown on the care of the Southern church. He had met during October the missionaries at Doaksville, the capital of the Choctaw nation, and had also addressed the Choctaw council.

One notable change in the practical administration of the departments of church work made by the Assembly was the abolition of Boards and the appointment of executive committees which were placed in different parts of the church. Dr. Wilson nominated Columbia as the location of the Committee of Missions, and offered as reasons (we quote from memory), that it was in a central position, that from the number of resident ministers a committee could be formed, and that it was in proximity to the sea-coast. He was placed in charge of the foreign missionary work, and "the sublime spectacle of faith was seen of a church hedged in by a cordon of armies, looking out upon the whole world as its field, and quietly preparing herself for work in the future." During the war the churches kept the Treasury of Foreign Missions well supplied with funds, which were sent to the Indian mission and to several Southern missionaries in various foreign fields.

He was at the Assembly in Columbia in 1863 when this venerable court was turned into a prayer-meeting, beseeching God to spare the life of Stonewall Jackson. Dr. Wilson rose with the body when it adopted the paper (brought in by Dr. Palmer) from which two sentences are taken: "The dispatches announcing the severe illness of this beloved servant of God, and invoking the prayers of the Assembly on his behalf, had scarcely aroused our alarm before the sad intelligence of his death fell, with its crushing weight, upon our hearts, and turned these prayers for him into weeping supplications for ourselves and for our beloved country. . . . In the army his religious influence diffused itself like the atmosphere around him, and by that strange magnetic power over minds which is given to all who are born to command, none were drawn into his

presence who did not bow before the supremacy of that
piety so silently, yet conspicuously, illustrated in the carriage of this Christian general.''

The report on Foreign Missions this year stated that
"a number of young men whose hearts are
deeply interested in this great cause have been
in correspondence with the Mission Rooms during the
year, the most of whom, it is believed, will be ready to
go as heralds of salvation to remote parts of the earth as
soon as the door is open for them to do so.''

Volunteers.

As the Committee of Domestic Missions which had
been placed at New Orleans was disbanded
upon the capture of that city in 1863, Home
and Foreign Missions were consolidated. This
opened up a wide field of immediate influence—the work
of the evangelization of the army. "The committee sol-
emnly resolved, with the help of God, to try to have one
chaplain, or permanent missionary from our churches, in
every brigade throughout our army.'' Commissioners
were appointed to the different armies so as to obtain a
general distribution of the ministerial forces. The Secretary sent out "a circular in the form of a personal call,
and addressed it to about eighty of the ministers of the
church who were thought qualified for the work, urging
them to leave their pastoral charges and spend at least
the summer months in labors in the field. . . . .
Before July sixty of these brethren were in the field.''
(This response of three-fourths of the called is an illustrious example of heroic consecration.) Dr. Wilson
visited several of the Synods, and they not only approved
of the general plan of the committee, but gave it their
hearty support, so the Presbyterian missionaries were
distributed throughout the army and supported by a
common fund. There were seasons of revival in the

Sixty out
of Eighty.

Confederate ranks, and soldiers of the South, under the outpouring of the Holy Spirit, enlisted in the army of the Great King. The Secretary used his practical wisdom and organizing skill to keep the work of the gospel alive during the tremendous struggle. He himself resided part of the time near Mayesville, and part of the time in the Seminary buildings at Columbia. During a few months of 1864 he acted as chaplain to a regiment on the sea-coast of South Carolina.

Dr. Dabney writes: "In 1865, being with the army in Petersburg, I met him there upon his business of supplying chaplains to the army. Upon a windy Sabbath in March he preached to a South Carolina regiment in the trenches, and even administered the Lord's Supper under a dropping picket fire. He returned to his lodgings greatly impressed with the terrible sufferings and hardships which the army was enduring in the trenches, and with their cheerful fortitude and devotion. The next day I went with him to the quarters of General Lee. Here he was received and had a full and frank conference with him concerning the spiritual wants of the army. The Commander-in-Chief was as thorough a Christian as a soldier. Dr. Wilson came away delighted with his reception and with the simplicity, dignity, and cordiality of the General."

In the Trenches.

Life in the trenches! Fifty thousand of the high-born sons of the South in the trenches! The contending armies, face to face, each protected by a mud embankment, and the men living in the ditch behind it, which in the rainy season was filled with mire. If a head were raised above the breastworks, the sharpshooters immediately made it a target for their rifles.

During the latter part of the war the difficulties of transportation became greater and greater, and often the troops were upon "short rations." Knowing the needs of the Virginia army, Dr. Wilson prevailed upon the government officials in Columbia to make extraordinary efforts to forward supplies of grain, and they arrived in a time of great need.

Short Rations.

Sad were the scenes that passed under his review. He beheld the ranks of the young men around his old home decimated as this one or that one fell in battle, or died in the hospital. Among these, two were his own beloved nephews. One was Mr. Leighton B. Wilson, the son of his brother Samuel, who died September 4, 1864, aged twenty-nine. He was a student for the ministry, but left Columbia Seminary and entered the army. Here a feeble constitution succumbed to the exposure incident to camp life, and he was brought home to die.

Leighton B. Wilson.

One of his favorite nephews was the Rev. Charlton H. Wilson, for four years a missionary to the Indians, where, "by his prudence, sagacity, frankness, and conciliatory manners, he brought the special work to which he was assigned out of great difficulties.' "Few modern missionaries have been better adapted to the work or have accomplished greater results in so short a time." In 1859, on account of the failure of the health of his family, he returned to South Carolina, and became the pastor of two churches in the Pee Dee Valley. The first missionary address to which the writer listened was from his lips. Rev. C. H. Wilson received his appointment as a missionary from his uncle, and was his constant correspondent, so there were strong ties to bind their hearts together. One of the saddest duties of Dr. Wilson's life was when he was called upon to preach a memorial sermon to the flock mourning for their departed under-

Rev. Charlton H. Wilson.

shepherd. His discourse, full of tender thoughts, and preached during the last throes of that mighty contest which convulsed the South, was printed on brown Confederate paper, (as this was the only kind printers could obtain,) and is a precious souvenir of the lovely preacher who had held the threefold office of missionary, pastor, and chaplain to the army. He delivered his last message to the cavalry of Holcomb's Legion from the words, "So teach us to number our days that we may apply our hearts unto wisdom."

Just after the close of the war, the sister who went to India and returned to pass her latter years in Easton, Penn., came South to visit the sister who had come back from Africa. The niece writes: "Our next meeting I shall never forget. Mother, after four weeks of travel, reached Mayesville early in the morning to find everything encased in ice from the tops of the tallest pines to the ground beneath our feet. The meeting between the sisters was a silent embrace, but mother read in the white hair, bent form, wrinkled face, shabby dress, the want of comforts about the house, what that loved one had gone through and suffered, both mentally and physically, though not a word of complaint was uttered, either then or afterwards."

CHAPTER XXIV.

Secretary of Domestic Missions.

THE war ended in April, 1865, and the tattered veterans returned to their native States, many of them to find black and smoking ruins to mark the spots which had been the homes of their childhood. The four million freedmen were politically the dominant race, the South was for some years a military despotism, and martial law through the Cotton States introduced a reign of terror. Many of the largest and most powerful congregations were in Macedonian poverty; others were left by the war without a church officer; some were mourning for the pastors who had been slain by the sword; many of the flocks were scattered as refugees and unable to return to their homes, while general ecclesiastical disorganization was experienced throughout the Southland. Ministers betook themselves to the plow to furnish bread for their wives and children; others were without pastoral charges; many were disheartened at the dark clouds overhanging the States, and not a few from necessity united secular labor with their ministerial avocations. In some sections of the Southern Zion, presbyteries were but the shells of organizations, with a thin clerical roll and a long list of vacant churches. The fathers had fallen asleep, the generation of young men who had escaped the sword had missed a collegiate career, the theological seminaries were closed, the colleges had lost their endowments, few were left to lead in public prayer, and the songs of Zion were sung by mourning women.

For fear that some who were not eye-witnesses may conclude that the picture is overdrawn, the writer will state that during his first seminary vacation, in 1869, he supplied two small churches; one of these at the beginning of the internecine struggle had thirty male members; of the three who survived, one was a grand old elder who died the day before his arrival and another was an aged, feeble man.   At the meeting of Presbytery we heard one of the ablest of our preachers report, "The church at —— pays me punctually and regularly twenty-five dollars a quarter."

The Southern church, however, lifted up her head and rejoiced in the thought that the Lord ruled in Zion, and that the functions of his kingdom were spiritual; her ministry preached the word and never alluded to the state of the country or the circumstances by which they were surrounded.

The direction of the affairs of the church is in the hands of the Master, but at special junctures he raises up and equips mighty leaders, just as when Israel's heart was about to fail, Caleb arose and said, "Let us go up at once and possess it, for we are well able to overcome it"; or as Chalmers at the disruption, when the five hundred ministers gave up their earthly livings and moved out of their manses, not knowing whither they went, organized the finance of the church and firmly established her in the land of John Knox; so at this crisis a man of practical wisdom, executive ability, and surprising magnetism was raised up to aid in rebuilding the waste places of Zion.   Just as Paul spent three years in the Arabian desert in preparation for his great work, so were the four years of the war which Leighton Wilson passed in sackcloth ordered by Providence to bring his heart into

The Chalmers of the Disruption.

close communion and sympathy with a brave people now crushed in the dust. No sooner did the bugle call to battle cease to be heard, than he seized the gospel trumpet and with its clarion notes summoned the church to action. He was a cheerful, hopeful leader, and his presence inspired faith and courage. He breathed upon the church the spirit of consecration; he awoke the slumbering energies of the people to fresh resolve; he gladdened the low-spirited and encouraged the faint. Combining the functions of Secretary both of Home and Foreign Missions, his office became the "connectional centre" of the church, and as a corresponding agent he was a chief director of her vast interests. In the Southern Synods no one has ever equalled him in the power for good he exerted, and we believe it is impossible in the future for any man to obtain the position of commanding influence that he exercised during the ten years following our civil struggle. Did a minister find it necessary to remove from his field on account of inadequacy of support? To Dr. Wilson he applied. Did a group of churches desire a pastor? To Dr. Wilson they wrote. While one was laboring in this vineyard and another in that, he, as a general, viewed the whole field, and it was his hand of practical finance that dispensed the funds contributed for the maintenance of struggling churches. Withal he was the meekest of men, the servant of Christ and of his brethren.

In 1865 his call to the Assembly was for the "restoration of our crippled and broken-down churches." "In many places our people are not only without houses in which to worship, but are without ministers to break unto them the bread of life."

In 1866 he presented the great sustentation scheme which has been the life of our new and border churches

for over a quarter of a century. Its founder, in his me-
Sustentation. morial, says, "In the present prostrated condition of the church and country, our great
work for the present is not so much to establish new
churches, as to keep life and energy in those already
organized. The broken walls of Zion must be rebuilt
before we can expect to accomplish much in the way of
direct, aggressive warfare. But what is the actual condition of a very large proportion of our churches at the
present moment? One of utter prostration and helpless-
ness! If we can rely upon the testimony of respected
brethren from different portions of the country, very
many of these prostrated churches must soon become
extinct, or pass into the hands of others, if we do not
hasten to their help. It is proposed that all funds raised
for sustentation, church erection, or missionary purposes,
should be lodged in the hands of the committee, to be
disbursed by them. Its design is to give strength and
vigor to our weaker churches, and unite the whole in one
close, compact brotherhood. To the Presbyteries is reserved the entire absolute ecclesiastical control of all
missionary operations within their bounds. It will be
for them to appoint the missionaries ; designate the places
where they are to labor ; superintend their work ; and to
the Presbyteries alone, under the Great Head of the church,
must the missionaries be responsible for the faithful discharge of their duties. The chairman of the Presbyterial
Committee of Missions should be the connecting link
between the Presbytery and the Central Committee, and
should be regarded as a corresponding member of the
Sustentation Committee. What your memorialist believes
is especially needed, under God, to give life and energy
to our schemes of benevolence is hearty, united, and harmonious coöperation among all our churches. During

the recent conflict for political independence, the great body of our churches acted upon this principle. We had but one treasury and one channel through which the beneficence of God's people flowed. The practical result was that nearly one-half of our whole ministerial force was in the field, as chaplains and missionaries, and for a time were well supported by the united liberality of the churches.''

The committee required that the congregation should do all that could be reasonably expected, that the minister should not combine with his sacred vocation a secular calling, and that the aid was to be given for a limited period. Practically it was found that in five years the churches were self-supporting.

Go through our Southern country and see the beautiful houses of worship erected in the modern style of church architecture, many of them supporting a missionary in the foreign field, and some also a home evangelist; on the roll of sustentation, twenty-five years ago, was found this same church. As Dr. Craig says: "In the first years after the war, many churches would have fallen into disorganization but for this effort.''

Dr. Wilson was gifted as a financier in three ways:

Financier.

First, In years of financial ruin he raised more money than perhaps any other man could have done. His appeals were so earnest and solemn that the people listened and gave with a self-denying hand. One of his brother secretarys said, "When the rest of us propose a matter in the Assembly, this one objects, and that one criticises, but when Dr. Wilson asks for a definite sum, they immediately grant it.'' Second, In times of threatened disaster he would go to the liberal Presbyterians of Kentucky and Missouri, spend a couple of months going from church to church, making soul-stirring addresses, and return home with several thousand dollars to replenish an impoverished treasury. An elect lady belonging to the other branch of the Presbyterian Church annually gave him $1,000 for Foreign Missions. Third, He wisely administered the moneys contributed, and they accomplished a vast amount of good all along. If one pointed to the small collections, the Secretary could show the balance-sheet and how these gifts had sustained weak and feeble churches and kept faithful preachers from pinching poverty. We doubt if the finance of the church, in any period of the history of God's people, can show greater returns from small investments than from the money spent in Home Missions during the decade succeeding the war.

He turned his eye to the trans-Mississippi department, for it was his fear that this great section would be lost to our church. We might give the names of noble preachers, who, by his influence, went to the Synod of Arkansas, some of whom have entered into their rest, while others still labor and are blessed in their labors.

The spiritual interests of the great empire of Texas were deeply graven on his heart. The committee soon after the war sent the Rev. Dr. A. A. Porter to visit the different sections of the State, and the appeals he made on his return were stirring. The Executive Committee resolved to send out and support five first-class men. The writer remembers to have heard Dr. Wilson say he wrote to twenty prominent ministers, but each in effect replied, " My church is in a flourishing condition, brotherly love prevails, why should I leave?" Others were found to go to the "Lone Star State." In a recent number of the *Christian Observer* Dr. Dabney said, "Dr. Wilson saved Texas to our church."

The "Relief Fund" was a tree of his favorite planting.

By this scheme churches paid $30 or $60 *per annum* for
their pastor, and at his death the family received
Relief Fund. the annuity of $200 or $400 for six consecu-
tive years. The families of some ministers who opposed
the plan received benefits from it. Some years afterwards it was merged into the Clergyman's Relief Association. In 1868 the "Invalid Fund" was established,
and a collection ordered for the relief of disabled ministers, and for the widows and orphans of deceased ministers, and many were the appeals this holy man of God
made in behalf of this large and destitute class. In 1871
a separate collection was ordered for the evangelistic
work, and the church began to look out upon the destitute fields where the people had no church privileges.

In 1872 the General Assembly elected as co-ordinate
secretary the Rev. Dr. Richard McIlwaine,
Dr. Mc-Ilwaine. now President of Hampden-Sidney College,
into whose hands principally the Home Mission department fell, and by whose wise, popular, and
energetic administration the sustentation and evangelistic work was pushed forward throughout our church.
For twelve years he was the colleague of the subject of
this sketch, who greatly admired his executive ability and
the efficiency with which he managed the great cause
committed to his care.

Dr. Wilson loved the Southern church with an intense
devotion. When in latter years there was
His Love for His Church. some talk of sacrificing her principles, he said
to Dr. Dabney with solemn pathos, "If the
church should betray her mission, then I crave to die, for
there would be nothing on earth to live for. Perhaps God
sees that I idolized my country and then my church. Perhaps he means to teach me that I should have no object
but him, should trust none but him, have nobody but him
to work for, and nothing else to love."

Secretary of foreign Missions.

THIS is the most important section in the life of John Leighton Wilson. It is a matter of devout thankfulness to Almighty God that the Head of the church, in his wise providence, gave unto the Southern church, at the beginning of her history, a man thoroughly accomplished in the science of missions. Had it been otherwise she might have waited for years trying to establish the home work before entering the field which is the world; also a minister might have been chosen to conduct her missionary operations who had not the slightest knowledge of how to lay the foundations of a great work in pagan lands, and so tens of thousands or dollars been wasted in unapostolic methods of evangelization.

Dr. Dabney writes, "To me it has always appeared a splendid evidence of the faith and courage of our Southern Assembly that they should have felt themselves either able or responsible for any foreign missionary work in the terrible prostration of their country, the disorganization of their home churches, and amidst the domestic and financial ruin that was spread around them. How naturally might they have justified themselves in saying that they owed no service to the heathen and were entitled to reserve all their means and efforts for their arduous home work. The Assembly, from the first, provided for the machinery of a Committee of Foreign Missions. This brave action was doubtless due in large part to Dr. Wilson's spirit and teachings. The church to this day is feeling the sacred influence of Dr. John Leighton Wilson in her foreign missionary work. Its wonderful power and progress are largely the result of his teachings, his sustained energy and statesmanlike plans."

Dr. Waddel says, "He received, in the providence of God, the very training most needful and appropriate for his life-work at the head of the foreign department. In the first place he went as a missionary personally and dwelt among the natives, learned their manners and customs, their wants (and how to supply them) and their traits of character (and how to understand them). These two facts meet in his history, viz., his thorough and practical training in the work, and his birthplace in the South, and both pointed to him unmistakably as the leader in this sphere of the work."

It is sometimes said of the editor and the author, "*nascitur non fit.*" It might be remarked of this great Secretary, *nascitur et fit.* He possessed all the high natural qualifications for the post; grace utilized, enlarged and quickened these and added to them manifold; then came experience with its thirty years in the field and in the office and presented to our little church one of the most thoroughly furnished men in Christendom for her foreign evangelistic work. Does not this seem to point to the fact that Providence calls upon Southern Presbyterians to take a leading part in the evangelization of the world?

The Red Men of the West first demanded his attention, and, as we have seen in a previous chapter, the *Five out of Eight.* missions among them were kept alive during the fearful civil war. Soon after its close, the Rev. E. B. Inslee, who had been a number of years in

China, offered himself for service under our committee, and so the mission at Hangchow was commenced. Not long after this occurred an event which stimulated the spirit of missions in our church. Out of the eight members of the graduating class at Union Seminary in Virginia in 1868, five volunteered for work in the foreign field, and this just three years after the surrender at Appomattox. The General Assembly passed the following resolution: "The great matter which claims the special attention of the Assembly at the present moment is the missionary zeal which has recently been enkindled in the hearts of many young men, disposing them to devote their lives to this great cause. Within a few months seven young men have placed themselves under the direction of the committee, whilst a number of others are in correspondence in relation to engaging in the work in foreign lands." The consecration of these young men greatly impressed the Secretary's heart. The next winter in the chapel of Columbia Seminary he spoke very feelingly "of the three who went to China; that they had gone out unmarried, fearing lest a wife might prove a hindrance to the work, and though he differed with them, yet he admired their self-denial."

Two from the class were sent to Brazil, and founded what has grown to be one of the finest missions that the modern apostolic movement has known. Oh! that the sainted Edward Lane, cut off in the prime of life by that fell scourge, yellow fever, could enrich these pages by a graphic description of what Dr. Wilson did for the United States of South America!

Brazil.

Dwelling in his home near Mayesville as a teacher was a Christian lady, a native of Italy, a person of fine talents, rare accomplishments and sterling Christian character. Dr. Wilson suggested

Miss Ronzone.

to her that she return to her own country as a messenger of the glad tidings, and so the Italian mission was begun. It may be taken as an example of the Catholic spirit with which the Southern missions are conducted, that it was understood the results of this work were to be gathered into the Waldensian Church.

Rev. M. B. Kalopothakes, a native Greek, but educated in the United States and a member of **Greece.** a Virginia Presbytery, asked to be sent out by our church. The mission, years before, had been founded by Southern men, the Rev. Dr. S. R. Houston and Rev. George W. Leyburn. Several valuable men were sent to this classic field during Dr. Wilson's administration.

The hearts of the Southern people were drawn to the great nation just beyond the Texas border, and **Mexico.** within eight years after the close of the war a mission was planted in the historic country of Mexico. Though the number of foreign missionaries has been small, yet through the labors of gifted native preachers a promising church has sprung up in this land of silver mountains.

At the semi-centennial of Columbia Seminary in 1881, Dr. Wilson said: "This brief survey of the missionary work of our church will show that she is no idle spectator of that mighty missionary movement which aims at the spiritual renovation of the whole family of man. Notwithstanding the poverty and prostration of the country at the time of her birth, yet at no period has she ever forgotten her obligations to the great Redeemer or to a perishing heathen world. To-day she can lift up her eyes over the benighted nations of the earth and count one hundred reapers, either sent forth from her own bosom, or trained by those who were sent out by her, who are gathering the rich harvest that is ripening in every direction. She can point to scores, and hundreds, and thousands of villages and towns in Mexico, in Greece, in Brazil, in China, among the American Indians, where the good seed has been sown in great abundance. If our beloved church has not abundant cause for gratitude to Almighty God for such distinguished honor bestowed upon her, then we know not what can be a legitimate cause for joy and thanksgiving."

If just following the close of the civil strife, amidst its deep poverty, the church could enter upon the conquest of the world, how much more might now be done when her cities are built, her institutions of learning established, and her churches enjoying a measure of prosperity!

Of his visit to the Indian Territory in 1874, leaving St. Louis February 3, he says: "Mr. Balentine was on hand in the course of an hour or two after my arrival at Vinita, and engaged a spring wagon to take me to his place about seven miles distant. It was snowing at the time, but I was well protected with blanket and umbrella. I was surprised when the vehicle drove up to see that I was to be escorted by three stout young Missourians, and the first impression was that this honorable escort was intended to be a sort of offset to the bad weather. We had not gone far, however, before I found out that two of these young men had come along to break a wild colt to the harness. They meant no harm, and as they were strong men and accustomed to manage wild horses, it resulted in no harm to me. . . . I was not impressed with the magnificence of Mr. Balentine's residence. It was a log cabin, precisely fourteen feet square, and eight feet high, and had two small shed-rooms of corresponding size. We found his house, though limited in accommodation, to be the very home of content and Christian cheerfulness. It is situated on the brow of a high hill, having a beautiful and commanding view to the West.

"I reached North Fork, the principal station in the Creek country, about 2 P. M. the next day. I had scarcely stepped upon the platform when two Indian women of very modest demeanor approached me and inquired if I was not 'Dr. Wilson, of South Carolina.' The name was well known, but I was a little surprised to hear it called so familiarly by apparent strangers in this far-off corner of the world. Upon answering them in the affirmative and inquiring how they came to know me, they informed me that they were school-girls at Tallahassee when I visited the country in 1855.

"I found upon inquiry that Mr. Perryman had made arrangements with a gentleman at North Fork to send me out to his station, twelve miles distant. Without much delay, a small open wagon, drawn by two spirited-looking ponies, and driven by a small Creek boy called Mike, presented itself to take me out to the Muscogee Institute. The road for a considerable part of the way lay along the eastern banks of the North Fork River, was exceedingly boggy, and in many places utterly impassable, except for horses of the best mettle. We had not gone far before we found ourselves on the edge of a deep creek, with a frightfully muddy and precipitous descent. My first impulse was to jump out of the wagon and walk down to the water, but this I found I could not do without getting knee-deep into the mud, besides which, I could see no way of crossing the water after I got to it. Mike did not seem to be at all alarmed, and finding no help for it, I clenched my teeth and perhaps shut my eyes, and bade him go forward. A few desperate plunges brought us through the mud into the water, where we were nearly submerged, but in a few moments our horses were floundering up the opposite bank, which was quite as muddy and steep as the one which we had just descended. When we were fairly out of danger, I could scarcely refrain from hurrahing for Mike and his ponies. This stream bears the unpoetic name of 'Coon Creek.' . . . The missionaries, as I learned from others, frequently sleep in the open prairie in the summer when on preaching tours, and I know of no ministers anywhere who seem to bear 'hardness' for the Master's sake with more cheerfulness.''

In the latter part of the same year he visited Brazil, sailing on the steamer *South Carolina*, November 23, 1874. He travelled twelve thousand miles going and coming; spent four weeks at Campinas, two weeks each at Rio de Janeiro and Pernambuco, and one week at Sao Paulo, besides visiting all the principal cities along the coast. He writes on board the ship: ''As we move over these calm waters, averaging two hundred miles a day or more, my mind is impressed with two important thoughts. One of these is the vastly improved modes by which missionaries are now conveyed to their fields of labor compared with what they were forty years ago. Then they had to perform voyages, varying from one to six months, in sailing vessels, with scarcely a single comfort. Sometimes these vessels were small and cramped, and life on board them was a matter of *endurance* from beginning to end. Now, almost every missionary station in the world can be reached by steamers which are provided with almost every possible comfort and convenience. I feel truly thankful that this is the case, and no doubt these outward improvements are brought about by the providence of God for the advancement of the Redeemer's kingdom. The other fact is the wonderful zeal and energy with which men of the world are pressing forward the interests of science and commerce. Of the young men on board, one goes to collect botanical specimens on the Amazon, one to survey a gold mine in the interior of Brazil, two as engineers on the railroads, two to engage in commerce, while only one goes to make known the unsearchable riches of Christ."

"We reached Sao Paulo about 6 P. M.," he writes, January 11, 1875, "and found the Rev. Dr. Chamberlain, of the Northern Board, waiting to take me to his house. Mr. Leconte had also come down from Campinas that morning to meet us. The next morning Mr. Chamberlain took me around to see a number of objects of interest. None of these were more so to me than the grave of Ashbel Green Symonton When he commenced his labors in Rio, he was there alone, and he well knew that in that great city of a half-million inhabitants there was not one who sympathized in the great object of his mission. On the other hand, he recognized the fact that there were thousands who not only looked upon him as an unwelcome intruder, but were ready to do everything in their power to defeat the object for which he had come; but he also knew he was there by the command of the Saviour, who had promised to be with him. . . . Mr. Lane came up about 2 P. M., when Mr. Leconte and I joined him and reached Campinas before night. At the depot we found Mr. Morton and Mr. Dabney waiting for us, and in fifteen minutes more we found ourselves on the porch of the Campinas Institute, where the ladies of our mission were assembled to give me a most cordial greeting. It will be ever remembered as an event of my life."

In his thrilling report to the General Assembly, he says, "The readiness which every man you meet manifests to converse on evangelical religion; the utter disfavor into which the Roman Catholic religion has fallen with at least four-fifths of the more intelligent classes of society; the unrestrained bitterness with which the ignorance and vices of the priesthood are denounced; the readiness with which the Bible is purchased, and the remarkable results which are beginning to develop from the perusal of the sacred volume; the eagerness with which the better classes place their children under the care and training of our missionaries; the fixed determination of the government to protect Protestant missionaries in preaching the gospel; the decided success with which God has been pleased to crown the labors of his servants, go to show that the whole country is now passing through a momentous crisis. If the Presbyterians could at once commission and send to Brazil forty or fifty missionaries of suitable qualifications, it is confidently believed, with the blessing of God, Presbyterian churches would be established in every town and village throughout the empire. Brazil stands before the church at the present moment like a tree loaded with the richest fruit, which she needs only to stretch forth her hands to gather.''

Dr. Wilson favored mission schools as an auxiliary to preaching the gospel, and in his administration sustained and fostered them. He once wrote, "The mission that neglects schools will be left in the lurch." Though he encouraged teaching, he insisted that the greatest prominence be given to the preaching of the gospel.

Mission Schools.

The Secretary relied on the power of the Holy Spirit to awaken the nations. He writes, in 1877, "I have read the proceedings of the Shanghai Conference, as published in the papers, with great in-

Holy Spirit.

terest. The opening sermon by Mr. John, on the necessity of the Holy Spirit, was much to my liking. I think there is a great tendency among missionaries to rely too much on the ordinary machinery for promoting evangelistic work, and too little on the Holy Spirit, who alone can build up the kingdom of Jesus.''

So fully absorbed was he in the work of Foreign Missions that he was ever on the alert to turn the tide of finance into the mission treasury. Twelve years ago, when on furlough, we heard the following incident: "A venerable and worthy elder from Middle Tennessee was a commissioner to the General Assembly, and was very anxious to have an interview with his relative, the Missionary Secretary. When they met, the elder gave, with much pride and enthusiasm, the narrative of their mutual ancestry, to which his auditor listened with close attention. At the close, instead of referring to the illustrious deeds of the generations passed away, Dr. Wilson said: "You are a man of handsome property, consecrated to the Lord; you are also a bachelor, and have no direct heirs; in your will I would urge you to give a portion of your estate to Foreign Missions.'' The good elder returned home grieved in spirit at the suggestion. When the writer told Dr. Wilson that he had offended his worthy cousin, he was highly amused and laughed very heartily.

The regular details of his office called for thousands of letters to be written to home pastors to keep alive the flame of missions in the Southern States. By the courtesy he manifested in all his relations to his brethren, he proved that he did not seek to be "a lord over God's heritage.'' Oh! the bushels upon bushels of letters he wrote, and how much pleasure they gave to the recipients!!

The Cousin and His Money.

Home Correspondence.

His duties were performed punctually and methodically. He wrote regularly monthly letters to his brethren in foreign lands, either to the station or to individuals. These epistles were looked forward to with interest and read with eagerness. They were not manuscript sermons, or homilies on religious topics, or exhortations to the inexperienced, or appeals about seeking a higher spiritual life, but kind, fraternal, sympathetic letters, laying down no rules, nor making any regulations, and expressed so kindly that it scarcely seemed to be advice. He gave all the items of news in the church, and told much that was of interest in the Foreign Mission work. The one who opened an epistle was sure to feel that within there was something cheery and pleasant. It made those in the field know that they had a friend at home, so the office became the heart, whence the blood circulated through all the arteries and veins of the missionary body.

For thirty years a part of his regular duties was to visit annually the "schools of the prophets" and lay before the students the great needs of the heathen world. Dr. Lefevre tells of his seminary days, "My personal acquaintance with Dr. J. Leighton Wilson began near the end of 1855, when he visited Princeton Theological Seminary for the purpose of presenting the claims of Foreign Missions to the senior class, especially the claims of Siam, then a new field. Three members of that class offered themselves for that field, Daniel McGilvary, Jonathan Wilson, and myself. At that time I observed Dr. Wilson with the closest scrutiny, for I had heard a few days before an eminent minister let fall the remark that the three wisest and best men in the whole church were Dr. Wilson, Dr. Boardman, and Dr. Hodge. The result of this visit to the seminary was that Messrs. McGilvary and Wilson were sent to Siam, whilst by Dr. Wilson's advice I was left at home. On account of my general debility and some hereditary pulmonary troubles, it was deemed unwise to accept my services. My two classmates urged so kindly and earnestly that I be sent with them, that, before their departure for Siam, more than a year later, Dr. Wilson and Mr. McGilvary visited me in Baltimore and urged me to go with my friends to that great field. But poor health and engagements forbade. These incidents are mentioned only to show under what circumstances my personal estimate of Dr. Wilson was formed. You have the testimony of a disappointed man. Of course the particulars of these interviews were too personal, and some of them too sacred, for publication; but the impression, left indelibly engraved on my mind, took its original form from that casual remark made in my hearing, shaped afterwards by more than fifteen years of intimate fellowship and co-working into its permanent form, viz., 'Dr. Wilson was the wisest and best man I ever knew.'"

His yearly visits were looked forward to with pleasure both by professors and pupils, and many were **A Stir.** the earnest and prayerful conversations he had with young ministers about their duty in reference to the foreign missionary work. Under date of March 1, 1883, he says in a letter to Soochow, "I wrote to the students of Union Seminary a few weeks ago, claiming in the name of the Master, from out of the twelve students that were about to graduate, three for the foreign field. It produced such a stir as I have never known before. Almost every member of the class has written to me since, submitting their different cases, presenting the difficulties and asking advice. One was perfectly willing to go, but he was deaf and had a very feeble wife.   In another case the physician pronounced the applicant utterly unsound in health.   A third applicant had a dependent mother, sister, etc.   One, and he is a most excellent man, I have secured, and I am hopeful of another, who is also a man of great promise.''

One of the most difficult and responsible duties that falls to the Secretary's office is the appointment of missionaries.   Sending out a man who is unsuited for an evangelist gives much trouble to his associates and annoyance to the office.   Appointing one who is in feeble health may cost the church thousands of dollars.   Dr. Wilson was granted the gift of the ''discerning of spirits,'' to know and judge of men and their adaptability to the foreign field. Especially was he gifted in the selection of elect ladies of high intelligence and deep piety for the work abroad. This latter department flourished under his administration. He was their wise counsellor, trusted friend, and earnest supporter.   And one who labored for twenty years in China and Japan pronounced his character a ''combination of manly dignity, united with womanly tenderness.''

The Missionary Secretary had to watch the interests of Foreign Missions on every hand.   Many generous Christians have a misguided zeal and a desire to fly off at tangents, and their benevolence must be directed in a right channel.   Special appeals have to be held in check and moneys expended on proper objects.   At the meetings of the General Assembly, where the privileges of the floor were granted him on all questions pertaining to Foreign Missions, he was continually on the alert, lest some action be taken that would prove injurious to the great cause that lay so near his heart.

The missionary work of the Southern church would never have assumed its present proportions during his term of service had he always re- mained at headquarters. His executive du- ties combined the functions of Secretary in the office and agent among the churches. Whenever he saw the funds running low he immediately visited the more prominent churches in some State and replenished the depleted treasury. He writes, August 27, 1875, "I have often desired to write to my missionary brethren person- ally, but I have been generally so pressed with labor that I have not been able to do so. During the last ten months I have been at home only two and a half, yet as far as correspondence is concerned I have been able to do the greater part of it." Great activity pervaded the ad- ministration during the first fifteen years succeeding the war. As with the Master so with the servant; he "dwelt among men." He felt the pulse of the church and kept in touch with all of its parts.

Field Secre-
tary.

Dr. Wilson not only witnessed the fearful desolations of the war, but he also passed through the years of financial depression that spread over the Southern country. The land was bankrupt, her people in great straits and her resources despoiled. During that period it was not the question of the exten- sion of the work, it was simply its maintenance. Many promising young men applied to be sent to heathen lands, but were refused on account of the want of funds. Then followed, on successive years, the fearful yellow fever scourge which raged through the Mississippi valley. Not only were business and travel suspended for months, but the benevolence of the country flowed towards the smitten districts and the church had to suffer in conse- quence. He writes, October 5, 1878, "The Southern

Financial
Depression.

country is terribly afflicted with the yellow fever and the pestilence still rages. All the money that can be raised goes to relieve this distress. In consequence of this our receipts have sadly fallen off, and we are in no little tribulation. I expect to leave on a six weeks' tour among the churches in North Carolina, South Carolina and Georgia. If no letters are received the next month, you will know the reason." These were years of great trial to his soul. At another time he writes to the field, "I have suffered great anxiety on account of our inability to reinforce the missions. Indeed, this is the chief source of my impaired health, or rather my inability to recover from it. This is all wrong I know. It is the Lord's ordering, and I know it will be for the best. He loves the missions more than any of us can do." Again, his words burn with a holy zeal for the extension of the kingdom, "It is a hard thing, my dear Du Bose, to fill the office of a foreign secretary; *to have to stand between a dying world and an indifferent, hesitating church."*

The Church and The Heathen.

One great desire of his heart in his latter years was to see the Foreign Mission moneys reach a hundred thousand dollars. Soon after his decease the contributions went far beyond that sum. Another burning hope was to see the church begin a mission in Africa. He presented his memorial to the Assembly and it was adopted, but it was not till three years after his burial that the Lord put it into the heart of the gifted and consecrated Samuel N. Lapsley to offer for this work, who, with his colleague, the Rev. W. H. Sheppard, was sent to the Congo Free State. The auspicious circumstances under which the mission was opened proved that the hand of the Lord pointed to this benighted land. Though Alabama's young son, after a ministry

Mission to The Congo.

of three years fell a prey to the destroying fever, yet he planted a mission, which, since reinforced, under the blessing of God, promises to be a light in the Dark Continent. The mission, though it came to birth after the Secretary, who loved Africa so dearly, fell on sleep, was designed and planned by his masterhand.

Though loving the church in every branch of her work, yet to him, the one great cause, we might say the one cause, was Foreign Missions. While he encouraged every forward movement of the church's progress, yet he guarded with a jealous eye every encroachment upon the cause so near to his heart. *The Father of The Work.* In trying to awake the energies of God's people to the lost condition of the heathen, all could see that the Saviour's last command was the moving spring of his life and labors. It was this intensity of interest in the cause of the world's salvation that made his words a power. The great principle which acted as the lever to his ministry was, "This gospel of the kingdom shall be preached in all the world for a witness unto all nations." What the work of the Southern Presbyterian Church *in partibus infidelium* may become in the generations to come, eye now hath not seen, but this we may without fear assert, that the place of the father of her foreign missionary work may be assigned to her first Secretary. It was his to awaken, to inspire, to plant, to carry onwards, till she had strengthened her stakes and enlarged her coasts. As he remarked to the writer, "My little universe is Foreign Missions."

CHAPTER XXVI.

Preacher and Editor.

DURING the time Dr. Wilson was in New York, he
edited the Missionary Department of the *Home and
Foreign Record*. This required a careful inspection
of the literature of the Mission Rooms, and the presentation of the most important and interesting
facts during the month. It was a laborious
task and performed with alacrity, though at
the same time he thought a journal of this
kind was but little read, the *Foreign Missionary* being
the monthly official journal.

Home and
Foreign
Record.

He established in 1866 *The Missionary*, the monthly
official journal of the foreign evangelistic
work, and for twenty years was its editor.
There were no special gifts displayed in this
department, yet there was a power in his plain statement
of facts, a glow in his appeals, and an enthusiasm as he
portrayed the needs of the heathen and the divine influence of the gospel. One special characteristic of his edi-
torial labors was *the hiding of himself;* he wrote little
with his own pen; he asked his brethren in the field to
send articles for publication. It was the publishing of a
number of letters from missionaries in different lands
which made the little journal so popular in his day. Regularly he urged his brethren to write; to write often; to
write carefully. He insisted continually that their best
thoughts and the ablest productions of their pens should
be given to *The Missionary*. The journal was every

month filled with new and fresh letters from the four quarters of the globe.

As to his being a prolific writer, the bound volumes of the *Missionary Herald* from 1834 to 1852 abundantly testify. It is from these papers that the materials for the sketch of the years he spent in Africa were principally obtained. He wrote seven annual reports on Home Missions, and thirty on Foreign Missions; also thirty articles for religious, literary, and scientific magazines. The pages of the *Southern Presbyterian Review* were enriched with the best articles from his pen. Urging the necessity of elaborate preparation, he mentioned to the writer that one of these articles had been printed bodily in one of the newspapers, and from this copied into others, and that he had written and re-written the same six times before sending it to the press. Once the remark was heard, "Dr. Wilson's style is sterotyped." This was true only partially, and resulted from the fact that his standing subject was foreign work. It was more so in the years of his vigorous work than in his ripe and mellow years. Strange to say, but it is nevertheless a fact, that the sun of literature shone brightest towards the evening of his life. Some of his latest articles were marked by sprightliness of style and rhetorical finish. As this little memoir is filled with quotations from his writings, the reader will no doubt come to the conclusion that Leighton Wilson's pen was mightier than the sword of many a noted chieftain.

There were three topics which specially engaged his best thoughts. One was, the powers of the foreign evangelist. For some years he was on a committee with Drs. Palmer, Peck, Lefevre, and Adger to prepare an amendment to the Book of Church Order. The Assembly did not accept the report of the committee, and so after much discussion in the papers, the subject was dropped. Dr. Wilson held that the foreign evangelist carried with him all the powers of the Presbytery.

The second topic that called forth some of his best efforts was the independence of the native church that it was not to be connected with or under **One Church.** the control of European or American judicatories. He held that the Gentile convert is the Lord's freeman, and entitled to his own status in the kingdom of Christ. The third was the union of Presbyterian bodies working in the same field in foreign lands. As far as the writer knows, he was the first publicly to advocate this measure, and his paper, read before the Pan-Presbyterian Council in 1880, was the first formal presentation of the subject. It has borne fruit in the formation of National Presbyterian Churches in several lands.

Dr. Wilson had but little opportunity to preach in English. For eighteen years he preached in Grebo **A Preacher.** and Mpongwe, and the rest of his life he was talking on missions. The writer only heard from his lips two sermons, one a funeral address at the burial of his beloved kinsman, Rev. W. W. Wilson; and the other in the fall of 1866, from the words, "We preach Christ crucified," etc., a plain, earnest, gospel discourse, delivered without notes. After the retirement of Father Reid, he supplied the pulpit of Mount Zion for six months, and contributed for the purchase of a manse the $500 paid him. His friends said that Sabbath after Sabbath he would present some new glory and beauty of the Redeemer, and that his preaching all led directly to Christ. It was a period of great spiritual growth in the church. He remarked in Baltimore, "I do not like it here; I have little opportunity to preach."

Dr. J. N. Waddell writes: "There no doubt burned

within him an earnest and ardent desire for the salvation of impenitent sinners, not only in heathen, but also in Christian lands. One illustration of this I witnessed on the occasion of a visit to a western church in which one of the Synods was holding its annual meeting. At a congregational assembly on the Sabbath, before the regular services began in the morning, he was addressing the audience on the solemn topic of their personal salvation, and he dwelt upon the peril of procrastination in its hardening and fatal results. He related the incident of an Indian who had undertaken to explore the celebrated Mammoth Cave of Kentucky; how he had insensibly penetrated into the subterranean cavern until he had gone into the darkness so deeply as to have lost his way beyond the possibility of retracing his steps, and perished. The dripping of the lime rock upon his lifeless body converted his entire form into the appearance of stone. Parties afterwards visiting the cave, found the stone-encrusted body of the Indian, the victim of rash and deadly curiosity. So earnestly and affectionately did he present the case, and so deep and earnest was his manner and style that accompanied the statement of the traditional story, that it brought to the minds of those he was addressing a realizing sense of the danger of delay in seeking and securing their return from their wanderings from God before it should be too late.''

His great pulpit work was his Foreign Mission addresses. Here was his forte. When the congregation saw him rise, instinctively there rose before them the picture of all the world guilty before God, and the Son of man stretching forth his arms to save. Mrs. J. L. Stuart says: ''I heard him speak several times, and was always impressed with his intense earnestness in the cause of Foreign Missions, which seemed to be a kind of passion with him. His talks to the children were specially interesting, full of apt illustration and stirring enthusiasm." In an address before the General Assembly at Staunton, Dr. Palmer said that "when he heard Dr. Wilson's voice before an audience pleading for Foreign Missions, it always brought tears to his eyes."

Rev. Dr. R. L. Dabney writes: "I met him for the first time in the autumn of 1855, at a meeting of the Synod of North Carolina at Greensboro. The Synod assigned an evening to hear him, when he addressed a crowded house with great gravity and earnestness. His theme was the duty of the Christian world to give the gospel to Africa. The impression which remains on my mind to this day, concerning this discourse, was prominently that of the honesty and earnestness of his faith. His countenance and voice convinced us that every word came from his heart. His style was marked by a statesman-like dignity and elevation of language which affected no rhetorical graces."

Statesman-like Dignity.

"During all the long period of his secretaryship of Foreign Missions," writes the Rev. Dr. C. A. Stillman, "his appearance before the General Assembly always called forth demonstrations of profound respect and of tender regard. They always welcomed him, and listened to him with confidence and interest. He was not an eloquent speaker, and had not a particle of sensationalism, yet his noble, honest face and tones of voice, his plain statements, and his earnest, often tearful, appeals, always drew out the response of genuine Christian sympathy. I can never forget his speech before the Synod of Alabama, at Gainesville, soon after the Sepoy mutiny in 1857, when, with almost choking utterance,

Dr. Stillman.

he detailed the horrors of that event, and the sufferings of our martyr missionaries. The large audience was melted into deep emotion, and could scarcely retain their seats. Though no mention had been made of such a thing, they could not leave the house until they had made a generous offering to the cause of missions.''

The vast number of his missionary talks must be taken into consideration. On his first furlough from Africa he spoke to vast assemblies, both at the North and at the South. During thirty years he was constantly called on to make addresses at missionary meetings, at the monthly concerts, and at anniversaries. He was the leading speaker on Foreign Missions before thirty assemblies, and attended about two hundred Synods. How many thousands of our ministers and elders had their hearts stirred by his burning words, and returned home' to kindle the zeal of God's children! Words do not perish; they live in the minds and hearts of men!

CHAPTER XXVII.

Residence in Salem.

JUST after the war he purchased from his sister the old family homestead, near Mayesville, Sumter county, and made it his residence during the time he was in South Carolina. It was within fifty miles of Columbia, where the committee held its monthly meet-

The Live-Oak.

ing. The house stood in a beautiful grove of the live-oak, whose leaves, untinged by autumn's frost or winter's snow, are evergreen, emblematic of the hero-saint. When a boy he went to the swamps and selected tall, straight, young trees, without a blemish, and planted them with his own hands. They grew to a great height and of beautiful proportions, and shaded the yard during the scorching suns of summer. Under these he played in his boyhood, studied the questions of church and missions during the prime of life, and there meditated in his old age. In this house he first saw the light, and from it his spirit winged its flight to the home prepared above. During these latter years precious were the memories of childhood, of the loving care of father and mother, of the merry plays with the goodly company of brothers and sisters, and of the happy, happy home!

His adopted daughter says: "While we lived near Mayesville he went once a month to Columbia to meet the committee. The missionaries al-

Daily Life.

ways visited us, and our house was frequently a home to the seminary students during vacation. The unbusiness-like carelessness of the people in the old Mount

Zion neighborhood worried him beyond measure. He was methodical and systematic, and could distinctly remember all that happened. I have often heard him say 'I forgot' was no excuse. He rose at about half-past six, and as soon as he came downstairs he went into the study which was built in the yard under the grand oaks. There he prayed and prayed aloud, and as my doll-house was in the next room I could often hear him. I made my missionary money by sweeping and dusting his study, and he allowed no one else to attend to it, and often praised me for not misplacing his papers. After prayer in the study he took a short walk, and always brought home a flower or something of interest. He was the most generally well-informed man I ever saw. When he walked in the woods, every tree, or plant, or flower, or bird, or cloud, gave him something to talk of, and always led his thoughts and conversation upwards.''

Though living so near to Columbia, there was one serious inconvenience. This was a delay of several hours at Kingsville, twenty-five miles below the capital. The importance of this place cannot be inferred from the royal appellation. He was often in company with the late Dr. Donald McQueen, the genial pastor of Sumter, and the only possible diversion at this swamp-begirt station was to watch four big hogs—the largest in the country—feeding in their pen. Dr. Wilson playfully complained of the injustice of the railway company, that just as he was preparing to move, they should run the road direct to Columbia, making it a journey of two hours.

Always crowded with work, he made no display of the press of business in the presence of others. He sometimes laughed about a minister of another denomination, the editor of a semi-religious paper, who, returning from his Sabbath appointment, was generally a fellow-passenger on the train, and who always had the seat in front of him spread with manuscript and proofs and clippings, as if a weight of literature rested upon his shoulders.

Immediately after the war, as the section of country was entirely bereft of educational advantages, he established at his home a school of high grade for girls. *The Home Institute.* Mrs. John S. Moore, of Sherman, Texas, who was connected with it during almost the whole of its history, writes thus tenderly of her great and noble friend: "When I opened *The Missionary* for October and saw his familiar face look out from one of its pages, a flood of tender memories came over me, and I felt it would be a privilege to lay a tribute of love upon his tomb. After the war, the schools for girls in the part of South Carolina in which he lived were broken up, the people had little money, and it seemed as if many of their daughters would have to go untaught through life, pending the establishment of new schools. Seeing this want, Dr. Wilson built a school-house in his own large yard, employed as many as five teachers at one time, and thus provided an education for the daughters of that country. He filled his own house and those of his neighbors with girls, and did a grand work for a number of years, until the necessity for such a school passed away. He did this at a financial loss to himself.

"He and his good wife would have enjoyed the restful quiet of their home, undisturbed by the constant presence of school-girls, but they allowed no selfish consideration to come between them and an opportunity of doing good to others. Many girls were blessed by the Christian influences of that home, and Dr. Wilson's presence there was ever an inspiration and a benediction. Always loving and thoughtful of those around him, his kind heart and rare wisdom made him a tower of strength to those associated with him.

"We think of him oftenest with the school-girls around him, a smile and pleasant word for all; and Sunday evenings, how many, many times, when gathered in the sitting-room, before retiring for the night, he would have them sing, always closing with,

'From Greenland's Icy Mountains.'

"When men and things went wrong, he would regret it deeply, talk about it earnestly and calmly, and while sometimes indignant, he seemed to have wonderful patience with human nature. He seemed rather to deplore the errors of Christian people than to rebuke them as faults, and often said, 'The great want of the world is grace and common sense.' The great desire of his heart was the growth of the church of God, especially in her foreign work, and he believed that the more earnest her efforts were in that direction, so much more would be her development at home."

Another writes: "He offered free tuition to all who could not pay, and to the children of ministers. Pupils came from four States. Mrs. Wilson was indeed his helpmeet in every good work, and it was owing to her generosity that this project was carried through, as she sold some property in Georgia to enable her husband to start the school. Their charities knew no bounds."

This school called forth severe criticism in one of the church papers, and the correspondent called at-
Criticism. tention to the fact that the Secretary's time was given to running a large school, which was a source of considerable income. The truth was that its management was entirely in the hands of the principal and his associates, and besides paying the salaries of the teachers,

19

and this at an expense to himself, his only connection with the Institute was conducting morning prayers.

A niece says: "Once when surrounded by the romping girls of Home Institute, Mrs. Wilson said, 'I do not think any one can imagine what a trial it is to me to have so many young people about. My solitary life in Africa for eighteen years has made me draw within myself.' I replied, 'I think uncle enjoys it, and he was out there the same length of time.' Mrs. Wilson responded, 'Oh! your uncle's big heart takes in the whole world.'"

While martial law prevailed in South Carolina, the freedmen throughout the State were in a state of great excitement. A house-servant reported Dr. Wilson to the Provost-Marshal, but upon his representation of the affair at the office, the case was dismissed. The following is a copy of the orders he received:

H. Q. U. S. FORCES, SUMPTER, S. C., *June 14, 1866.*

Dr. Wilson:

SIR,—The Freedman Harrison English Complains at this office that you have accused his wife, Julia, of thieving without cause, and turned her out of your employ, paying no regard to your contract with her. this conduct is rong, the woman says she wants to work for you till Janry next. if she has done any rong, prosecute her, and the court, if she is found guilty, will relieve you from the contract. otherways if you do not permit her to return to her work, will hold you responsible for her wages and Board.

M. BOYEN,
Provost-Judge.

The estimate in which he was held by the colored people was shown in a very practical way. Emancipation

seemed to develop an appetite for fried chicken, so in
the barnyards of the planters there was a scarcity
Chickens
  Safe.   of poultry. While others could not protect
their fowls by night with lock and key, Dr.
Wilson's chickens roosted in the trees, and not a feather
was ever touched.

He was never unmindful of the wants of the sons of
Africa. A night-school was kept up for them
Mount Sinai. for years, and a house provided in which they
could worship on the Sabbath. He ever stood ready to
preach to them and to teach them the Bible whenever
they should come. One summer he employed a young
man from the Seminary to do missionary work among
them. During the last year of his life, he refused to
preach at Mount Zion, the church with a white member-
ship, but he was always ready for service at Mount Sinai,
where the colored people worshipped, a church which he
aided in building. His last sermon was to his friends of
African descent.

His love for gardening, which was developed so fully
in Africa, was again seen in Salem. His gar-
The Garden. den was his pride. Missionaries from many
lands sent him rare seeds, and he watched the growth of
the plants with great interest. He had a fine assortment
of vegetables throughout all of the summer season.

A nephew, a worthy elder, writes: "You know how
poor we soldiers were after the war ended. Some friend
of his sent him a cloth coat to be sold to the negroes. It
was such a good coat that he and his wife came to see if
I was too proud to wear it. It fit me as if made for me,
and they made me a present of it. I kept it as a dress-
coat, and wore it when three of my children were baptized, and when my boy was ready for college, I gave it to
him.

Rev. J. L. Stuart, of Hangchow, writes of a visit to the old home : "Greatness and goodness were
Simplicity of
His Habits. conspicuous traits of his character which were known to me a long time before another trait was brought to my knowledge.   It was on a visit to his own house in the country, which it was my privilege to pay him in 1874, that I was so surprised and gratified to observe the simplicity of his habits.   I well remember that short but delightful visit to the quiet and simple home of this grand man.   He treated me with such kindness and cordiality as to win my heart completely, and the place in my affections, which had remained vacant since the death of my own father, came as near being filled by this dear *father* as possible.   Ever after that I looked up to him more than to any other man on earth, as unto a father, and I felt sure his big heart would act a father's part by me if ever there should be a need of an appeal to him.   Only one night was spent under his roof, but how vividly the picture of that old-fashioned house, and especially of the simply-furnished room occupied by me, remains in my memory !   At bed-time he showed me to my room, he looked around to see that everything was in order, he gave directions to me to call him if there should be need of his service in the night, then with his benediction he left me.   But just as he left he called my attention to the button on the door-frame and said, 'You may bolt your door if you like.'   And the thoughts that occurred to my mind at that time have lingered there ever since, and they most fittingly sum up his chief characteristics as they have occurred to me.   They were these : How strange, yet how pleasant it is, to see one who is so great, at the same time so kind in manner and so simple in habits.''

CHAPTER XXVIII.

Love for Children.

THE Master said, "Except ye be converted and become as little children ye shall not enter the kingdom of heaven." Nothing goes to show, in a greater degree, the simplicity of character of the great Missionary Secretary than his love for children. We have never known any other Secretary, there may have been others who would write to the children of missionaries in the field, but he counted it a pleasure, when writing to the father on business, to enclose a line to his far-away little friends. He knew their names and took the warmest interest in their welfare. He carried on a brief correspondence with numbers of children throughout the church who had missionary hens or canaries, and who used their tiny efforts to send the gospel to those who worshipped stocks and stones. The children in the households of his friends were his special pets, and many a little tot from hearing his African stories had a longing desire to go and teach the heathen.

His niece tells of his coming home on furlough from the mission field: "Aunt Jane had written that she had a parrot for me, so one day my brother Leighton and I were playing in the front yard of a large country house when we noticed a carriage drive up with a parrot's cage hanging in front. We little things rushed into the house and announced the fact that Uncle and Aunt Africa had come and brought

my parrot, which greatly amused him when told of it,
and up to the last of his life he often referred to the name
I gave him. Father told him he ought to feel compli-
mented that 'even the children in America knew him by
his work.' We sat, the one on one knee, and the other
on the other, and were fascinated with his stories of
African life.''

The following picture of home life is from Miss Johnson's
pen: ''Adele Wilson and Dora Hudson, both his
Doll Party. nieces, were my best friends, and we often invited him to our doll tea-party in the room adjoining his
study. He always accepted the invitation and drank
hot-water tea. He took great interest in his garden, and
once the pets were some fine tomatoes which he watched
with interest. We children were also watching them,
and when they looked ripe we gathered them for our
doll party and invited him to dine with us, and I can
never forget how kindly he told us never to pull those
tomatoes, but gave us permission to take what we wanted
of other vegetables. A request from him was enough.
I never heard him give an order. He treated a child
with as much courtesy as he did a guest.''

A lady missionary, whose father (Dr. Woodrow) was a
most intimate friend of the subject of this memoir, writes,
''Dr. Leighton Wilson was one of the first and dearest
friends that I remember having as a child, for he was
always so kind to children. We welcomed the time
when he came to our home in Columbia to attend the
meeting of the Committee of Foreign Missions, for he
had a great store of amusing anecdotes of his life in
Africa that he was always willing to tell us. He seemed
to enjoy remembering, as we did hearing of, his many
adventures among these wild people. As a child I made
him and Mrs. Wilson a good many visits, and shall always

think of the time spent in their happy home with the greatest pleasure.''

Another, now laboring in China, says, ''As a child I was impressed with his beautiful home life, the gentleness, courtesy, and consideration which marked his intercourse with those around him. Often he would come in from his day's work, and throwing himself on his lounge he would say to me, 'My dear, if you will come and comb my hair, I will tell you about Africa.' I need not say that I desired no greater incentive, for his talks about his life and experiences in that Dark Continent had a peculiar fascination for me. Sometimes his pathetic stories would bring tears to my eyes and, again there would be a hearty laugh over his funny experiences. His heart was full of love for the work there and for the people of that land. It was during these days of early childhood spent under his roof that the desire to be a missionary was first implanted in my heart. Once I said, 'Uncle Leighton, I would like to be a missionary some day.' He replied, 'My dear, nothing would give your uncle more joy than to have you become one. He was very fond of children, and took great delight in giving them pleasure. When I was eight

Birthday.

years old Aunt Jane gave me a birthday party. Uncle Leighton came from Columbia just a few hours before my little guests arrived, bringing me all sorts of things that would gladden the heart of a child. He came in and watched us at our games, even taking part in them and crowning me with a wreath of roses woven by young friends, and finally took tea with us. I remember we all thought this a great honor. He had a great deal of quiet humor about him which showed itself in his home life.''

Dr. Wilson was great in the kingdom because he became as a little child. He had what the philosopher Mencius terms "The child's heart." He associated with divines, ecclesiastics, and theologians, and with them discussed the great questions of the church, but he could turn aside from these to the children, join in their games, and play with them in as childlike a way as if he himself were a little child.

CHAPTER XXIX

Life in Baltimore.

IN 1876 the office of Foreign Missions was removed to Baltimore, in order to secure a better financial centre than Columbia at that time afforded. This was the last scene of his labors. Here he enjoyed the society of noble men, and was specially intimate with his brethren on the committee, Drs. Bullock, Lefevre, and Murkland, and with Messrs. J. Harman Brown, J. F. Weeks, Geo. F. Anderson, C. F. McKay, LL. D., and other worthy ruling elders. He sat under the ministry of Dr. Murkland in the Franklin-street Church, and enjoyed his eloquent evangelical sermons. He was once confined to his room for three months with rheumatism, and Dr. Murkland visited him regularly, and conferred with him in regard to spiritual hope and experience. The hearts of the aged and the young minister were drawn very closely together during the time the former lay upon a couch of suffering.

His family physician was Dr. Carey Gamble, who was not only a distinguished practitioner, but also a most enthusiastic and devoted friend. He watched over Dr. Wilson closely during this term of years, and was his constant visitor and admiring companion. Dr. Wilson reciprocated to the fullest extent the loving sympathy and tender regard of this "beloved physician."

Dr. Gamble.

One marked feature of Dr. Wilson's administration was his securing able and trusted counsellors. The two resi-

dent ministers, Drs. Lefevre and Murkland, were consulted on every important step in the direction
of the missionary work.   Thus, when his views
were brought before the committee they were
fully matured, and generally met with a hearty approval.
This trait of his character is to be specially emphasized:
his readiness to listen to the views of his younger brethren, and to adopt them if they commended themselves to
his judgment.   One of the highest marks of wisdom is
"not to rely on your own understanding."   Dr. Murkland
says: "He was one of the best and noblest men I ever had
the privilege of knowing, and he honored by his life and
counsels the holy cause to which that life was consecrated."

As Dr. Wilson's ministry was given to earnest appeals in behalf of a dying world, he appeared
to many as a solemn man.   To those who knew
him well he was jovial and full of humor, and though
seldom given to joking, he laughed heartily at a good
anecdote and enjoyed merry company.   This led some of
his brethren on the foreign field to adopt the vivacious
style in addressing their communications to the Secretary.
He so thoroughly enjoyed the amusing side of life in the
Orient, seemed so entertained by striking incidents, and
replied so spicily, that his young correspondents were
disposed to let their letters to the Rooms be a relaxation
from the severer duties of evangelistic labor.   So close was
the connection between the field and the office, that when
Dr. Wilson withdrew from the work the writer felt that
the portcullis was dropped, and he was separated from
the home-land; but happily the human heart can form
new ties and relationships.

In 1878, in the midst of financial ruin of the country,
he writes: "I have often felt tempted to send out all the

missionaries who apply, irrespective of the debt that

would be incurred, but I suppose if I were to
do so in the existing circumstances, I would be

Hunting Rabbits.

sent back to the swamps of South Carolina,
not to hunt rabbits as in my younger days, but to be as
Jeremiah in the boggy dungeon, which I confess I do
not covet with my present stiff limbs.''

Miss Johnson says: ''While we boarded at the Albion,

there was a social club composed exclusively of
the gentlemen and ladies of the house, and he

Kings and Queens.

was invited to lecture. He began very humor-
ously by telling them he felt honored in being invited to
address so select an audience, but then he was accustomed to honors. Once, for example, he had kings for
his cooks and queens for his porters, and went on to
mention the various instances where he received distinguished honors upon the shores of Africa. He mentioned that once he had fifty queens and prominent
women offered to him as wives, and upon his declining,
the animosity of the tribe seemed to be aroused on this
account, and the guides heard them saying that they
would kill him and see how white flesh tasted, and so he
thought it expedient to leave the cannibal country in the
middle of the night. He was very popular in every circle he moved in. I have often noticed that in a large
boarding-house every one loved him, and he had a kind
word for all.''

During the last two years in Baltimore he submitted
everything he wrote for publication to Mrs. J. N. Craig
for criticism. It is stated that he considered her ''the
most intellectual lady he had ever met with.'' She
writes, ''He would submit his papers to me because I
had leisure, and would patiently and interestedly attend
to what he had to say. At such times he would tremble

with excitement at the unavoidable conviction that the affairs of the church were slipping beyond his cognizance and control."   Miss Johnson says, "Once I heard him read an article to Mrs. Craig for her approval, and in the next paper Mrs. Wilson read it and told him that some one else had his views on the subject, and begged him always to wait, and that some other minister would save him the trouble of writing upon the questions before the church, that he was always too ready to rush into print. She had not noticed that the article was from her husband's pen."

His niece records the following incidents: "One day he was reading *Harper's Magazine* attentively, and I remarked, 'You seem to have changed your mind about Harper.'   'Yes, this is really a fine number, but for months I have not seen an article worth reading.   I wonder why they will publish things nobody cares to read.'   I said, 'I do not know what you think of your wife and niece, whether we are anybody or not, but we read most of the articles with interest;' and then added, 'I am willing to wager anything that this particular number has something about Africa, and that is the reason you think it is such a good number.'   He laughed heartily, and said, 'You audacious witch! how did you know it was about Africa that I was reading, and how dare you talk to your old uncle in that way!'

"He went to dine with a cousin of his wife's who was an infidel, but a gentleman of rare cultivation, who knew perfectly well how to adapt himself to those in whose company he was thrown; quite a versatile man, and not only a good talker, but also a good listener.   Uncle did not want to go, but on his return he said, 'Anna, daughter, I think there must be some mistake about your Cousin ——'s religious opinions.   He is intensely interested on the subject of missions.' I exclaimed, 'Cousin —— interested in missions! they are his special detestation.' Aunt Jane laughed and said, 'He asked your uncle some leading questions about Africa, and he talked the entire time on that subject. I noticed as soon as Mr. Wilson began to talk about missionary work, Mr. —— would put in a question that would bring him back to the general subject of the country and people, and on leaving he thanked your uncle for the very lucid way in which he had explained some points he had not previously understood about the tribes, languages and customs.' Our cousin was really very much interested in the conversation, and said he had gained a great deal of information. He afterwards said to me, ' If all Christians were like that uncle of yours, I might say, *Almost thou persuadest me to be a Christian.* But, Anna, can you imagine a man to have lived to his age, travelled as much as he has, met with various classes of people at home and abroad, and yet have but one idea?'

One Idea.

I replied, 'The grandeur of that man's character is its oneness. His motto evidently is, *This one thing I do*, and from the time he rises in the morning and addresses the throne of grace, asking for guidance through the day, until he retires at night with thanksgiving for the wisdom given in answer to prayer, everything that he hears, reads, or talks about is some way or other connected with his life's work. He so realizes the vastness of the work that he is overwhelmed, therefore calls on God that his strength may be made perfect in weakness, and consequently he is sublime in his own childlike simplicity and God-given strength.' He said, 'I do not understand it, but there is something grandly simple in him that I never saw in another.'"

His long experience in the field with a true and worthy helpmeet, led him to encourage missionary candidates to lead about a sister as Peter or other of the apostles. He writes from Baltimore, "—— has been appointed to China. He is a pious man, a good scholar and very gentlemanly in deportment. He has not selected a *victim* to go with him, and I do not know whether he understands the art of *skirmishing*, without which it will be almost impossible to find the right one."

Encouraged Marriage.

The death of young brethren in the field caused him much grief. Under date of June 17, 1880, he says, "The sudden and unexpected death of Mr. Thompson of Pernambuco has created quite a sensation throughout the church, and I earnestly hope it will be overruled for good. Mr. Wardlaw, as soon as he heard of the death of his friend, telegraphed that he would be ready to go by the July steamer, provided the committee was ready to send him."

In 1879 he writes, "On the 25th of this month I shall be threescore and ten. I am aging fast, because I cannot get Christian people to feel as they ought to do in relation to the great work of evangelizing the world; still, I believe we are making progress, but it is slow."

At Seventy.

Two years before this he says: "In every way I was comforted by my visit to South Carolina. The people have no money, but their prospects are cheering. Wade Hampton is a prince. The legislature really looks like old times; only a few negroes to be seen in either body. All the carpet-baggers and scalawags are either in jail or have fled."

Wade Hampton.

One after another of the Wilson family dropped off as they reached a ripe old age: "Baltimore, June 3, 1881,

I have just heard of the death of dear Brother Flinn.
How little did I anticipate this when I saw you both
a month ago.   He is gone to a better world;
you are to remain here a while longer, and then
to follow.   I have no doubt about his preparation for the change, and I have as little doubt
about your preparation to follow him when the time
comes for your departure. We are timid and fearful
about the approach of death, but simple trust in Jesus
Christ as our Saviour is all the preparation that any of us
need.   You will no doubt feel the loss of Flinn as a part
of your being, and will be reaching out your hands to
touch him from time to time.   He and I have been intimate for near seventy years, and I cannot recall that
there was ever an unkind feeling between us. You have
to look steadily to Jesus in this trying dispensation.
He alone can sustain and strengthen you, and he will
not be slow to hearken to your prayers.''

To Mrs. Mills: ''January 22, 1884, I received a letter
from Brother Robert last night informing me of the
death of our dear Sister Mary [Mrs. Flinn Wilson].   It
did not occasion either surprise or grief.   I was rather
comforted at the thought that she was at rest.   But how
we are being reduced as a family ; only you, Robert, and
myself!''

The writer met him in Columbia in 1881, at the Synod
of South Carolina.   He remarked, ''I have just come
from the death-bed of my brother Samuel.''   ''Is there
no hope for his recovery?'' was the inquiry.   ''I do not
want him to get well,'' was the reply.   When a few
days afterwards we saw the giant but wasted form of the
grand old elder, now unable to know what was passing
around, we appreciated his words.

While in Baltimore he quietly passed the fiftieth anni-

Golden
 Wedding.

versary of his marriage. What a happy union! It was May 21st, and the General Assembly wired its congratulations to the aged servant of Christ and his faithful wife. We are of the opinion that this is the only time in the history of the church that its highest court pronounced its parting benediction upon a united couple now celebrating their marriage jubilee. They had passed the spring-time of life at Cape Palmas and the Gaboon diligently sowing the seed; they had spent the summer of toil in New York and Carolina; now the golden autumn was calmly gliding by in Baltimore ; but no chill winter comes to the noble old hero and heroine of the cross, for luminous in the western sky is the radiance of the setting sun.

Losing
 Strength.

Mrs. J. N. Craig writes: ''There are few things that can be said of his last days in Baltimore. They were so quiet, and yet so busy; his mind too active for a body that was fast failing. It was sad for us who loved him to see the great strong man gradually yielding to the mortal. Some days, after working vigorously for hours at the office, he would start up the familiar street which for years his feet had walked in safety and strength, when suddenly the mind would become bewildered, and the limbs refuse to act, and some kind passer-by would see his condition and lead him to his rooms. He would suffer great mortification when his will-power would re-assert itself, at the thought that he had become timid and helpless as a child. I have never seen a stronger will, nor so gentle and sweet a nature. It was this will which enabled him to exercise such control in Africa when often his life was in the hands of savages, and this gentleness which made all little children love and revere him. He sought by every opportunity to do good, and I never knew him to be thrown with a young person, or to take a little child upon his knee, that he did not in some kind and cheerful way seek to impress some thought that might yield future results.

"I suppose the very last talk he made upon his work in Africa was at Orkney Springs, Va., in 1884. Quite a crowd of guests from the hotel and cottages gathered late Sunday afternoon under the shade of a wide-spreading tree.

Last Missionary Address.

The surroundings seemed to inspire him, and he became eloquent in his appeals; but the effort was too much for him, and was as though the fire of his youthful enthusiasm had burst forth once more for a moment, then went out. The excitement made him restless and sleepless for days and nights. It was during this summer that I had the privilege of daily companionship with him, and I watched with interest his anxiety about the future of the church. His faith in God was implicit; his peace of mind with regard to himself and his own personal affairs was perfect."

"He continued to serve the church," says Dr. Waddel, "until he was reluctantly permitted to retire to that quiet, private life he had merited

Resignation.

so long by arduous and faithful service, and which he was admonished by the pressure of advancing age, with its infirmities, was absolutely essential. He sent his letter of resignation to the General Assembly at Houston, Texas, the substance of which is given: Referring to his past labors in the office of Secretary, he expresses his grateful sense of the great kindness and repeated words of the Assembly's appreciation of his work. He speaks of the painfulness of separating from a work which, for an unusually long period, had been the chief joy of his life; but as he had attained the seventy-seventh

20

year of his age, he considers it justice to the General Assembly, and to the work of missions, that he should withdraw from a position which could be more effectively maintained by a younger and more vigorous servant of the church.   Cordially he congratulates the General Assembly upon the favorable circumstances under which he is permitted to withdraw from service, and at so auspicious an era in the work of missions, when it combines within itself all the essential elements of hope and prosperity.   He closes his letter by expressing to the Assembly the profound gratitude he feels for the confidence that has been extended to him during all these years, the remembrance of which will be the chief solace of his remaining days. Secondly, with characteristic, affectionate unselfishness, he bespeaks for his successor in office, and for the executive committee, the same kindness and confidence which he himself had enjoyed, and with his native tenderness of heart he reminds the Assembly that all the sympathy that can be extended to them will be needed ; nor does he forget to bear cheerfully his testimony that each of the committee had uniformly discharged his responsible duties with singular ability, and he bespeaks for them the thanks of the whole church.''

The General Assembly adopted the following resolution : ''While we think it due to him that he be released from the burdens and responsibility of the office, yet believing it would be injurious to this great cause for his connection with it to be severed, we recommend that his resignation as Secretary of Foreign Missions be accepted in so far as to relieve him of all work and responsibility, and that he be appointed Secretary Emeritus, and that he be entitled to draw a salary of one thousand dollars annually, so long as God continues him among us.''

Dr. M. H. Houston had been elected Assistant Secretary the year before. Writing to Mr. William
E. Mills, June 10, 1884, Dr. Wilson says,
"The Assembly has given me a most excellent
assistant in Dr. Houston. He has already lightened my
burdens. A better man could not have been found in
the whole church. He is pious, talented, level-headed,
and truly loyal to the Southern church. He could have
had a professorship in Union Seminary, but he preferred
the missionary work, and I am glad of it."

His Suc-
cessor.

Mrs. Craig continues, "In the fall of 1884, soon after
he returned to Baltimore, he made up his mind
to retire to private life. There are days and
scenes which come but once in a generation,
and such a day and scene was that when this mighty
man of God, this valiant servant of Christ, bade farewell
to his co-laborers in the Mission Rooms in Baltimore,
and quietly and serenely walked out from the place
where his strong spirit had ruled with wisdom and faithfulness for thirty-three years. He laid down his life-
work as calmly, and with the same *sublime faith in God
and consciousness of duty performed*, as on that day when
in his strong young manhood he entered the jungles of
Africa as a pioneer missionary."

Leaving
The Office.

He came into the office one morning and talked with
the Secretaries of Home and Foreign Missions. He said
that the night before he began to think upon some church
question, but that he became so nervous and excited that
he thought he would die there in his room, and that he
was convinced that it was time for him to withdraw from
active service. He talked cheerfully till the time for the
train to leave, then arose, and shaking hands, said,
"Good-bye Brother Craig," "Good-bye Brother Houston," and walked away with a firm, stalwart step, leav-

ing the Secretaries with tearful eyes standing fixed in
their places.   Dr. Craig said, "Brother Houston, we
shall never see a sight like this again in our lives.   A
man after a half-century's toil for Foreign Missions laying down his commission and going home so calmly to
die."   It was a fitting *finale* to his official career.

CHAPTER XXX.

His Last Year.

D R. WILSON left the office to retire to his home in
Salem, and here, in green old age, unable to work
actively in the Lord's vineyard, he interested himself in the farm and garden, watched with interest the
growing corn and the beautiful fields of cotton, looked
after the stock on his place, and thus kept himself employed with easy out-door exercise, much to the delight
of his friends, who feared if he should relax his efforts
that he would immediately fall into a decline. Dr.
Cozby, in the memorial adopted by Synod, says, "From
an almost daily intercourse with this man of God, after
his retirement from official responsibilities, the writer is
able to say Dr. Wilson was to the last the same great-
hearted man that he had ever been. His zeal for the
cause of Christ did not flag, even when his bodily infirmities increased, his interest in the church never abated.
Even when he had taken his bed to die, and when too
feeble to converse, he would request that the church
news be told him in as few words as possible."

Miss Johnson writes, " During the last year of his life
his eye-sight became very poor, and with the
Failing Sight. exception of reading the Bible in the morning,
that being good type, he was unable to use his eyes
during the day, and I often, during the heated discussions that were going on at that time about evolution,
read to him several hours a day."

Mrs. Craig says, "No record of Dr. Wilson's life would be perfect without some reference to the orphan girl whom he brought up and educated, and whose presence cheered and ministered to his last days with great faithfulness, and whose hand he held in his as he went down into the valley of the shadow of death. Alice is the daughter of a Presbyterian minister, her father and mother both being dead. Dr. Wilson heard of her in 1870 and received her into his family. When she was quite a child he desired that she should take his name, and was much impressed by her refusal, on the ground that her father's name was Johnson and she preferred to keep it. He seemed gratified at her affectionate devotion to her father, and asked, 'Will you be as faithful to my memory when I am dead?' She nobly rewarded their faithful care, and the affection between herself and Dr. Wilson was very beautiful. There was never a time that he did not show the utmost devotion to her, and he and Mrs. Wilson stated repeatedly that they desired she should stay by them and be their support and comfort in declining years."

Second Adopted Daughter.

Fifty-one years had passed since the young missionary, returning from his first voyage to Africa, led his bride to the altar. Now comes the time when the aged husband and wife must part. She died after a brief illness, July 16, 1885, in the seventy-ninth year of her age. She made one request, and that was that no obituary notice of her should be published; so in the religious papers appeared simply the announcement, "Our dear friend, Mrs. J. Leighton Wilson, is dead. She enjoyed the consolations of God in all her sickness, and with a comforting faith in Jesus Christ she quietly fell asleep. Her beloved husband, with whom she had walked for more than fifty years, was with her to

Death of Mrs. Wilson.

the last moment of her life. The grace of God sustains him in this sore bereavement.''

''Before leaving home,'' says Miss Alice Johnson, ''for a visit to the New Orleans Exposition and to friends in Texas, Mrs. Wilson told me that she felt she would not live long, but as for three years she had often said this, I did not attach any importance to her words. She told me in case she died she wanted my promise that I would take care of Dr. Wilson. I had not been in Texas three weeks before I received a telegram telling me of her death. I can never forget the night I arrived home. Dr. Wilson had given directions to Adele, who was stay- ing with him, to tell me to go to him as soon as I arrived. He broke down completely, and 'my child!' were the only words spoken as he folded me in his arms.''

Mrs. Essie Wilson Price gives the following description of Mrs. Wilson's funeral: ''At Mount
Her Burial. Zion cemetery a great number of friends and relatives had gathered to pay their last tribute of affec- tion to his beloved wife. The coffin was borne to the grave by the loving hands of nephews and grand-nephews. As we stood around the grave some thoughtful friend brought a chair for Uncle Leighton, who was quite feeble at that time. He would not sit down, but supported himself by resting his hands on the back of the chair. After the grave had been covered with flowers and the benediction pronounced, he, with his head still un- covered, and with that old-fashioned courtesy so char- acteristic of him, said distinctly, but with a voice trem- bling with emotion, 'My friends, I thank you.' And afterwards as friends gathered around to offer their sympathy I merely went up and slipped my hand in his. He turned immediately and, kissing me on the forehead, said, 'Poor child, you have lost a dear friend!' thus

showing in his deep grief his forgetfulness of self and thoughtfulness of others.''

Going back to his silent home he found there a letter from the new Secretary of Missions, making inquiries about some special matter. He sat down immediately and replied that he had just returned from the funeral of his wife, he mentioned her sickness and her calm, happy death, then answered fully all the questions that were asked in reference to the work in a plain, business-like way.

The China Mission at its fall meeting appointed one of their number to write a letter to the venerable Secretary, expressing their sympathy for him in his bereavement, assuring him of their prayers for him in his declining years, and referring with gratitude to the fact that he had loved this mission before any of those who signed their names had come to the field. He wrote in answer his last letter to the mission:

"MAYESVILLE, S. C., *March 1, 1886.*

"*Rev. H. C. Du Bose and the Members of the China Mission:*

"VERY KIND FRIENDS.—Your favor of 27th October, 1885, was received about ten days ago. I cannot express to you in any language that I can command the true amount of comfort it afforded and will afford me till the close of life. I have ever felt the deepest interest in the China Mission and the great work in which you are engaged. Then the perfect harmony that has always existed between you and myself is one of the greatest and sweetest recollections of my old age. You and your work are almost constantly before my mind, and particularly so in my approaches to a throne of grace. Be patient, be persevering, and always trusting in the Lord, and your reward will certainly come in due time.

"I am living a very quiet and peaceful life in the old homestead where I was born, which I suppose Brother Du Bose remembers. Alice Johnson, an adopted daughter, whom Mrs. Randolph probably remembers, lives with me, takes care of me, and is all to me that a daughter could be. I am surrounded with friends who love the missionary cause. I will be seventy-seven years old on the 25th of the present month, if I live to that time. My decline in strength is very gradual, and is alleviated by many mercies. I look to the end with much comfort, having learned from my dear wife how to die, if I may say so. My vision is declining very sensibly. I can neither write or read without difficulty. Alice reads to me one or two hours every night.

"Dr. Lefevre, Chairman of the Committee of Foreign Missions, did me the great favor to make me a visit last week, coming all the way from Baltimore for that purpose. We had much talk about the missionary work in which he feels very great interest. And now, dear friends, my prayer is that God s best blessing may rest upon you and yours, and the great work in which you are engaged.

"Very affectionately,

"J. Leighton Wilson."

At the quarter-centennial of the Assembly, a letter was received from Dr. Wilson, of which extracts are given:

"Old Homestead, Mayesville, S. C., *May 22, 1886.*
"*To the Venerable General Assembly about to convene in Augusta, Ga.:*
"The writer takes the liberty to address a word of cheer and encouragement. He aided in organizing the Pres-

byterian Church in the United States twenty-five years ago, and has been engaged in her public service, except the last year, ever since that time. He has done, with the help of God, what he could to promote her best interest at home, and through her agency to extend the blessings of salvation to the distant nations of the earth. The only possible object he could have for wishing to live longer here below would be to promote these same great objects. It would be both a pleasure and a privilege to meet brethren in the approaching Assembly, but the condition of his health is not sufficient to authorize him to undertake the journey. He can, therefore, only tender his sympathies and his prayer that the Holy Ghost may preside over the proceedings, infuse them with the wisdom and grace that cometh down from on high, and that our beloved church may enter upon a new course of usefulness, and become one of God's favored instruments for extending his kingdom over the earth. With sentiments of unfeigned Christian affection," etc., etc., etc.

A special committee, consisting of the Rev. J. N. Waddel, D. D., LL. D., the ex-Chancellor of the South-Western Presbyterian University, the Rev. W. T. Richardson, D. D., editor of the *Central Presbyterian*, with ruling elder, the late Hon. J. D. Armstrong, of Romney, West Va.,—all members of the Assembly of 1861—was appointed, to whom this letter was referred for reply, the substance of which is here recorded:

AUGUSTA, GA., *May 27, 1886.*

"*To the Rev. J. Leighton Wilson, D. D.:* •

"VENERABLE AND BELOVED FATHER.—The General Assembly acknowledges, with sincere gratification, your

most interesting and welcome communication, and are
thankful that you send us this 'word of cheer and encouragement.' We bear in mind the fact that you are
one of those who twenty-five years ago aided in organizing our beloved church, and we shall ever cherish the
memory of the great kindness of our Heavenly Father in
granting us your wise and efficient aid and counsel on
that memorable occasion. No less gratefully do we recognize the fact that God has spared you for so long a
period to be to us a guide and leader in that department
of church work to which your life has been consecrated.
We sympathize most profoundly and tenderly in the infirmities of age which press upon you, and we pray God
that he be merciful and gracious to you. It would have
afforded your brethren of the Assembly a great pleasure
to have been allowed to grasp your hand and look upon
your face once more, but as God has denied us this gratification, we thank you for your fervent prayers in behalf
of our beloved church. The General Assembly in session take great pleasure in assuring you of their undi-
minished esteem and brotherly love for you. We pray
that God the Father, the Son, and the Holy Ghost may
be with you, and as the time of your departure draws
nearer day by day, you may be comforted by the assurance that 'there is a crown of righteousness laid up for
you which the Lord, the righteous Judge, shall give you'
in the coming day of your everlasting rest. With affectionate greetings from all your brethren, and prayers for
your increasing joy and comfort in the Lord, we are
your brethren in the same Saviour.

JOHN N. WADDEL, *Chairman Committee.*"

Of the time referred to in the letter to the China Mission, given above, Dr. Lefevre writes: "I visited him in

Nearness to Heaven. the last year of his life at his home. There in the home of his childhood, under trees of his own early planting, and in walks that he loved from youth, he discoursed of personal experience, of the preciousness of Christ, of the work of Foreign Missions, and of heaven. I could hardly refrain from putting into his mouth the words of the great apostle—words which his pure and humble spirit would never have dreamed of appropriating to himself in their external conception—'I have fought a good fight, I have finished my course, I have kept the faith, henceforth there is laid up for me a crown of righteousness'; but the reverence I felt for the venerable dying saint and hero would not allow me to mar the holy simplicity of his experience. Besides, at the very time of the temptation, I suddenly remembered once in the General Assembly, where others and myself were referring to him as 'that venerable servant of God,' etc., etc., he came to me and said with tearful voice: 'Don't speak of me in that way; it pains, and humiliates, and crushes me.' This last interview was some months after the death of his venerable, and noble, and tenderly-loved wife, the companion and solace of his whole life. His own followed in less than a year. From the moment of this bereavement his steps seemed to be willingly quickening their speed towards the goal of human life. Her presence with Christ made heaven so near, and dear, and real, that if ever man since the 'roll' of the ancient worthies was made up had a faith which was the 'substance of things hoped for and the evidence of things not seen,' he was that man. All the tenderness of his great heart, all his consecration to Christ, all his intense and consuming zeal for the filling of the whole world with the glory of God's grace, burned and shone in a mighty flame that knew no unsteadiness or variation. Blessed memories! It was a precious privilege to hold communion with that great, and good, and wise man on the verge of heaven at the completion of his 'course.'"

His wife's niece, Mrs. Dr. Crane, visited him constantly, and would remain for days and minister to his comfort. Mrs. Joseph Scott, the adopted daughter of their earlier years, with her own daughters would come to see him and rejoice his heart, for he loved her very dearly, and so many thousand memories clustered around the years she played upon his knee.

The last sermon he preached was at Mount Sinai, the church of the colored people, from the words, **Last Sermon.** "Let this mind be in you which was also in Christ Jesus,' and was delivered in a very simple, pathetic style. Miss Johnson writes, "The last year of his life his health failed steadily. In February he had a slight attack, and although afterwards able to ride and take his usual walk, he never regained his strength, and the next two months was several times confined to his bed for a day or two. About the 1st of June he was taken sick, and although our dear physician, Dr. Hudson, was not uneasy at first and encouraged him to go to Asheville, yet it was not until the 26th of June that the doctor became alarmed, and calling me aside told me that there were bad symptoms and he feared the worst. Dr. Crane was called in for consultation, and the two physicians did all they could, but from the first had little hope. Dr. Wilson knew that he was ill and expected to die.

"On the 29th, as I was watching by his bedside, Mrs. **A Rose.** Crane handed me some lovely roses, one of which was his special favorite, and I can never forget his loving expression as he took it from my hand.

He had always been fond of violets and roses, and displayed his love for the beautiful just before entering the paradise above. He told me that when he was gone I could never reproach myself for not doing for him all that was possible, that he left me in the care of our Heavenly Father, and that even in heaven he himself would never forget nor cease to love me.'' He commended her. now left a second time an orphan, to the affectionate care of his family.

Dr. Wilson had previously requested his near kinsmen, Col. Harvey Wilson and Mr. Robert E. Wilson, to nurse him in his last sickness. These gentlemen left their homes, abode with him night and day, took the entire care of him, and ministered to him very gently and tenderly. His pastor says: ''His illness was protracted through several weeks, but loving ones stood by him day and night, ministering to his every want. With others we esteemed it a great honor and privilege to lift in its weakness that stalwart frame that for the love of Christ had been in journeyings often—in perils in the wilderness, in perils in the sea, in perils among the heathen—and to moisten with cold water the tongue that moved our church, as no other had done, to carry the water of life to the perishing millions of the earth. He conversed but little during his illness, being for the most part in a semi-conscious or sleeping state.''

During the last months of his life, his experience was not that of the valley and shadow of which the sweet Psalmist spake, but it was rather that of **On Mt. Pisgah.** the great prophet who had led his people out of Egyptian bondage, and who, standing on Pisgah's summit; looked across the plains of Canaan to Mount Zion, and to the General Assembly and church of the first-born, so much higher and more glorious than the many General Assemblies and great congregations he had attended on earth. His was the pathway of a conquering saint; no shadows, no darkness; only "an abundant entrance." He for a long time knew that there was "a decease to be accomplished," and quietly tarried till his Lord should come.

An eye-witness said: "He only ceased breathing, and then we saw that he was dead." This was July 13, 1886, a year lacking three days since the departure of his wife. It was in the seventy-eighth year of his age.

A vast assembly filled the ancestral church to listen to the funeral discourse from his bosom-friend of five and twenty years, the Rev. Dr. James Woodrow, who, before the casket which held the mortal remains of the aged preacher was sealed, kissed the forehead of the man he had loved so long and so well. The Rev. Dr. Edmunds, of Sumpter, assisted the pastor, the Rev. J. S. Cozby, in the services, and the Rev. W. A. Gregg offered a most earnest and fervent prayer that the church might not forget to send the gospel to the heathen.

Funeral.

The hymn was announced—the hymn the patriarch had before so often given out—

"From Greenland's icy mountains."

We use the word *announced* designedly, for out of the vast assembly met to pay their last respects to the deceased, only one or two voices were heard in song. Grief found expression in silence. As the news went through the Southland, many tears were shed, and when the tidings reached foreign shores, not a few felt there was within the breast an empty void. One of the ministers found expression in the language of the prophets:

' My father, my father, the chariot of Israel and the horse-men thereof.'' '' Know ye not that there is a prince and a great man fallen this day in Israel.''

When his will was opened, it was found that he left the sum of four hundred dollars to FOREIGN MISSIONS.

CHAPTER XXXI.

Character and Influence.

"The righteous shall flourish like the palm tree;
He shall grow like a cedar in Lebanon;
They that be planted in the house of the Lord
Shall flourish in the courts of our God,
They shall still bring forth fruit in old age,
They shall be fat and flourishing,
To show that the Lord is upright;
He is my rock, and there is no unrighteousness in him.'

THE subject of this memoir was one of the trees of the Lord. The Lord planted it. The Lord watered it. The Lord pruned it. The Lord rejoiced in it. If David called the stately cedars of Lebanon "trees of the Lord," how would his soul have gone out into lofty flights of holy meditation had he beheld the forests of California! In the kingdom of our Lord, Leighton Wilson was one of the monarchs of Yosemite; in its branches the birds of the air found lodging, and under its shade the pilgrims of earth joyfully rested.

In stature he was one or two inches over six feet, with broad shoulders, and a full, well-rounded frame. His form was erect and very symmetrical, and as he arose in the pulpit his audience was impressed with the dignity and nobleness of his presence. He was blessed with a sound body, and, with the exception of a few seasons of illness, enjoyed uninterrupted health throughout life. Thus in body he was fitted for the work before him, and, as the body reacts on the mind, he looked at things in a normal way, and not through a distorted medium.

His was a life of faith, and he could truly say : "The life which I now live in the flesh I live by the faith of the Son of God." By faith, like Abraham, he went out not knowing whither he went. By faith he depended upon God for the support of his missionary laborers. By faith he looked for a spiritual harvest. Though he did not see Africa evangelized, yet by faith he beheld the triumphs of the cross. He was one of those who "died in faith, not having received the promises, but having seen them afar off, and were persuaded of them and embraced them, and confessed that they were strangers and pilgrims on the earth." Thus "he became heir of the righteousness which is by faith."

Faith.

The Scriptures say, "And Barnabas was a good man." So was Leighton Wilson. He had no special or glaring fault, as with so many of the bright lights of the church. Goodness, with its deep, silent current, bearing unnumbered blessings, flowed on through all of his life. He fed the hungry, clothed the needy, adopted the orphan, educated the destitute, comforted the sorrowing, healed the sick, and preached the gospel to the poor.

Goodness.

His life was marked by the warmest attachments of his friends. He was the "beloved disciple" who leaned on the Master's bosom, and this seemed to attract those that were like-minded. There was, perhaps, never a man who held more intimate communion with those dear to him than did the subject of this sketch. Friendship was to him a sacred and blessed tie, and few men have ever lived in the church who enjoyed the heart-fellowship of a larger number of eminent and godly min-

Friendship.

isters. His affection for his personal friends was tender and ardent. He delighted in their society, rejoiced in their success, and counted their blessings his own. The testimony of some of these will be given:

"My relations with him were very tender. He wanted me associated with him in his work twenty *Conversation.* years ago. In all our talks there was much that was pleasant, for he breathed his holy and consecrated spirit in the ordinary conversations of every day. Every one felt the power of his personality. His words were weighty, because his character and his life were behind them. His pleadings for missions and for Christ went to the heart, because his own consecrated spirit made them effective. I loved to sit near him and hear him talk. I loved the shadow of his great loving presence."—*E. M. Green.*

Dr. Wilson was preëminently noted for wisdom. Since the days of the royal preacher of Jerusa- *Wisdom.* lem, perhaps, no one was so universally spoken of in the church as distinguished for wisdom. "When he left New York to cast in his lot with the South in 1861, it was reported that Dr. Charles Hodge said of him, 'The wisest man among us has gone out.' This remark made the first impression on my mind that I remember to have had concerning Dr. Wilson. When I first met him, in 1868, this first impression was confirmed, and during the years following, as I served as a missionary under his superintendence as Secretary, this impression was constantly deepened and strengthened up to the time of his death. It seems to me that the most striking characteristic of the grand old man was his wisdom. This feature of his character shone out strongly in his management of the cause of Foreign Missions in the early years of our church. He had charge in the beginning, when the foundations had to be laid. Many new and perplexing questions arose in starting our work in strange and distant lands. Principles had to be settled, plans adopted, methods tried, and errors and mistakes guarded against. New workers in new fields had to be counseled and directed. For such a time and for such a work his great wisdom and his previous experience gave him special and preëminent fitness. He was wise and judicious in counsel, wise and careful in speech, wise and prudent in action. His advice and directions given to the missionaries before starting and after arrival on the field were always regarded by them as wise and judicious. In the early days of our mission he wrote us frequent letters, and these were always looked forward to with interest and read with pleasure. He took broad and liberal views, and brought many points to our attention which we might not have otherwise considered.

"But if wisdom was the characteristic of his mind, kindness was the expression of his heart. His **Kindness.** official letters always breathed the spirit of kindness, and were clothed in the language of courtesy. He had sometimes to give advice, or to communicate directions from the committee, which he knew would not agree with the views of some or of all the members of the mission, and in such cases he was specially careful to make the communication in the least objectionable form, and thus relieve it as far as possible of unpleasant features. His kindness to all, and his consideration for the feelings and opinions of others, were marked features in his dealings with the mission."—*J. L. Stuart.*

"Were I called to name the characteristic which impressed me most in the noble life of Dr. J. Leighton Wilson, I would without hesitation designate *love.* I

have seen him in circumstances very trying to his faith
and forbearance, especially towards men much
younger than himself, yet love was the guiding star, and the law of kindness was in his lips.   This
love in his heart made him, as it ever makes men, wise.
The disciple whom Jesus loved has told us 'he that lov-
eth his brother walketh in the light.'   The clear dis-
cernment, the intuitive perceptions of what ought to be
done and said in circumstances that perplexed others,
though springing from an intellect naturally well-balanced and strong, was the result of a permanent habit of
viewing every question in the light of love.   Dr. Wilson
had what the Bible calls 'an understanding heart.'

    Love.

"Another trait rising from the same golden source,
which often impressed me in Dr. Wilson, was
his humility.   In the presence of the youngest
men around him he placed himself in the attitude of an
inquirer, of one who sought counsel and was willing to
accept it, if it were good.   This trait made him prompt
to accept suggestions when they were wise.   He was
ready to listen to any one who could give him information or counsel in a matter that was before him, and it
was usually on a broad basis of inquiry that his mind
was made up.   His conclusions, therefore, were well-
rooted and strong.   It is such men that God sets on
high.   About a year before his death one quoted in his
presence the words of Christ, 'He that humbleth himself shall be exalted.'   Dr. Wilson turned, and evidently
summing up the experience of his life, said, 'That is
true.'

    Humility.

"It was his spirit of love, and the clearness of his
convictions, which made him stand firm as an
oak in every matter affecting the interests of the
Foreign Mission work.   He knew that it concerned the

    Firmness.

eternal happiness of millions of his fellow-men.   To
promote it, his own personal interest, or the personal interest of any one else, should be entirely waived.   This
refusal to consider personal wishes, when he believed
them to contravene the requirements of the mission service, sometimes brought him in conflict with others.   I
can truly say that I have never known a man whose aim
seemed to be more entirely single for the high interests of
God's service."—*M. H. Houston.*

"I think his greatest work, and that which will tell
most on time and eternity, is his work in the
South.   In arousing the churches and organizing the missionary work, only Leighton Wilson could have done it, and he did it in the best manner
possible.   He is the most striking instance of what one
talent can accomplish when put out to usury.   His common sense, consecrated to God, and concentrated on the
one idea of fulfilling the command, 'Go preach my gospel,' made of him such a power, that not only the savage African felt and obeyed his will, but the rulers of
the earth sought his counsel, and wealth, beauty, and
rank loved and revered his great goodness.   He was great
in goodness, and was trusted as I have never known
another man to be.   He has blessed many, many hearts,
and has left his impress on many, many lives.   The remembrance of him is precious."—*J. R. Eckard.*

"He was singularly modest.   He did his work well,
seeking divine approval.   Simple-hearted and
loyal to his Master, he went on his way not
seeking applause, and not frequently dismayed
by opposition.   His time was so filled with the Lord's
work that he had no chance to write about himself, and
much that we would like to know must remain in obli-
vion until 'the day shall declare it.'   His life is written

on the characters he renovated, on the lives he bright-
ened and blessed, and on the church he loved so well and
served so faithfully.

> 'To those who knew thee not, no words can paint,
> And those who knew thee, know all words are faint.'"
>
> —*Leighton Wilson Eckard.*

"Dr. Wilson was as near perfect as any one could become. He was generous; he never thought of himself
in the expenditure of money, nor in seeking his own
pleasure in any way. He was just; his judgment was
good, and he could intuitively see the truth in any question that came before him. In his opinions he was chari-
table, and I have never heard him, but once, distrust his
fellow-men. During all the agitations and discussions
in which our church was involved and in which he took
a prominent part, he was always perfectly sincere and
frank. The interest of the church was always upper-
most in his heart."—*Alice Johnson.*

"He was a man for whom I always entertained the
highest respect and admiration, and his parting benediction has remained with me all these
years. He was so simple in his greatness, yet
he was one of the great men of the church, and eternity
alone can reveal how much his life, his work, and his
example did to promote the cause of Foreign Missions."
—*Mary Horton Stuart.*

His Bene-
diction.

"The Psalmist's devotion to Zion, when he wrote the
one hundred and thirty-seventh Psalm, was
hardly greater or more heroic than Dr. Wilson's to the church of Christ in his day. Our
version is a true expression of his whole life:

Love for
Zion.

> 'For her my tears shall fall,
> For her my prayers ascend;
> To her my cares and toils be given,
> Till toils and cares shall end.'"
>
> —*Amicus.*

"His life was not what might be termed eventful, but was more like the easy flow of a mighty river when at its average height, bearing immense cargoes to their destination, and yet doing it with so much ease and quietness as scarcely to attract any attention. He did attract attention, and had a host of admirers, but it was not so much because of what he said or did here or there, as because of his uniformly wise counsels and powerfully controlling influence. He made no effort to soar above his brethren—he would have scorned the very thought of such a thing—but he was so opened-hearted, pure, humble, wise, and zealous, that by the common consent of almost the whole Christian world he ranked among the greatest of his day and generation."—*W. W. Mills.*

The Mighty River.

"It was one of the privileges of my life that I was associated with that great and good man for so many years. He was a true gospel representative of the Christian ministry, full of love and of entire consecration to the evangelization of the world. As for years a member of the Committee of Foreign Missions, I can truly say I was impressed with his profound wisdom, his perfect self-forgetfulness, and his supreme consecration to the cause of Foreign Missions. I believe that was the impression of every member of the committee. He always acted with an eye single to the glory of God, and to the best interest of the cause. While Dr. Wilson was a man of great modesty and humility, he possessed strong convictions when he had studied a subject, and was a man of inflexible determination. I never saw one who spoke less about himself, and who more completely hid himself behind the Master and his cause."—*J. J. Bullock.*

His Eye Single.

"Dr. Wilson's great qualities were his unfeigned

Christian faith and his intuitive sagacity. He wielded
more real power in the Southern Presbyterian
Influence. Church than any other man in it; a power,
indeed, more enviable and prevalent than I have ever
seen possessed by another. And this influence was accorded him, not by reason of any assumption, dogma-
tism, or imperiousness on his part, but because of the
contrary traits. Every one was certain of the purity of
his aims. They knew that Christ and his cause were always foremost with him. Always modest and conciliatory, even one's opposing opinions were listened to with
respect, and yet he was perfectly candid and manly in as-
serting his own. He practiced no arts nor policies, but
relied solely upon the appeals of facts and reasoning to
the consciences of his brethren. Hence his influence
with the Assembly was ever solid and usually prevalent.
He was marked by a uniform, gentle dignity. His manners were always those of the elevated and polished gentleman. His public discourses contained no slang, no
levity, no sensational catches. His style and manner
were those of the cultivated statesman, softened by evangelical unction."—*R. L. Dabney.*

"Nothing gives me greater pleasure than to think, talk,
and even write about our venerated and be-
Transparent. loved Dr. John Leighton Wilson. It was my
privilege, my highly appreciated honor, to be intimately
acquainted and associated with him for many years. I
think I knew him well—indeed, it was not hard to know
him—he was such a grand figure, and he was so transparent. I always regarded him as one of the best and purest
of men; honest as the light of day, just and true to all
men and his God; full of charity and benevolence, and
entirely free from dissimulation. His aim ever seemed
to be to speak the truth in love, and to do the just and
right thing in the kindest way.

"He was not an intellectually great man, but his well-balanced mind, his sound judgment, his admirable common sense, his pure and lofty purposes, his devout and humble piety, his consecration to God, and his self-denying devotion to doing good, gave to his character all the essential elements of the truest greatness. The estimation in which he was held by our church, especially in her best days, and in the times of her best and greatest men, is a monument of his worth which will never perish while his contemporaries live and their successors keep up the history of the past.

"I never knew a more humble great man. He never assumed superiority over any person or class. He was simple as a child. 'We be all brethren' was the expression of all his talks and conferences. I always looked up to him as my wise father, but he treated me as if I were his equal, and consulted me as if I had superior wisdom, and yet no one could accuse him of the least disposition to flatter. I have seen him in times of sore trouble and perplexity in regard to the interests of the church he loved. His heart was often crushed, but his faith never gave way.

"He was a most agreeable companion; cheery, never morose; genial, fond of humor, and always added to the joy of fraternal intercourse. His purity, faith, kindliness and hopefulness were sunshine. How I miss him! his talks, his letters, his sweet counsel. When he died a large part of life passed from me. His influence in the church was greatest always for good. He lived a grand life, and his memory is precious."—*C. A. Stillman.*

"Dr. Wilson has a commanding presence. His features are clearly marked, and indicate physical and intellectual strength. His manly form is graced with great dignity. Affable and courteous in address, he exerts over those about him a great charm. His varied information makes him the attractive centre of the

Executive Ability. social circle. He is just in judgment, wise in counsel, practical in methods, and endowed in an eminent degree with executive ability. His life has been devoted to Foreign Missions, both in the active service in the field, and in the direction and management of the work from the office at home. In this work he has achieved his greatest distinction, and for it will be long remembered. His public life has now covered fifty years. These fifty years have recorded wonderful progress in the Foreign Mission work. They constitute a great missionary age in the history of the church. It is only fair to remark that among the great workers in this branch of Christian service, the able and efficient Secretary of Foreign Missions for the Southern Presbyterian Church stands with the first."—*G. L. Petrie, in The Presbyterian Cyclopædia.*

"Dr. Wilson was the wisest and best man I ever saw. He was a man of inflexible righteousness, and

Symmetry. yet without any scrupulous crotchets; of the deepest and tenderest affections, and yet without weak and foolish fondness; of the most profound and intuitive judgment, and yet totally free from that logical guile that snatches at any argument; consecrated to the cause of Foreign Missions, to which he devoted more than half a century of active work, and yet without a taint of that fanaticism which mars the efforts of so many of its advocates; always manifesting the sacred and awful presence of Christ in his spirit as his Lord and Saviour, and yet a perfect stranger to the least appearance or tinge of mystical enthusiasm. His whole life and all his works testify to the fact that he was a great, good, and symmetrical leader of God's people. His wonderful and sweetly controlling influence in the church courts, over corporate bodies associated with him in church work, and no less in personal intercourse, all testify to the pre-ëminent greatness of the man. He possessed and wielded this influence because all felt and most knew that he deserved it.

"There was harmony and unity wherever Dr. Wilson was leader. His biography, if it should recount only the annals of his life, will surely make the impression of his greatness, and goodness, and wisdom, and self-sacrifice—but that will be a cold marble stature—one must have had long association with him to know the living Christian hero. The symmetry of his gifts and graces necessarily made him marvelously brave, but that same symmetry saved him from the least admixture of daring, or that audacity which is so painfully visible and offensive and un-Christian in a large class of truly brave and good men. The memory of Dr. Wilson is to me not only or chiefly one of those beautiful models of a Christian man, but also a warm, living impulse that salts and sweetens my own declining years."—*J. A. Lefevre.*

"Of the life and labors of Dr. Wilson as the Missionary Secretary of our church, the importance and value of which is so well known to us all, I need not speak. But let me say, John Leighton Wilson was no ordinary man. The very form of his countenance must have impressed every stranger as noble. There have been many distinguished Wilsons, but which of them lived a more honorable or useful life? 'That life is longest which best fulfils life's great end.' When I think of those eighteen years of devoted Christian service spent by him among the savages of the Western coast of Africa, with no companion but his excellent wife,

my heart melts in admiration of the grandeur of his life.
It was given him to be the father of nations, for any man
deserves to be called the father of a people who first re-
duces her language to writing, and then teaches them
to read it and write it themselves.   Yes, and even more,
that man is the father of a people who takes them in their
heathenish darkness and makes them, by the grace of
God, acquainted with the salvation of Christ.

"Wilson may truly be called a great man.   He was
great in his unselfishness.   Think of his abandonment
of that sphere in which he moved in his native State,
and with no motive of reward on earth, going forth to
spend the whole of his life in savage Africa!   It makes
us recall to mind the greatness of Father Abraham, who
obeyed when required to go forth he knew not whither.

"Great, also, was Wilson's unconsciousness of self.
To a small man, his personal convenience and his own
selfish enjoyments are the great things of the world in
which he lives.   But a man like Wilson will always
find some object to pursue that is bigger than himself,
and in the pursuit of which himself is entirely absorbed.

"Great, too, was Wilson's humility.   No man ever
knew him to exhibit the slightest self-conceit.   'Seekest
thou great things for thyself? seek them not,' saith the
prophet, and Wilson was an humble servant of his Lord
and Master, with no ambition for preëminence.   And so
in comparison with his brethren generally, Wilson must
be acknowledged to have been great in faith and in zeal
and love for his Lord and mankind.

"But these are moral qualities, and what am I to say
of him intellectually considered?   I cannot say that he
was great in metaphysics or in the classics, but I do say
his common sense was great, and that his judgment was
generally admirable.   I say that he had the intellectual

qualities of a statesman. His mind was broad enough and strong enough to grasp the interests of whole tribes of men. He could carry on his shoulders the weight of a great cause like the foreign propagation of the faith. He could take upon his single soul the affairs of his own conquered people and their impoverished and almost despairing church, and bear them through the dark days to brighter ones. Yes, he was a statesman, though his statesmanship may have admitted some errors. What statesman ever lived that proved to be infallible? Dear, faithful, honest-hearted, humble-minded, unselfish, ever-loving brother, thou art gone to be forever with thy Lord!"—*J. B. Adger.*

This soldier of the cross possessed a deep and tender sympathy for his brethren and sisters on the mission field. He had spent two-fifths of his ministry in rugged contact with heathenism in its lowest forms. He had experienced the hardships of life under a burning sun, and felt the most tender solicitude for those who in distant climes were bearing the heat and burden of the day. The tenderness of woman's nature was united with the chieftain's courage. In the exquisite compassion of his soul, he gave proof of his union with the great High Priest, and thus his young co-laborers across the sea knew that they had not a Secretary which could not be touched with a feeling for their trials and difficulties. This oneness of mind and heart made them catch higher views of the meaning of the blessed Master's words, "I in them and thou in me, that they may be made perfect in one, and that the world may know that thou hast sent me, and hast loved them as thou hast loved me."

We have in his life and character the highest internal evidence of the truth of Christianity. Can we picture him from childhood to old age without the gifts and graces of religion? We would have a just, honorable, polite citizen of the country. But where the power of an endless life? Where the power of Christ's resurrection? Where the power to witness unto the uttermost parts of the earth? Without Jesus, he would have been aimless, godless, hopeless.

The Power of Christ.

In the subject of this memoir we behold the developing power of the Foreign Mission life and work. How it kindles all that is tender and gentle, awakens zeal, gives new impulse to prayer, expands the heart till it takes in the whole family of man, and gives glorious views of the wonders of redemption. The promises of the future glory of Messiah's kingdom were to him living realities, and by faith he dwelt in the millennial days. The world's evangelization was the mainspring of his religious life. If the induction be true, that this grand character was built upon the ascension command, then the church militant may glory in her call to Foreign Missions.

The Developing Power.

When we contemplate a ministerial life of three and fifty years intensely fixed upon one end, enthusiastically and heroically devoted to one object, and that the spreading the news of salvation throughout the earth; when we consider the seed sown broadcast in many lands, and watered by prayers and tears, we must exclaim, What will the harvest be? His influence was like a mighty river, which combines the waters of the Congo, the Amazon, and the Yangtse, and flowing through Africa, Brazil, and China, empties in the sea of latter-day glory, when Christ will be King of nations, as he is now King of saints. The doctrine of awards, so mysterious to the believer, is dis-

The Judgment.

tinctly taught in the Scriptures: "Who will render to every man according to his deeds; to them who by patient continuance in well-doing seek for glory, and honor, and immortality, eternal life." "And they that be wise shall shine as the brightness of the firmament; and they that turn many to righteousness, as the stars for ever and ever." Leighton Wilson kindled the fire of missions on the altars of ten thousand hearts, and each light becomes a living flame, which, igniting other torches, glows and burns, till with the brightness of their beams they shine with unwonted splendor and illuminate the earth. How glorious will this saint appear before the throne of the King in the presence of the angels. The sweet surprises on that day of days! He invested his all in the evangelization of the world, and will receive compound interest for a thousand years! "He being dead yet speaketh." "The righteous shall be in everlasting remembrance."

The graves of Dr. and Mrs. Wilson are side by side in the cemetery of Mount Zion Church, where sleep the holy dead of several generations. Two plain stones of Italian marble stand near the roadside. Traveller, rein your steed and uncover your head, as you read:

REV. JOHN LEIGHTON WILSON, D. D.,

THE FOREIGN MISSIONARY,

BORN MARCH 25, 1809,

DIED JULY 13, 1886.

EIGHTEEN YEARS A MISSIONARY ON THE WESTERN COAST OF AFRICA.

THIRTY-THREE YEARS SECRETARY OF FOREIGN MISSIONS.

"He rests from his labors, and his works do follow him."

"Go ye into all the world and preach the gospel to every creature"

PREACHING IN SINIM,

—OR THE—

Gospel to the Gentiles,

WITH HINTS AND HELPS FOR ADDRESSING A HEATHEN AUDIENCE.

BY

HAMPDEN C. DuBOSE, D. D.,

MISSIONARY IN CHINA.

PRICE, CLOTH, $1.00; PAPER, 60 CENTS.

This little volume on preaching in China is the work of one who can speak from experience, the author being for "twenty-one years a missionary at Soochow" and a zealous, indefatigable preacher. The author's aim, as stated in the preface, is to offer aid to newly-arrived missionaries and to present hints on preaching, which may be useful to ministers in other lands.

Presbyterian Committee of Publication,

Richmond, Virginia.

The Dragon,
Image and Demon,

—OR THE—

Three Religions of China: Confucianism, Buddhism and Tao-ism.

GIVING AN ACCOUNT OF THE

MYTHOLOGY, IDOLATRY AND DEMONOLATRY OF THE CHINESE,

BY

HAMPDEN C. DuBOSE, D. D.,

MISSIONARY IN CHINA.

PRICE, $2.00.

A. C. ARMSTRONG & SON,
NEW YORK.